Tome of Wondrous Items

AUTHOR
Ken Spencer

DEVELOPERS
Zach Glazar
Edwin Nagy
Matt Finch

EDITOR
Jeff Harkness

LAYOUT
Suzy Moseby
Rich Oliver

COVER ART
Artem Shukaev

INTERIOR ART
Brett Barkley
Colin Chan
Julio De Carvalho
Adrian Landeros
C.J. Marsh
Santa Norvaisite
Thuan Pham
Sid Quade
Hector Rodriguez
Artem Shukaev
Quentin Soubrouillard
Erica Willey

ART DIRECTOR
Casey Christofferson

©2022 Necromancer Games. All rights reserved. Reproduction without the written permission of the publisher is expressly forbidden. Necromancer Games, and the Necromancer Games logo, *Tome of Wondrous Items* is a trademark of Necromancer Games. All rights reserved. All characters, names, places, items, art, and text herein are copyrighted by Necromancer Games. The mention of or reference to any company or product in these pages is not a challenge to the trademark or copyright concerned.

NECROMANCER Games
ISBN: 978-1-6656-0205-1
5e Hardcover
PRINTED IN USA

TABLE OF CONTENTS

Chapter One: Introduction 1
  Chapter Breakdown 1
    Chapter One: Introduction 1
    Chapter Two: Armor 1
    Chapter Three: Otherworldly Items 1
    Chapter Four: Rings 1
    Chapter Five: Rods 1
    Chapter Six: Potions 1
    Chapter Seven: Scrolls 1
    Chapter Eight: Staves 1
    Chapter Nine: Wands 1
    Chapter Ten: Weapons 1
    Chapter Eleven: Wondrous Items 1
    Appendix A: New Monsters 1
    Appendix B: New Spells 1
    Appendix C: Magical Tattoos 1
  Alchemical Formulas 2
  New Magical Item Rules 2
    Esoteric Conjunction 2
    Effects of Complementary Conjunction 2
    Effects of Antagonistic Conjunction 2
  Panoply 2

Chapter Two: Armor 3
    Alcaeus' Lion Skin 3
    Ancient King's Harness 3
    Antelope Skin of Enkidu 3
    Behir Armor 3
    Blister Beetle Armor 3
    Blood Orchid Armor 3
    Bronzewood Breastplate 3
    Bronzewood Shield 3
    Centurion's Lorica Segmentata 4
    Centurion's Scutum 4
    Coat of Many Metals 4
    Coral Plate 4
    Couatl Armor 4
    Crocodile Armor 4
    Ethereal Armor 4
    Flying Shield 5
    Ghast Armor 5
    Goat-Faced Shield 5
    Golden Crab Manica 5
    Hoplomachus' Manica 5
    Hoplomachus' Shield 5
    Jousting Armor 6
    Lobster Armor 6
    Mimic Armor 6
    Ooze Armor 6
    Remorhaz Armor 6
    Retiarius's Manica 7
    Rhinoceros Armor 7
    Rock Troll Armor 7
    SandWalker's Armor 7
    Salamander Armor 7
    Scrolled Shield 7
    Spider Silk Armor 7
    Tortoise Shell Shield 7
    Tribune's Cuirass 7
    Wall Passer 8
    Warded Plate 8

Chapter Three: Otherworldly Items 9
  Using Otherworldly Items 9
  Relics of the Cometfall 9
    Energy Disk 9
    Energy Projector 9
    Flight Belt 9
    Golem Suit 10
    Merfolk Suit 10
    Needle Projector 10
    Otherworldly Potions 11
    Potion Ampoule 11
    Potion Wand 11
    Power Disk 11
  Relics of Distant Worlds 11
    Boom Club 11
    Iron Horse 12
    Talker 12
  Relics of Strange Worlds 13
    Arm Bug 13
    Armor Bug 13
    Brain Jar 14
    Brain Jar Attachments 14
    Etheric Projector 15
    Helm Bug 15
    Revivification Serum 15
  Other Otherworldly Item 15
    Crystal Icosahedron 15
    Sky Throne 16

Chapter Four: Rings 17
    Message Rings 17
    Piscean Ring 17
    Ring of Absorption 17
    Ring of the Barrier 17
    Ring of Blindsight 17
    Ring of Burrowing 17
    Ring of Charidis 17
    Ring of Climbing 17
    Ring of Darkvision 17
    Ring of the Imposter 17
    Ring of Kicking 18
    Ring of the Library 18
    Rings of Life Sharing 18
    Rings of Life Stealing 18
    Rings of Love 18
    Ring of Rings 18
    Ring of Scyllabis 18
    Ring of Severing 18
    Ring of the Shield 18

Ring of the Smoke Wyrm. 19
Signet Ring of Summoning and Binding 19
Ring of Tremorsense 19
Vampire Ring. 19

Chapter Five: Rods **20**
Rod of Abjuration 20
Rod of Air 20
Rod of Conjuration 21
Rod of Disruption 21
Rod of Divination 21
Rod of Dragons 21
Rod of Earth 21
Rod of Enchantment 22
Rod of Evocation. 22
Rod of Fire 22
Rod of Illusion. 22
Rod of the Land 23
Rod of Necromancy. 23
Rod of Nine Lives 23
Rod of Transmutation 23
Rod of Water 23
Tribune's Baton 24

Chapter Six: Potions **25**
Draught of Hope 25
Draught of Madness. 25
Draught of Terrors 25
Elixir of Lethe 25
Elixir of Undoing. 25
Elixir of Youth. 25
Potion of Coziness. 25
Potion of Ectoplasm. 25
Potion of the Feast 25
Potion of the Fey Walk 26
Potion of Ice 26
Potion of Luck 26
Potion of Magma 26
Potion of Origination. 26
Potion of Poetry. 26
Potion of Smoke 26
Potion of the Clouds 26
Potion of the Fishes 26
Potion of Transference. 26
Potion of Translocation 26
Wolf-fanged Elixir. 26

Chapter Seven: Scrolls **27**
Casting Tablets 27
Cursed Scroll 27
Cursed Scroll 27
Mirror Scroll 27
Script of the Evil Eye 27
Scroll of Abjuration. 28
Scroll of Abjuration. 28
Scroll of Abjuration ,Blank 28
Scroll of Answers 28
Scroll of Armor 28
Scroll of the Artisan. 28
Scroll of the Camp. 28

Scroll of Communion 28
Scroll of Elemental Air 28
Scroll of Elemental Earth. 28
Scroll of Elemental Fire. 29
Scroll of Elemental Water 29
Scroll Familiar. 29
Scroll Of the Garden of Monsters 29
Scroll of the Menagerie 29
Scroll of Resistance 29
Scroll of Trapping 29
Scroll of the Unarmed 29

Chapter Eight: Staves **30**
Staff of the Arch-Spider. 30
Staff of Beasts 30
Staff of Death 30
Staff of the Eternal Stone. 31
Staff of the Exquisite Flame 31
Staff of the Four Winds 31
Staff of Hiking. 31
Staff of Knowledge 31
Staff of the Oasis. 31
Staff of the Pillar. 32
Staff of Plants 32
Staff of Vaulting 32
Staff of Vaulting, False 32
Staff of the Waves 32
Thrysus 32

Chapter Nine: Wands. **33**
Wand of the Cobra. 33
Wand of Colors 33
Wand of Conducting 33
Wand of the Dead 33
Wand of Dispelling 33
Wand of Distant Touch 33
Wand of Entombment 33
Wand of the Fist. 33
Wand of Flies. 33
Wand of Flight 33
Wand of Hands 34
Wand of the Hedgerows. 34
Wand of Horror 34
Wand of the Hourglass. 35
Wand of Mapping 35
Wand of Misdirection 35
Wand of Roses. 35
Wand of Runes 35
Wand of Rust. 36
Wand of Sleep and Waking 36
Wand of Spiders 36
Wand of Swine 36
Wand of the Route 36
Wand of the Twice Blessed 36
Wand of Trapping 36
Wand of Whispers 36

Chapter Ten: Weapons. **37**
Alcaeus' Arrows 37
Alcaeus' Club 37

Ancient King's Sword	37
Axe of the Water Warrior	37
Banner of the Desert Prince	37
Baton of Banishment	37
Bident of Wealth	38
Blade of Truth	38
Bow of the Air Warrior	38
Centurion's Gladius	38
Crystal Weapons	38
Cursed Clay Bullets	38
Desert Prince's Scimitar	38
Fan of the General	39
Fan of Lightning	39
Fan of Thunder	39
Giant Slayer Axe	39
Goad of the Ghost Elephant	39
Goblin Stones	39
Golden Arrow	39
Golden Arrow of Madness	39
Hammer of the Dwarven King	40
Hammer of the Worthy	40
Heptascopic Blade	40
Hoplomachus' Spear	40
Interrogator's Razor	40
Killed Weapons	40
Jawbone of Slaying	40
Lead Arrow	40
Leafy Sword	40
Lion-Tailed Whip	40
Marlin-Spiked Cutlass	41
Maul of the Earth Warrior	41
Nine Arrows Bow	41
Ox-Headed Mace	41
Quill of the Assistant	41
Razor of Beauty	41
Retiarus's Net	42
Retiarius's Trident	42
Scepter of the Heavens	42
Sickle of Parthenos	42
Scorpion Bow	42
Spearhead of the Thunderbolt	42
Spear of Jumping	42
Spear of Lengthening	42
Spiny Lance	42
Sword of the Dawn Star	42
Sword of the Fire Warrior	43
Sword of the Night Orb	43
Sword of Seven Lightnings	43
Tribune's Spatha	43
Unfinished Dagger	43
Wave Steel Blades	44
Wind-Splitting Sword	44
Chapter Eleven: Wondrous Items	**45**
A Sunny Day at Southdale	45
Aba of the Dancing Queen	45
Aba of Dislocation	45
Aba of Mislocation	45
Albert's Chum Bucket	46
Amulet of Protection from the Evil Eye	46
Amulet of Resurrection	46
Amulet of Resurrection, False	46
Animal-Headed Canopic Jar	46
Ancient King's Horned Helm	47
Ancient Spell-stone	47
Ancient Pass-stone	47
Armband of the Ring Giver	47
The Astrological Book of ibn Farabi	47
Antitheirka Mechanism	47
Antitheirka Mechanism Effects	48
Automata Cart	50
Baetylus	50
Bag of Silver	50
Bane Jar	50
Banner of the Lion	50
Batrachite Stone	50
Battle of the King's Road	50
Binnacle of True Sight	51
Blade Oil	51
Bone Flute	51
Book of Libraries	51
Boon Jar	51
Bowl of Miscibility	51
Box of Evils	51
Brazier of Lies	52
Brazier of Divination	52
Brick of Building (structure)	52
Brick of Building (wall)	53
Brick of Building (well)	53
Bronze Hippoi	53
Bronze Watchdogs	53
Bull's Yoke	53
Bust of Kell	53
Caduceus of the Legions	53
Centaur's Halter	53
Canopic Urn of Revenge	54
Canopic Jar of Eternal Life	54
Canopic Urn of the Undead, Lesser	54
Canopic Urn of the Undead, Greater	54
Cauldron of Swarms	54
Cave Pigments	55
Chariot of the Sun	55
Capstan of the Miser	55
Centurion's Galea	55
Chessboard of the Long Moment	55
Cinnabar Rouge	55
City in A Bottle	56
City in A Bottle, Cursed	56
Cursed City in a Bottle Grand Task	56
Clay Seal	57
Cloak of the Dead	57
Cloak of the Dwarven King	57
Cloak of Many Weapons	57
Cloak of Disarming	57
Commander's Shako	57
Cooling Fan	57

Cottage of Confinement	57
Cube of the Tower	58
Cup of Phyrga	58
Curse Bag	58
Crown of the Dwarven King	58
Crown of the Heavens	59
Dancer's Anklets	59
Dancer's Castanets	59
Dancer's Veils	59
Deconjunctionifier	59
Desert Prince's Keffiyeh	59
Desert Prince's Saddle	60
Desert Prince's Thawb	60
Diadem of the Spider	60
Drums of Summoning	60
Eagle Throne	61
Ellidi	61
Everchanging Dresser	61
Everlasting Cart	62
Eyes of Conjunction Detection	62
Fan of Concealing	62
Fascinator of Fabulousness	62
Fibula of Armor	62
Fibula of Binding	62
Fibula of the Wardrobe	62
Figurine of Wondrous Power	62
Fire Cloth	63
Flayed Man's Cowl	63
Flayed Man's Gloves	63
Flayed Man's Pants	63
Flayed Man's Shirt	63
Girdle of Passage	63
Girdle of the Twins	64
Glade with Unicorn	64
Ghost Stone of the Tower of Screams	64
Golden Fiddle	65
Gourd of Capture	65
Gryphon Pepper Pot	65
Hand of the Beggar	66
Hand of Doom	66
Hand of Holding	66
Hand of Many Hands	66
Hand of the Prisoner	66
Hand of the Thief	66
Halter of the Steed	66
Hat of the Eternal Storm	66
Helm of the Choosers	67
Helm of the Air Warrior	67
Helm of the Fire Warrior	67
Helm of the Earth Warrior	67
Helm of the Water Warrior	67
Hennin of the Princess	67
Hoplomachus's Helm	68
Horn of Fog	68
Horn of Pricus	68
Honeyed Head	68
Horn of the Great Feast	68
Horn of Warning	68
ibn Farabi's Planar Astrolabe	69
Ibn Farabi's Pen	69
Ideal Forge	69
The Idol of Tindlehaven	69
Imperial Death Masks	70
Imperial Death Mask Subjects	70
The Ironshaker	70
The Knidian	71
Knight Errant	71
Knot of Worldly Attachment	71
Kohl of Clear Sight	71
Kohl of Far Sight	71
Kohl of Night Sight	72
Kohl of True Sight	72
Krater of Endless Libation	72
Laurel of the Athlete	72
Laurel of the Conqueror	72
Laurel of the Hero	72
Laurel of the Poet	72
Libra of Justice	72
Lotus Sandals	72
Lute of Dancing	73
Lute of Suggestion	73
Luck Bag	73
Lucky Dice	73
Manna Box	73
Medusa's Head	74
Metate of the Three Sisters	74
Mirror of Revealing	74
Mosaic of Far Stepping	74
Mosaic of the Bedchamber	75
Mosaic of the Dining Hall	75
Mosaic of the Garden	75
Mosaic of the Hidden Chamber	75
Mosaic of the Protected Room	75
Mukissi	76
Ornmathur's Arm	76
Ornmathur's Eye	76
Ornmathur's Hand	77
Ornmathur's Leg	77
Ostraka of Cursing	77
Necklace of Missiles	77
Oxhide Ingot	77
Patent of Ennoblement	77
Paper Lantern of Conflagration	78
Paper Lantern of the Courier	78
Paper Lantern of Seeking	78
Paper Lantern of the Storm	78
Paper Lantern of Transformation	78
Paper Lantern of Transformation Creatures	78
Paper Lantern of Wind Journeys	78
Paper Lantern of True Love	78
Parasol of Ninety-Nine Demons	79
Parasol of Flight	79
Parasol of the Water Strider	79
Pipa of Weather Control	79
Pipa of Weather Control Effects	79
Pipes of Flame	80

v

Plow of Reaping	80
Pomegranate Seed of Knowledge	80
Portal to the Home of the Dwarven Gods	80
Powdered Instant Death Watch Beetle	80
Powdered Instant Gelatinous Cube	80
Powdered Instant Gorgon	80
Powdered Instant Ooze	80
Powdered Instant Salamander	80
Powdered Instant Spell Parrot	81
Powdered Instant Troll	81
Powdered Instant Unicorn	81
Powdered Instant Winter Wolf	81
Powdered Instant Wraith	81
Powdered Instant Xorn	81
Praxiteles' Birds	81
Putto	82
Quern of Grinding	82
Rake of Meditation	82
Ranger's Beret	82
Rat Whisker Slippers	82
Retiarus's Girdle	83
River Boatman	83
River Bridge	83
Robe of Flailing	83
Robe of the Heavens	83
Salmon of Truth	83
Sandals of the Chariot Runner	83
Sash of the Air Warrior	83
Sash of the Earth Warrior	84
Sash of the Fire Warrior	84
Sash of the Sun and Moon	84
Sash of the Water Warrior	84
Scarab of Devouring	84
Scarab of Embalming	84
Scarab of Mummification	85
Scarab of Resurrection	85
Seahorse Saddle	85
Seamless Globe	85
Senatorial Sandals	86
Senatorial Stylus	86
Senatorial Tablet	86
Senatorial Toga	86
Shaduf of Irrigation	87
Sharbat Cup	87
Sharktooth Necklace	87
Shovel of Posting	87
Shroud of Reanimation	87
Shroud of Resurrection	87
Silver Canoe	87
Singing Heads	87
Skeleton of Inovax of Kratir	87
Skirt of Many Pockets	88
Sky Barge	88
Sky Galley	88
Slippers of the Night's Wind	88
Slippers of the Narrow Gulf	88
Slippers of the Smoking Inferno	88
Slithering Rope	88

Statue of Town Defense	88
Stele of Binding	89
Stele of Commandments	89
Stele of Exorcism	89
Stamp of the Heavenly Empire	89
Bear Stone of Harva'roth	90
Dragon Stone of Harva'roth	91
Giant Stone of Harva'roth	91
Lion Stone of Harva'roth	92
Mammoth Stone of Harva'roth	93
Wolf Stone of Harva'roth	93
Studious Robes	94
Swan Helmet	94
Thawb of the City Dweller	94
Thawb of the Sage	94
Thimble of Mending	94
Throne of the Heavens	94
Token Balls	94
Tracking Feather	95
Tribune's Toga	95
Tome of Fate and Prophecy	95
Ushabti Locations	96
Ushabti People	96
Ushabti Vehicles	97
Weather Stone	97
Wheel of Earth	97
Wheel of Fire	97
Wheel of Water	97
Wheel of Wind	97
Whistle of the Middle-Sky	98
Wotan's Cloak	98
Appendix A: New Monsters	**99**
Beetle, Giant Death Watch	99
Caryatid Column	99
Cave Lion	100
Coral Golem	100
Giant Tortoise	101
Glyptodont	101
Hippopotamus	101
Megaloynx	102
Mi-Go	102
Prehistoric Honey Badger	103
Prehistoric Beaver	103
Scroll Familiar	104
Smoke Wyrm	104
Spell Parrot	105
Appendix B: New Spells	**106**
Analyze Conjunction	106
Drain Charge	106
False Attunement	106
Fuel Charge	106
Locate Panoply	106
Major Enchantment	106
Minor Enchantment	106
Suppress Conjunction	106
Suppress Item	106
Transfer Charge	106

Appendix C: Magic Tattoos **107**
    Arrows 107
    Clan Mark 107
    Cloak Clasp 107
    Crossed Weapons 107
    Dragon 107
    Dragon Tattoo Colors 108
    Falcon 108
    Fangs 108
    Flowers 108
    Geometric 108
    Heart 108
    Horse 108
    Mountain 108
    Palm of Energy 108
    Red Eyes 108
    River 108
    Scroll 108
    Shield 108
    Society Mark 109
    Snake 109
    Spear 109
    Tiger 109
    Third Eye 109
    Wolf 109

viii | Tome of Wondrous Items

CHAPTER ONE: INTRODUCTION

Magic items: the best part of treasure other than, well, treasure. In some campaigns they are rarer than hen's teeth; in others, so common you can buy them on the open market. In either case, what you want is more magic items, and then some more. This tome offers you just that: more magic items than you will ever need, and then a few on top of that. Inside, you will find something for every taste, be it subtle magic or booming thunder or arcane might, items of utility and items of raw power, and even items that are cursed or require a steep price to be paid to gain their powers.

Enough preamble; let's get onto the catalog of magic items you now hold in your hands (or view through the magic tablet of reading).

CHAPTER BREAKDOWN

CHAPTER ONE: INTRODUCTION

Aside from this chapter breakdown that you're currently reading, Chapter One includes a short discussion of some of the new magic items "tags" we're introducing and a bit of other information on how to get the most out of this wondrous tome.

CHAPTER TWO: ARMOR

Need protection? You have come to the right place, my friend. Magical armor can spell the difference between life and death for the adventurer, or for their foes. Many of the magical armors here are part of panoplies: sets of magical items that gain power the more of the set you have.

CHAPTER THREE: OTHERWORLDLY ITEMS

Not all magic is of this world. Some things — and it is hard to classify them by the common types of magic items — come from other worlds, other times, and even the mysterious space outside of our realities. Use of these otherworldly items often comes at some cost or great peril. That is if you can figure out how to use them at all. Normal identification magic yields nothing and not even the gods know of these things other than their existence. The only sure way is a combination of research into dusty tomes, or playing around with the items and hoping they don't just go off in your face.

CHAPTER FOUR: RINGS

Why just one ring? No, you need one for each finger when you go looking for magical rings. You'll find them here in spades, enough for both hands at the least.

CHAPTER FIVE: RODS

The power of magical rods is great; they are more than just larger, thicker wands. Yet they are one of the rarest of magical items. Here are a plethora of new rods, many tied to magical feats of daring for those spellslingers out there.

CHAPTER SIX: POTIONS

Consumable magic items are really a win-win. They can affect the game in an interesting way, players enjoy finding them, and once they are gone, they're gone. This section provides lots of new potables and a few that might be better thrown.

CHAPTER SEVEN: SCROLLS

Unrolling a long parchment scroll to save the day with a little extra spell power makes a spellcaster look like a *real* caster, not some conjurer of cheap tricks. You can never have too many of them.

CHAPTER EIGHT: STAVES

What is a mage without a staff, or other spellcasters for that matter? This chapter gives you new staves with which to wield ultimate power, crush your foes, and make the deserts flow with milk and honey. Yes!

CHAPTER NINE: WANDS

Wands, the ultimate point-and-click magical item. Great for spellcasters, but many are useful for everyone. Grab one of these wands, maybe two or three, and see what wonders you can work.

CHAPTER TEN: WEAPONS

Magical weapons are more than just swords. In this chapter, you will find bows, maces, and even magical whips. These are often part of a panoply that combines with armor and other items to grant greater power. All are potent in their own right, although some may be too powerful for your own good (and cursed, don't forget the cursed ones).

CHAPTER ELEVEN: WONDROUS ITEMS

The largest and most diverse chapter in this book, wondrous items run from the useful utility item to near artifact power levels. They are usable by everyone, and frankly are some of the most fun and interesting treasures those pesky characters will uncover. Some of the wondrous items present here are not portable, at least not easily so.

APPENDIX A: NEW MONSTERS

Some of the magic items summon monsters, and we have included their statistics here for your ease and enjoyment. Others eat, hunt, or otherwise interact with magical items, so be wary of the spell moth and the ring warden lest you lose that fancy enchanted baubles (or in the latter case, your finger as well).

APPENDIX B: NEW SPELLS

Two new rules for using magic items, conjunction and panoplies, are introduced below. Among the new spells are ones that interact with these magical phenomena, as well as spells such as *obfuscate nature* and *suppress item* that allow you to alter, change, and otherwise manipulate magic items.

APPENDIX C: MAGICAL TATTOOS

As a bonus, and because the author loves his tattoos and skin art in general, this appendix covers magical tattoos, how to get them, how to use them, and their power. Tattoos, magical or non, come with pain. It's part of the process, and magical tattoos often come at a cost.

ALCHEMICAL FORMULAS

Certain magic items in this book have alchemical formulas included in the descriptions. These formulas refer to **The Tome of Alchemy** sold separately by **Necromancer Games** and are useful for creating magical items.

NEW MAGICAL ITEM RULES

The following new rules systems are designed to enhance the way magical items work and to allow for new ways to view magical items. Conjunction represents the esoteric linkages that some magical items (but by no means all) contain. These effect the other magical items you own, sometimes boosting them or sometimes negatively altering their powers. Panoplies are collections of magical items linked by common theme and thaumatological import. As you collect more of a set of items from the same panoply, all or some of the items gain power.

ESOTERIC CONJUNCTION

Some magic items produce magical fields that interact with similar magic items. These might be magic items that were created by the same craftsfolk or through the same process, or those whose natures or means of production are complementary or antagonistic. The vast majority of magic items do not have any esoteric conjunction; their creation and nature are so idiosyncratic that they do not interact with the magic of other relics.

Esoteric conjunction differs from a panoply in that the conjunction is not designed to be part of the relic; instead, it is a supernatural phenomenon with unintended consequences. Often esoteric conjunction occurs without warning, though someone testing two magical items to determine if they have esoteric conjunction may attempt a DC 18 Intelligence (Arcana) check.

Magic items are conjoined if they share complementary or antagonistic keywords in their descriptor line. A keyword is complementary if it is the same. For example, two items with the Earth keyword are complementarily conjoined. Antagonistic keywords can be found on **Table 1–1** below.

COMPLEMENTARY CONJUNCTION KEYWORDS

Keyword …	is Complementary with
Earth	Water
Fire	Air
Sulfur	Azoth
Mercury	Salt

ANTAGONISTIC CONJUNCTION KEYWORDS

Keyword …	is Antagonistic with
Earth	Air
Fire	Water
Sulfur	Salt
Mercury	Azoth

EFFECTS OF COMPLEMENTARY CONJUNCTION

Two types of effects exist for complementary esoteric conjunction: general and idiosyncratic. General effects are listed below; idiosyncratic effects are listed in the descriptions of individual magic items.
- Two complementary magical items count as only one for the purposes of attunement.
- If two or more complementary items are being carried by the same person, each complementary magical item gains an additional charge or use depending on the magic items in question.

EFFECTS OF ANTAGONISTIC CONJUNCTION

Two types of effects exist for antagonistic conjunction: general and idiosyncratic. General effects are listed below; idiosyncratic effects are listed in the descriptions of individual magic items.
- You cannot attune to multiple items with antagonistic conjunction.
- If two or more antagonistic items are being carried by the same person, each antagonistic magical item reduces its charges or uses by one (to a minimum of one charge or use) depending on the magic items in question.

PANOPLY

Some magic items are created to work together, forming a panoply. Such items have the keyword Panoply (name) in their descriptor to make them easier to find. While each panoply has its own unique effects based on what items are in a collection, they all share some common features. A person has to be attuned or in possession of the items to gain the benefits. Furthermore, a panoply, no matter how many items are in it, counts as two items for attunement purposes. However, you may only have attuned pieces of a single panoply at a time.

CHAPTER TWO: ARMOR

ALCAEUS' LION SKIN
Armor (hide), panoply (Alcaeus), unique (requires attunement)

Ancient legends speak of a great hero who slew a lion of prodigious size. This hero, Alcaeus, had the mighty lion's skin made into a cloak-like suit of armor. Thusly clad and with the lion's head serving as a helmet that framed his own, Alcaeus went on to have many adventures. Which of the hundreds of adventures that have been recorded during the days of the empire and since are true and which are fiction is unknown, as is the final fate of Alcaeus' lion skin.

That the skin existed is well documented. Records dating to the earliest days of the empire mention the lion skin being worn by various heroes and generals. Emperor Haro donned it for his coronation and often wore it while presiding over religious ceremonious. It passed from the imperial treasury into private hands in the dynastic struggles of the later empire and has been reported as recently as last year being worn by a bandit chieftain in distant lands.

Once attuned to *Alcaeus' lion skin*, your armor class is 14 + your Dexterity modifier (maximum +2), and you gain resistance to piercing and slashing damage. Additionally, once per day as a bonus action you may let loose a mighty roar. All foes within a 15-foot cone centered on you must succeed at a DC 13 Wisdom saving throw or become frightened of you until they can no longer see you. Creatures who cannot hear your roar are immune to its effects. You regain the use of this feature each day at dawn.

If worn as part of a complete *panoply of Alcaeus*, as a bonus action you may cause the loose paws of the lion skin to strike at a foe. You gain a +1 bonus to hit with this attack and inflict 1d6 slashing damage if successful.

ANCIENT KING'S HARNESS
Armor (breastplate), panoply (ancient king's), very rare (requires attunement)

The ancient kings were buried in great barrows sealed with stone doors and often topped with stone altars and circles where sacrifices to the dead could be conducted. The kings were buried in the finest raiment adorned with precious stones, gold, and the teeth of fearsome beasts. Alongside these kings were placed the bodies of their spouses and most loyal followers, as well as hunting dogs and horses. These first deaths served to enchant the barrow and provide the first sacrifices to a great king's memory.

The *ancient king's harness* is a breastplate made of bronze adorned with the teeth and fangs of the beasts the king slew in life. Enchanted, these breastplates survived the passage of millennia and are as bright and shiny as when they were first entombed. Many a great hero of the Northlands wore an *ancient king's harness* taken from the animated corpse of one of these long-dead warrior-kings. Once you have attuned to the *ancient king's harness*, your armor class is 16 + your Dexterity modifier (maximum +2).

If worn as part of a complete set of *ancient king's panoply*, you gain advantage on death saves. Additionally, as a bonus action, you may command the teeth adorning your armor to attack a foe within five feet of you. You gain a +1 to hit with this attack and inflict 1d6 + 1 slashing damage to the target if successful.

ANTELOPE SKIN OF ENKIDU
Armor (hide), conjunction (earth), rare

This crudely cut, whole antelope skin has the hair on the hide. It can be draped over your body to form a simple type of clothing that is held in place by leather thongs and careful placement. When worn, your armor class is 13 + your Dexterity modifier. Furthermore, while wearing the *antelope skin of Enkidu* you gain advantage on any attempts to grapple or escape from a grapple, your speed increases by +10 feet, and you can cast *speak with animals* as an action three times per day.

BEHIR ARMOR
Armor (hide), very rare (requires attunement)

This dark blue suit of armor is crafted from the hide of a slain behir so that the head of the beast forms the helmet. When wearing *behir armor*, your armor class is 13 + your Dexterity modifier and you gain resistance to lightning damage. As an action, you may fire a bolt of lightning in a line five feet wide and 15 feet long. Any creature caught in that line must succeed at a DC 15 Dexterity saving throw or suffer 4d6 lightning damage, or half as much on a successful save. You may fire one bolt of lightning from the armor. You regain use of this feature at sunset.

BLISTER BEETLE ARMOR
Armor (hide), very rare (requires attunement)

This rounded body armor is made from the shell of the blister beetle. When wearing *blister beetle armor*, your armor class is 13 + your Dexterity modifier and you gain resistance to acid damage. As a bonus action, you may cause a single melee weapon you are wielding to become envenomed. The next creature struck by that weapon in the next hour must succeed at DC 15 Constitution saving throw or suffer 4d6 poison damage and gain the poisoned condition for one hour, or half as much and not poisoned on a success. You may envenom one melee weapon and regain use of this feature at sunset.

BLOOD ORCHID ARMOR
Armor (hide), very rare (requires attunement)

This bright red and green armor is made from the wood and petals of the blood orchid. When wearing *blood orchid armor*, your armor class is 13 + your Dexterity modifier and you gain resistance to thunder damage. As a bonus action you may touch a creature. The touched creature must succeed at a DC 15 Constitution saving throw or its hit point maximum is reduced by 1d10. This reduction lasts until the creature takes a long rest. If this loss reduces the creature to 0 hit points, it dies. You regain hit points equal to the amount you drained, up to your maximum hit points. You may use this feature three times and regain its use at sunset.

BRONZEWOOD BREASTPLATE
Armor (breastplate), rare

This breastplate is made from bronzewood, a rare wood that can be carefully steamed into shape and then hardens to be as strong as steel. When wearing *bronzewood armor*, your armor class is 15 + your Dexterity modifier. The *bronzewood breastplate* also acts as a druidic focus.

BRONZEWOOD SHIELD
Armor (shield), rare

This crescent-shaped shield is made from bronzewood, a rare wood that can be carefully steamed into shape and then hardens to be as strong as steel. When wielding the *bronzewood shield*, you gain a +3 bonus to your armor class. The *bronzewood shield* also acts as a druidic focus.

CENTURION'S PANOPLY

In ages long past, a powerful empire ruled much of the world. The might of this empire was so great that they freely created magical items for their soldiers. The common soldiers had to make do with a handful of potions or maybe a scroll, but their officers were granted more powerful items. The *centurion's panoply* is one such gift. Upon first attaining this rank, usually by working one's way up through the ranks, a piece of the panoply was granted to the newly minted centurion. As they gained fame, rank, and the notice of their superiors, centurions were granted additional pieces of their panoply.

When they retired or died, their panoply was supposed to be returned to the imperial armories, but this did not always happen. As a result, piece of the panoply made their way into private hands and the illicit trade. The successor kingdoms to that great empire developed the tradition of granting pieces of this panoply to heroes, nobles, or to seal treaties. Today, while it is rare to find a complete set of the centurion's panoply, the pieces turn up from time to time.

CENTURION'S LORICA SEGMENTATA

Armor (splint), panoply (centurion's panoply), rare (requires attunement)

This finely crafted metal breastplate is chased in gold and decorated with the heraldry of an imperial legion. It is composed of bands of metal hoops that overlap across the chest, as well as tassets and pauldrons. A short skirt of metal studded leather, dyed in legionary colors, hangs from the lower edges of the armor. It is not unusual to find the name of the centurion the armor was made for engraved on the inside of the plates in inlaid gold script. The armor never tarnishes. When you are attuned with the *centurion's lorica segmentata*, your armor class is 20 and you do not suffer disadvantage on Stealth checks normally caused by wearing splint armor.

If worn as part of the *centurion's panoply* with the *centurion's galea*, as a bonus action you may cause the armor to shed bright light in a 20-foot radius and dim light 10 feet beyond that.

If worn as part of a complete set of the *centurion's panoply*, you have advantage on death saving throws.

CENTURION'S SCUTUM

Armor (shield), panoply (centurion's), rare (requires attunement)

This finely wrought shield is rather large, easily three-and-a-half-feet tall and a foot-and-a-half wide, with a convex cross-section. It is made from sturdy wood lined with leather and reinforced with steel straps and boss. The front is painted in a variety of colors (red being the most common) and features distinctive legionary heraldry. It is not unusual to find the name of the centurion for whom the shield was made on the inside of the shield in inlaid gold script. The shield never tarnishes.

You gain a +3 bonus to your armor class when you are attuned with the *centurion's scutum*. Additionally, you can use your move to remain stationary and ground your shield. If you do so, you gain the benefits of half cover until the end of your next turn.

If worn as part of the *centurion's panoply* with the *centurion's gladius*, you may use your bonus action to attack with the *centurion's scutum*, and if you hit, inflict 1d6 bludgeoning damage and the target must succeed at a DC 13 Strength save or fall prone.

If worn as part of a complete set of the *centurion's panoply*, you have advantage on Strength checks to bash down obstacles or force open obstacles.

COAT OF MANY METALS

Armor (scale), rare (requires attunement)

This coat of scale mail is made from a single tiger skin turned so that the stripes are on the inside. The coat is faced with large metal scales of different types, enamels, and styles. Once you have attuned to the coat, your armor class is 15 + your Dexterity modifier (maximum 2). As an action, you can expend one charge from the coat, take it off, whip it around your body, and place it back on. When you do this, you must choose one of the following damage types: acid, bludgeoning, cold, fire, lightning, necrotic, piercing, poison, radiant, slashing, or thunder. You gain resistance to that damage type for one hour. You may repeat the process on your next turn while expending two charges to gain immunity to the chosen damage type for one hour. The *coat of many metals* offers protection against one damage type at a time. The *coat* has three charges. It regains 1d3 charges each morning at dawn.

CORAL PLATE

Armor (plate), panoply (coral knight), conjunction (water), very rare (requires attunement)

Despite being made from blocks of coral, this armor is as light and flexible as well-crafted steel plate. The coral is living and gives *coral plate* a bright rainbow pattern. Once attuned to *coral plate*, your armor class is 19. While wearing the *coral plate*, you may breathe water as easily as air, gain a swim speed equal to your normal speed, and are unhindered by being underwater. Furthermore, you may immerse yourself in sea water for an hour to provide all the nourishment you need for a day. If you take a short rest while immersed in sea water, you regain half (rounded down, minimum 1) any hit dice you spend during the short rest. You may use the *coral plate* to regain hit dice once and regain use of this feature following a long rest.

If worn while seated in the *seahorse saddle*, your mount gains a number of additional hit dice equal to your Charisma modifier.

If worn while wielding the *spiny lance* you may use the lance's ink blast property an additional time.

If worn as part of a complete panoply of the coral knight, you may perform a one-hour ritual above a natural coral reef. At the end of this ritual, a section of the reef awakens as a coral golem (see Appendix A: New Monsters). The coral golem serves you until the next tide ends and then returns to its home and natural state.

PANOPLY OF THE CORAL KNIGHT

Scholars disagree on who created the *panoply of the coral knight*. Some maintain that it is a suit of armor created for merfolk or another aquatic people. Others point to the armor's ability to provide for breathing underwater as a sign that it was created by natural air breathers. These scholars lay the credit on the Order of the Sunken Reef, paladins in the service of a lawful good sea deity who protect shipping and travelers along a stretch of dangerous coast.

COUATL ARMOR

Armor (hide), very rare (requires attunement)

This brightly colored armor is made from the hide and feathers of a couatl. When wearing couatl armor, your armor class is 13 + your Dexterity modifier and you gain resistance to radiant damage. At will, you may cast any of the following spells using the armor: detect evil and good, detect magic, and detect thoughts.

CROCODILE ARMOR

Armor (hide), rare (requires attunement)

This suit of armor is fashioned from the hide of a giant crocodile. The crocodile's head forms the helmet and frames your face, while your limbs are clad in the beast's thick hide and claws. The tail is cut short so as not to interfere with your movement while still being long enough to serve as a majestic train. When you don *crocodile armor*, your armor class is 13 + your Dexterity modifier (maximum 2). Furthermore, once you are attuned to the armor, once per day you may use an action to change shape into a **giant crocodile** as the druid's wild shape class feature.

ETHEREAL ARMOR

Armor (leather), rare

This suit of leather armor seems to shimmer in and out of reality in pieces. For example, the chest piece fades away while the shoulder guards remain, the belts and buckles phase in and out of our reality, and the color seems to change from warm tanned leather to a faded and dull shadow. When you wear this armor, your armor class is 12 + your Dexterity modifier. You may use a bonus action each round to magically shift from the Material Plane to the Ethereal Plane or vice versa for 10 minutes. During this time, you can see 60 feet into the Ethereal Plane when you are on the Material Plane and vice versa. You may do this once and regain use of this ability each day at sunset.

> ## HIDE ARMOR ADVENTURE HOOKS
>
> Several armors listed here are made from the hides of living creatures (or whatever an ooze is, ick). An entire adventure can be made out of finding the right mage or alchemist (or maybe both) who can turn the freshly peeled skin into the right kind of armor.
>
> *Flawed Making.* The magic armor is done, but something went wrong and it picked up an esoteric conjunction. A new quest must be conducted to find someone to fix the thing.
>
> *For the King.* A great king wants a suit of hide armor made from a certain creature. The characters are hired to acquire the hide, find someone to enchant it, and bring it back to the king. Alternately, a powerful figure has a suit of enchanted hide armor, and a relative of the skin's original owner wants it stolen so that their loved one can finally rest in peace.
>
> *Unwilling Wonder Worker.* Someone capable of making the magic hide armor is found, but they do not want to do the task. Perhaps they are simply too busy, maybe they dislike the person making the request (or the person who made it), or maybe they are offended by the type of enchanted hide armor. Can the characters find a way to convince the wonder worker to help them?

FLYING SHIELD

Armor (shield), rare

This golden shield is composed of a pair of foot long metal wings joined at the middle. When wielding the *flying shield*, you gain a +3 bonus to your armor class. You may speak a command word to have the *flying shield* take flight for an hour, and for as long as you have one hand on the shield, you can go along for the ride. The *flying shield* has fly 40 feet and can hover. When the duration of the flight ends, the shield falls if it is still in the air. You may use this feature once and regain its use at midday.

GHAST ARMOR

Armor (hide), very rare (requires attunement)

This suit of armor is made from the flayed flesh of a ghast and has a ghoulish gray color as well as the texture of coarse skin. When wearing *ghast armor*, your armor class is 13 + your Dexterity modifier and you gain resistance to necrotic damage. You may use a bonus action to touch a creature. The touched creature must succeed at a DC 15 Constitution saving throw or become paralyzed for one hour. You may use this feature once and regain use of it at sunset.

GOAT-FACED SHIELD

Armor (shield), rare

This large round bronze shield has a lifelike goat's face molded into the boss. The rim of the shield is decorated with twining vines that have leaves shaped like small flames. The *goat-faced shield* is a *+1 shield*. In addition, it has three charges, and you may expend a charge to command the *goat-faced shield* to:

Bray. Speak with a braying goatish voice as a free action. The shield is not intelligent but you can record up to 10 different messages, each of no more than 20 words.

Cone of Flame. As a bonus action, the *goat-faced shield* breathes a 15-foot-long cone of flame. All creatures caught in this cone must succeed at a DC 15 Dexterity save or suffer 14 (3d6) fire damage, or half damage with a successful save.

Fly. As an action you may command the *goat-faced shield* to cast the *fly* spell, targeting you. However, you must retain your grip on the shield or fall as the *goat-faced shield* flies off without you into the distance.

The *goat-faced shield* regains 1d3 charges every sunrise.

GOLDEN CRAB MANICA

Armor (shield), very rare

This manica — an armored sleeve that extends from the neck to the gauntleted hand — is made of gold-plated steel and shaped like a crab's claw. The gauntlet is a large claw with razor-sharp edges. You may not use the hand that is wearing the *golden crab manica* to hold a weapon, cast spells, or manipulate an object. It certainly can be used to lift and carry things. While wearing the *golden crab manica*, your armor class increases by +3. Additionally, your Strength score increases by +2; this can raise your Strength score above 20. Finally, the arm wearing the *golden crab manica* can make an attack with the claw, gaining a +1 to hit and inflicting 2d6 +1 piercing damage with a successful hit. A creature hit by the claw is grappled (escape DC 8 + your Strength modifier + your proficiency bonus). You may use an action to either restrain a creature you have grappled or to inflict 1d6 + 1 piercing damage to it.

HOPLOMACHUS' MANICA

Armor (shield), panoply (hoplomachus), very rare (requires attunement)

The hoplomachi gladiators were noted for their heavy armor and sturdiness in combat. Often the largest gladiators in any given arena's stable, hoplomachi were trained to stand and fight while lighter gladiators tried to find a weak spot in the armor. A *hoplomachus's manica* is an armored sleeve and shoulder guard that fits one arm from the neck to the gauntleted hand.

Once attuned to a *hoplomachus's manica*, your armor class increases by +2 and you gain advantage on Dexterity saving throws. Although the *hoplomachi's manica* is treated as a shield, it leaves the hand free to hold a weapon or even another shield. However, if used to hold another shield, your speed is decreased by 10 feet.

If worn as part of a *panoply of the hoplomachus* with a *hoplomachus' spear*, you gain a +1 to hit and damage with the *hoplomachus' spear*.

If worn as part of a complete set of the *panoply of the hoplomachus*, you may throw *hoplomachus' spear* and the spear reappears in your hand at the end of your turn.

HOPLOMACHUS' SHIELD

Armor (shield), panoply (hoplomachus), very rare (requires attunement)

This heavy concave shield is not as large as the famed shields of the imperial legionnaires, but it is heavier and better suited to individual combat. Made from solid metal, these shields are heavy and only the strongest gladiators could hope to perform while carrying one. The face of the shield is decorated with relief images of glorious arena combats, often notable combats from the recent past. Once attuned to a *hoplomachus' shield*, you gain a +1 to your armor class in addition to the shield's normal bonus. Additionally, as a bonus action you may make a melee attack with your shield, inflicting 1d6 bludgeoning damage and forcing your target to succeed at a Strength saving throw with a DC equal to 8 + your proficiency bonus + your Strength modifier + your proficiency bonus (if applicable) or fall prone.

If carried as part of a *panoply of the hoplomachus* with *hoplomachus' helm*, you have advantage on Strength checks and saving throws, including uses of the Athletics skill.

If worn as part of a complete set of the *panoply of the hoplomachus*, as an action you may cast the *shield of faith* spell.

> ## ADVENTURE HOOK: ARENA OF DEATH
>
> The *panoply of the hoplomachus* and *panoply of the retiarius* are based off sets of armor and weapons worn by gladiators. The characters are captured and forced to fight in an arena against a variety of deadly opponents. These fights are always to the death. The jaded audience's bloodlust is not sated by mere combat, and they require a magical component. The characters are armed with magical items such as the above mentioned panoplies. The enchantment on the arena prevents the items from being removed (at least until the characters lead their gladiator uprising and smash the wards). Some highlights of this adventure:
>
> *Capture the Flags.* The characters and their opponents are each given one piece of several panoplies. The fight is over once one gladiator has an entire set. At the start of the fight, *false attunement* (see **Appendix B: New Spells**) is cast on all gladiators, so they have only 10 rounds to win!
>
> *Fight Until Resurrected.* Everyone fights for 24 hours straight and receives a *resurrection* spell if they die before being put right back into the fight. The winner is the one who dies the least.
>
> *Wheel of Doom.* Sets of traps filling the arena can be activated or deactivated by spinning a great bronze wheel set in the middle of the arena. The gladiators are divided into teams. It would be evil to split the party, so do so.

CHAPTER TWO: ARMOR | 5

JOUSTING ARMOR
Armor (plate), rare

This very fancy plate mail is designed for ease and comfort while mounted on a steed. While wearing *jousting armor*, your armor class is 19. Any creature you mount as a steed counts as being trained for combat and wearing a saddle (if the creature is sapient it must be willing to be mounted). You can mount and dismount a steed without sacrificing any movement. A mount you control may use one of its attacks as an action. Finally, you may not be forcefully dismounted.

LOBSTER ARMOR
Armor (plate), very rare (requires attunement)

This articulated suit of plate armor bears a striking resemblance to the carapace of a lobster. Two antennae sprout from the helmet, the gauntlets look like pincers, and a short tail-like set of tassets hang off the back. While wearing *lobster armor*, your armor class is 19. The armor has three charges and regains charges after soaking in saltwater for one hour. As an action, you may expend one charge to use the following properties:

Aquatic Adaptation. You adapt to water, being able to breathe water and gain a swim speed of 30 feet. However, you no longer are able to breathe air and your walking speed becomes 15 feet. This effect lasts until you expend a charge to revert to your normal means of respiration and movement.

Antennae. You gain darkvision 60 feet and tremorsense 30 feet but only when within water for the next hour.

Claws. For the next hour, you may use a bonus action to attack with one of your claw-like gauntlets. This attack gains a +1 to the attack roll and inflicts 1d8 + 1 bludgeoning damage and the target is grappled (escape DC + 9 + your Strength modifier + your proficiency bonus).

MIMIC ARMOR
Armor (hide), very rare (requires attunement)

This armor can take on any hue or shape. When wearing *mimic armor*, your armor class is 13 + your Dexterity modifier and you gain resistance to acid damage. As an action, you may command the *mimic armor* to change form to appear as some other kind of armor or clothing. Once it changes form, this new shape has all the normal features of *mimic armor* but is indistinguishable from what it appears to be. You can also alter the color, decorations, and general appearance of the armor.

OOZE ARMOR
Armor (hide), very rare (requires attunement)

This gooey mess of armor is made from the carefully treated remains of a variety of oozes. When wearing *ooze armor*, your armor class is 13 + your Dexterity modifier and you gain resistance to psychic damage. Once per day, you may use an action to change your body's substance to become that of an ooze for up to an hour. This allows you to squeeze through any opening no smaller than three inches in height and you become semi-translucent, granting advantage on Dexterity (Stealth) checks. Returning to your normal state can be done as a bonus action. If you return to your normal state while in an area smaller than you, you take 3d10 force damage an are ejected to the nearest available space.

REMORHAZ ARMOR
Armor (hide), very rare (requires attunement)

This blue-white armor is made from the hide of a remorhaz. When wearing *remorhaz armor*, your armor class is 13 + your Dexterity modifier and you gain resistance to cold damage. You may use an action to cause the armor to heat up for one minute. During this time, a creature that touches you or hits you with a melee attack while within five feet of you takes 1d6 fire damage. You may use this feature once and regain use of this feature at the next sunrise.

RETIARIUS'S MANICA
Armor, panoply (retiarius) very rare (requires attunement)

Of the styles of gladiators that fought in magically enhanced combats, the retiarius was one of the most impressive. Great walls of magical force were summoned so that the arena could be filled with seawater. The retiarius fought against summoned or captured sea monsters within these arcanely created arenas. The *retiarius's manica* is an armored sleeve and shoulder guard that fits one arm from the neck to the gauntleted hands. It is usually lightly adorned but gilding or engravings depicting sea life is common. Once you attune to the *retiarius's manica*, your armor class increases by +2. Additionally, as a reaction, if an enemy succeeds on a melee attack against you, you may intercede your armored arm between you and a foe. You make an attack roll, and if you succeed, the attack is negated.

If worn as part of the *panoply of the retiarius* with *retiarius's net*, as a bonus action you may recall *retiarius's net* to your hand, teleporting the net from a distance of up to 60 feet.

If worn as part of a complete set of the *panoply of the retiarius*, you may cast *speak with animals* at will, but the animals targeted must be aquatic.

RHINOCEROS ARMOR
Armor (hide), rare (requires attunement)

This suit of armor is fashioned from the hide of a large rhinoceros, complete with the head serving as the helmet (horn attached), the forelimbs covering your arms and legs, and even the short tuft tail protruding from your backside. When you don *rhinoceros armor*, your armor class is 13 + your Dexterity modifier (maximum 2). Furthermore, once you are attuned to the armor, once per day you may use an action to change shape into a **rhinoceros** as the druid's wild shape class feature.

ROCK TROLL ARMOR
Armor (hide), very rare (requires attunement)

This stony armor is made from the hide of a rock troll. When wearing *rock troll armor*, your armor class is 13 + your Dexterity modifier and you gain resistance to force damage. As an action, you may cause your next successful attack to be counted as if made by a magic weapon. You may do this three times and regain expended uses at sunset.

SANDWALKER'S ARMOR
Armor (any), rare

Most commonly made of leather, chain, or splint mail, *sand walker's armor* is enchanted to enable the wearer to survive in the heat of the open desert while wearing stiflingly hot armor. When worn, you do not suffer any ill effects from extreme heat, can survive without drinking water, and ignore the effects of difficult terrain that is the result of heat or sand. Additionally, you have a +1 bonus to your armor class in addition to any normally given by the armor.

SALAMANDER ARMOR
Armor (any), rare

This glowing red-and-orange armor is made from the hide of a salamander. When wearing *salamander armor*, your armor class is 13 + your Dexterity modifier and you gain resistance to fire damage. As an action, you may breathe a 15-foot-long cone of fire. Any creature caught in this cone must succeed at a DC 15 Dexterity saving throw or suffer 4d6 fire damage, or half as much on a success. You may breathe one cone of fire from the armor and regain use of this feature at sunrise.

SCROLLED SHIELD
Armor (shield), rare (requires attunement)

This curved round shield is made of a shiny purple metal that never tarnishes. On the inside curve is an engraving of a blank scroll. Once you attune to the *scrolled shield*, you gain an additional +1 bonus to your armor class. You may spend an hour mediating on the shield and a *spell scroll* with a spell on it with a casting time of 1 action or 1 bonus action that you are holding in your hand. At the end of this time, the *spell scroll* crumbles to dust and is written on the inside of the shield. You may use a bonus action to cast the spell.

SPIDER SILK ARMOR
Armor (chain shirt), rare

This gossamer armor is made from the spun and enchanted fibers of various monstrous spiders. When wearing *spider silk armor*, your armor class is 13 + your Dexterity modifier. You gain a climb speed equal to your normal speed and may climb difficult surfaces, even hanging upside down, without requiring an ability check.

TORTOISE SHELL SHIELD
Armor (shield), uncommon

This shield is made of a single large turtle or tortoise shell with simple leather straps on the inside curve. The *tortoise shell shield* increases your armor class by +3 when you use it. Additionally, you can command the shield to become a small boat (speed 3 mph, AC 18, 150 hp, cargo 500 pounds) for eight hours. The boat needs to be rowed or poled and can hold six people. The boat becomes a shield when you utter the same command, or when the duration elapses. If the *tortoise shell shield* is destroyed in boat form, the magic dissipates and it becomes a normal, although wrecked, boat.

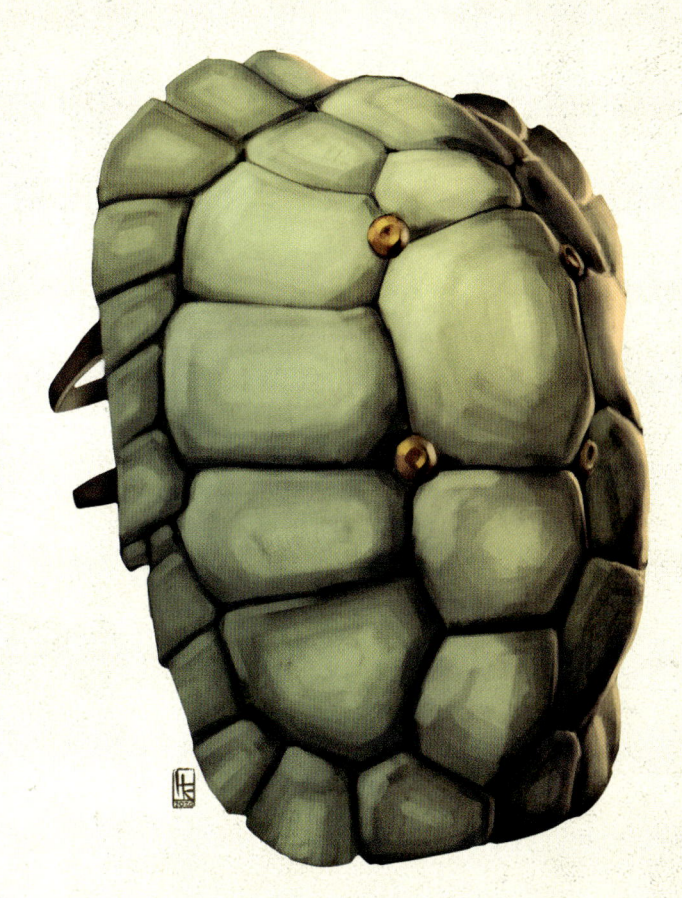

TRIBUNE'S CUIRASS
Armor (breastplate), panoply (tribune's panoply), very rare (requires attunement)

Bearing the heraldry of an imperial legion as well as the marks of the Imperial Smiths and the Imperial College of Wizardry, this cuirass is decorated with intricate scenes of warfare and sculpted to resemble a heavily muscled torso. The creators spared no expense, and the armor is dripping with gold leaf and other adornments. The name of the tribune it was awarded to, as well as the date of awarding and the name of the emperor presenting it, are engraved in the inside of the armor in glowing script. The cuirass never tarnishes or rusts. When you are attuned with the *tribune's cuirass*, your armor class is 16 + your Dexterity modifier (maximum +2).

If worn as part of the *tribune's panoply* with the *tribune's spatha*, as an action, you may cast *hold person*. You may do this once and regain use of this feature following a short rest.

If worn as part of a complete set of the *tribune's panoply*, you add +2 to your Strength score. This may raise your Strength score above 20.

WALL PASSER

Armor (leather), very rare

This gray-dyed suit of leather armor has no obvious buckles or straps, yet it easily fits itself to the wearer. When wearing this armor, you have AC 12 + your Dexterity modifier. As an action, you can make yourself incorporeal for 10 minutes. You appear as a ghostly image of yourself, translucent and insubstantial. While in this incorporeal form, you can move through other creatures and objects as if they were difficult terrain. You suffer 10 force damage if you end your turn inside an object. You may not interact with the physical world and gain advantage on any Dexterity (Stealth) checks. Finally, you gain resistance to acid, cold, fire, and lightning damage, as well as bludgeoning, piercing and slashing damage from nonmagical attacks while you are incorporeal. During this duration, you can become corporeal again and switch back to being incorporeal at will. You may do this once and regain the use each sunset.

WARDED PLATE

Armor (plate), very rare

This ornate suit of plate armor is engraved on the inside with golden arcane script. When wearing *warded plate*, your armor class is 18. Each suit of warded plate is tied to one specific type of creature. The specified type of creature must succeed at a DC 15 Charisma saving throw to approach within 10 feet of you, and even if it makes its save, it suffers disadvantage on attack rolls made against you, and you gain advantage on saving throw made against any effect the creature causes.

WARDED PLATE SPECIFIED CREATURE

1d10	Creature Type	1d10	Creature Type
1	Aberrations	6	Fey
2	Beasts	7	Fiends
3	Celestials	8	Giants
4	Dragons	9	Monstrosities
5	Elementals	10	Undead

8 | Tome of Wondrous Items

CHAPTER THREE: OTHERWORLDLY ITEMS

Not all magical items found in the Lost Lands are native to that world and plane. While many of the extraplanar items belong to the faithful of one deity or another, others come from someplace else, somewhere that lies beyond even divine knowledge. A few otherworldly relics are the result of visitors from other planes and realities. One of the events, the Cometfall, has provided numerous items that have perplexed scholars and driven treasure hunters to extreme ends to acquire.

USING OTHERWORLDLY ITEMS

Otherworld relics are not like more common magical items. *Identify* and similar spells do not give insight into their use, nor can one study them and easily figure out how to use them. You must experiment with the item by pressing buttons, turning dials, and investigating how the item operates. Their very nature is so far beyond that of mortals, and even many gods, that no shortcuts exist in figuring out how to use them. Also, no one may be considered proficient in the use of an otherworldly item unless so stated in the item's description.

RELICS OF THE COMETFALL

Decades ago, an unexpected comet was spotted in the sky. Astrologers and sages had long charted the regular celestial visitors, and the appearance of a rogue comet elicited a great shock. The learned argued and studied while the ignorant feared an evil portent. The rogue comet's appearance was brief and fiery, and it left a trail of smoke and flame across the sky that spanned from the east to the farthest west before impacting somewhere in wild untamed country. Although many expeditions have been mounted, none found the crater that no doubt resulted from the impact.

The rogue comet shed pieces of itself across the world during its long, slow plummet to the ground, and some of these pieces survived. It has been determined from these fragments that the comet was composed of a strange metal fused with a substance as light as glass yet flexible and difficult to cut. Some relics have been found within these cometary fragments, and these have served only to spur greater interest in scholarly circles and among the more foolish treasure hunters.

ENERGY DISK

Otherworldly Item, uncommon

Energy disks are thin, three-inch diameter disks made from a colored material similar in texture to fine porcelain but incapable of being shattered without great force (AC 19, 55 HP). A small depression on one side is the same size and shape as a *power disk*. They are slightly convex, and one side has a button in a contrasting color that glows when pressed. The button starts to flash six seconds after being pressed. Six seconds after that, the *energy disk* emits a flash of light that matches its color and affects all creatures within a 30-foot cube who must succeed at a DC 15 Dexterity saving throw or suffer the effects of the blast. After releasing its stored energy, the disk becomes inert until a *power disk* is place upon it. This drains the *power disk* of all of its charges. There are five types of *energy disk*, each with different effects. An *energy disk* can be thrown up to 50 feet away as an action.

Black. A black *energy disk* emits a flash of darkness that causes all caught within its area of effect to fall asleep for 2d6 hours. This is not a magical sleep and can affect elves and others immune to magical sleep.

Red. A red *energy disk* emits a flash of flame that inflicts 18 (4d8) fire damage on all caught within its area of effect.

Green. A green *energy disk* emits a cloud of gas that inflicts 18 (4d8) poison damage on all caught within its area of effect.

Yellow. A yellow *energy disk* emits a bright flash of light that blinds those caught within its area of effect for 24 hours.

Purple. A purple *energy disk* translocates all those caught within the area of effect. Those affected are teleported 2d10 miles in a random direction. They will not rematerialize inside a solid object or creature, in a dangerous location, or in open air, but are instead shunted to the nearest safe location.

ENERGY PROJECTOR

Otherworldly Weapon, rare

This metal and ceramic device consist of an open armature that slides over the forearm and allows you to grasp a protruding handle. A foot-long tube extends from an eight-inch rectangular box that is fitted to the top of the armature. The handle has three small studs that can be depressed, and the box has a dial and a row of lights. From left to right, the lights are red, yellow, and green. A slot on the underside of the box next to the handle is the thickness and depth of a *power disk*. Using an action to press a stud causes the weapon to fire. The *energy projector* adjusts your aim when you fire, granting you a +1 bonus to the attack roll.

The topmost stud causes the *energy projector* to fire a beam of blue light at a target (range 120/480 ft.) You make a ranged attack, and if you hit a living creature, that creature must succeed at a DC 15 Constitution saving throw or be stunned for one minute.

The middle stud causes the *energy projector* to fire a beam of red light at a target (range 120/480 ft.). You make a ranged attack, and if you hit a living creature, that creature suffers 2d8 fire damage and must succeed at a DC 15 Dexterity save or be lit on fire. A creature lit on fire suffers 1d6 fire damage at the start of its turn and can use an action to put out the flames.

The bottommost stud causes the *energy projector* to fire a black beam of light at a target (range 120/480 ft.). You make a ranged attack, and if you hit a living creature, that creature suffers 27 (6d8) necrotic damage.

The dial has three settings labeled in an unknown language (if using magic to determine the language, the settings are 1, 2, and 3. Setting 1 is the standard and does not change the effects listed above. Setting 2increases the save DC of the beam fired by the topmost stud by +2, and the damage of the other two studs by +2d8. If placed on Setting 3, the *energy projector* fires a 15-foot cone instead of a beam.

The three lights indicate power level. The *energy projector* holds 20 charges (though you will not know that exact number). A green light indicates it has between 15 and 20 charges. The yellow light indicates there are between 5 and 14 charges left. When the red light comes on, the *energy projector* holds 4 or fewer charges. It can be fully recharged with a *power disk*, which drains the power disk in the process.

Each use on Setting 1 uses one charge. Setting 2 uses three charges and Setting 3 uses 10 charges. Each use of the bottommost stud uses an additional charge. If the *energy projector* does not have enough charges to fire a beam on a setting, it will not fire and your action to fire it is wasted.

FLIGHT BELT

Otherworldly Item, rare

This 60-inch-long and three-inch-wide belt of a flexible metallic cloth has a large buckle hidden within a three-inch-square metal box. The box has a slot the same thickness and depth as a *power disk*, a pair of dials, a pair of switches, a red button, a flat black glass plate, and a line of colored lights (red, yellow, and green from left to right). If the *flight belt* is attached to a living creature and has any charges, the red button activates it. Once the belt is activated, the creature, if it is Large or smaller, hovers a few inches above the ground.

The left-hand dial controls horizontal movement, while the right-hand controls vertical movement. It takes an action to operate the *flight belt*. Following 80 hours of practice, you can control the belt to a point that it grants you a fly speed of 30 feet as long as it has adequate charge. However, the *flight belt* moves exactly 30 feet on any turn you use it. You need to figure out the controls yourself. Until you refine your control of the *flight belt*, you must succeed on a DC 13 Dexterity check every time you use it to move, and move in a random direction (three dimensionally) if you fail. Every minute of operation uses one charge.

The left-hand switch overcharges the pulse reactor, increasing the flight speed to 60 feet. This uses one additional charge per minute of operation. The switch must be returned to its off position in order to stop the overcharge effects.

The right-hand switch dampens the pulse reactor, decreasing flight speed to 15 feet. This allows the *flight belt* to use one charge for every two minutes of operation. The switch must be returned to its off position to stop the dampening effect.

The flat black glass plate displays altitude and a three-dimensional map of the surrounding cubic mile. The numbers are meaningless without the use of *comprehend languages* or similar means. A successful DC 13 Intelligence check deciphers the map.

The three lights indicate the number of charges remaining in the *flight belt*. Green indicates 50 to 60 charges. A yellow light indicates 10 to 49 charges, while the red light comes on when there are fewer than ten charges left. Once the red light comes on, the overcharge effect of the left-hand switch no longer functions, and the belt's maximum speed is 15 feet. Once the *flight belt* has a single change left, safety protocols kick in and the *flight belt* descends at a rate of 10 feet per round for two minutes (and thus uses up the last charge) or until you reach a solid surface, and the controls no longer function. If the *flight belt* runs out of charges while in descending safety mode, it ceases to function and you begin to fall.

The *flight belt* holds 60 charges, and a single *power disk* can recharge up to 20 charges. If out of charges, the *flight belt* does not operate.

GOLEM SUIT
Otherworldly item, very rare

This oddly shaped, nine-foot-tall suit of armor is made of a dense material that is somewhere between metal and ceramic in composition. It has a fully enclosed helmet without any visor or other opening, two arms and two legs, and the joints are covered in large spheres. None of the pieces can be separated from the whole. A large backpack of similar material is attached to the suit as if an integral part of it. The left arm ends in a three-fingered hand, and the right arm has a long hollow tube attached to it under the arm that extends two feet past the hand. All told, the suit weigh 800 pounds.

The left side of the *golem suit* has nine latches that recess into the suit. A latch must be depressed to access it, at which point it pops out and may be worked. Once all nine latches are open, the suit can be manually pried open with a successful DC 18 Strength check. The inside is hollow and has several metal wires with rubbery disks attached to them. The wires run into the suit's inner surface. The helmet has a flat curve of very fine black glass. If the suit is closed and latched, it seals against the outside environment. Anyone trapped inside begins to suffocate in five minutes. The suit fits a Medium-sized humanoid snugly. The user must be naked to comfortably wear the suit, and any clothing interferes with the suit's operations. Small or smaller creatures cannot get the suit to activate, and Large or larger creatures simply will not fit.

If the *golem suit* has sufficient charges to be activated, it can be activated by attaching the rubbery disks to the temples, wrists, chakra points along the spine, back of the knees, ankles, and over the heart. These disks are self-adhesive and pull away any body hair where they are attached.

Once activated, the black glass panel lights up to reveal a highly detailed view of the outside world as seen from the front of the suit's helmet. Icons flash along the edges of the panel to display the outside atmosphere, suit integrity, power level, view options, wearer's health status, and target-tracking information. These will likely be confusing for the user.

Also, once activated, the suit extends several sets of tubes into the wearer. One set allows for bodily waste to be excreted and passed outside of the suit or held inside in an internal reservoir that can contain one gallon of waste. Needle-tipped tubes penetrate the user's inner elbows and allow for various medications to be dispensed.

When wearing the suit, your armor class becomes 20 and your Strength score becomes 24. Your speed increases to 40 feet. If you figure out which icon to use, the suit allows you to use a bonus action to perform a rocket-assisted leap of 50 feet vertically or 60 feet horizontally using one charge. The target-tracking system grants you advantage on all attack rolls made while wearing the suit.

The view options include an electronic version of darkvision 120 feet, the ability to zoom in to 100x magnification, and signal amplification that allows you to ignore penalties due to fog, smoke, or other obscurement. Auto dampeners prevent loss of vision due to sudden changes in light as well as brightly lit conditions. Finally, the viewscreen can be set to show any 180-degree arc from the helmet.

The suit monitors the user's vital signs and dispenses medications from an onboard reservoir that contains 10 doses of each of the following. It automatically stabilizes you if you are reduced to 0 hit points. It can dispense stimulants to remove one level of exhaustion per 24-hour period. It can dispense more powerful stimulants whose effects are the same as the *haste* spell, although at the end of the duration you gain a level of exhaustion. Finally, it can dispense medications to remove any one of the following conditions at the start of your turn: blinded, charmed, frightened, paralyzed, stunned, and unconscious.

The suit has a built-in weapon system in the form of an energy projector. Each use of this projector uses one charge. The projector cannot be removed from the suit without damaging both.

The suit has other minor functions. It can be set to surveil the area while you sleep and awaken you if a creature approaches within 30 feet (and can be fine-tuned to determine which creatures are allies and set to assume that a certain-sized creature or smaller is not a threat). It can induce sleep. It can be locked in position and the gripping hand can be locked to hold an item.

The suit's backpack holds 100 charges, and if there are no charges in the backpack, the suit cannot activate. When it reaches zero charges, it automatically unlatches and opens the suit, although it can still manually be closed or prevented from opening. The suit uses one charge every hour or partial hour of operation.

MERFOLK SUIT
Otherworldly item, rare

This odd suit of armor consists of a helmet, a skintight cloth garment that covers the entire body, a square metal backpack with cloth straps, and two shoes shaped like fins that strap onto the feet. The garment covers the entire body from the neck down and includes gloves and booties. A metal ring around the neck allows the helmet to be latched on with an airtight seal. The booties do not split the toes into separate sections like a glove would and have attachment points for the fins. The gloves have pressure points that activate and control the suits functions. These require a finger movement that is simple enough to use quickly in an emergency. Anyone playing around with the suit figures these out if they experiment with finger movements. The pressure points can be felt in the fingertips of the gloves. Internal and external straps allow the suit to be changed to fit a creature from size Small to Large.

The helmet is made of a shiny metal that is resistant to corrosion. There is no visor, but the front of the helmet is covered in a clear glass-like material that is resistant to being shattered. Four small circles of the same glass-like material surround the face plate, and behind them are odd mirrors and objects. Three flat glass panels inside the helmet have radial displays showing numbers. The leftmost decreases as you descend beneath the waves; the middle points an arrow at the location where you were when you turned on the helmet; and the rightmost decreases the longer the suit is operational. On the back of the helmet are a hollow ring of metal and a smaller ring of metal filled with blunt needles.

The right glove has three pressure points in the fingers. If you press the right hand's index finger, the helmet's internal black glass disks come on. The right pinky activates the four clear glass circles on the helmet to create a 30-foot cone of bright light that sheds dim light for 20 feet beyond it. If you press the pressure point on the right hand's middle finger, it activates the backpack's breathing function. The left hand's glove has five pressure points, all of which control the directed thrust system. Beginning with the left hand's pinky, the controls are on/off, hover, direction, speed 1, speed 2.

The backpack has two shoulder straps that can be adjusted to various sizes to fit Small to Large creatures. A short hose on the backpack's top connects to a ring of metal on the back of the helmet, and a short cable of some leather-like substance that ends in a rectangular piece filled with tiny holes connects to the matching port on the helmet. Once these are connected the backpack provides power and air to the rest of the suit. The backpack holds 20 charges and can be recharged by leaving it in bright sunlight, where it regains a charge every two hours.

While wearing a *merfolk suit*, you gain resistance to cold damage. If the helmet is worn and connected to the backpack and the backpack has power, it draws dissolved gasses from water and provides you with breathable air, using one charge every two hours for a Small creature, one charge every hour for a Medium creature, and one charge every half hour for a Large creature. Use of the lighting system does not consume a charge.

The backpack also has a ducted thrust system that expels water across micro fans to allow for rapid travel underwater. When combined with the fins, this gives you a swim speed of 30 feet (20 feet without the fins) and consumes one charge per hour or partial hour of use. You can increase this speed to 120 feet, consuming one charge per minute or partial minute of use.

NEEDLE PROJECTOR
Otherworldly item, rare

This device vaguely resembles a crossbow. There is a curved grip with three buttons on the left-hand side, roughly where a right-handed person's thumb would rest while holding the grip. Above the grip is a boxy portion with a three-inch-long hollow tube. In front of the grip is an open cavity that fits a *potion ampoule*. The butt of the *needle projector* is hollow and holds a special charge block that contains enough charges and ammunition for 20 shots.

The *needle projector* can be fired by using an action to press down one of the buttons. The bottommost of three thumb buttons fires a single needle (range 20/80 ft., 1d4 piercing damage, light property). If the middle thumb button is pressed, the *needle projector* fires a barrage of needles

10 | Tome of Wondrous Items

(+1 to hit, increases damage to 1d8, uses five shots). The topmost button activates an internal mechanism that coats all needles fired with whatever substance is in an attached *potion ampoule*. One *potion ampoule* can coat up to 20 shots from a *needle projector*. Targets struck with a coated needle suffer the effects of whatever potion fills the ampoule, although likely in a greatly reduced fashion versus injecting or consuming the entire contents (GM's discretion).

OTHERWORLDLY POTIONS
Otherworldly item, rarity varies

Otherworldly potions are found in *potion ampoules* or already loaded into *potion wands*. The following potions are labeled by color.

Black: A creature with 0 hit points is stabilized. A creature with at least 1 hit point, they must succeed on a DC 15 Constitution saving throw or suffer 21 (6d6) poison damage.

Blue: The creature is cured of any diseases, even magical disease, that they are suffering from and they cannot be infected with any diseases, mundane or magical, for the next 365 days.

Brown: The creature must make on a DC 15 Constitution saving throw. On a failure, the creature is paralyzed, while on a success the target takes 10 (3d6) poison damage on a success.

Gray: The creature must make a DC 15 Constitution saving throw. On a failure, the creature is petrified while on a success the target takes 10 (3d6) poison damage .

Green: The creature recovers 21 (6d6) hit points.

Indigo: The creature must make a DC 15 Constitution saving throw, taking 21 (6d6) poison damage on a failure or half as much on a success.

Orange: The creature must succeed on a DC 15 Constitution saving throw or be stunned for 1d6 + 1 rounds.

Purple: The creature is affected as per the spell *haste*, but at the end suffers two levels of exhaustion.

Red: The creature is placed into a healing coma for 1d4 days. They may not be awakened during this time. At the end of this time, the creature awakens with full hit points and hit dice, and all conditions affecting them are removed.

White: One level of exhaustion is removed from the creature.

Yellow: The creature must succeed at a DC 15 Wisdom saving throw or suffer the effects of the *confusion* spell. After the duration of the spell ends, they immediately gain the benefits of an *augury* spell.

POTION AMPOULE
Otherworldly item, uncommon

These two-inch-long, half-inch-wide glass tubes hold a liquid of some kind. One end is rounded and blunt, while the other is capped with a hollow metal cap. Inside the hollow is a rubber gasket with a needle protruding from it. A *potion ampoule* can be placed in the appropriate receptacle on a *needle projector* or *potion wand* or used on its own by pressing the uncapped end against flesh. Several types of otherworldly potions are available, and a *potion ampoule* can be opened, filled, and resealed with any liquid.

POTION WAND
Otherworldly item, rare

A rectangular block of metal top this four-inch-long opaque glass cylinder. The cylinder has six buttons on it, which are green, red, blue, black, purple, and white from top to bottom. If a button is depressed, nothing happens unless the box end is being held against living tissue. If the box end is being held against living tissue, the *potion wand* dispenses medicines according to the color of the button pressed. The *potion wand* holds up to 10 doses in each internal reservoir and can be refilled at a medical dispenser or from a *potion ampoule*.

POWER DISK
Otherworldly item, uncommon

This inch-diameter blue disk of a ceramic-like substance is perfectly smooth. It has a small, recessed light on one surface that glows either red or green. There is no obvious means of operating the *power disk*. If it has at least one charge, the *power disk*'s light glows green; if no charges remain, it glows red. The *power disk* holds up to 20 charges for use with otherworldly relics. If placed within an item that uses *power disks*, it transfers its remaining charges into the item until that item's internal storage of charges is filled. A *power disk* can be recharged using the following means: one hour placed in direct sunlight yields one charge, 10 hours in a fire of at least 500º yields one charge, and being placed in a recharging receptacle for one minute completely recharges the *power disk*.

RELICS OF DISTANT WORLDS

Wizards are odd sorts and tend to delve into things others would not even imagine. Not a few wizards have used their magical knowledge to peer into other worlds, distant cosmoses, and even alternate realties. These are beyond the planes known by many scholars but are strange places where great birds of steel fly the skies like proud dragons, people dress in bizarre fashions and seem to be sporting parasitic metal boxes attached to their hands and ears, and glass boxes flicker with alien life.

Sometimes the wizards go to these realms and return with things that should not exist in the world — objects of great power and wonder that are magical in effect, but not magical in nature. These are those otherworldly items from distant worlds. Oddly, these otherworldly items often have writing on them in Common. Weird, huh?

BOOM CLUB
Otherworldly weapon, very rare

Only a handful of these weapons have been brought back from distant worlds. There are two types, the *lesser* and *greater boom club*, but both work roughly the same. *Boom clubs* are metal and wooden weapons that bear a slight resemblance to a warclub with a shaft of metal (or metal and wood), and a striking surface of wood. You can use a *boom club* as a club, and the *greater boom club* has the versatile property. However, if you do so, there is a 15% chance that the *boom club* is destroyed in the process.

Lesser Boom Club. This one-handed metal club has a curved wooden striking surface, a rotating piece near the striking surface, and a long hollow metal handle. You can use it like a club, but it is better held by the striking surface with the handle pointed at a target. When you do so, you may use an action to make a ranged weapon attack with the *lesser boom club*, range 40/120 ft., damage 2d8 bludgeoning. The *lesser boom club* holds six uses as a ranged weapon and after that functions only as a club.

Greater Boom Club. This long club has a lever near the curved wooden striking surface, a wood frame, and a long hollow metal tube along the handle. You can use it like a club, but it is better held by the striking surface with the handle pointed at a target. When you do so, you may use an action to make a ranged weapon attack with the *greater boom club*, range 200/ 800 ft., damage 2d10 bludgeoning. Once fired, a bonus action must be used to work the lever for the *boom club* to be able to fire again. The *greater boom club* holds 14 uses as a ranged weapon and after that functions only as a club.

Chapter Three: Otherworldly Items | 11

IRON HORSE

Otherworldly weapon, very rare

One of the complexities of these other worlds seems to be machines that act as horses, or that at least serve the same role. The *iron horse* is a metal device with a leather saddle, two handles that rise up from the front end, a pair of rubber wheels, and a complex assortment of metal parts and tubes in the middle. The *iron horse* is very loud and spews large clouds of black smoke when it is used. When you sit upon the leather saddle and grasp the raised handles, you can manipulate the various levers, pedals, and twisting portions of the handle to make the *iron horse* move at speed 80, and hopefully steer it. The *iron horse* has a very limited amount of uses; it can run only for 50 hours before it sputters and dies, no doubt unable to exist in our magic rich environment.

TALKER

Otherworldly item, very rare

This flat rectangular box made of gleaming, smooth metal and some sort of fine ceramic has one surface covered in a flat black glass. The box is only a quarter-inch thick but is four inches long and two inches wide. There are two buttons; one is embedded in the lower fifth of the flat glass panel, while the other is on the upper right-hand side. A folding wire stand on the back allows it to be carried in one hand or propped up in either a horizontal or vertical position. The *talker* seems to never need a charge or other means of power.

If it has a *power disk* with at least one charge in it, the *talker's* black glass panel lights up with several strange images. It can function for up to eight hours with one charge. The images seem to vary from *talker* to *talker*, but all have the following images. Pressing an image on the flat glass activates it.

Black Box with Numbers: This image flashes, and then the glass shows an empty white box at the top, rows of numbers below 0–9, and a column of odd symbols to the right.

Blue Box with Compass: This image flashes and then the glass shows a compass pointing north. As you move, the compass needle keeps turning to point toward north. The compass also shows degrees from north.

Green Handle with Bubble: This image flashes, and then the glass shows an 11-digit code at the very top, a white field with a smaller outlined white box just below, and another smaller outlined white box in the middle. A box displaying an alphabet fades into view along the lower third of the glass. If you enter a numeric designator in the top box, you can communicate textually to the *talker* linked to the numeric designator.

Green Handle with Two Bulbs: This image flashes, and then the glass shows. This image flashes, and then the glass shows an 11-digit code at the very top, an outlined white box, and a list of 1d4 11-digit codes, and then a large green button at the bottom. If you touch the outlined white box, a row of numbers from 0–9 fades in along the bottom third of the glass. If you enter an 11-digit numeric code into the white outlined box or touch one of the 11-digit codes in the list and then press the green button, you can communicate verbally with the linked *talker*. The list of codes keeps a log of the last 10 *talkers* you have connected with.

Red Box with Small Circle in Middle: This image flashes, and then the glass shows a detailed painting of the area the back of the *talker* was pointed at as well as a red button. The painting changes as you move the *talker* about. If you press the red button, the painting freezes in place and you hear a loud click.

Red Box with Small Tabs on Top: This image flashes, and then the glass shows tiny paintings, including any you captured by depressing the red box with a small circle in the middle image. You can touch one of these paintings and expands to fill the glass.

Talkers might have up to 1d6 additional images, such as the following:

Black Box with White Circle and Two Arms: This image flashes, and then the glass shows a white circle with three black arms inside pointing at numbers ranging from 1–12 spaced evenly around the outside of the circle. One arm is long and touches the edge of the circle; this one moves rapidly around, making a full rotation at a slow count of 60. The shorter arm moves slowly, making a full rotation every 24 hours. The middle arm moves moderately fast, making a full rotation every hour of the day. The arms are highly accurate and never seem to lose even a fraction of time. If you touch the circle, a set of arms in red appear; you can move these arms to different positions. Once you do so and stop touching the image, the *talker* makes a loud alarm noise every day at the assigned time.

Blue Box with Bar and Hanging Orbs: This image flashes, and then the glass shows a list of odd phrases. The *talker* emits music if you touch one of these phrases. There are hundreds of phrases in the list.

Gray Box with Warrior: This image flashes, and then the glass shows a moving painting of a city from a distant world. At the bottom corners of the painting are glowing symbols, hearts on the left and odd rounded cylinders on the right. Shapes move in the background and sometimes get close. As they near, flashes appear for their hands and the hearts decrease. You can use your fingers to move the view of the painting around and make a flash appear in the painting, though when you do the latter, the number of rounded cylinders decreases. If all of the hearts disappear, the painting flashes red and the words, "you lose," appear on the painting. If the number of rounded cylinders becomes 0, the flashing no longer happens.

Orange Box with Open Book: This image flashes, and then the glass shows several small paintings. When you touch one of these paintings, it opens and fills the screen with text as if from a book.

Purple Box with Running Figure: This image flashes, and then the glass shows a number that increases each time you take a step.

Yellow Box with Raccoon Face: This image flashes, and then the glass shows a list of words. If you touch the word, the *talker* translates a language associated with that name into Common if someone is speaking that language within 30 feet. The translation appears as text on the *talker*. All of the common languages of your world are there, but the names are all different than what you are used to.

Yellow Box with Starburst: This image flashes, and then the glass shows several rows of strange symbols. There are yellow crescents, black stars, blue orbs, green squares, and purple triangles in random arrangements. If you touch one of these, it disappears and the symbols above drop down the column. Should this cause two symbols of the same type to now be vertically adjacent, those disappear as well, and so forth until there are no longer any adjacent symbols of the same type in that column. New symbols fall down into the columns to fill the empty spaces. Numbers off to the side keep increasing: One set increases with every breath, while the other tracks how many symbols you have caused to disappear. A third number at the top starts at 10 and increases regularly. At first, if you spend one minute making symbols disappear and make 10 or more disappear, the columns reset with new symbols and the number at the top increases to 20. This cycle continues, and if you continue to make the minimum number of symbols disappear before the breath counter to the side increase from zero to 60. If you fail to do this, the glass flashes, and the top number resets to 10. Should you spend more than five minutes making symbols disappear, you must succeed at a DC 15 Wisdom saving throw or be forced to spend at least one hour per day making symbols disappear.

RELICS OF STRANGE WORLDS

These relics came from an unknown plane of existence, some scholars believe from several planes. They are not native to the known planes, and indeed, their form might be strange to us but their composition is certainly like that of this world. Their use is certainly dangerous, both to the user and to whomever they might be targeting.

ARM BUG

Otherworldly weapon, very rare (requires attunement, see below)

This three-foot-long insect looks much like a large beetle or cockroach. It has a shiny black carapace, a pair of antennae at one end, and a soft underbelly. There is no obvious mouth or other orifice. It has six jointed legs that are too short to allow for movement; indeed, the creature does not move at all.

The *arm bug* attaches to the arm of the person who attunes to it. Which arm is up to you, but it cannot be changed once the bug attaches. The attachment process is painful, and the *arm bug* inflicts 14 (4d6) piercing damage when it attaches (this damage ignores any damage resistance as it occurs inside you). During this process, it latches its six legs around your arm and extends two tubes from its soft underbelly into your forearm. The first tube crawls under your skin and grows around your fist, rendering that hand useless save for firing the weapon by squeezing the soft pulpy sack that now fills the spaces between your fingers and palm. The second tube is the feeding and aiming tube. It enters into the forearm and travels along the bones, branching at the shoulder to extend one tendril into the liver and the other into the brain.

Once the attunement process is complete, you cannot remove the *arm bug* without destroying it and inflicting 33 (6d10) piercing damage on you (this damage ignores any damage resistance as it occurs inside you). This severs your hand in the process. You may make an attack with the *arm bug*, gaining a +2 to hit and inflicting 9 (2d8) piercing damage plus 7 (2d6) acid damage, range 120/480 ft. The *arm bug* feeds on your blood, draining 1 hit die every 24 hours. When it attunes, it produces 20 projectiles; it expels these small, winged insects by forming an orifice on its "barrel" end. As a bonus action, you may expend 1 hit die to have the *arm bug* generate an additional 20 projectiles, to a maximum of 60 projectiles stored in the *arm bug*. The *arm bug* is considered a part of you and may not be attacked separately.

ARMOR BUG

Otherworldly armor, very rare (requires attunement, see below)

The *armor bug* looks much like a large black crab with long jointed limbs but no pincers, eyes, or mouth parts. It is covered in a shiny black carapace save for its soft underbelly. The *armor bug* attaches to the chest of the person who attunes to it. When it does so, the long spidery legs wrap around your torso and pierce your body. A feeding tube extends from the soft underbelly and sinks into your liver. These attachments inflict 21 (6d6) piercing damage (this damage ignores any damage resistance as it occurs inside you).

Once attached, the *armor bug* rapidly grows and a carapace forms between the legs and the body of the bug. Within seconds, you are covered from neck to groin with thick, flexible plates of chitin. New legs sprout from the pulsating mass on your chest and extend along your arms and legs. These armor plates are flexible but cannot be removed without inflicting horrible pain and 55 (10d10) piercing damage to you. You may not wear any other armor while wearing an *armor bug*, and clothing needs to be made to suit. The *armor bug* extends into your excretory system, covering and protecting it while allowing effluent to be absorbed by the *armor bug* and recycled into a nutritious fluid.

While wearing the *armor bug*, your armor class is 18 plus your Dexterity modifier. You gain resistance to bludgeoning, piercing, and slashing damage from nonmagical attacks. You gain advantage on Dexterity (Stealth) checks. The *armor bug* stores rehydrating sustenance paste filtered from your excretions; you (or ick, someone else) may drink from this storage through a feeding sphincter on one of the bug's legs. One day's worth of food and water is produced every three days. However, the *armor bug* draws its nourishment from your blood, draining 1 hit die every 24 hours. The *armor bug* is considered a part of you and may not be attacked separately.

CHAPTER THREE: OTHERWORLDLY ITEMS | 13

BRAIN JAR

Otherworldly item, very rare (requires attunement, see below)

This brass-framed glass cylinder is three feet high and two feet wide. It is filled with a strange glowing fluid that sloshes around on its own accord. One end has three sockets, while the other is flat and smooth. The top of the cylinder unscrews.

The *brain jar* can be attuned only to a living brain placed within it. The brain must be removed from a body, and the strange magic of the jar allows the brain to be up to one day "dead" before being placed in the jar. However, the brain must be intact. Once placed within the jar and the lid screwed back on, thin threads extend from the bottom of the jar and penetrate the brain. The *brain jar* can keep the brain inside alive indefinitely. The brain is protected by the jar, which has AC 20 and 50 hit points, is immune to psychic and poison damage, and is resistant to acid cold, fire, lightning, and thunder damage, as well as bludgeoning, piercing, and slashing damage from nonmagical attacks. If your jar is destroyed, your brain is exposed to the elements and loses its life-supporting magic. You begin to die.

Once attuned to the *brain jar*, you are conscious but have no sensory input. You must succeed at a DC 15 Wisdom saving throw every 24 hours or go insane from the isolation. You may not cast any spells that require material, somatic, or verbal components. You may manipulate up to four *brain jar attachments* attached to your *brain jar*. You no longer have a Strength or Dexterity score, and your Constitution score applies only to your brain. Your Intelligence, Wisdom, and Charisma scores remain unchanged. You retain your hit dice, but your brain's hit points are reduced to 1.

BRAIN JAR ATTACHMENTS

Otherworldly item, very rare

These otherworldly devices attach to a *brain jar*. All save the *crawling apparatus* attach to one of the attachment ports on the top of the cylinder. A *brain jar* can have only three attachments hooked up to its attachment ports at a time, plus the *crawling apparatus*. Each attachment can be targeted separately from the main jar and has its own AC and hit points. Once an attachment is plugged into your *brain jar*, you may use it as if it were an extension of your body. In a very real sense, these attachments are your body.

Crawling Apparatus. These three articulated brass legs are connected to each other by an intricate girder work. Once attached to your *brain jar*, they give you a move speed 30 feet, a climb speed of 30 feet, and you can climb upside down on horizontal surfaces. The apparatus gives you a Dexterity of 10 and a Strength of 12. The apparatus is noisy and you suffer disadvantage on all Dexterity (Stealth) checks. The *crawling apparatus* has AC 18 and 15 hit points, is immune to psychic and poison damage, and is resistant to acid cold, fire, lightning, and thunder damage, as well as bludgeoning, piercing, and slashing damage from nonmagical attacks.

Death Ray. This long rubber hose ends in a narrow cone. As an action, you may make an attack with the *death ray*, projecting a 15-foot cone of purple-green energy. All creatures caught in the cone must make a DC 15 Dexterity saving throw, suffering 21 (6d6) necrotic damage with a failure, or half as much with a success. The *death ray* has AC 14 and 10 hit points, is immune to psychic and poison damage, and is resistant to acid, cold, fire, lightning, and thunder damage, as well as bludgeoning, piercing, and slashing damage from nonmagical attacks.

Manipulator. This three-foot-long articulated brass arm ends in a pair of pincers. You can manipulate objects as if with a hand, even performing delicate tasks. As an action, you may make a melee attack with the *manipulator* and inflict 1d8 bludgeoning damage. The *manipulator* has effective ability scores of Strength 18 and Dexterity 12. The *manipulator* has AC 16 and 20 hit points, is immune to psychic and poison damage, and is resistant to acid, cold, fire, lightning, and thunder damage, as well as bludgeoning, piercing, and slashing damage from nonmagical attacks. The *manipulator* does not have a true sense of touch. You can feel heat and cold, as well as tell the position of the *manipulator* relative to your brain, and have enough of a sense of touch to know you are gripping something and how you are holding it. You cannot feel texture, pain, or pleasure through the *manipulator*.

Mental Control Device. This two-foot fan of red metal can be unfolded into a roughly, six-foot-diameter dish shape. As an action, once per long rest, you may cast *dominate person* with a DC 15 saving throw.

Mind Transfer Device. This pair of bronze antennae can be extended from mere nubs sunk into the connection port to two-foot-long rods of metal. As an action, once per day, you may target one creature within 30 feet that you can sense. That creature must succeed on a DC 18 Wisdom saving throw or have its consciousness exchanged with yours in the jar. The creature is now inhabiting your brain and you are inhabiting their body. You retain your Intelligence, Wisdom, and Charisma scores as well as any proficiencies you might have. The creature transferred into your brain in the jar is stunned until the end of their next turn. Best run for it now.

Sensor Suite. This two-foot-diameter brass dish grants you normal sense of hearing and sound, as well as darkvision 120 feet and blindsight 60 feet.

Speaker. This four-foot-long, 16-inch-wide brass cone allows you to speak. You can adjust the volume to barely a whisper or up to deafening levels. As an action, once per short rest, you may project a 15-foot cone of sound from the *speaker*. All creatures caught in that cone must make a DC 15 Constitution saving throw. A creature who fails takes 14 (4d6) thunder damage and is deafened for one hour, while a creature who succeeds takes half as much damage and is not deafened.

Thought Projector. This two-foot-long brass box opens to reveal a spinning void of color and nothingness. You may project your thoughts as realistic images in a 160-foot radius around you, the only limit being your imagination. Creatures who view these images may mistake them for reality. If they interact with these images, they must succeed on an Intelligence (Investigation) saving throw with a DC equal to 8 + your proficiency bonus + your Charisma modifier or assume the images are real.

ETHERIC PROJECTOR

Otherworldly item, very rare (requires attunement)

This strange helmet made of brass and rubber has a large square mesh dish on the top that makes wearing it a strain on the neck muscles. Two wooden handles extend from the top of the helmet and allow you to rotate the dish on top. Once you attune to the *etheric projector*, you can issue a command to have it project an invisible 25-foot cone of energy. Within that cone, the ethereal plane is revealed for all to see. Creatures who are invisible are also clearly shown, as are creatures that are ephemeral. The *etheric projector* functions as long as you are grasping the handles, but each minute of use causes a level of exhaustion.

HELM BUG

Otherworldly item, very rare (requires attunement)

This black, spongy lump of flesh quivers and pulsates as if to a heartbeat. To attune to the item, you must place it on your bare head. After the attunement process ends, you suffer 1d6 piercing damage and 1d6 psychic damage as the *helm bug* expands to encompass your entire head and face, sending tendrils through your ears, nose, and eyes, as well as into your skull. A large tendril rolls down your throat, splitting to send tubes into your lungs and stomach. The process is very uncomfortable.

Once attuned, you are blind and deaf. You cannot breathe save through the *helm bug* nor can you eat or drink. The *helm bug* provides clean air for you no matter the environment you find yourself in. An orifice on the helm allows you to put any water and organic matter in, which the *helm bug* cleans and converts into the sustenance you need. When you desire to speak, the *helm bug* picks up your thoughts and transmits them outside the helmet as a droning, vibrating hum that closely mimics speech. Finally, the *helm bug* transmits its own senses to you, allowing you to see and hear normally, as well as providing you with darkvision 120 feet.

The *helm bug* exacts a price from you. It drains 1 hit die from you every 24 hours. The *helm bug* is treated as a part of you and cannot be targeted separately. If the *helm bug* is removed, you suffer 10d8 piercing damage and are left blind and deaf.

REVIVIFICATION SERUM

Otherworldly item, very rare

A greenish-yellow fluid fills this glass vial that is attached to a very long, large-bore brass needle. Two finger loops on the needle allow you to work the plunger and inject the fluid into a target. If the target is living, it must succeed at a DC 15 Constitution saving throw, dying on a failure, and suffering 22 (5d8) necrotic damage on a success. If the target is a humanoid corpse or a living humanoid target that failed its save and died, the target rises within 1d8 minutes as a zombie with double hit dice. This zombie is not under anyone's control.

OTHER OTHERWORLDLY ITEM

The Crystal Icosahedron does not fit in the categories scholars have long used to classify otherworldly items. Where they came from is even more of a mystery than the *arm bug* or *energy disk*. Indeed, these otherworldly items might be unique in this world, or disturbingly common in others.

CRYSTAL ICOSAHEDRON

Otherworldly item, very rare

This regular 20-sided polygon is made from smoothly cut semi-translucent blue crystal. Citrine flashes of light appear inside among clouds of purple gas. Each face of the icosahedron has a different golden symbol etched into it. Just holding the polygon exudes a feeling of power and anticipation, mixed with vague dread.

You activate the *crystal icosahedron* by using an action to blow upon it and then roll it like a die on a flat surface. It does not work if rolled upon a book, paper, or other similar surface, and the surface it is rolled on must be flat; throwing the *crystal icosahedron* into the dirt has no effect, nor does rolling it on an incline or in the palm of your hand. You may use a shallow box to contain the die's rolling, and some past owners have used complex mechanisms to cause the *crystal icosahedron* to bounce about more as it tumbles to the ground. Shaking it in a mug or cup before rolling it is permissible, but loud. If a box or other object is not used to contain the *crystal icosahedron* when it is rolled, it disappears afterward, teleporting itself 1d100 feet away, or 1d10 miles away if a feline observes the rolling.

Once rolled, the effects of the *crystal icosahedron*'s effects occur immediately and cannot be adjusted by any trait, feat, or spell. A single person can only roll the crystal icosahedron once per year with any effect.

CRYSTAL ICOSAHEDRON SIDES

d20	Symbol	Effect
1	A	You gain the ability to cast the *tongues* spell on yourself at will. However, this ability degrades with each use, with the translation becoming more garbled until after five uses, any time you are the beneficiary of a *tongues* spell all you get is gibberkol, dhjuhjkes, kuwbuus.
2	B	You become the proud owner of a house somewhere in the world. You always know the exact distance and direction of this house. As the proud (and legal) owner of the house, you feel a strong desire to go there and make sure it is in good repair. The first time you are in sight of your house each year, you must succeed on a DC 15 Wisdom saving throw or be compelled to spend at least 10,000 gp refurbishing it.
3	G	A magic club appears in your hand. You gain a +1 bonus to attack and damage rolls when you use the club. However, the club is a sapient magic item and has a distinct personality that is cynical, snarky, and passive aggressive.
4	D	A door opens within 10 feet of you. Beyond the door lies another plane of existence or perhaps whatever world from which the *crystal icosahedron* came. You can see a tall table, several people gathered around it like scribes, while one stands behind some sort of short divider. The door remains open for 1d4 rounds and then closes.
5	E	You can scry on one target as per the spell *scrying*, using an ability score of your choice as your spellcasting ability score. You must do this immediately or lose the ability, and may do this only once.
6	Z	A giant hook appears out of thin air within five feet of you and drags one target of your choice that you can see within 30 feet of you into an extradimensional space. The target must succeed at a DC 15 Charisma saving throw or be pulled into an extradimensional space for 1d4 rounds. When the target reappears, it is covered in rotten tomatoes and wears a blonde wig with long braids.
7	H	You disappear into an extradimensional space where you are put on trial for all your crimes, even things that you only thought about doing. You must argue your case, and if you succeed in convincing the jury that you can do better with a DC 15 Charisma (Deception or Persuasion) check, you are returned to where you disappeared from. If you do not convince the jury, you are sent to a prison, where you remain for 20 years and then are returned to where you disappeared from. In either case, you return 1d4 rounds after you disappeared with only vague memories of what happened (and possibly 20 years older).
8	F	A golden chariot appears within 10 feet of you. The chariot does not need horses to pull it and moves by command. It is a bonus action to command the chariot, and it has a speed of 50 feet. The chariot follows the commands of whoever is holding the reins.
9	I	You gain the ability to cast the spell *arcane hand* as an action, using an ability score of your choice as your spellcasting ability score. However, each time you use this ability, the hand created shrinks in size from Large to Medium, Medium to Small, and Small to Tiny. After that, you lose the ability to cast the spell through any means.

CHAPTER THREE: OTHERWORLDLY ITEMS | 15

d20	Symbol	Effect
10	K	The palms of your hands become coated in a film of a sticky substance that you continue to generate for 1d4 days. This substance is so sticky that anything you grasp cannot be taken from your hands by force, nor can your hand be pried off a surface. You can wiggle your hands off things, though it takes some effort. You gain a climb speed of 30 feet and can climb sheer and horizontal surfaces.
11	L	A shepherd's hook appears in your hand (treat as a *+1 quarterstaff*). Furthermore, the hook allows you to cast *beast friend* and *speak with animals* at will, but only on sheep, using an ability score of your choice as your spellcasting ability score. If you ever eat lamb or mutton, the hook disappears.
12	M	For the next 1d4 days, every time you open your mouth a font of water, as per a *decanter of endless water*, pours forth from your mouth. This does not affect your ability to breathe; indeed, you can now breathe in water as easily as air. Both effects end when the duration of the spewing water ends.
13	N	For the next 1d4 days, you have disadvantage on every ability check, saving throw, attack roll, and initiative check.
14	X	You can command the earth to split open and a 50-foot-tall, 10-foot-diameter pillar of stone to rise up. You may do this once, and regain the use following a long rest. The pillar is a permanent feature.
15	O	As a bonus action, you may remove one of your eyes and place it in a location, toss it, or have others move it away from your body. As long as the eye is within one mile, you know its exact location and can see through it. While looking through this eye, you must keep your other eye closed. As a bonus action, you may put the eye back in your head and it functions as normal.
16	π	For the next 1d4 days, you cannot speak or even open your mouth. During this time, you gain the ability to telepathically communicate with any living creature within 60 feet of you and do not need to eat, drink, or breathe.
17	P	For the next 1d4 days, you may remove your head, which does not kill you. It just pops right off. You can still operate your body as long as it is within 60 feet and receive sensory signals from it. You may replace your head on your body at any time and take it off again but need at least one hand free to do so.
18	S	A galley appears within 50 feet of you, complete with sails and oars. It does not need a crew or the wind, and operates by command. Whoever stands at the tiller may use a bonus action to direct the galley, which moves at a speed of 60 across water.
19	T	You gain 3d100 gp in wealth per day for the next 1d4 days. This wealth is not in coin but in a quantity of goods such as livestock, bolts of cloth, sacks of grain, and so forth. The wealth is yours and you are responsible for it, which can be a problem when you accidentally unleash 200 gp worth of live chickens in the marketplace.
20	Y	Your eyes swell up and turn reddish. For the next 1d4 days, you gain a gaze attack. When a creature that can see your eyes starts its turn within 30 feet of you, you must force it to make a DC 15 Constitution saving throw if you are not incapacitated and can see the creature. On a failure, the creature is blinded for one minute. Unless surprised, a creature can avert its eyes to avoid the saving throw at the start of its turn. If the creature does so, it can't see you until the start of its next turn, when it averts its eyes again. If the creature looks at you in the meantime, it must immediately attempt the save. While averting its eyes, any attacks on you are done at disadvantage.

SKY THRONE
Otherworldly item, very rare

This ornate throne is made from strange metals polished to a high sheen and decorated with otherworldly gems. It is not comfortable, and you will probably want to get a cushion if you plan to use it. On its own, the *sky throne* is just a fancy chair, but to anyone capable of spellcasting and knowledgeable in how to mount it in a ship, the *sky throne* is a powerful tool.

In order to function, the *sky throne* must be properly mounted to a vessel of some kind. This can be any ship or boat. The proper mounting is a laborious process that takes at least one week. The directions to do so can be found in musty tomes long lost in ancient ruins. Or maybe the local bookstore. Who knows?

Once mounted on a ship, a spellcaster must sit upon the throne and meditate for one hour. At the end of the hour, the spellcaster gains control of the throne and the ship to which it is attached. The vessel gains the ability to fly at a speed of 60 mph, hover in place, and ascend beyond the clouds. The throne generates an envelope of atmosphere around the vessel that permits breathing in even the rarified air of the highest elevations, and possibly beyond. It also generates a magical gravity so that the deck is always down while within 10 feet of the vessel. It does not regulate temperature, however, and you should probably wear a coat.

This amazing effect comes at a cost. The spellcaster expends 2d6 spell slots to power the *sky throne* for one day. If they do not have enough spell slots, the throne does not function. Every dawn, an additional 2d6 spell slots must be fed into the throne for it to continue to function. As this feeding of mystical energy must be done by the person sitting on the throne, and said person has control over the vessel, it is recommended that it be voluntary.

CHAPTER FOUR: RINGS

MESSAGE RINGS
Ring, common (requires attunement)

These paired copper rings have a gaudy glass jewel in their settings. Each *message ring* comes as part of a set, usually a pair, but sets of up to six have been found. Each person attuned to a *message ring* can mentally communicate with anyone else attuned to a ring in the same set. This mental communication functions as the spell *sending*. Each ring can send a message 10 times per day, regaining all uses at midnight.

PISCEAN RING
Ring, very rare (requires attunement)

This simple brass ring features two fish leaping along the band. A favorite of fisherfolk and others who work the sea, these rings have become increasing more difficult to find as their users tend to meet their demise in the ocean's depths. Once attuned to the *piscean ring*, as an action, you may cast *locate animals and plants* or *speak with animals*, but the target must be a sea creature. Furthermore, you gain a swim speed of 30 feet. You may breathe underwater. Finally, once per day, you may cast *conjure animals* as a ritual, but the animals must be sea creatures.

RING OF ABSORPTION
Ring, very rare (requires attunement by a spellcaster)

This golden ring absorbs one type of damage and transforms it into magical energy. Each type of *ring of absorption* absorbs a certain type of damage, and the gem set in it is a clue to what it absorbs. Each time you suffer the linked type of damage, you may funnel that damage into the ring to become one charge, and not take any damage. The ring can store up to three charges. If it is full, you cannot use it to absorb damage. While casting a spell, you may expend one charge. When you do, the spell you cast is cast as if using a spell slot one level higher.

1d10	Damage Type	Gem
1	Acid	Pearl
2	Cold	Tourmaline
3	Fire	Garnet
4	Force	Sapphire
5	Lightning	Citrine
6	Necrotic	Jet
7	Poison	Amethyst
8	Psychic	Jade
9	Radiant	Topaz
10	Thunder	Spinel

RING OF THE BARRIER
Ring, rare

This platinum ring has an inscription in the inside that speaks of strange locales and endless vistas one can never reach. The ring has three charges. While wearing the ring, you may use an action to expend a charge to create an invisible *wall of force* 20 feet high and up to 60 feet long. This wall remains up to one minute as long as you spend a bonus action to maintain it each round. You can use an action to move the wall. Any creature caught in the wall when it is created or moved must make a DC 15 Dexterity saving throw. On a failure the creature suffers 2d6 force damage, while on a success it suffers half that damage. In either case, the creature is shifted aside. The wall has AC 20 and has 75 hit points, is immune to psychic and poison damage, and is resistant to bludgeoning, piercing, and slashing damage from nonmagical attacks.

The ring regains 1d3 expended charges each day at sunset.

RING OF BLINDSIGHT
Ring, rare

This dark gold ring has a single trihedral piece of obsidian set in it. You gain blindsight 60 feet while wearing this ring.

RING OF BURROWING
Ring, uncommon

This band of stone has a small piece of flint set into it. You have a burrowing speed of 40 feet while wearing this ring.

RING OF CHARIDIS
Ring, very rare (requires attunement)

This silver ring is made of dozens of small tentacles that wrap around each other to form a ring shape. Once attuned, the ring grows a number of tentacles equal to one more than the number of fingers you have on your hand: one wraps around your wrist, while the other spreads to your fingers and creates small loops. This does not hamper your use of that hand. However, while wearing the ring, you must kill a living creature each day or suffer 4d10 psychic damage. When given a command word, the *ring of Charidis* extends one or more tentacles as you will it toward targets within 30 feet of you. You can target a creature with more than one tentacle or target as many creatures as you have fingers on the hand wearing the ring. Each target must make a DC 13 Dexterity saving throw, taking 4d10 bludgeoning damage on a failure, or half damage on a success. Each use reduces the number of tentacles the ring has available, and when the last tentacle is used, the ring drops off and crawls through a tiny dimensional portal to seek a new host.

RING OF CLIMBING
Ring, uncommon

This silver ring is fashioned to look like a network of spider webs set with diamond chips. You have a climbing speed of 40 feet while wearing this ring, and can scale difficult surfaces, even hanging upside down, without requiring an ability check.

RING OF DARKVISION
Ring, uncommon

This band of silver twined with threads of copper wire is set with a bright moonstone. While wearing this ring, you gain darkvision 60 feet.

RING OF THE IMPOSTER
Ring, uncommon (requires attunement)

Every time you look at this ring it has a different appearance, but all are plain bands of some material that lack a gemstone. While wearing this ring, you may cause it to alter how you are perceived. You do not change shape but instead others think of you as a creature of a different type. For example, you can use the *ring of the imposter* and assume the semblance of an undead creature, and other creatures consider you to be undead. However, this change come as a price, and any effect that would target the creature type you are masquerading as affects you as well.

CHAPTER FOUR: RINGS | 17

RING OF KICKING

Ring, uncommon (requires attunement)

This plain steel band is shaped like an arm with a foot instead of a hand. While wearing this ring, your unarmed combat attacks inflict damage one die type larger. For example, a non-monk character has an unarmed attack that inflicts 1 + Strength modifier bludgeoning damage; with the *ring of kicking*, you inflict 1d4 + Strength modifier bludgeoning damage. Die sizes increase from 1d4 to 1d8 to 1d10 to 1d12 to 2d6 to 2d8, and so forth.

RING OF THE LIBRARY

Ring, panoply (scholarly mage), conjunction (azoth), very rare (requires attunement by a wizard)

This gold ring is set with two sapphires impossibly cut to appear as two books set in it. Once attuned to the *ring of the library*, you may link it to a library or other repository of knowledge. While in the linked library, you know the location and condition of every book in the library, can read every book that is part of the library, and can summon any book in the library to you at will.

If you are wearing the *ring of the library* and the *studious robes*, all books in the linked library gain the same resistances as you have and their AC becomes 18.

If you are wearing the *ring of the library* and carrying the *quill of the assistant*, the quill has seven charges and regains 1d6 + 1 charges at sunrise.

If you are wearing the *ring of the library* as part of a complete *panoply of the scholarly mage*, you may fold up the linked library and take it with you, books, building, and all. The linked library is held in stasis in an extradimensional space and cannot be accessed. You may unfold the library as a one-hour ritual, bringing it into existence in an area that can contain it.

RINGS OF LIFE SHARING

Ring, rare (requires attunement)

This matched pair of gold rings have star-shaped rubies set in them. Each pair of *rings of life sharing* is uniquely marked in some manner. When wearing a *ring of life sharing*, during a short rest you may call upon the person wearing the matched *ring of life sharing*, exchanging hit dice between you. Also, you may use a reaction when you suffer damage to transfer any or all of the damage to the person wearing the matched *ring of life sharing*. However, the person wearing the matched *ring of life sharing* must consent to these transfers.

RINGS OF LIFE STEALING

Ring, rare (requires attunement)

These rings look like *rings of life sharing* and operate like them in all ways save that one ring shares hit dice and receives damage, while the other receives only hit dice and shares damage. Which ring is the sharer and which the receiver changes periodically. Roll 1d6 every 24 hours: 1–3, no change; 4–5, the roles of the two rings switches; 6, the rings work like *rings of life sharing*.

RINGS OF LOVE

Ring, uncommon (requires attunement)

This matched pair of gold rings have heart-shaped rubies set in them. Each pair of *rings of love* is uniquely marked in some manner. As the rings must be attuned, they require consent to be used. While wearing a *ring of love*, you are charmed by the person wearing the matched ring, and vice versa. Also, you always know the immediate needs of the person wearing the matched ring, as well as their emotional and physical state.

RING OF RINGS

Ring, very rare (requires attunement)

This gold band is engraved with linked rings forming an intricate knot pattern. While wearing this ring, once per week you may command the ring to activate. When you do so, it changes; roll on the table below to determine the effects. Unless otherwise noted, the ring remains in its new form for 24 hours and then reverts to a *ring of rings*.

RING OF RINGS FORMS

1d12	Form
1	*Ring of kicking*
2	*Ring of warmth*
3	Nine golden rings worth 100 gp each. Eight of these rings are permanent; the ninth is the *ring of rings* and reverts as normal.
4	*Ring of climbing*
5	*Ring of water walking*
6	*Ring of jumping*
7	*Ring of mind shielding*
8	The *ring of rings* disappears and finds a new owner
9	*Ring of darkvision*
10	*Ring of burrowing*
11	*Ring of the imposter*
12	A pair of *messenger rings*; after 24 hours, one vanishes and one becomes the *ring of rings*.

RING OF SCYLLABIS

Ring, very rare (requires attunement)

This plain ring made of verdigris-covered bronze bears a single aquamarine stone held in a setting shaped like a great mouth. When worn and thrust into a natural body of water, the ring creates a massive whirlpool that can sink ships and even slay small creatures. You must remain stationary at the center of the whirlpool for it to gain strength; if you move more than five feet away from the point at which you activated the ring, the whirlpool ends. The whirlpool takes three rounds to grow to full power. On the first round, all movement in the water within 30 feet of the whirlpool is treated as occurring on difficult terrain. On the second round, any creature within 30 feet of the whirlpool that wants to move away from you must succeed on a DC 15 Strength (Athletics) check to do so. On the third round, all creatures within the whirlpool must succeed at a DC 13 Strength saving throw or be sucked into the ring. Ships less than 30 feet long caught within the whirlpool on the third round are destroyed. Creatures sucked into the ring are trapped, alive and unharmed, inside it. The whirlpool dissipates after three rounds These creatures may be disgorged from the ring upon command, and the *ring of scyllabis* cannot create a whirlpool if creatures are within it. The *ring of scyllabis* can be used three times either to create a whirlpool or to disgorge creatures from the ring, after which it crumbles to dust. When found, roll 1d3 to determine the number of uses it has left. If the number is even, creatures are trapped in the ring.

RING OF SEVERING

Ring, very rare

This ring appears much like a different magic ring, even to spells such as *identify*. Its effects when worn are the same as the ring it is mimicking. When you next roll a 1 on any attack roll, saving throw, or skill check, the *ring of severing* cuts off one of your fingers and teleports away.

RING OF THE SHIELD

Ring, uncommon

This steel ring has a large kite shield set in it with enameled coat of arms. The ring has seven charges. While wearing this ring, you may use a bonus action to expend a charge to cause the ring to project a spectral blue shield as if the hand the ring is worn on is holding the shield. This shield grants you a +3 bonus to AC. The spectral shield remains for one minute or until you issue a command to cancel it, at which point it vanishes. You may not set the shield down or otherwise lose your grip on it.

The ring regains 1d6 + 1 expended charges each sunrise.

RING OF THE SMOKE WYRM
Ring, conjunction (mercury), rare (requires attunement)

For a time, Talvan of Reme funded his research by crafting these rings and giving them as "gifts" to local officials who then managed to see that funding was funneled into Talvan's hands. Each ring is a golden dragon that coils around the finger, its head lying atop the finger with the mouth gaping open. Often the eyes were inset with chips of precious stones.

As an action, once per day, you may issue a command word to the *ring of the smoke wyrm*. A dense fog pours from the dragon's mouth and forms into a draconic shape. This smoke wyrm can be commanded to perform one task such as to fetch a single person and bring them back, attack a target, or fly over an area and return. The smoke dragon dissipates at the next sunrise whether it completed its task or not. You can use the *ring of the smoke wyrm* once, and regain use of it at the next new moon.

If you possess and have on you a magical item with esoteric conjunction (air), the smoke wyrm dissipates in 24 hours as opposed to with the next sunrise, and its speed is doubled.

SIGNET RING OF SUMMONING AND BINDING
Ring, very rare (requires attunement)

This golden ring has a large face embossed with a circle surrounding a square, with a triangle inside the square. Arcane sigils form a band around the circle. Once attuned, you may use the ring to summon and bind creatures from other planes. The *ring of summoning and binding* has three charges. You can use one charge to summon a celestial, elemental, fey, or fiend. You can also use a charge to bind a celestial, elemental, fey, or fiend creature. Finally, you may expend a charge to cast one of the following spells: *banishment, detect evil and good, protection from evil and good,* or *magic circle.*

The ring provides the power and knowledge to summon but does not provide the ability to do so safely. To summon a creature, you must perform a complex hour long ritual and make a successful Intelligence (Arcana) check. The DC for this check is equal to 10 + the Challenge of the creature you are summoning. If you succeed, the summoned creature arrives and is stunned until the end of its next turn. If you fail, you summon something (GM's choice) and the summoned creature is not stunned.

Likewise, the *ring of summoning and binding* provides the means and knowledge to bind a creature, but not the ability to do so with ease. As an action, you may attempt to bind a celestial, elemental, fey, or fiend you can see and that is within 30 feet of you. To do so, you must be able to speak. The targeted creature must succeed at a Wisdom saving throw whose DC is equal to 8 + your Intelligence modifier + your proficiency bonus. A bound creature is restrained and obeys your commands but is free to interpret the words as it sees fit. While bound, you may use an action to release the creature from being restrained, place it back under restraint, or use an action to inflict 4d10 psychic damage to the creature. The creature remains under the effects of the binding until the next sunrise or sunset.

The ring regains 1d3 expended charges each sunset.

RING OF TREMORSENSE
Ring, uncommon

This bronze ring has a single amethyst set in it. While wearing the ring, you gain tremorsense 60 feet.

VAMPIRE RING
Ring, uncommon (requires attunement)

This black enameled ring has two tiny prongs that lie along your finger. Each prong is tipped with a tiny ruby chip as if they were a drop of blood. Once attuned to the ring, you can use an action to touch a target as a melee attack. If successful, the target suffers 1d8 necrotic damage. You recover hit points equal to half of the damage you cause with the *vampire ring*.

CHAPTER FIVE: RODS

ROD OF ABJURATION
Rod, conjunction (azoth), very rare (requires attunement by a spellcaster)

This rod of lead alloy is tipped with a bright flawless diamond. The rod has seven charges. Once you have attuned to the rod and are holding it, aberrations, celestials, elementals, fey, fiends, and undead have disadvantage on attack rolls against you, and you have advantage on saving throws against effects they generate that target you or include you in an area of effect. You may use an action to expend one charge from the *rod of abjuration* to use one of the following properties:

Attack. The wand can be used as a mace for one minute, granting you +1 bonus to attack and damage rolls when making attacks with it.

Aura. The rod may be used to draw a protective circle on the ground as per the spell *magic circle* but requiring no material components. This protective circle lasts as long as the rod is not moved.

Spells. You can cast one of the following spells using the rod (spell save DC 15): *banishment*, *dispel magic*, or *planar binding*.

Additionally, you may use a reaction and expend one charge from the *rod of abjuration* to cancel an effect generated by a *rod of conjuration*. Should a *rod of abjuration* come into contact with a *rod of conjuration*, both rods disappear in a blinding flash that fills a 40-foot cube with arcane energies. Any creature caught in this area must make a DC 18 Dexterity saving throw, suffering 5d10 force damage on a failure, or half as much with a success.

The *rod of abjuration* regains 1d6 + 1 charges at sunrise. If the last charge in a *rod of abjuration* is used, roll 1d20. On a 1, the rod crumbles to dust.

ROD OF AIR
Rod, conjunction (air), very rare (requires attunement by a spellcaster)

This rod of pure sapphire bound in gold wire feels much lighter than it should. The rod has seven charges. Once attuned to the rod and holding it, you gain resistance to lightning damage and a fly speed of 30 feet. As an action, you may expend one charge from the rod to do one of the following:

Control Air Elementals. You target a creature of the elemental (air) type that you can see within 60 feet. That creature must succeed on a DC 15 Wisdom saving throw or you gain control of it as per the spell *dominate monster*.

Mace of Air. The *rod of air* becomes a mace that effects only creatures of the Plane of Earth. You gain +1 bonus to attack and damage rolls with this mace and are considered to be proficient with it. When you successful hit a creature of elemental earth, the mace inflicts an additional 2d6 lightning damage. This property lasts for 10 minutes and then the *rod of air* reverts to its normal form.

Spells. You can cast one of the following spells using the rod (spell save DC 15): *cloud kill*, *gaseous form*, or *cloud kill*.

Additionally, you may use a reaction and expend one charge from the *rod of air* to cancel an effect generated by a *rod of earth*. Should a *rod of air* come into contact with a *rod of earth*, both rods disappear in a blinding flash that fills a 40-foot cube with arcane energies. Any creature caught in this area must make a DC 18 Dexterity saving throw, suffering 5d10 force damage on a failure, or half as much with a success.

The *rod of air* regains 1d6 + 1 charges when exposed for eight hours to the open air during which time it may not be touching the ground. If the last charge in a *rod of air* is used, roll 1d20. On a 1, the rod crumbles to dust.

> ### RODS OF THE SCHOOLS OF MAGIC
> It is said that these were created in ancient times by a powerful and learned master mage who sat as the head of an arcane schools. Each rod was held by the dean of a school of magic and served not just as powerful magic items, but as symbols of their authority and scholarship. Sadly, such mighty schools of magical learning are long gone, but the rods of the schools remain. Perhaps if all eight and the master *rod of the loremaster* is found, such an august body of mages could be reassembled for the benefit of the land.
>
> Then again, this may all be stories told around tankards at the local tavern.

ROD OF CONJURATION

Rod, conjunction (azoth), very rare (requires attunement by a spellcaster)

This rod of polished wood is tipped with a single large garnet. The rod has seven charges. Once you have attuned to the rod and are holding it, any creature you summon using a spell from the conjuration school, including those summoned with this rod, gain additional hit dice equal to your spellcasting ability score modifier. You may use an action to expend one charge from the *rod of conjuration* to use one of the following properties:

Assume Command. You target a single creature you can see within 30 feet that was summoned by a spell from the conjuration school or similar effect that you do not have control of. That creature must succeed at a DC 15 Wisdom saving throw or become under your control as per the spell or effect that summoned it.

Doorway. You open a doorway to another place you know on the plane you are occupying. This doorway allows passage between this point and where you are currently standing. The doorway lasts until the end of your next turn, and then closes.

Spells. You can cast one of the following spells using the rod (spell save DC 15): *conjure elementals*, *conjure woodland beings*, or *spirit guardians*.

Additionally, you may use a reaction and expend one charge from the *rod of conjuration* to cancel an effect generated by a *rod of abjuration*. Should a *rod of conjuration* come into contact with a *rod of abjuration*, both rods disappear in a blinding flash that fills a 40-foot cube with arcane energies. Any creature caught in this area must make a DC 18 Dexterity saving throw, suffering 5d10 force damage on a failure, or half as much with a success.

The *rod of conjuration* regains 1d6 + 1 charges at sunrise. If the last charge in a *rod of conjuration* is used, roll 1d20. On a 1, the rod crumbles to dust.

ROD OF DISRUPTION

Rod, conjunction (azoth), rare (requires attunement by a cleric or paladin)

This rod of platinum is engraved with burning runes of fiery copper. The rod has seven charges. Once attuned to the rod and while holding it, you may use an action to expend a charge to target a single undead creature you can see within 60 feet. That creature suffers 2d6 radiant damage and must succeed at a DC 15 Charisma saving throw or be frightened of you until the end of its next turn.

The *rod of disruption* regains charges when you spend an action to use your channel divinity class feature on it, regaining one charge per funneled channel divinity. The rod may not hold more than seven charges.

ROD OF DIVINATION

Rod, conjunction (azoth), very rare (requires attunement by a spellcaster)

This rod of lacquered wood forks at the end to produce two tips, one with a single large emerald, the other with a single large sapphire. The rod has seven charges. Once you have attuned to the rod and are holding it, any spell of the divination school you cast as a ritual takes half the time and requires half of the usual material components. You may use an action to expend one charge from the *rod of divination* to use one of the following properties:

Pansophical. For the next hour, you act as if under the effects of the following spells: *detect evil and good*, *detect magic*, *detect poison and disease*, and *detect thoughts*.

Prescient. Within the next minute, you may reroll one attack roll, ability check, or saving throw, taking whichever result you want.

Spells. You can cast one of the following spells using the rod (spell save DC 15): *arcane eye*, *locate creature*, or *legend lore*.

Additionally, you may use a reaction and expend one charge from the *rod of divination* to cancel an effect generated by a *rod of illusion*. Should a *rod of divination* come into contact with a *rod of illusion*, both rods disappear in a blinding flash that fills a 40-foot cube with arcane energies. Any creature caught in this area must make a DC 18 Dexterity saving throw, suffering 5d10 force damage on a failure, or half as much with a success.

The *rod of divination* regains 1d6 + 1 charges at sunrise. If the last charge in a *rod of divination* is used, roll 1d20. On a 1, the rod crumbles to dust.

ROD OF DRAGONS

Rod, very rare (requires attunement)

This rod is shaped like a dragon's neck and head, the mouth open and snarling, and the eyes set with a precious gem. There are 10 different types of *rod of the dragon*, each tied to one type of dragon. The color of the rod and the gems set in its eyes match those of the dragon to which it is tied, as do the rod's properties. While attuned to and in possession of a *rod of dragons*, you gain the resistance type and movement type associated with that rod. Once per long rest, you may use the rod's attack form, projecting the attack from the mouth of the rod once and regain expend uses following a long rest. Those caught in the attack type's area of effect must make the DC 15 saving throw of the listed type or suffer 4d8 of the damage type for that rod.

ROD OF DRAGONS TYPES

Dragon Type	Description	Attack Type Resistance	Movement Type	Save
Black	black enameled steel, onyx eyes	acid	swim 30 ft.	15-ft. cone of acid (4d8)
Blue	blue enameled steel, sapphire eyes	lightning	burrow 30 ft.	15-ft. line of lightning
Brass	brass with garnet eyes	fire	burrow 30 ft.	15-ft. cone of fire
Bronze	bronze with sapphire eyes	swim 30 ft.	lightning	15-ft. line of lightning
Copper	copper with tanzanite eyes	acid	climb 30 ft.	15-ft. cone of acid
Gold	gold with diamond eyes	fire	swim 30 ft.	15-ft. cone of fire
Green	green enameled steel, emerald eyes	poison	swim 30 ft.	15-ft. cone of poison gas
Red	red enameled steel, ruby eyes	fire	climb 30 ft.	15-ft. cone of fire
Silver	silver with hematite eyes	cold	fly 30 ft.	15-ft. cone of cold
White	white enameled steel, diamond eyes	cold	swim 30 ft.	15-ft. cone of cold

ROD OF EARTH

Rod, conjunction (earth), very rare (requires attunement by a spellcaster)

This rod of pure agate bound in platinum wire feels much heavier than it should. The rod has seven charges. Once attuned to the rod and holding it, you gain resistance to acid damage and a burrow speed of 30 feet. As an action, you may expend one charge from the rod to do one of the following:

Control Earth Elementals. You target a creature of the elemental (earth) type that you can see within 60 feet. That creature must succeed on a DC 15 Wisdom saving throw or you gain control of it as per the spell *dominate monster*.

Mace of Earth. The *rod of earth* becomes a mace that affects only creatures of the Plane of Air. You gain a +1 bonus to attack and damage rolls with this mace and are considered to be proficient with it. When you successfully hit a creature of elemental air, the mace inflicts an additional 2d6 acid damage. This property lasts for 10 minutes and then the *rod of air* reverts to its normal form.

Spells. You can cast one of the following spells using the rod (spell save DC 15): *glyph of warding*, *stone shape*, or *wall of stone*.

Additionally, you may use a reaction and expend one charge from the *rod of earth* to cancel an effect generated by a *rod of air*. Should a *rod of earth* come into contact with a *rod of air*, both rods disappear in a blinding flash that fills a 40-foot cube with arcane energies. Any creature caught in this area must make a DC 18 Dexterity saving throw, suffering 5d10 force damage on a failure, or half as much with a success.

The *rod of earth* regains 1d6 + 1 charges when buried for eight hours in natural soil. If the last charge in a *rod of earth* is used, roll 1d20. On a 1, the rod crumbles to dust.

ROD OF ENCHANTMENT

Rod, conjunction (azoth), very rare (requires attunement by a spellcaster)

This rod of redwood is tipped with a perfect emerald. The rod has seven charges. Once you have attuned to the rod and are holding it, people are naturally drawn to you. When you make a Charisma check, you do so with advantage. You may use an action to expend one charge from the *rod of enchantment* to use one of the following properties:

Beguile. You touch one creature with the rod, and that creature must succeed at a DC 15 Wisdom saving throw or be overcome with emotion, becoming paralyzed until the end of their next turn.

Force Emotions. You target one creature you can see within 30 feet. That creature must make a DC 15 Wisdom saving throw. On a failure the target gains your choice of the following conditions until the end of their next turn: blinded (anger), charmed (love), frightened (fear), or one level of exhaustion (depression), and suffers 2d8 psychic damage. On a success, the target takes half as much damage and does not succumb to a condition.

Spells. You can cast one of the following spells using the rod (spell save DC 15): *confusion*, *modify memory*, or *suggestion*.

Additionally, you may use a reaction and expend one charge from the *rod of enchantment* to cancel an effect generated by a *rod of necromancy*. Should a *rod of enchantment* come into contact with a *rod of necromancy*, both rods disappear in a blinding flash that fills a 40-foot cube with arcane energies. Any creature caught in this area must make a DC 18 Dexterity saving throw, suffering 5d10 force damage on a failure, or half as much with a success.

The *rod of enchantment* regains 1d6 + 1 charges at sunset. If the last charge in a *rod of enchantment* is used, roll 1d20. On a 1, the rod crumbles to dust.

ROD OF EVOCATION

Rod, conjunction (azoth), very rare (requires attunement by a spellcaster)

This rod of bronze is tipped with a bright fire opal. The rod has seven charges. Once you have attuned to the rod and are holding it, any evocation spell you cast counts as being cast with the next higher level of spell than you cast it with. You may use an action to expend one charge from the *rod of evocation* to use one of the following properties:

Circle of Evocation. You are surrounded by a five-foot ring of energy that lasts until the end of your next turn. During that time, any creature that tries to pass through your space or attempts a melee attack against you must succeed on a DC 15 Dexterity saving throw or suffer 2d8 damage of a type you choose when you use this property: acid, cold, fire, force, lightning, or thunder.

Evoked Immunity. You create a field around your body that grants resistance to one of the following energy types for 10 minutes: acid, cold, fire, force, lightning, or thunder.

Spells. You can cast one of the following spells using the rod (spell save DC 15): *fireball*, *ice storm*, or *wall of force*.

Additionally, you may use a reaction and expend one charge from the *rod of evocation* to cancel an effect generated by a *rod of conjuration*. Should a *rod of evocation* come into contact with a *rod of transmutation*, both rods disappear in a blinding flash that fills a 40-foot cube with arcane energies. Any creature caught in this area must make a DC 18 Dexterity saving throw, suffering 5d10 force damage on a failure, or half as much with a success.

The *rod of evocation* regains 1d6 + 1 charges at sunrise. If the last charge in a *rod of evocation* is used, roll 1d20. On a 1, the rod crumbles to dust.

> ### ELEMENTAL RODS
> Were they created by a powerful cabal of elemental wizards? Gifts from great powers of the elemental planes? Perhaps they were given to warlocks who had elemental patrons, and since were lost.

ROD OF FIRE

Rod, conjunction (fire), very rare (requires attunement by a spellcaster)

This rod of pure ruby bound in copper wire feels warm to the touch. The rod has seven charges. Once attuned to the rod and while holding it, you gain resistance to fire damage and can walk across fire as per the spell *water walk*. As an action, you may expend one charge from the rod to do one of the following:

Control Fire Elementals. You target a creature of the elemental (fire) type that you can see within 60 feet. That creature must succeed on a DC 15 Wisdom saving throw or you gain control of it as per the spell *dominate monster*.

Mace of Fire. The *rod of fire* becomes a mace that affects only creatures of the Plane of Water. You gain a +1 bonus to attack and damage rolls with this mace and are considered to be proficient with it. When you successfully hit a creature of elemental water, the mace inflicts an additional 2d6 fire damage. This property lasts for 10 minutes and then the *rod fir air* reverts to its normal form.

Spells. You can cast one of the following spells using the rod (spell save DC 15): *haste*, *scrying*, or *wall of fire*.

Additionally, you may use a reaction and expend one charge from the *rod of fire* to cancel an effect generated by a *rod of water*. Should a *rod of fire* come into contact with a *rod of water*, both rods disappear in a blinding flash that fills a 40-foot cube with arcane energies. Any creature caught in this area must make a DC 18 Dexterity saving throw, suffering 5d10 force damage on a failure, or half as much with a success.

The *rod of fire* regains 1d6 + 1 charges when exposed for eight hours in a natural fire. If the last charge in a *rod of fire* is used, roll 1d20. On a 1, the rod crumbles to dust.

ROD OF ILLUSION

Rod, conjunction (azoth), very rare (requires attunement by a spellcaster)

This rod looks like it is made of silver that is tipped with a bright blue sapphire but it is really just a plain wooden stick with a chunk of rock at one end. The rod has seven charges. Once you have attuned to the rod and are holding it, illusions you create are more real. If the illusion affects a limited number of senses, it affects one more sense. In all cases, the DC to save against any illusion spell you cast is increased by +1. You may use an action to expend one charge from the *rod of illusion* to use one of the following properties:

False Shapechange. You assume the appearance of any creature of any size. The magical aura of this effect is cloaked so that it appears to be a transmutation spell. Creatures that attempt to interact with this false image must succeed at a DC 15 Intelligence (Investigation) check to perceive the truth.

Skittering Sounds. You target a creature that you can see within 60 feet of you. That creature is haunted by illusions you generate of moving shadows, strange noises behind them, and other distractions. Until the end of your next turn, the target suffers disadvantage on all attack rolls, ability checks, and saving throws.

Spells. You can cast one of the following spells using the rod (spell save DC 15): *greater invisibility*, *hypnotic pattern*, or *seeming*.

Additionally, you may use a reaction and expend one charge from the *rod of illusion* to cancel an effect generated by a *rod of divination*. Should a *rod of illusion* come into contact with a *rod of divination*, both rods disappear in a blinding flash that fills a 40-foot cube with arcane energies. Any creature caught in this area must make a DC 18 Dexterity saving throw, suffering 5d10 force damage on a failure, or half as much with a success.

The *rod of illusion* regains 1d6 + 1 charges at sunrise. If the last charge in a *rod of illusion* is used, roll 1d20. On a 1, the rod crumbles to dust.

ROD OF THE LAND
Rod, very rare (requires attunement, see below)

This rod of varnished wood wrapped in purple-dyed leather gives a feeling of home when you hold it, of warm hearths, close friends, and good cheer. To attune to the *rod of the land*, you must be the legal owner or ruler of a territory of at least 10 square miles. The *rod of the land* is attuned to you and the land. The rod has seven charges. You may perform an eight-hour ritual to expend one charge from the *rod of the land* to use one of the following prosperities:

Blessing of Fecundity: All plants in the area produce yields double what they normally would, and all animal life becomes fertile and bears young if the natural prerequisite for such exists. This effect lasts until the next equinox or solstice. Any harvest or young are produced in the natural course of affairs, but to greater effect.

Blessing of Fortune: Any mines or other resource extraction enterprises within the area yield twice as much as normal with the same amount of effort. This effect lasts until the next equinox or solstice.

Spells. You may cast one of the following spells using the rod, requiring no material components, and the area of effect stretches to encompass the entire 10-square-mile area: *control weather*, *hallucinatory terrain*, or *scrying*.

The *rod of the land* regains expended charges only at the solstices and equinoxes and only when within the boundary of the land to which it is attuned, gaining 1d3 expended charges each solstice and equinox. If the last charge in a *rod of the land* is used, roll 1d20. On a 1, the rod crumbles to dust and the land suffers the effects of the spells *earthquake*, *plague of insects*, and *storm of vengeance* but the area of effect extends to the entire 10-square-mile area (spell save DC 15).

ROD OF NECROMANCY
Rod, conjunction (azoth), very rare (requires attunement by a spellcaster)

This rod of bone is tipped with a single finger bone bearing a white pearl in its nail. The rod has seven charges. Once you have attuned to the rod and are holding it, undead treat you as one of their own. Mindless undead will not attack you, and willful undead do not consider you prey but still might think of you as a threat. You may use an action to expend one charge from the *rod of necromancy* to use one of the following properties:

Assume Command. You target a single undead creature you can see within 30 feet. That creature must succeed at a DC 15 Wisdom saving throw or become under your control for one hour.

False Death. You become temporarily undead. You are no longer living and thus do not need to eat, drink, or even breathe. You retain your normal abilities save any that strictly rely on being alive. You gain immunity to poison damage. You remain in this undead state for one hour or until you choose to become a living creature again.

Spells. You can cast one of the following spells using the rod (spell save DC 15): *animate dead*, *contagion*, or *harm*.

Additionally, you may use a reaction and expend one charge from the *rod of necromancy* to cancel an effect generated by a *rod of enchantment*. Should a *rod of necromancy* come into contact with a *rod of enchantment*, both rods disappear in a blinding flash that fills a 40-foot cube with arcane energies. Any creature caught in this area must make a DC 18 Dexterity saving throw, suffering 5d10 force damage on a failure, or half as much with a success.

The *rod of necromancy* regains 1d6 + 1 charges at sunset. If the last charge in a *rod of necromancy* is used, roll 1d20. On a 1, the rod crumbles to dust.

ROD OF NINE LIVES
Wondrous item, conjunction (salt) uncommon

Talvan of Reme created this item to get around one of his pet peeves: the general inability of arcane magics to heal others. He had an adversarial relationship with Sir Elvatar, a paladin Talvan adventured with for decades. Following the end of that adventuring partnership, Talvan vowed to never adventure with, "god-prodders" again. Toward that end, he stocked up on healing potions and went to work on the *rod of nine lives*.

The *rod of nine lives* is deceitfully designed. It is a three-foot rod of ivory polished to a high sheen that bears ancient runes of healing. The rod is tipped with a clear diamond in a platinum setting. A false aura upon the rod causes any attempts to determine the magical schools it uses to read as evocation. The *rod of nine lives* actually uses necromantic magic to affect the semblance of healing. As an action, you can touch the rod to a living creature and grant it 1d6 + 4 temporary hit points. You may do this nine times and then the rod crumbles to dust.

ROD OF TRANSMUTATION
Rod, conjunction (azoth), very rare (requires attunement by a spellcaster)

This rod changes shape every time you hold it. The rod has seven charges. Once you have attuned to the rod and are holding it, any transmutation spell you cast has its duration doubled. You may use an action to expend one charge from the *rod of transmutation* to use one of the following properties:

Fool's Gold. You may change one pound of matter you touch into a similar type of matter. This change lasts for one hour and then the matter reverts to its normal form. You may not change matter from one state to another: liquids can be changed into other liquids, not into solids or gases.

Undo. You touch the *rod of transmutation* to an object or creature that has been affected by transmutation magic. The effect ends if it has a duration, and if a permanent change, the magic is suppressed for one hour.

Spells. You can cast one of the following spells using the rod (spell save DC 15): *flesh to stone*, *gaseous form*, or *polymorph*.

Additionally, you may use a reaction and expend one charge from the *rod of transmutation* to cancel an effect generated by a *rod of evocation*. Should a *rod of transmutation* come into contact with a *rod of evocation*, both rods disappear in a blinding flash that fills a 40-foot cube with arcane energies. Any creature caught in this area must make a DC 18 Dexterity saving throw, suffering 5d10 force damage on a failure, or half as much with a success.

The *rod of transmutation* regains 1d6 + 1 charges at sunset. If the last charge in a *rod of transmutation* is used, roll 1d20. On a 1, the rod crumbles to dust.

ROD OF WATER
Rod, conjunction (water), very rare (requires attunement by a spellcaster)

This rod of pure aquamarine bound in bronze wire feels cold to the touch. The rod has seven charges. Once attuned to the rod and holding it, you gain resistance to cold damage and a swim speed of 30 feet. As an action, you may expend one charge from the rod to do one of the following:

Control Water Elementals. You target a creature of the elemental (water) type that you can see within 60 feet. That creature must succeed on a DC 15 Wisdom saving throw or you gain control of it as per the spell *dominate monster*.

Mace of Water. The *rod of water* becomes a mace that affects only creatures of the Plane of Fire. You gain a +1 bonus to attack and damage rolls with this mace and are considered to be proficient with it. When you successful hit a creature of elemental fire, the mace inflicts an additional 2d6 cold damage. This property lasts for 10 minutes and then the *rod of water* reverts to its normal form.

Spells. You can cast one of the following spells using the rod (spell save DC 15): *control water*, *ice storm*, or *wall of ice*.

Additionally, you may use a reaction and expend one charge from the *rod of water* to cancel an effect generated by a *rod of fire*. Should a *rod of water* come into contact with a *rod of fire*, both rods disappear in a blinding flash that fills a 40-foot cube with arcane energies. Any creature caught in this area must make a DC 18 Dexterity saving throw, suffering 5d10 force damage on a failure, or half as much with a success.

The *rod of water* regains 1d6 + 1 charges when submerged for eight hours in a natural waterway. If the last charge in a *rod of water* is used, roll 1d20. On a 1, the rod crumbles to dust.

TRIBUNE'S BATON
Rod, panoply (tribune's panoply), very rare (requires attunement)

This ivory baton is simply dripping with gold leaf, intricate carvings, and imperial heraldry. Issued to the most trusted tribunes of the empire's legions, the baton was a symbol of authority as well as a potent magic item. Each has the name of the tribune awarded the baton engraved on it in a glowing gold script, as well as the date it was awarded and the emperor's personal signature.

While you are attuned with the *tribune's baton*, you gain a +1 bonus to your armor class and as a bonus action you may touch a living creature and grant it 1d4 + 2 temporary hit points. You may do the latter once and regain the use of that property following a long rest.

If worn as part of the *tribune's panoply* with the *tribune's toga*, as an action you may cast the *zone of truth* spell. You may do this once and regain use following a long rest.

If worn as part of a complete set of the *tribune's panoply*, you have advantage on Charisma (Intimidation and Persuasion) checks. Additionally, you have advantage on Charisma (Performance) checks that involve oratory.

TRIBUNE'S PANOPLY

The great empire that once ruled most of the world had a system of government where senators made the grand decisions in consultation with the emperor. (Or not. It varied by who sat the imperial throne.) But the tribunes handed the day-to-day affairs. These elected (or appointed, again it varied by emperor) officials most often led the imperial armies. Even tribunes who were not placed in charge of military forces were treated as military commanders due to long tradition.

The main signifier of tribunal rank was the baton. As the empire gained power, magical items became increasingly common, and the tribune's baton became a standardized enchanted item. Over time, an entire panoply was granted to those of tribunal rank upon election or appointment. This panoply was more than a mark of status; the pieces provided important tools for the fulfillment of a tribune's duties.

Tribunes who died in service or retired were supposed to have their panoplies cremated with them. However, this did not always happen and sometimes the massive pyres did not destroy the magical items adorning the corpse. It is rare to find even a single piece of a *tribune's panoply*, much less a complete set. Collectors try to acquire sets with the name of a single tribune, most often one famous or infamous in history.

CHAPTER SIX: POTIONS

DRAUGHT OF HOPE
Potion, uncommon

Upon draining this sparkling rainbow-colored liquid, you are filled with a wave of positive emotions. If you are under the effects of a mind-affecting effect such as being charmed or frightened, you may immediately make a saving throw with advantage to recover from the effect. You may reattempt this saving throw at the start of each of your turns for the potion's duration. Furthermore, you gain advantage on saving throws against mind-affecting effects for the duration of the potion. The effects of a *draught of hope* lasts for 10 minutes, after which you feel somewhat depressed as the artificial hope fades away.
Alchemical Formula: Rare Earth, Mercury (any), Emotion

DRAUGHT OF MADNESS
Potion, uncommon

This vial of liquid bears a striking resemblance to another potion and reveals itself to be an entirely different potion upon inspection (a successful DC 15 Intelligence (Arcana) check shows its true nature). Upon imbibing this potion, you must succeed at a DC 15 Constitution saving throw or suffer the effects of the *confusion* spell for 1 hour.
Alchemical Formula: Rare Earth, Mercury (any), Mind

DRAUGHT OF TERRORS
Potion, rare

This dark liquid has the viscosity of cold syrup and the flavor of rusty blades mixed with iodine. Upon imbibing this potion you may hold it in your mouth up to a number of rounds equal to your Constitution modifier, after which you must either use it or swallow it. While holding it in your mouth you may use an action to exhale the potion in a 10-foot cone originating from your mouth. All creatures caught in that cone must succeed at a DC 15 Wisdom saving throw or be overcome with visions of their greatest fears for 1d8+1 rounds. Creatures overcome thusly may not willingly take actions and must roll on the following table to determine their behavior for the duration of the effect. If you swallow the potion, either through choice or ignorance of its effects, you suffer as above, but may not make a saving throw to resist.

DRAUGHT OF TERRORS EFFECTS

1d8	Effect
1	The creature screams in fear and cowers, effectively stunned.
2	The creature flies into a rage and may only move towards a target or engage in melee combat. The target attacks the nearest creature, friend or foe, and if no targets are within sight attacks inanimate objects.
3	The creature flees, using its move action and taking the Dash action, in a random direction. The creature attempts to avoid dangerous terrain if possible.
4	The creature chooses a randomly determined creature it can see within 100 feet; that creature is the cause of its terror. They attempts to slay that creature using whatever means at hand, ignoring all others. If no creature is within range, the effected creature cowers as in 1 above.
5	The creature voids their bowels and bladder, shreds their clothing, tosses aside anything it holds in their hands, and screams nonsense for the duration of the potion. They may only take either a move action to escape or an attack action against a creature or object blocking their escape.
6	The creature's psyche flees the psychic assault, resulting in the creature having a new personality, allegiances, and goals. They may take actions to fulfill this new persona.
7	The creature wanders aimlessly about in random directions. They may only take a move and may not take an action. They do not interact with their environment, but simply stares slack-jawed at the world.
8	The creature flies into a rage and must make a ranged attack on its turn against a randomly chosen target within range and sight. It continues to stand in place and make ranged attacks until it is out of ammunition and may only move to gain a new ranged weapon. If none are within sight and within 30 feet, the creature finds something to throw, even if it is just a shoe.

Alchemical Formula: Rare Earth, Mercury (any), Emotion, Fear

ELIXIR OF LETHE
Potion, rare

Upon drinking this watery black liquid you must succeed at a DC 15 Wisdom saving throw or forget the past 1d10 + 5 years of your life. The memory does not return; it is gone forever. This may cause you to lose levels or other traits if you gained them during that time.
Alchemical Formula: Rare Earth, Mercury (any), Memory

ELIXIR OF UNDOING
Potion, very rare

Upon consuming this thick clear liquid you gain the ability to completely destroy an object. The next object you touch is unmade, falling apart into its component pieces. Buildings become piles of lumber and bricks, swords become coal and iron ore, cloth unravels into threads. This does not affect magical items and items held or in the possession of another creature allow their owner to make a DC 15 Charisma saving throw.
Alchemical Formula: Rare Earth, Azoth (any), Mercury (any), Emotion, Decay (x2 from 2 different sources), Transmutation

ELIXIR OF YOUTH
Potion, uncommon

This blue liquid has a strange shimmering gold film on top and tastes like pomegranate and cherry. Upon imbibing it you reverse the effects of aging, physically becoming 1d10 +5 years younger.
Alchemical Formula: Rare Earth, Mercury (any), Decay, Life

POTION OF COZINESS
Potion, uncommon

This red liquid is always just warm enough to be comfortably drunk and tastes like cinnamon and cloves with a hint of brown sugar or chocolate. It can be shared with up to six willing companions, each taking a sip. Those effected by the *potion of coziness* are immune to cold and fire damage, are kept comfortably safe and warm no matter the climate and may sleep for 6 hours despite distractions or other concerns (though they can awaken if they so choose). The potion lasts for 8 hours, after which it fades away leaving a warm glow and sense of fulfillment.
Alchemical Formula: Rare Earth, Fire (any), Mercury (any), Cold

POTION OF ECTOPLASM
Potion, rare

This thick sludge-like, yellow-green liquid tastes like ashes and sea foam. After drinking it your body and all equipment you are wearing or carrying become insubstantial for 1 hour. During this time you gain resistance to bludgeoning, slashing, and piercing damage from nonmagical attacks as well as acid, cold, fire, lightning, thunder, and radiant damage. You gain advantage on Dexterity (Stealth) checks. Furthermore, you may move through other creatures and objects as if they were difficult terrain. You suffer 10 force damage if you end your turn inside an object and may not end your turn inside a creature. However, any physical attack you make using a weapon that is insubstantial has its damage reduced by half and you cannot interact with physical matter while insubstantial.
Alchemical Formula: Rare Earth, Azoth (any), Mercury (any), Water (any), Armor, Protection, Planar, Stealth

POTION OF THE FEAST
Potion, rare

After consuming this gravy like liquid, you feel bloated as if you had just partaken of a massive feast. One drink of this potion provides a day's worth of food and drink. Once before you take a short or long rest you may use an action to disgorge the contents of your bloated stomach at a single target within 5 feet. This target must make a DC 15 Dexterity saving throw, taking 4d10 acid damage on a failure, or half as much on a success.
Alchemical Formula: Rare Earth, Earth (any), Acid

CHAPTER SIX: POTIONS | 25

POTION OF THE FEY WALK
Potion, rare

This amber colored liquid tastes of honeysuckle and chrysanthemum. After consuming a *potion of the fey walk*, for the next ten minutes you may use a bonus action to step through the land of fey and reappear. When you do so you disappear from your current location and reappear at the end of your turn at a location within 60 feet of your point of origin and visible from it. There is some risk in stepping through the land of the fey, and each time you do so there is a cumulative 5% chance some fey creature has taken notice and follows you into the mortal world. The chance resets to 5% after a long rest.

Alchemical Formula: Rare Earth, Sulfur (any), Luck, Planar

POTION OF ICE
Potion, uncommon

This light blue liquid is cold to the touch. When the *potion of ice* touches any liquid it immediately freezes the liquid to ice. A single *potion of ice* can freeze solid up to 40 cubic feet of liquid but must be used all at once as the potion interacts with moisture in the air. The *potion of ice* can be used as a weapon. Throw the potion at one creature within 30 feet that you can see. That creature must make a DC 15 Dexterity saving throw taking 4d10 cold damage on a failure, or half as much on a success. Drinking the *potion of ice* is lethal, you must make a DC 18 Constitution saving throw If you fail, you drop to 0 hit points. If you succeed you suffer 5d10 cold damage.

Alchemical Formula: Rare Earth, Mercury (any), Cold (x2)

POTION OF LUCK
Potion, very rare

Drinking this bright gold ham flavored liquid brings you incredible luck. You gain 5 luck dice, which are d8s. You may expend a luck die to add its result to any ability check, attack roll, initiative roll, or saving throw you make. Once expended the luck dice are gone.

Alchemical Formula: Rare Earth, Sulfur (any), Luck (x3)

POTION OF MAGMA
Potion, rare

This reddish-orange liquid is always hot and tastes like cayenne and chocolate. Upon imbibing a *potion of magma*, your body temperature increases to 150° F, although this does not cause you any harm. For the next hour, if you are hit by a melee attack that causes slashing or piercing damage the creature that hit you suffers 2d6 fire damage as your blood explodes out and turns into a stream of lava. Furthermore, while the *potion of magma* is affecting you, you gain immunity to fire damage and vulnerability to cold damage.

Alchemical Formula: Rare Earth, Fire (any) (x3), Mercury (any), Transmutation

POTION OF ORIGINATION
Potion, very rare

This jasmine scented green liquid allow you to make massive alterations to your body and mind. After imbibing a *potion of origination*, as an action you may alter your psychical form. You may change your race to another of the same size, and change your gender, or physical appearance. By spending ten minutes in concentration you may swap two of your ability scores, such as exchanging your Strength for Intelligence. The effects of the *potion of origination* last for 1 hour.

Alchemical Formula: Rare Earth, Mercury (any), Sulfur (any), Transmutation (x3)

POTION OF POETRY
Potion, uncommon

This golden liquid has a strong flavor of spices and vanilla. Upon consuming a *potion of poetry*, for the next hour you gain advantage on Charisma checks. You may end the duration of the potion in order to charm a single creature within 100 feet that you can see. The targeted creature must succeed at a DC 15 Wisdom saving throw be charmed by you for 1 hour, after which they know you have used mind-affecting powers on them.

Alchemical Formula: Rare Earth, Mercury (any), Water (any), Mind, Transmutation

POTION OF SMOKE
Potion, rare

This black foamy liquid tastes like smoked pork and sauerkraut. Upon imbibing a *potion of smoke*, for the next ten minutes every time you open your mouth a 10-foot diameter cloud of smoke issues from your mouth. These clouds remain until dispersed by high winds, driving rain, or similar phenomena. The clouds of smoke are thick and block line of sight through them, granting concealment to any creature within one. During the duration of the potion you cannot speak or cast spells that require a vocal component. However, you are immune to poisonous gases, and do not need to breathe.

Alchemical Formula: Rare Earth, Fire (any) (x2), Mercury (any), Stealth

POTION OF THE CLOUDS
Potion, very rare

This white foamy liquid tastes strongly of milk and honey. After drinking a *potion of the clouds*, for the next hour you may walk upon air as if it were solid ground. You ascend or descend as if climbing stairs and can even stand in open air. When the effect ends, if you are not on solid ground, you fall.

Alchemical Formula: Rare Earth, Air (any), Earth (any), Mercury (any), Transmutation

POTION OF THE FISHES
Potion, rare

This thick dark liquid tastes like seaweed and old fish. When you drink a *potion of the fishes*, for the next hour your gain the ability to speak with sea life as per the spells *speak with animals* and *speak with plants*. Furthermore, you may breathe water as easily as air and are not hampered by moving underwater.

Alchemical Formula: Rare Earth, Mercury (any), Water (any), Mind, Transmutation

POTION OF TRANSFERENCE
Potion, very rare

This light-colored potion tastes like anise and allspice and is always found in a bottle with two mouths. Two creatures must consume the potion at the same time. The minds of the two creatures are transferred between their bodies. Each creature keeps its class and class abilities, skills and other proficiencies, as well as their Intelligence, Wisdom, and Charisma scores. The bodies retain their hit points totals, physical features such as from race, and their Strength, Constitution, and Dexterity scores. Ongoing physical effects such as conditions suffered remain with the bodies, and mental effects likewise remain with the minds. The effects of the *potion of transference* last for 1 hour, after which the minds return to their original bodies. If a body dies while swapped using the *potion of transference*, the mind inhabiting that body dies as well and the partner swapped mind remains in its new body. A *resurrection* or similar spell can return a body and mind that was lost, but the effects of the *potion of transference* are then permanent.

Alchemical Formula: Rare Earth, Azoth (any), Mercury (any), Water (any), Body (x2) (different sources), Mind (x2) (different sources

POTION OF TRANSLOCATION
Potion, very rare

This blue-green viscous liquid tastes of purple and lightning. After drinking a *potion of translocation* you immediately must teleport, as per the spell *teleport* to a new location. If you have the potion in your hand you may consume it as a reaction.

Alchemical Formula: Rare Earth, Air (any), Azoth (any), Transportation

WOLF-FANGED ELIXIR
Potion, very rare

This dark red potion tastes of pine and fresh blood. Once you have drunk a *wolf-fanged elixir* you take on the shape of a hybrid wolf, growing fangs and claws, sprouting hair, and gaining the ability to run on all fours as well as darkvision 60 feet, the ability to track and detect scents, and advantage on all Wisdom (Perception) checks. You gain a bite attack that inflicts 1d8 piercing damage and a claw attack that inflicts 1d6 slashing damage and may use either attack as a bonus action as if fighting with two weapons. Furthermore, your speed increase to 40 feet. The effects of a *wolf-fanged elixir* last for 1 hour.

Alchemical Formula: Rare Earth, Earth (any), Mercury (any), Salt (any), Agility, Body, Speed, Transmutation

CHAPTER SEVEN: SCROLLS

CASTING TABLETS
Scroll, varies

These fried clay tablets have spells incised on them in cuneiform and function like *spell scrolls* in all ways except for the following: Instead of reading the spell, if the spell is on your spell list, as a bonus action you may break a *casting tablet*. If you do so, the spell incised into it is lost, but you regain an expended spell slot of the same level as the spell that was on the tablet.

CURSED SCROLL
Scroll, rare

This scroll appears to be a different type of magical scroll. You may read it as an action, and when you do, you are affected by the scroll's curse.

Cursed. The curse affects you as soon as you read the scroll. There are many types of cursed scrolls; roll on the table below to discover what new and wondrous thing has entered your life. The effects of the curse are permanent until dispelled with *remove curse* or similar magic.

CURSED SCROLL

1d6	Curse	Effect
1	Lycanthropy	You are cursed with lycanthropy. (Roll 1d6: 1, werebear; 2, wereboar; 3, wererat; 4, weretiger; 5 werewolf: 6 were-creature of GM's choice.)
2	Shapechange	You shapechange into a creature as per the spell *shapechange*. (Roll 1d6: 1, bat; 2, dire wolf; 3, common dog; 4, common cat; 5, horse; 6, elephant).
3	Love	You are charmed by the first sentient creature you see after reading the scroll.
4	Misfortune	You suffer disadvantage on all attack rolls, ability checks, and saving throws. Furthermore, things go bad all the time: you trip while running, are mistaken for someone else, and otherwise have ill luck.
5	Haunted	You become the target of a minor fey creature or undead spirit. While not deadly in itself, the creature haunting you plays pranks, distracts you, or otherwise hampers your enjoyment of life.
6	Creeping Anxiety	Nothing happens at first but you know you are cursed. This is not to say something bad won't happen, but the Sword of Damocles is set, the candle is lit, and the waiting begins …

MIRROR SCROLL
Scroll, uncommon

This scroll has a glossy sheen and the words are written in reflective silver. As an action, you may read this scroll, after which the scroll turns into a mirrored surface. The scroll remains intact as a mirror you can roll up or unfurl for 10 minutes, after which the scroll crumbles to dust. Paper Portal

Scroll, very rare

This massive scroll is 10 feet long and six feet wide. The edges of the scroll are covered in arcane writing and appear dull and faded. You must unroll the *paper portal* and string it so that it hangs between two sturdy objects, with all four corners tied down taut. Once this is done, you may use an action to read the script, after which the words glow green and a portal to another world opens on the blank interior of the scroll. This portal is a two-way passage and lasts for one hour or until the scroll is damaged or rolled up (even one corner will do). When the portal closes, the *paper portal* crumbles to dust. Each *paper portal* is keyed to a specific plane; when a *paper portal* is discovered, roll on the following table to see where it leads:

PAPER PORTAL RANDOM PLANE TABLE

1d20	Plane
1	Elemental Air
2	Elemental Water
3	Elemental Fire
4	Elemental Earth
5	Ethereal
6	Alternate Material Plane
7	Private Demiplane
8	Astral Plane
9	Fey Planes
10	Shadow Planes
11	Elemental Chaos
12	Plane of lawful evil gods
13	Plane of neutral good gods
14	Plane of chaotic evil gods
15	Endless plane of white space
16	1d100 years into the past
17	1d100 years into the future
18	An exact, but opposite, version of the plane from which the doorway is opened
19	A plane composed entirely of sentient mustard
20	A different point on the same plane from which the doorway is opened

SCRIPT OF THE EVIL EYE
Scroll, common

This small scrap of paper has a curse written on it in elegant cursive, but the name of the target is left blank. You may complete the curse by writing the name of a creature upon it with a pen and quill. This name must be a proper full name, not a nickname or type of creature. Once you write the name, you must burn the *script of the evil eye*. If the target is on the same plane as you, it suffers the effects of the *bestow curse* spell (DC 15 spell save).

SCROLL OF ABJURATION
Scroll, varies

The intricately worded glowing words on this scroll can be read aloud to hold at bay a specific type of creature. You use an action to read from the scroll to cause a shimmering 10-foot ring of magical writing to form at your feet. Creatures of the type the scroll abjures must succeed at a DC 15 Wisdom saving throw to cross the ring of writing. Even if they succeed on their saving throw, the creature suffers disadvantage on all attack rolls, ability checks, and saving throws if they begin their turn inside the ring. While the *scroll of abjuration*'s power is in effect creatures inside the ring gain advantage on saving throws against any effect the targeted creature type produces. The protective ring of writing remains for 10 minutes, after which it fades away and the scroll crumbles to dust.

SCROLL OF ABJURATION

Creature Type	Rarity
Aberrants	Rare
Beasts	Uncommon
Celestials	Very Rare
Constructs	Rare
Dragons	Very Rare
Elementals	Rare
Fey	Uncommon
Fiends	Very Rare
Giants	Rare
Humanoids (specific species)	Uncommon
Monstrosities	Rare
Oozes	Uncommon
Plants	Uncommon
Undead	Uncommon

SCROLL OF ABJURATION BLANK
Scroll, very rare

The intricately worded glowing words on this scroll can be read aloud to hold at bay a specific creature. You must know the creature's true name and must be able to write it in the blanks on the scroll. You use an action to read from the scroll to cause a shimmering 10-foot ring of magical writing to form at your feet. The specified creature must succeed at a DC 15 Wisdom saving throw to cross the ring of writing. Even if they succeed on their saving throw, they suffer disadvantage on all attack rolls, ability checks, and saving throws if they begin their turn inside the ring. While the *scroll of abjuration*'s power is in effect creatures inside the ring gain advantage on saving throws against any effect the targeted creature produces. The protective ring of writing remains for 10 minutes, after which it fades away and the scroll crumbles to dust.

SCROLL OF ANSWERS
Scroll, uncommon

As an action, you can open the blank scroll and ask it a single question. The answer to that question appears in a glowing script on the scroll and remains until the end of your next turn, at which point the scroll disintegrates. The scroll can answer any question whose answer is not protected by magic or the gods.

SCROLL OF ARMOR
Scroll, varies

The bright red script on this scroll forms an image of a person wearing armor. As an action, you may read this scroll, after which it crumbles to dust. The dust whirls around you and becomes a suit of armor, fastening itself in place if you are currently not wearing armor, or falling to the ground in pieces if you are. The armor remains for one hour, after which it crumbles to dust.

SCROLL OF ARMOR

Armor	Rarity
Breastplate	Uncommon
Chainmail	Uncommon
Chain shirt	Uncommon
Half plate	Uncommon
Hide	Uncommon
Leather	Common
Padded	Common
Plate	Rare
Ring mail	Rare
Scale mail	Uncommon
Shield	Common
Splint	Rare
Studded Leather	Common

SCROLL OF THE ARTISAN
Scroll, rare

This scroll has a large blank space in the middle and intricate calligraphy around the outer edge. As an action, you may read the scroll and draw a mundane item on the scroll that is worth less than 1,001 gp. Once you finish drawing the item, the scroll crumbles to dust and the item becomes real. The quality of the item is dependent on your artistic skills, but at the least is minimally functional.

SCROLL OF THE CAMP
Scroll, uncommon

This worn scroll has brown lettering that takes the shape of a campsite. As an action, you may read the scroll. The campsite springs off the scroll and becomes real, complete with tents and bedrolls for six people, a burning fire, a latrine dug safely away from the camp, stools for sitting around the fire at night, and a complete cast-iron cook set. Food simmers and sizzles on the pans, and enough water hangs in a large goatskin for six people to eat three meals. The tents and bedrolls are appropriate for the environment and protect against natural weather and temperatures ranging from −30° Fahrenheit to 120° Fahrenheit. The fire burns for the duration of the scroll. The camp disappears after 24 hours.

SCROLL OF COMMUNION
Scroll, uncommon

This scroll has a large drawing of an eye and a line of red script beneath it. *Scrolls of communion* are linked; each such scroll is mystically tied to another. As an action, you may read one of the pair of scrolls to activate them, and they remains active for one hour. While active, you may hold one scroll up and communicate with the linked *scroll of communion*. Your face appears on the linked scroll, and your words come from it as if from your own mouth, and likewise for anyone speaking on the other end. When the duration ends, both *scrolls of communion* crumble to dust.

SCROLL OF ELEMENTAL AIR
Scroll, conjunction (air), rare

Each *scroll of elemental air* is tied to the Elemental Planes of Air and is written in Primordial. As an action, you may read from the scroll. Once read, the scroll grants you control of a single creature native to the Elemental Plane of Air that you can see and that can hear you within 30 feet as per the spell *dominate monster* with a DC 15 spell save. Once used, even if the target resists the spell, the scroll crumbles to dust.

SCROLL OF ELEMENTAL EARTH
Scroll, conjunction (earth), rare

Each *scroll of elemental earth* is tied to the Elemental Plane of Earth and is written in Primordial. As an action, you may read from the scroll. Once read, the scroll grants you control of a single creature native to the Elemental Plane of Earth that you can see and that can hear you within 30 feet, as per the spell *dominate monster*, with a DC 15 spell save. Once used, even if the target resists the spell, the scroll crumbles to dust.

SCROLL OF ELEMENTAL FIRE
Scroll, conjunction (fire), rare

Each *scroll of elemental fire* is tied to the Elemental Plane of Fire and is written in Primordial. As an action, you may read from the scroll. Once read, the scroll grants you control of a single creature native to the Elemental Plane of Fire that you can see and that can hear you within 30 feet, as per the spell *dominate monster*, with a DC 15 spell save. Once used, even if the target resists the spell, the scroll crumbles to dust.

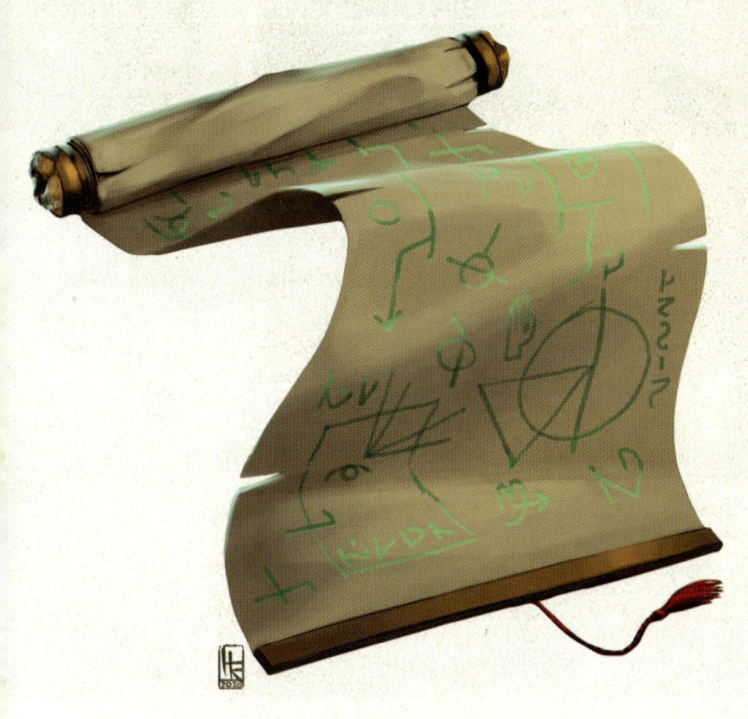

SCROLL OF ELEMENTAL WATER
Scroll, conjunction (water), rare

Each *scroll of elemental water* is tied to the Elemental Plane of Water and is written in Primordial. As an action, you may read from the scroll. Once read, the scroll grants you control of a single creature native to the Elemental Plane of Water that you can see and that can hear you within 30 feet, as per the spell *dominate monster*, with a DC 15 spell save. Once used, even if the target resists the spell, the scroll crumbles to dust.

SCROLL FAMILIAR
Scroll, uncommon

Only spellcasters can use this complexly worded scroll. You may use an action to read this scroll, after which the scroll animates as your companion as if using the spell *find familiar*. The scroll remains your familiar until you dismiss it or until it dies. It has the statistics of a **scroll familiar** (see **Appendix A: New Monsters**).

SCROLL OF THE GARDEN OF MONSTERS
Scroll, rare

This enchanted scroll is covered in a script that gets smaller as you read down the page, until at the end you are squinting to make out the words. As an action, you may read the scroll. You and up to four other willing creatures within 30 feet of you and any items on their person or being carried are shrunk down to Tiny size. Affected creatures remain shrunken for 24 hours and then revert to their normal sizes.

SCROLL OF THE MENAGERIE
Scroll, rare

This scroll has a large blank space in the middle and intricate calligraphy around the outer edge. As an action, you may read the scroll and draw a beast of up to Challenge 5 on the scroll. Once you finish drawing the item, the scroll crumbles to dust and the item becomes real. The beast is under your control for one hour; afterward, it behaves as a normal example of its species. The quality of the beast is dependent on your artistic skills, but at the least will have its statistics.

SCROLL OF RESISTANCE
Scroll, very rare

This scroll is written in a flowing script. You may use an action to read the scroll, after which you gain resistance to a type of damage for one hour. Each *scroll of resistance* protects against one of the following damage types: acid, bludgeoning, cold, fire, force, lightning, necrotic, piercing, poison, psychic, radiant, slashing, or thunder. If you read a *scroll of resistance* while under the influence of one, the effects of the previous one end.

SCROLL OF TRAPPING
Scroll, rare

This scroll appears to be a different type of magical scroll. As an action, you may read this scroll and then become subject to its curse.
Cursed. When you read this scroll, you must succeed at a DC 15 Wisdom saving throw or be converted into text and placed upon the scroll. If a creature is already trapped inside the scroll (50% chance when a *scroll of trapping* is found), the trapped creature appears in the same location you were in when you read the scroll. Unlike other scrolls, the *scroll of trapping* does not crumble to dust when read.

SCROLL OF THE UNARMED
Scroll, varies

The blue script of this scroll takes the form of a weapon. As a bonus action, you may read from this scroll, which causes the scroll to crumble to dust. The dust whirls into one of your hands and forms into the shape of a weapon. This weapon reverts to dust after one hour.

SCROLL OF THE UNARMED

Weapon	Rarity
Battleaxe	Uncommon
Dagger	Common
Greatsword	Uncommon
Handaxe	Common
Light crossbow and 10 bolts	Uncommon
Longbow and 10 arrows	Uncommon
Longsword	Uncommon
Shortsword	Common
Spear	Common
Warhammer	Uncommon

CHAPTER EIGHT: STAVES

STAFF OF THE ARCH-SPIDER
Staff, very rare (requires attunement by a spellcaster)

This ebony staff is carved with intricate spider webs along its full length. You may use the staff as a magic quarterstaff that grants a +2 to attack and damage rolls made with it.

The staff has 10 charges. It regains 1d6 + 4 expended charges each day at sunset. If you expend the last charge, roll 1d20. On a 1, the staff loses its properties and becomes a nonmagical staff.

As an action, you may expend one or more charges to use one of the following properties:

Poisoned Bite. For the one minute when you strike a creature with the *staff of the arch-spider*, the target must make a DC 15 Constitution saving throw. On a failure it takes 4d8 poison damage and is poisoned until the end of its next turn. On a success it takes half as much damage and is not poisoned.

Spells. You can cast the following spells using the staff, requiring no material components: *animal messenger* (one charge, must be a spider), *bestow curse* (2 charges), *conjure animals* (2 charges, must be a spider of some kind), *protection from poison* (1 charge), *vampiric touch* (2 charges), or *web* (1 charge).

As long as you are attuned to and holding the *staff of the arch-spider*, you can use an action to cast any of the following spells at will, expending no charges: *darkvision*, *speak with animals* (spiders only), and *spider climb*.

STAFF OF BEASTS
Staff, very rare (requires attunement by a druid)

This oaken staff is carved to look like a series of woodland animals standing on top of one another, wrapping around the staff until they reach the top which is a great bear's head. You may use the staff as a magic quarterstaff that grants a +2 to attack and damage rolls made with it.

The staff has 10 charges. It regains 1d6 + 4 expended charges every sunrise. If you expend the last charge, roll 1d20. On a 1, the staff loses its properties and becomes a nonmagical staff.

As an action, you may expend one or more charges to use the following properties:

Spells. You can cast the following spells using the staff, requiring no material components: *animal messenger* (1 charge), *conjure animals* (2 charges), *conjure woodland beings* (3 charges), *insect plague* (3 charges).

You can also spend an action to use the staff to cast *speak with animals* without using any charges.

Transform. You plant the *staff of beasts* in the ground and call upon it to transform into a living beast of no more than Challenge 2. The beast obeys your commands and considers you a close friend. The staff remains transformed until you choose to end the effect, the beast is killed, or after one hour has passed. At that point, it reverts to the *staff of beasts*. If the creature the staff becomes is slain, the maximum number of charges the staff holds is reduced by 1. If the maximum number of charges is reduced to zero, the staff loses all its magical abilities.

STAFF OF DEATH
Staff, very rare (requires attunement by a druid, cleric, ranger, sorcerer, warlock, or wizard)

This staff of polished bone topped with a skull exudes feelings of ill ease and dread. You have resistance to necrotic damage while holding this staff.

The staff has 10 charges. While holding it, you can use an action to expend one or more charges to cast one of the following spells from it, using your spell save DC: *animate dead* (3 charges), *blight* (4 charges), or *false life* (1 charge).

The staff regains 1d6 + 4 expended charges daily at sunset. If you expend the last charge, roll 1d20. On a 1, the staff turns to bone dust and blows away.

30 | Tome of Wondrous Items

STAFF OF THE ETERNAL STONE

Staff, conjunction (earth), very rare (requires attunement by a druid, cleric, ranger, sorcerer, warlock, or wizard)

This staff can be wielded as a magical quarterstaff granting you +2 to attack and damage rolls made with it. While attuned to the *staff of the eternal stone*, you gain resistance to acid damage. Furthermore, if you are on the Elemental Plane of Earth, you adapt to that plane, being able to breathe, eat, drink, and sleep as if a native, and while there gain a burrowing speed of 30 feet.

Once attuned, you can use the following properties of the *staff of the eternal stone*:

Command Earth Elementals. As an action, you may use a charge to attempt to command an earth elemental or other creature native to the Plane of Earth within 30 feet that can see and hear you, as per the spell *dominate monster*. Use your own spell save DC.

Earth Travel. As an action, you may expend two charges to transfer you and everything you are carrying as well as up to your spellcasting ability score in additional creatures within 30 feet of you to or from the Elemental Plane of Air. Creatures who do not want to travel with you must succeed at a Wisdom saving throw to resist the effect using your spell save DC.

Spells. Spells require an action to cast and use your spell save DC and spell attack bonus. The following spells expend one charge: *acid arrow*, *create food and drink* (food only), *meld into stone*, *pass without trace*. The following spells expend two charges using your spell save DC and spell attack bonus: *stone shape*, *stone skin*. The following spells expend three charges: *banishment*, *conjure minor elementals*, *planar binding*.

The staff has 10 charges and regains 1d4 + 2 charges at dawn every day.

STAFF OF THE EXQUISITE FLAME

Staff, conjunction (fire), very rare (requires attunement by a druid, cleric, ranger, sorcerer, warlock, or wizard)

This staff can be wielded as a magical quarterstaff granting you +2 to attack and damage rolls made with it. While attuned to the *staff of the exquisite flame*, you gain resistance to fire damage. Furthermore, if you are on the Elemental Plane of Fire, you adapt to that plane, being able to breathe, eat, drink, and sleep as if a native, and while there you are immune to fire damage.

Once attuned, you can use the following properties of the *staff of the exquisite flame*:

Command Fire Elementals. As an action, you may use an action to attempt to command an fire elemental or other creature native to the Plane of Fire within 30 feet that can see and hear you, as per the spell *dominate monster*. Use your spell save DC.

Fire Travel. As an action, you may expend two charges to transfer you and everything you are carrying as well as up to your spellcasting ability score in additional creatures within 30 feet of you to or from the Elemental Plane of Fire. Creatures who do not want to travel with you must succeed at a Wisdom saving throw to resist the effect using your spell save DC.

Spells. Spells require an action to case and use your spell save DC and spell attack bonus. The following spells expend one charge: *burning hands*, *continual flame*, *flaming sphere*, *pass without trace*, *scorching ray*. You may expend two charges to cast one of the following spells, using your spell save DC and spell attack bonus: *flame strike*, *magic circle*. You may expend three charges to cast one of the following spells: *banishment*, *conjure minor elementals*, *planar binding*.

The staff has 10 charges and regains 1d4 + 2 charges at dawn every day.

STAFF OF THE FOUR WINDS

Staff, very rare (requires attunement by a druid, cleric, ranger, sorcerer, warlock, or wizard)

This staff can be wielded as a magical quarterstaff granting you +2 to attack and damage rolls made with it. While attuned to the *staff of the four winds*, you gain resistance to lightning damage. Furthermore, if you are on the Elemental Plane of Air you adapt to that plane, being able to breathe, eat, drink, and sleep as if a native, and while there you gain fly 30 feet.

Once attuned, you can use the following properties of the *staff of the four winds*:

Air Travel. As an action, you may expend two charges to transfer you and everything you are carrying as well as up to your spellcasting ability score in additional creatures within 30 feet of you to or from the Elemental Plane of Air. Creatures who do not want to travel with you must succeed at a Wisdom saving throw to resist the effect.

Command Air Elementals. As an action, you may expend a charge to attempt to command an air elemental or other creature native to the plane of Air within 30 feet that can see and hear you, as per the spell *dominate monster*. Use your spell save DC.

Spells. Spells require an action to case and use your spell save DC and spell attack bonus. The following spells expend one charge: *fog cloud*, *gust of wind*, *fly*, *lightning bolt*, *pass without trace*, *wind walk*. You may expend two charges to cast one of the following spells: *freedom of movement*, *magic circle*. You may expend three charges to cast one of the following spells: *banishment*, *conjure minor elementals*, *planar binding*.

The staff has 10 charges and regains 1d4 + 2 charges at dawn every day.

STAFF OF HIKING

Staff, uncommon (requires attunement)

This sturdy but well-worn staff is shod with a copper sheath at its base. You may use this as a magical quarterstaff, gaining a +1 bonus to attack and damage rolls when you wield it. While attuned to and holding the staff, you ignore the effects of nonmagical difficult terrain and never fatigue or tire no matter how far you walk. Other sources of exhaustion are possible, such as lack of sleep or certain spells, but you never tire from walking.

STAFF OF KNOWLEDGE

Staff, panoply (scholarly mage), conjunction (azoth), very rare (requires attunement by a wizard)

This simple staff has a handle carved like a rolled scroll. You may use the *staff of the scholar* as a magical quarterstaff, gaining a +1 bonus to attack and damage rolls when you wield it. The staff has seven charges and regains 1d6 + 1 charges at sunrise. You may expend one or more charges to use the following properties:

Pontificate. The staff knows much and has seen much. As an action, you may command the *staff of knowledge* to speak on one of the following topics: arcana, history, nature, or religion. When it does so, it grants you advantage on your next skill checks involving that topic.

Spells. You may expend one or more charges to cast the following spells from the staff, requiring no material components: *augury* (2 charges), *clairvoyance* (2 charges), *comprehend languages* (1 charge), or *private sanctum* (3 charge).

Storage. As part of a 10-minute ritual, you may expend one charge to store a text in the *staff of knowledge*. The staff may store up to seven texts. These texts are recorded into the staff; as a bonus action, you may command the staff to project a single text it has stored.

If you wield the *staff of knowledge* while carrying the *quill of the assistant*, you may exchange charges between the two items.

If you wield the *staff of knowledge* while wearing the *studious robes*, when you cast *private sanctum* from the *staff of knowledge*, you cast the spell as if using a 6th-level spell slot.

If you wield the *staff of knowledge* as part of a complete *panoply of the scholarly mage*, the *staff of knowledge* has 10 charges and regains 1d8 + 2 charges each sunrise.

STAFF OF THE OASIS

Staff, rare (requires attunement by a druid or ranger)

This knobby staff is carved from a date palm. Several small water gourds hang from its top. You do not need to eat or drink while holding this staff, and you do not suffer exhaustion from excessive heat. Additionally, you are unhampered by terrain that is difficult due to being hot, sandy, or otherwise natural to a desert environment.

Once attuned, you can thrust the staff into any natural soil and cause a small oasis to spring up. This oasis covers 30 acres in area and replaces the natural terrain. The oasis has a small pond of freshwater that is free of taint and full of fish. Several trees grow around the edges of the water and provide dates, figs, and olives. Underbrush between the trees is heavy with berries. A few small goats graze about, and there are rabbits ready to snare. While resting at the oasis you can name up to your Wisdom score in creatures; these named creatures are then welcome at the oasis. All others must succeed at a DC 15 Wisdom saving throw to enter the oasis, being unable to pass its margins if they fail. Furthermore, the oasis acts as a *magic circle*. The oasis lasts until you pull the staff from the ground.

STAFF OF THE PILLAR
Staff, rare

This staff is carved from a single piece of basalt shaped to look like natural wood. Despite its heft and weight, you can still wield it as a weapon, gaining a +1 bonus to attack and damage rolls. The staff has three charges. It regains a spent charge when placed upright in natural soil for six hours. As an action, you thrust the staff into the ground and spend one charge to cause it to grow into a 50-foot-tall, 60-foot-diameter pillar of basalt that you may ride up to the top if you so desire. This pillar is a permanent structure until you spend an action and one charge to make it shrink back down into a staff. You and any allies on the top of the basalt pillar are gently lowered to the ground; everyone else on top of the pillar when it reverts to a staff are not so lucky.

STAFF OF PLANTS
Staff, very rare (requires attunement by a druid)

This oaken staff is carved to look like dozens of vines coiling around each other until reaching the top to form the canopy of a mighty tree. You may use the staff as a magic quarterstaff that grants a +2 to attack and damage rolls made with it.

The staff has 10 charges. It regains 1d6 + 4 expended charges every sunrise. If you expend the last charge, roll 1d20. On a 1, the staff loses its properties and becomes a nonmagical staff.

As an action, you may expend one or more charges to use the following properties:

Spells: You can cast the following spells using the staff, requiring no material components: *conjure woodland beings* (3 charges), *plant growth* (2 charges), *spike growth* (1 charge), or *tree stride* (3 charges). You can also use the staff to cast *speak with plants* without using any charges.

Transform: You plant the *staff of plants* in the ground and call upon it to transform into a living plant of no more than Challenge 2 that obeys your commands and considers you a close friend. The staff remains transformed until you choose to end the effect, until the plant is killed, or after one hour has passed. At that point, it reverts to the *staff of plants* form. If the creature the staff becomes is slain, the maximum number of charges the staff holds is reduced by one. If the maximum number of charges is reduced to zero, the staff loses all its magical abilities.

STAFF OF VAULTING
Staff, uncommon

This long staff is narrow and very flexible. You may use this as a magical quarterstaff, gaining a +1 bonus to attack and damage rolls when you wield it. The staff has seven charges and regains 1d6 + 1 charges every sunrise. You may use this staff to make incredible leaps, provided you hold onto the staff the entire time. As an action, you may expend one charge to plunge one end of the staff into the ground and vault over an obstacle, clearing up to 10 vertical feet and 100 horizontal feet.

STAFF OF VAULTING, FALSE
Staff, uncommon

This long staff is narrow and very flexible. You may use this as a magical quarterstaff, gaining a +1 bonus to attack and damage rolls when you wield it. The staff has seven charges and regains 1d6 + 1 charges every sunrise. You may use this staff to make incredible leaps, provided you hold onto the staff the entire time. As an action, you may expend one charge to plunge one end of the staff into the ground and vault over an obstacle, clearing up to 10 vertical feet and 100 horizontal feet.

Cursed. This magical staff is cursed. Every time you expend a charge to use its vaulting property, there is a 35% chance the staff lets go of you midleap, letting gravity and momentum take their toll. The staff laughs wickedly as it falls away, and then disappears in a puff of green smoke.

STAFF OF THE WAVES
Staff, very rare (requires attunement by a druid, cleric, ranger, sorcerer, warlock, or wizard)

This staff can be wielded as a magical quarterstaff granting you +2 to attack and damage rolls made with it. While attuned to the *staff of the waves*, you gain resistance to cold damage. Furthermore, if you are on the Elemental Plane of Water, you adapt to that plane, being able to breathe, eat, drink, and sleep as if a native, and while there you gain a swim speed of 30 feet.

Once attuned, you can use the following properties of the *staff of the waves*:

Command Water Elementals. As an action, you may attempt to command a water elemental or other creature native to the Plane of Water within 30 feet that can see and hear you, as per the spell *dominate monster*. Use your spell save DC.

Spells. Spells require an action to case and use your spell save DC and spell attack bonus. The following spells expend one charge: *create/destroy water, pass without trace, sleet storm, water breathing, water walk*. You may expend two charges to cast one of the following spells: *control water, magic circle*. You may expend three charges to cast one of the following spells: *banishment, conjure minor elementals, planar binding*.

Water Travel. As an action, you may expend two charges to transfer you and everything you are carrying as well up to your spellcasting ability score in additional creatures within 30 feet of you to or from the Elemental Plane of Water. Creatures who do not want to travel with you must succeed at a Wisdom saving throw to resist the effect using your spell save DC.

The staff has 10 charges and regains 1d4 + 2 charges at dawn every day.

THRYSUS
Staff, very rare (requires attunement)

Created by a fringe sect of worshipers of the god of wine, the *thyrsus* is a long staff tipped with a fennel cone and adorned with vines heavy with grapes. Its use was banned within the empire, and the sect that created it was violently repressed. Only a handful of examples of this powerful staff were saved, and it is thought that nearly all of them have been either destroyed or taken into custody by a temple of the god of wine. You can use the *thyrsus'* following properties:

Break. You may break the staff as an action. All creatures within a 300-foot cube centered on you must make a DC 15 Wisdom saving throw or suffer a long-term madness, or suffer a short-term madness on a successful save.

Feed the Multitudes. As an action, you may expend one charge to cast *create food and drink*, though the drink created is some form of alcoholic beverage.

Fennel-Tipped Spear. As a bonus action, you may expend one charge to cause the fennel cone tip to become as sharp and hard as a steel spearhead, making the *thyrsus* a magical spear that grants you a +1 bonus on attack and damage rolls with it.

Spells. As an action, you may expend one charge to cast the spells *charm person* or *hideous laughter*. You may expend two charges to cast one of the following spells: *dream, modify memory*, or *hypnotic pattern*. The spells have a DC 15 spell save.

Touch of Confusion. As an action, you may expend one charge to touch a creature, and the target must succeed on a DC 15 Wisdom save or suffer the effects of a *confusion* spell.

A *thyrsus* has 10 charges and regains 1d8 + 2 charges following a long rest.

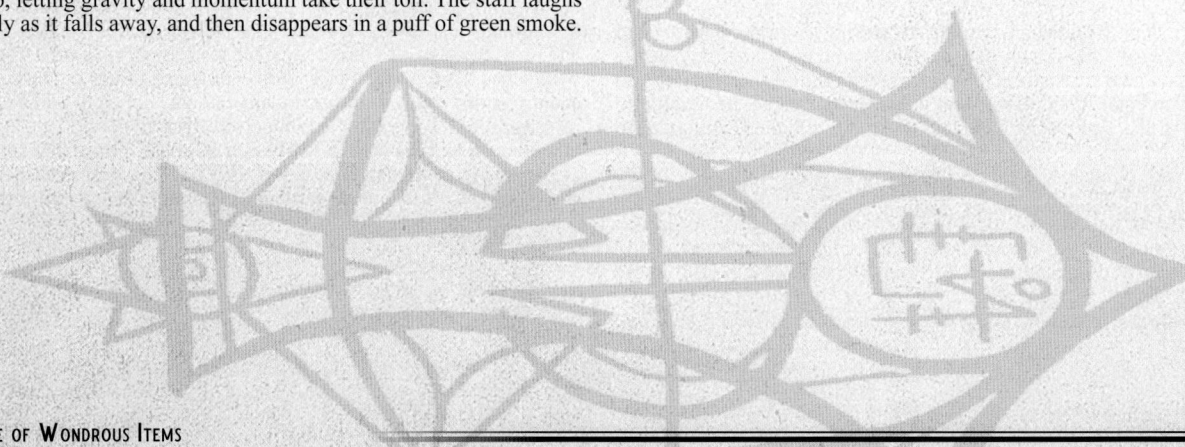

32 | Tome of Wondrous Items

CHAPTER NINE: WANDS

WAND OF THE COBRA
Wand, rare

This black-and-gold painted wooden rod is in the shape of a cobra, its hood flared and ready to strike. The wand has three charges. While holding it, you may use a reaction to expend one of its charges to target a creature who has just successfully attacked you in melee. The cobra head on the wand animates and attacks the target who must succeed on a DC 15 Dexterity check or suffer 1d6 piercing plus 2d6 poison damage.

The wand regains 1d3 expended charges each day at sunset. If you expend the wand's last charge, roll 1d20. On a 1, the wand crumbles into ashes and is destroyed.

WAND OF COLORS
Wand, uncommon

This rainbow-colored wand is tipped with a clear crystal that splits light that passes through it. The wand has seven charges. While holding it, you can use an action to expend one or more of its charges to cast the *color spray* spell from it. For one charge, you cast the 1st-level version of the spell. You can increase the spell slot level by one for each additional charge you expend. Alternately, you can expend one charge to change the color of one creature, suit of clothing, suit of armor, or object up to five cubic feet in size.

The wand regains 1d6 + 1 expended charges each day at sunrise. If you expend the wand's last charge, roll 1d20. On a 1, the wand crumbles into colored glitter and is destroyed.

WAND OF CONDUCTING
Wand, uncommon

This plain black wand is highly polished and tipped in silver. The wand has seven charges. While holding it, you can use an action to expend one charge per hour of work to aid in the completion of a group task. Target up to 10 willing creatures within 60 feet of you who are engaged in completing a single task such as building a wall or digging a well. The task is completed in half the time, requires half the usual amount of materials, and if the task requires a check of any kind, the workers have advantage on it.

The wand regains 1d6 + 1 expended charges each day at sunrise. If you expend the wand's last charge, roll 1d20. On a 1, the wand crumbles into ashes and is destroyed.

WAND OF THE DEAD
Wand, conjunction (salt), rare

This wand is carved from the bones of a humanoid forearm bound together by wires. The wand has three charges. While holding it, you may use an action to expend one of its charges to target an undead creature you can see within 30 feet. That creature must succeed on a DC 15 Charisma saving throw or be charmed by you for one hour.

The wand regains 1d3 expended charges each day at sunset. If you expend the wand's last charge, roll 1d20. On a 1, the wand crumbles into ashes and is destroyed.

WAND OF DISPELLING
Wand, conjunction (azoth), very rare

This crooked stick is actually a powerful wand that has three charges. While holding it, you can use an action to expend one or more of its charges to cast *dispel magic* from it, but you must touch the target with the wand. When you use the wand to dispel magic, it makes a spellcasting check at +4. For each charge above one that you expend when invoking the wand, the spellcasting bonus increases by one. The wand is automatically successful at dispelling the effects of a spell cast with a spell slot equal to or lower than the spellcasting bonus used. For example, with two charges, it automatically dispels spell effects of fifth level or lower, and has a +5 bonus to a spellcasting check to dispel higher level spell effects.

The wand regains 1d3 expended charges each day at sunrise. If you expend the wand's last charge, roll 1d20. On a 1, the wand crumbles into ashes and is destroyed.

WAND OF DISTANT TOUCH
Wand, uncommon

This wand is carved to look like a hand with a single pointing finger. The wand has seven charges. While holding it, you can use a bonus action to expend one of its charges to manipulate an item within 30 feet that you can see as if you were touching. You can flip a lever, push a button, open a chest, or even use thieves' tools (provided you have thieves' tools handy and know how to use them).

The wand regains 1d6 + 1 expended charges each day at sunset. If you expend the wand's last charge, roll 1d20. On a 1, the wand crumbles into ashes and is destroyed.

WAND OF ENTOMBMENT
Wand, very rare

This wand of hard stone has a hollow groove along its length. The wand has three charges. While holding it, you can use an action to expend one of its charges and touch a target with the wand. A fissure in the earth opens up under the target. The target must succeed on a DC 15 Dexterity saving throw or be caught in the fissure. While the creature is caught, it is grappled and restrained (escape DC 15). At the beginning of your next turn, the fissure closes and traps the target within. The target suffers 27 (5d10) bludgeoning damage and begins to suffocate.

The wand regains 1d3 expended charges each day at sunrise. If you expend the wand's last charge, roll 1d20. On a 1, the wand crumbles into ashes and is destroyed.

WAND OF THE FIST
Wand, uncommon

This oak wand is carved with a very realistic fist at its tip. The wand has seven charges. While holding it, you may use an action to expend one of its charges to target one creature you can see within 60 feet. Make an attack roll against that target using your choice of ability score + your proficiency bonus as a modifier to the attack roll. If you hit, the target suffers 2d8 bludgeoning damage as a spectral fist slams into it.

The wand regains 1d6 + 1 expended charges each day at sunset. If you expend the wand's last charge, roll 1d20. On a 1, the wand crumbles into ashes and is destroyed.

WAND OF FLIES
Wand, rare

This wand is cleverly carved and painted to look like a fly's leg. The wand has three charges. While holding it, you can use an action to expend one of its charges to summon a swarm of biting flies. This swarm fills a 10-foot cube you can see within 60 feet of you and has a fly speed of 35 feet. As a bonus action, you can cause the swarm to move up to its full speed. The swarm lasts for 1d6 + 1 rounds and dissipates at the end of your turn. The swarm blocks line of sight through it, and any creature that ends its turn within the swarm suffers 2 piercing damage and must succeed at a DC 15 Constitution saving throw or become stunned (swatting at flies) until the end of their next turn.

The wand regains 1d3 expended charges each day at sunrise. If you expend the wand's last charge, roll 1d20. On a 1, the wand crumbles into ashes and is destroyed.

WAND OF FLIGHT
Wand, uncommon

This yellowwood wand has a white stripe down the middle of it. This wand has seven charges. While holding it, you can use an action to expend one of its charges to cast the *expeditious retreat* spell. While under the effects of the spell cast from this wand you do not provoke attacks of opportunity. However, you must use this extra movement to move away from danger. If you move closer to a foe or cause damage, the effect ends.

The wand regains 1d6 + 1 expended charges each day at sunrise. If you expend the wand's last charge, roll 1d20. On a 1, the wand crumbles into ashes and is destroyed.

CHAPTER NINE: WANDS | 33

WAND OF HANDS
Wand, uncommon

This oak wand is tipped with two realistically carved clasping hands. The wand has seven charges. While holding the wand, you may use a bonus action to expend one of its charges to activate it for one hour. While active the wand floats beside and acts as an extra hand under your control. You can carry an item, wield a weapon, or manipulate an item. At the end of the hour, the wand of hands it drops whatever it is holding and returns to your hand, if one is available, otherwise it drops to the ground along with whatever it was holding.

The wand regains 1d6 + 1 expended charges each day at sunrise. If you expend the wand's last charge, roll 1d20. On a 1, the wand crumbles into ashes and is destroyed.

WAND OF THE HEDGEROWS
Wand, very rare

This thorny wand is carved from a slender piece of blackthorn. The wand has three charges. While holding the wand, you may use an action to expend one of its charges to draw a doorway in the air that fills a 10-foot-by-10-foot space you can see within 30 feet of you. This doorway opens onto another plane; roll randomly on the table below to determine where it leads. The doorway remains open until the end of your next turn and then closes. The doorway is a one-way opening; you and creatures from your side can pass through, but nothing can come from the other side.

The wand regains 1d3 expended charges each day at sunset. If you expend the wand's last charge, roll 1d20. On a 1, the wand crumbles into ashes and is destroyed.

WAND OF THE HEDGEROWS RANDOM PLANE TABLE

1d20	Plane
1	Elemental Air
2	Elemental Water
3	Elemental Fire
4	Elemental Earth
5	Ethereal
6	Alternate Material Plane
7	Private Demiplane
8	Astral Plane
9	Plane of Faerie
10	Plane of Shadows
11	Elemental Chaos
12	Nine Hells
13	Elysium
14	Abyss
15	Endless plane of gray space
16	1d100 years in the past
17	1d100 years into the future
18	An exact, but opposite, version of the plane from which the doorway is opened
19	A plane composed entirely of sentient mayonnaise
20	A different point on the same plane from which the doorway is opened

WAND OF HORROR
Wand, rare (requires attunement by a spellcaster)

This black oak wand is tipped with a small animal's skull. This wand has seven charges. While holding it, you can use an action to expend one of its charges and choose a target you can see within 120 feet of you. The target can be a creature, an object, or a point in space. Roll 1d100 and consult the following table to discover what happens.

If the effect causes you to cast a spell from the wand, the spell's save DC is 15. If the spell normally has a range expressed in feet, its range becomes 120 feet if it isn't already.

If an effect covers an area, you must center the spell on and include the target. If an effect has multiple possible subjects, the GM randomly determines which ones are affected.

The wand regains 1d6 + 1 expended charges each day at sunset. If you expend the wand's last charge, roll 1d20. On a 1, the wand crumbles into ashes and is destroyed.

WAND OF HORROR EFFECTS

1d100	Effect
01–05	You cast *vampiric touch*.
06–10	You cast *false life*.
11–15	You are paralyzed with terror until the start of your next turn.
16–20	You cast *speak with dead* on the target, or if the target is not dead, the nearest appropriate corpse. If something dead is within 120 feet, even if it is an insect, the spell takes effect. If no possible corpse is available, the charge is wasted.
21–25	You cast *blindness/deafness*. If the target was not a creature, you suffer 1d6 necrotic damage.
26–30	You cast *fear*.
31–33	The sky rains bloody worms in a 60-foot radius centered on the target. The area becomes lightly obscured, and the ground becomes difficult terrain. The bloody worms fall until the end of your next turn and then melt into piles of red goo.
34–36	An undead creature appears in the unoccupied space nearest the target. The undead creature isn't under your control and acts as it normally would, meaning it likely seeks the warm flesh of the living to satiate its vile appetites. Roll 1d100 to determine which undead creature appears. On a 1–25, a **wight** appears; on a 26–50, a **wraith** appears; on a 51–100, a **zombie** appears.
37–46	You cast *animate dead* or, if the target is not dead, on the nearest appropriate corpse. If something dead is within 120 feet, even if it is an insect, the spell takes effect. If no possible corpse is available, the charge is wasted.
47–49	A cloud of 600 jabbering skulls fills a 30-foot radius centered on the target. The area becomes heavily obscured. Any creature that ends its turn within the area of effect suffers 1d6 psychic damage as the jabbering skulls speak of horrid crimes and terrible desires. The skulls remain for 10 minutes.
50–53	You cast *ray of enfeeblement*.
54–58	You cast *darkness*.
59–62	All vegetation dies within a 60-foot radius centered on the target. If a creature of the plant type is within that area, it suffers 4d10 necrotic damage. Furthermore, all nonmagical items made of plant material, such as wood or rope, rots away to black dust over the next 1d4 rounds.
63–65	An object of the GM's choice decays to black dust. The object must be neither worn nor carried, within 120 feet of the target, and no larger than 10 feet in any dimension.
66–69	You cast *bestow curse* on yourself.
70–79	You cast *black tentacles*.
80–84	You cast *inflict wounds*, but with the wand's range counting as your touch range.
85–87	Weeping sores form on the target's flesh. If you chose a point in space or an object as the target, the sores appear on the creature nearest to that point. The sores remain for 24 hours and cause no harm but look horrid and revolting. The target suffers disadvantage on any Charisma checks with people that can see the weeping sores.
88–90	A stream of 1d4 × 10 disembodied bleeding tongues shoots from the wand's tip in a line 30 feet long and five feet wide. Each tongue deals 1 slashing damage, and the total damage of the tongues is divided among all creatures in the line. The tongues bear piercings, each holding a tiny gemstone worth 1 gp.

1d100	Effect
91–95	A burst of greenish-purple energy extends from you in a 30-foot radius. You and each creature in the area must succeed on a Constitution saving throw or become poisoned for one minute.
96–97	The target takes on the appearance of a rotting corpse for 1d10 days. If you chose a point in space, the creature nearest to that point is affected. If you chose an object, that object appears to be rotting and decayed.
98–00	If you targeted a creature, it must make a Constitution saving throw. If you didn't target a creature, you become the target and must make the saving throw. If the saving throw fails by 5 or more, the target dies and reanimates as a **wight** in 1d6 days. On any other failed save, the target begins to rot away, suffering 2d10 necrotic damage at the start of its turn. A rotting target may repeat the saving throw at the end of each of its turns, ending the effect on a success.

WAND OF THE HOURGLASS
Wand, very rare

This wand is carved from soft maple into the shape of an hourglass. The wand has three charges. When you are holding the wand, you may use an action to expend one of its charges to throw yourself back in time 1d6 minutes. You remain in that time for one minute and then snap back to the moment you left. After the third charge is used, the wand moves forward or backward in time 1d10 years and recharges.

WAND OF MAPPING
Wand, uncommon

This plain, slightly bent twig has a very sharp point. This wand has seven charges. While holding it, you can expend one of its charges to command it to draw a map of the surrounding 10 miles. This takes one minute to complete, and it must have a surface to work on, even if it is the dirt at your feet. The map shows major physical features, settlements, political boundaries, trails, and roads. It also displays dangers, ruins, and similar features of interest. It does not show anything hidden by magic or any detail that is less than a mile square.

The wand regains 1d6+1 expended charges each day at sunrise. If you expend the wand's last charge, roll 1d20. On a 1, the wand crumbles into ashes and is destroyed.

WAND OF MISDIRECTION
Wand, uncommon

This plain, slightly bent twig has a very sharp point. This wand has seven charges. While holding it, you can expend one of its charges to command it to draw a map of the surrounding 10 miles. This takes one minute to complete, and it must have a surface to work on, even if it is the dirt at your feet. The map shows major physical features, settlements, political boundaries, trails, and roads. It also displays dangers, ruins, and similar features of interest. It does not show anything hidden by magic, or any detail that is less than a mile square.

The wand regains 1d6 + 1 expended charges each day at sunrise. If you expend the wand's last charge, roll 1d20. On a 1, the wand crumbles into ashes and is destroyed.

Curse. The wand is cursed and houses a mischievous spirit. The *wand of misdirection* appears to be a *wand of mapping* to spells such as *identify*. The map this wand creates is flawed in some way. Dangers are unmarked or mismarked, trails veer off course, and sites of interest are not where they should be. The wand does not cause any gross changes such as moving mountains or ignoring a river; that would give away the deceit. Instead, the map is subtly inaccurate in the most amusing manner possible.

WAND OF ROSES
Wand, uncommon

Three branches of rosewood wrap around each other to form a small bouquet of three roses. This wand has seven charges. While holding it, you may use an action to expend one of its charges to target a creature. The targeted creature must succeed at a DC 15 Wisdom saving throw or be charmed by you (as the spell) for one hour. However, you are likewise affected by the wand in the same manner, becoming charmed by the target.

The wand regains 1d6 + 1 expended charges each day at sunrise. If you expend the wand's last charge, roll 1d20. On a 1, the wand crumbles into ashes and is destroyed.

WAND OF RUNES
Wand, conjunction (azoth), legendary (requires attunement by a spellcaster)

This plain ash staff is carved with 24 runes carved into it. The wand likewise has 24 charges. While holding this wand, you may use an action to expend one of its charges to activate a rune, creating the effect linked to that rune. Each rune may be used once, and then it disappears. Once all 24 runes are used, the wand crumbles into ashes and is destroyed.

WAND OF RUNES EFFECTS

Rune	Effect
f (fehu)	100 head of cattle appear within 120 feet of you, each branded to show your ownership. Within the next 30 days, you must give at least 25 of these cattle to worthy individuals or all of the cattle disappear.
u (ūra)	A clear freshwater spring appears from the ground at a point within 120 feet of you.
th (thurisaz)	A **hill giant** appears within 120 feet of you and serves you loyally unto death for the next hour. After this time expires, the giant is free to go about its business. It may continue serving you, attack you, or just wander off depending on how you treated it.
a (ansuz)	When you activate this rune, you must tear one of your eyes out. In exchange, your Intelligence, Wisdom, and Charisma scores all increase by +1.
r (radiō)	You and up to six willing creatures within 60 feet of you are transported to a point you declare anywhere on the same plane you are on.
k (kenaz)	The *wand of runes* glows brightly for 24 hours. You can increase or decrease this glow as an action from as bright as a beacon to as dim as a single torch.
g (gebō)	When you activate this rune, choose one creature you can see within 60 feet of you. That creature must succeed at a DC 15 Charisma saving throw or be forced to enter into a reciprocal gift exchange with you. You offer one item you own; the target offers a similar item in return.
w (wunjo)	Choose a target you can see within 120 feet of you. That target is healed of all injuries, recovers from any disease or poison affecting it, and loses any negative conditions it currently suffers.
h (hagalaz)	Rains fall over a 10-mile area. The rains are gentle but constant for the next 2d4 hours. If the current climate permits, this rain may become a snowfall.
n (naudiz)	Choose a target you can see within 120 feet of you. That target must succeed on a DC 15 Wisdom saving throw or all of the possessions they are carrying disappear. Furthermore, they are restrained (escape DC 15) for one hour.
i (īsaz)	When you activate this rune, you must thrust the *wand of runes* into a body of water. That body of fresh water freezes over with ice thick enough to ride a horse over. The ice remains or melts as normal for the current climate.
j (jēra)	When you activate this rune, you must wave it over a field or orchard. The plants contained within the boundaries of that field or orchard sprout, mature, and bear fruit in a bountiful harvest over the next hour.
œ (ihwaz)	Name a creature that has died within the past century. That creature is subject to a *resurrection* spell.
p (perth)	You learn a spell from a spell list belonging to any class you do not have access to. This spell must not appear on any spell list you have access to from your class or classes. You may cast this spell as if it were on a spell list you have access to, and if you have a limited number of spells you can know, does not count against that total.

Rune	Effect
z (algiz)	Your body sprouts horn-like growths. Until the end of your next turn, anyone who hits you with a melee attack is pierced by one of these thorns, suffering 2d8 piercing damage.
s (sōwilō)	The *wand of runes* projects a 30-foot cone of blinding light. All creatures caught in that area must succeed at a DC 15 Dexterity saving throw or be blinded until the end of their next turn. Additionally, if a creature caught in the area of effect is a fiend, fey, or undead, they suffer 5d10 radiant damage on a failed save, or half as much on a success.
t (tíwaz)	A *spear of jumping* appears in your hand. You may use this spear once and then it disappears.
b (berkanan)	For the next 24 hours, you do not need to breathe, drink, eat, or sleep. Furthermore, you gain immunity to cold, fire, lightning, and thunder damage.
e (ehwaz)	You summon a **warhorse** (with a speed of 80 feet) from the celestial realms. This horse serves you loyally for 24 hours without tiring, does not need to breathe, drink, eat, or sleep, and then disappears. Furthermore, it ignores all forms of difficult terrain and can even run across water as if solid ground.
m (mannaz)	You summon 2d4 **berserkers** from the halls of the dead. They serve you faithfully for 24 hours and then disappear.
l (laguz)	You point the wand at a stand of trees or a pile of lumber. At the end of your next turn, the wood tears itself apart and flies together into a longship. This ship requires no crew and rows at your command, the oars dipping on their own accord. The longship steers whatever course you command, and the wind always fills it sails no matter what point it might blow from. The ship remains yours for 24 hours and then disappears.
eng (ingwaz)	You point the wand at a willing target. That target is fertile to a high degree for the next month. Each mating the target consents to produces a child, if appropriate, based on their biology and the biology of their partner(s).
d (dagaz)	The sun rises and the following day is clear, bright, and comfortably warm.

WAND OF RUST
Wand, uncommon

This iron rod is covered in deep pockets of rust. This wand has seven charges. While holding it, you may use an action to expend one of its charges to target a metal object. If that object is being held by a creature, the creature must make a DC 15 Charisma saving throw or the item suffers a permanent and cumulative −1 penalty to all rolls made with it. If the item is a suit of metal armor, its AC drops by 1. If the total penalties reach −5, the item is destroyed. Unattended items do not make a saving throw.

The wand regains 1d6 + 1 expended charges each day at sunset. If you expend the wand's last charge, roll 1d20. On a 1, the wand turns into powdered rust and is destroyed.

WAND OF SLEEP AND WAKING
Wand, uncommon

This ivory wand bifurcates into two heads, one tipped with onyx and the other with amber. This wand has seven charges. While holding it, you may use an action to expend one of its charges to target a creature. Choose if you are causing the target to awaken or sleep. If you choose to awaken the target, it must succeed at a DC 15 Wisdom saving throw or the target becomes awake. If the target had been asleep for more than an hour, it awakes as if it had a full night's sleep. If you choose to put the target to sleep, it must succeed at a DC 15 Wisdom saving throw or fall into a deep slumber for one hour or until physically wakened. In either case, the target can choose to fail the saving throw.

The wand regains 1d6 + 1 expended charges each day at midday. If you expend the wand's last charge, roll 1d20. On a 1, the wand crumbles into ashes and is destroyed.

WAND OF SPIDERS
Wand, rare

This wand is cleverly carved and painted to look like a spider's leg. The wand has three charges. While holding it, you can use an action to expend one of its charges to summon a swarm of spiders. This swarm covers a 10-foot area you can see within 60 feet of you and has a climb speed of 35 feet. As a bonus action, you can cause the swarm to move up to its full speed. The swarm lasts for 1d6 + 1 rounds and dissipates at the end of your turn. Any creature that ends its turn within the swarm suffers 2 piercing damage and must succeed at a DC 15 Constitution saving throw or become poisoned until the end of their next turn.

The wand regains 1d3 expended charges each day at sunrise. If you expend the wand's last charge, roll 1d20. On a 1, the wand crumbles into ashes and is destroyed.

WAND OF SWINE
Wand, rare

This bronze wand is tipped with a single large ruby. The wand has three charges. While holding it, you may use an action to expend one of its charges to target a creature you can see within 60 feet. The target must succeed at a DC 15 Wisdom saving throw or be changed into a pig as per the spell *animal shapes*.

The wand regains 1d3 expended charges each day at sunrise.

WAND OF THE ROUTE
Wand, common

This simple twig bears a crude compass carved on one tip. The wand has seven charges. You may use an action to expend one of its charges to speak the name of a location or specific creature, after which you throw the wand into the air. The *wand of the route* lands with the compass tip pointing in the direction of the location or creature you named.

The wand regains 1d6 + 1 expended charges each day at sunset. If you expend the wand's last charge, roll 1d20. On a 1, the wand crumbles into ashes and is destroyed.

WAND OF THE TWICE BLESSED
Wand, uncommon

This highly detailed and painted wooden wand is shaped like a serpent with a head for a tail. The wand has seven charges. While holding the wand, you may use an action to expend one of its charges to grant an advantage to a creature you can see within 30 feet on its next attack roll, ability check, or saving throw. When you do so, you must also grant advantage to another creature you can see within 30 feet other than yourself.

The wand regains 1d6 + 1 expended charges each day at sunset. If you expend the wand's last charge, roll 1d20. On a 1, the wand crumbles into ashes and is destroyed.

WAND OF TRAPPING
Wand, rare

This wand looks much like a long piece of chalk yet does not produce dust or wear down. The wand has three charges. While holding the wand, you may use an action to expend one of its charges to draw a trap on a solid surface. This trap takes whatever form you wish and inflicts 2d6 of your choice of bludgeoning, piercing, or slashing damage. The trap can be detected with a DC 15 Intelligence (Investigation) check and disarmed with a DC 15 Intelligence (Arcana) check. It effects the first creature to cross the lines you draw of the trap. The trap can fill up to a 10-foot-by-10-foot area.

The wand regains 1d3 expended charges each day at sunset. If you expend the wand's last charge, roll 1d20. On a 1, the wand crumbles into ashes and is destroyed.

WAND OF WHISPERS
Wand, uncommon

This short wand is painted black and white in alternating stripes. The wand has seven charges. While holding the wand, you may use an action to expend one of its charges to speak with another creature as per the cantrip *message*. Alternately, you can expend one charge to listen to a conversation occurring within 120 feet of you. You do not need to be able to see the conversation, but you must be familiar with either the people holding the conversation or the location in which it is being held.

The wand regains 1d6 + 1 expended charges each day at sunset. If you expend the wand's last charge, roll 1d20. On a 1, the wand crumbles into ashes and is destroyed.

CHAPTER TEN: WEAPONS

ALCAEUS' ARROWS
Weapon (arrow), panoply (Alcaeus), very rare (requires attunement)

During one of the many adventures of Alcaeus, the great hero of a long lost land slew a serpent whose very blood was poison. Alcaeus dipped six of his arrows in the serpent's blood, tainting them for all time. Scholars believe that these arrows are still deadly, a fact reinforced by the accidental death of Sigmund the Wise while he studied one of the arrows. Each arrow is a simple arrow that is three feet in length (and thus suited to use with a longbow) with a purplish stain on its tip. It should be noted that you only need to have attuned to one of *Alcaeus' arrows* to gain the benefits of attuning the entire panoply. Once attuned to *Alcaeus' arrows*, you gain a +1 to hit and damage with the arrow. A creature hit with *Alcaeus' arrow* must succeed on a DC 15 Constitution save or suffer 5d10 poison damage.

If carried as part of a complete *panoply of Alcaeus*, a fired *Alcaeus' arrow* returns to your quiver or hand, your choice, at the start of your next turn.

ALCAEUS' CLUB
Weapon (maul), panoply (Alcaeus), unique (requires attunement)

The great hero Alcaeus lived long before the empire fell. He was a warrior of incomparable skill and strength, but also cursed with misfortune and never able to find solace in the simple joys of home and hearth. Many tales of his deeds, not all of which scholars consider to be true accounts of a man who no doubt once lived, speak of him using a great club of oak ringed in stout bands of bronze to slay fearsome beasts.

Alcaeus' club is less well recorded than his famed lion skin. Although often depicted in art wielding the club, the club is mentioned only three times in known documents. Plaubius' account of the coronation of Emperor Haro describes the emperor as wearing the entire panoply of Alcaeus. After that, the great club is not mentioned again until it was reported lost with the warrior-wizard Gaius when he drowned off the coast of the Talanos Peninsula. *Alcaeus' club* reappears in the historical record as part of the treasure trove of Verithix the Foul, a dragon slain by the Friends of Corimi in the Green Mountains. Once attuned to *Alcaeus' club*, you gain a +1 to hit and damage with the club. Additionally, as a bonus action, if you successfully hit a creature with *Alcaeus' club* on this turn, you may attempt to stun that creature. The target must succeed at a DC 13 Constitution saving throw or be stunned until the end of its next turn.

If carried as part of the *panoply of Alcaeus*, you may throw *Alcaeus' club* with a range of 20/40 feet. The club returns to your hand at the end of your turn.

ANCIENT KING'S SWORD
Weapon (greatsword), panoply (ancient king's), very rare (requires attunement)

While there were many weapons buried with the ancient kings, the most commonly found are great swords made of bronze. These weapons are often adorned with runes etched along their blades and gold wire wrapped around their hilts and guards. These greatswords would have been soft and easily bent if not enchanted, but magicked as they are, they are as strong as steel. Once you have attuned to an *ancient king's sword*, you gain a +1 bonus to hit and damage with the sword.

If worn as part of a complete set of *ancient king's panoply*, you may use the following properties once each, and regain use of them following a long rest:

Challenge. As a bonus action, you may challenge one foe within 30 feet that you can see and that can see you. You have advantage on attack rolls against the challenged creature. The challenged creature must target you for any attacks it makes, though it if it succeeds at a DC 13 Wisdom saving throw, it may attack as it wills on its turn, but must reattempt to do so on each of its following turns. The challenge remains for as long as you and the targeted creature both live or until you attack a different creature. You may not challenge more than one creature at a time.

Spell. As an action, you may cast the *thunderwave* spell.

AXE OF THE WATER WARRIOR
Weapon (battleaxe), (panoply of the water warrior), conjunction (water), rare

This finely crafted battleaxe is forged from float stone found on the Elemental Plane of Water. It is amazingly light for a weapon its size. Once attuned to the *axe of the water warrior*, you gain a +1 bonus to attack and damage rolls made with it. Additionally, you may use the following properties of the *axe of the water warrior*:

Drink. The *axe of the water warrior* may absorb up to three pints of a liquid and release it later. Releasing the liquid is a bonus action. You may release this liquid into you (even storing and consuming a potion) or onto the blade (useful for applying a poison or other deadly substance).

Throw. You may make a ranged attack with the axe (range 20/80 feet). The axe doesn't leave your hand; instead, it mystically freezes the target, inflicting 7 (2d6) cold damage and the target must succeed on a DC 15 Wisdom saving throw or be petrified until the end of their next turn. You may use this ability once and regain its use following a long rest.

You are considered proficient in the following skills as long as you are also wearing the *sash of the water warrior*: athletics, acrobatics, sleight of hand, and stealth. Furthermore, you gain resistance to cold damage.

If you wield the *axe of the water warrior* with a complete *panoply of the water warrior*, you gain a swim speed of 30 and the ability to breathe water as well as air. Additionally, you may use an action to cast one of the following spells: *conjure elementals* (water only), *protection from evil and good*, and *magic circle*. You may use this feature only once and regain its use following a one-hour ritual that requires you to expose the *panoply of the water warrior* to flowing water and leaves you with a level of exhaustion.

BANNER OF THE DESERT PRINCE
Weapon (lance), legendary (requires attunement)

This banner of green silk bears the words "Rebirth and Revenge" on it. While many desert princes sought to unite the desert tribes and restore their long-lost empire and each had his own personal *panoply of the desert prince* created for him, only one *banner of the desert prince* exists. A key component to becoming the next desert prince (as chosen by prophecy and acclaimed by the tribal leaders) is to locate the *banner of the desert prince*. When the desert prince falls, the banner teleports itself to a hidden location somewhere in the deserts. Its current whereabouts are unknown.

The *desert prince's banner* grants you +1 to attack rolls and damage rolls made with it. It has three charges. You may use an action to expend charges to perform the following:

Charge! You may expend one charge to cast *expeditious retreat* on you, your mount, and any living creatures you choose within 30 feet who can see you.

Hold Steady! You may expend two charges to cast *heroism* on up to six creatures within 30 feet who can see you.

Rally! You may expend two charges to cast *mass healing word* using your Wisdom modifier as the spellcasting ability.

Strike! You may expend two charges to cast *lightning bolt* with a spell save DC of 15.

Succor. You may expend three charges to cast *mass cure wounds* using your Wisdom modifier as the spellcasting ability

The spells do not require concentration checks and last until dispelled, until another charge of the banner is used, or until the normal duration of the spell ends.

The *desert prince's banner* regains 1d3 expended charges at each sunrise.

BATON OF BANISHMENT
Weapon (mace), rare

This ornate baton ends with a hand grasping a golden pomegranate. Its haft is carved with arcane sigils and mystical symbols. You gain a +1 bonus to attack and damage rolls made with the *baton of banishment*. Furthermore, against celestials, elementals, fey, or fiends, the baton inflicts an additional 7 (2d6) force damage and ignores the target's damage resistances. Finally, you may use the *baton of banishment* to cast the spell *banishment* (save DC 15) requiring no material components once and regain the use following a long rest. However, the range of the spell is reduced to touch, but you can use a bonus action to cast the spell on a creature you have successfully hit with the baton on your turn.

BIDENT OF WEALTH
Weapon (spear), rare

This two-headed spear is one single piece of steel, including the shaft. The heads are thin, more like tines, but still strong enough to pierce even the toughest hide. Often, these enchanted spears are decorated with small golden pomegranates in clusters around the head. When wielded as a weapon, the *bident of wealth* gives you a +1 bonus to hit and damage. If you score a critical hit with the *bident of wealth* against a living creature, the spear transmutes some of the blood spilled into gold, with each critical hit yielding gold splatters worth the amount of damage inflicted in gold pieces.

BLADE OF TRUTH
Weapon (longsword), rare (requires attunement)

This slightly curved longsword has a jet black blade and a pommel that sports a single large ruby. You gain a +1 bonus to attack and damage rolls when you use the *blade of truth*. As an action, you may hold the blade to a creature's throat and ask it a single question. The creature must succeed at a DC 15 Wisdom saving throw or be compelled to answer. If the answer is dishonest or untruthful, the color of the ruby drains into the sword, tinting it red. The redder the sword is tinted, the more egregious the falsehood. You gain an additional +1 to attack and damage rolls against the liar until you complete a long rest or until you question another creature.

BOW OF THE AIR WARRIOR
Weapon (longbow), panoply (air warrior), conjunction (air), rare

This finely made longbow is carved from a single limb of the yatal tree that grows in the Elemental Plane of Air. It is amazingly lightweight for a weapon of its size. Once attuned to the *bow of the air warrior*, you gain a +1 bonus to attack and damage rolls made with it. Additionally, the bow creates its own ammunition. As soon as you pull the string, an arrow appears notched and ready to fire. Also, you may use a bonus action to declare a single creature you can see within 150 feet as the bow's target. The next arrow the bow creates inflicts an additional 2d6 lightning damage to the target if it hits. You may do this once and regain the use of this ability following a long rest.

You are considered proficient in the following skills as long as you are also wearing the *sash of the air warrior*: arcana, nature, medicine, and religion. You also gain resistance to lightning damage.

If you wield the *bow of the air warrior* with a complete *panoply of the air warrior*, you gain a fly speed of 30. Additionally, you may use an action to cast one of the following spells: *conjure elementals* (air only), *protection from evil and good*, or *magic circle*. You may use this feature only once and regain its use following a one-hour ritual that requires you to expose the *panoply of the air warrior* to the wind and leaves you with a level of exhaustion.

CENTURION'S GLADIUS
Weapon, panoply (centurion's), rare (requires attunement)

This well-made shortsword bears the crafting marks of the imperial smiths and the imperial college of wizards. The hilt bears imperial heraldry, and the pommel features the heraldry of the legion of the centurion for whom the sword was made. Often, the centurion's name is engraved on the blade in golden script. The weapon never tarnishes and is always razor sharp.

When you are attuned with the *centurion's gladius*, you gain a +1 bonus to hit and damage rolls when using the *centurion's gladius*.

If worn as part of the centurion's panoply with the *centurion's scutum*, as a reaction when you are hit by a melee attack, you may make an attack roll and if your result is higher than the attack that hit you, that attack is parried.

If worn as part of a complete set of centurion's panoply, the sword gives you an additional +1 bonus on attack and damage rolls.

CRYSTAL WEAPONS
Weapon, rare, (requires attunement by a spellcaster)

Weapons made of carefully worked solid crystal have been found across the Lost Lands. These are thought to have been crafted before recorded history for the greatest heroes of the age, but their purpose other than being well wrought and enchanted weapons is unknown. The largest collection of crystal weapons can be found in the Academy of Sculpture. To date, the following weapons have been found as crystal weapons: battleaxe, dagger, great axe, handaxe, mace, maul, spear, and quarterstaff.

Despite being made of clear quartz crystal, crystal weapons are as strong as steel. They grant you a +1 bonus to attack rolls to use them. In addition, as a free action, crystal weapons can be made to glow with a clear light that illuminates a 20-foot sphere. Finally, once attuned to the weapon, you can issue a command word to cause a crystal weapon to store up to two levels worth of spells you know. These stored spells can be cast from the crystal weapon as a bonus action. It takes an action to transfer a spell into the crystal weapon and uses a spell slot. The spells remain in the weapon until used. When discovered, a crystal weapon has 1d2 levels of spells stored within.

CURSED CLAY BULLETS
Weapon (sling bullet), conjunction (salt), very rare

These sling bullets are made from twice-fired hard clay and are inscribed with a single line of cuneiform text that describes a horrid curse upon those struck by the stone. When using a *cursed clay bullet*, you gain +1 bonus to hit and damage. A target hit by the bullet must succeed at a DC 15 Wisdom saving throw or suffer the effects of a *bestow curse* spell. The exact effect is randomly determined for each stone when found; roll 1d4 and consult the spell description.

DESERT PRINCE'S SCIMITAR
Weapon (scimitar), panoply (desert prince's), rare (requires attunement)

This scimitar is made from folded steel that shows intricate random patterns along the blade. It's cross guard is ornamented in different jewels for each *desert prince's scimitar* (guess what color jewels were placed in the scimitar of Black Prince Faisal ibn Nassir). A silk tassel often matching the color of the matched *desert prince's thawb* extends from the pommel.

Once you have attuned to the *desert prince's scimitar*, you gain a +1 bonus to attack rolls and damage rolls made with the scimitar. As a reaction, you may attempt to parry a single melee attack made against you. You must make an attack roll with the *desert prince's scimitar*, and if the result is higher than that of the melee attack you are parrying, the attack does not hit.

If carried with the *desert prince's thawb*, as a bonus action you may hold the *desert prince's scimitar* aloft to grant all allies within 30 feet who can see and hear you 5 temporary hit points. You may do this once and regain the ability at the next sunrise.

If worn as part of a complete *desert prince's panoply*, as a free action you may coat the *desert prince's scimitar* in either fire or lightning for one minute. During this time, the scimitar inflicts an additional 2d6 damage of that type. You may do this once and regain the ability at the next sunrise.

38 | Tome of Wondrous Items

FAN OF THE GENERAL
Weapon (sickle), rare (requires attunement)

This folding fan is made of metal, with the ribs ending in sharp points and the outer edge of the blade being razor sharp. The blade is enameled in red and gold figures of a battle upon a black enamel background. You can use the *fan of the general* as a sickle gaining a +1 bonus to attack and damage rolls. On any turn you are wielding the *fan of the general* in one hand, you may use a bonus action to increase your armor class by +1 until the end of your next turn.

The true power of the *fan of the general* is evident only once you have attuned to it. Once attuned, you gain a number of command dice equal to 2 + your Charisma modifier + your proficiency bonus. If you gain command dice from another source, such as a class feature, these stack with the command dice from the *fan of the general* and can spend command dice from any source on the abilities granted by the *fan of the general*.

You may use a bonus action to expend a command die to perform one of the following abilities. Expended command dice return following a long rest. These abilities affect only allies that are within 30 feet who can see and hear you. The effects of any of these abilities last until the start of your next turn.

Encouragement. You encourage your allies to charge forward. All affected allies may use their reaction to take a Dash action.

Comfort. With stern yet comforting words you grant each ally affected advantage on saving throws.

Tactics. You call out a tactic designed to take advantage of the situation. Each affected ally gains advantage on their next attack roll.

FAN OF LIGHTNING
Weapon (sickle), panoply (thunder and lightning), rare

This folding paper fan is a deep blue with golden lightning bolts playing across the blades. The handle is of wood carved into the shape of a lightning bolt. You gain a +1 bonus to attack and damage rolls made with the *fan of lightning*. Also, as a free action you may cause the *fan of lightning* to become engulfed in crackling lightning that inflicts an additional 2d6 damage lightning damage when you hit with a melee attack. Finally, you may cast the spell *lightning bolt* from the fan, requiring no material components. You may do this once and regain its use following a long rest.

If you are wielding the *fan of lightning* alongside the *fan of thunder*, you gain a fly speed of 30 feet and may use the *fan of lightning's* lightning bolt two times per long rest.

If you are wielding the *fan of lightning* alongside the *hat of the eternal storm*, you gain resistance to lightning damage. Additionally, when you suffer lightning damage, you gain temporary hit points equal to the amount of damage you suffer after applying your damage resistance. You may use this ability once and regain use of it following a long rest.

If you are wielding the *fan of lightning* as part of a complete *panoply of thunder and lightning*, as an action you may jump between any two lightning bolts on the same plane, disappearing into one where it strikes the ground and reappearing into another where it strikes the ground.

FAN OF THUNDER
Weapon (sickle), panoply (thunder and lightning), rare

This folding paper fan is a deep blue with golden lightning bolts playing across the blades. The handle is of wood carved into the shape of a lightning bolt. You gain a +1 bonus to attack and damage rolls made with the *fan of thunder*. Also, as a free action you may cause the *fan of thunder* to emit a sharp roll of thunder that inflicts an additional 2d6 thunder damage when you hit with a melee attack. Finally, you may cast the spell *shatter* from the fan. You may do this twice and regain use of it following a long rest.

If you are wielding the *fan of thunder* alongside the *fan of lightning*, you gain darkvision 60 feet. Additionally, your vision is not hampered by fog, mist, rain, or other natural atmospheric conditions. Finally, you may use the *fan of thunder's shatter* ability three times per long rest.

If you are wielding the *fan of thunder* alongside the *hat of the eternal storm*, you gain resistance to thunder damage. Also, when you suffer thunder damage, you gain temporary hit points equal to the amount of damage you suffer after applying your damage resistance. You may use this ability once and regain use of it following a long rest.

If you are wielding the *fan of thunder* as part of a complete *panoply of thunder and lightning*, as an action you may disappear in a burst of thunder that fills a 30-foot cube centered on yourself. All creatures within the area of effect must succeed at a DC 15 Constitution saving throw, suffering 8d8 thunder damage on a failure, or half as much on a success. You reappear in a random location 1d100 miles away. You do not reappear in a dangerous area such as a pit of lava or underwater.

GIANT SLAYER AXE
Weapon (warhammer), unique (requires attunement by a dwarf of the clan that forged it)

Forged by the *ideal forge*, the giant slayer axe is a massive double bit greataxe made of mithril. Only a dwarf of the clan that forged it may attune to it; any others who attempt die, with no saving throw and no chance of resurrection save by the whim of a dwarven deity. When you wield the *giant slayer axe*, you gain a +2 bonus to attack and damage rolls, which increases to +4 when fighting giants.

If you hit a giant with the *giant slayer axe*, that giant must make a DC 18 Constitution saving throw. On a failure it drops to 0 hit points, while on a success it takes an additional 10d6 slashing damage.

The *giant slayer axe* has a few secondary powers. It senses giants within 100 feet and alerts its wielder by glowing deep red as if freshly taken from the forge. If a giant is struck with the axe, you ignore any damage resistances the giant might have. Finally, as an action you may toss the *giant slayer axe* into the air. It lands blade down in the ground (no matter the substance, it embeds itself into it) with the hilt pointing in the direction of the nearest giant.

GOAD OF THE GHOST ELEPHANT
Weapon (war pick), rare

The shaft of this six-foot elephant goad is wrapped in fine-grained leather that has been dyed red and green. The head is steel with gold inlays in geometric patterns that blend into the inlays on the tapered head. When you attack with the *goad of the ghost elephant*, you add +1 to your attack and damage rolls.

You may use the *goad of the ghost elephant* to summon a spectral **elephant**. While it is semi-transparent and a magical construct, it has all of the normal statistics and behaviors of an elephant. The spectral elephant is under your command, and you may use a bonus action to control its actions or issue a general order such as to go in a specific direction, guard a person or area, or attack a specific target. The spectral elephant remains for eight hours or until it is reduced to 0 hit points. You may use this feature once and regain use of it at dawn.

GOBLIN STONES
Weapon, rare

Falsely credited to the goblinoid races, *goblin stones* are a term used for stone arrow and spear heads commonly turned up by plows. Most of these stone projectile points are not enchanted, but every now and then such a one turns up. The projectile points must be attached to a shaft of some kind to be used; otherwise, they make poor weapons. *Goblin stones* can be found as arrowheads, javelin heads, or spearheads. A *goblin stone* gives you a +1 bonus to hit and has the additional property of being able to damage ethereal or other insubstantial creatures. They do not lose their magical properties when they hit a target.

GOLDEN ARROW
Weapon (arrow), rare

This arrow is of solid gold yet is as light and as aerodynamic as a normal arrow of wood. The head is wickedly sharp, and the shaft is undecorated. A target hit by the arrow does not suffer any damage; instead, they fall in love with the first person they see. If the person is of a species and gender to which the target is attracted, the target treats the person as their true love for the next hour; otherwise, the *golden arrow* has no effect. During this duration, the target is treated as charmed by that person.

GOLDEN ARROW OF MADNESS
Weapon (arrow), rare

This gold arrow shaft has fletching of carved ivory and a head tipped with a single ruby shaped like an arrowhead. You may fire this arrow from any bow, and it magically resizes itself to match your draw length. You gain a +1 to hit rolls when using the *golden arrow of madness*. If you hit a target, the *golden arrow of madness* does not cause any damage; instead, the target is under the effects of a *confusion* spell. Once fired, the *golden arrow of madness* disappears into the flesh of the target. It can be recovered with a successful DC 15 Wisdom (Medicine) check, but the target should be dead or restrained in order to do so.

HAMMER OF THE DWARVEN KING

Weapon (warhammer), panoply (dwarven king), unique, (requires attunement by a dwarven king)

Forged from a single block of mithril adorned with engraved carvings filled with gold, the *hammer of the dwarven king* is as much a work of art as it is a weapon. The oak haft is wrapped in a silk-like cloth made from the first beard growths of a thousand adolescent dwarves, each clipped with mithril shears and consecrated on an altar of the dwarven gods. Only the rightful ruler of a dwarf hold can attune to the *hammer of the dwarven king*; all others die if they attempt to wield it in battle.

When you wield the *hammer of the dwarven king*, you gain a +3 bonus to attack and damage rolls. Furthermore, the hammer holds five charges. It regains charges when you spend an hour sitting upon the *throne of the dwarven king*. You may expend a charge to perform one the following:

Thundering Strike. As a bonus action, you may cause the hammer to inflict an additional 2d6 thunder damage with every successful attack for the next 10 rounds.

Thundering Sweep. As an action, you may sweep the hammer at your foes to create an effect as per the spell *thunderwave* cast at 6th level.

If you wield the *hammer of the dwarven king* while wearing the *crown of the dwarven king*, as an action you may hold the *hammer of the dwarven king* aloft and issue a single command to all allies within 60 feet who can hear you. This command must be no more than three words long. The affected allies may choose to use their reaction to take any action needed to complete that command, such as moving or attacking.

If you wield the *hammer of the dwarven king* as part of a complete *panoply of the dwarven king*, the hammer warns you when the following creatures enter your rightful domain: aberrations, celestials, dragons, fey, fiends, giants, goblins, hobgoblins, orcs, and undead. You know such a creature has entered your domain and its location, but not the number of said creature or its intentions.

HAMMER OF THE WORTHY

Weapon (warhammer), very rare (requires attunement, see below)

This simple warhammer does not radiate magic of any type nor does it give itself away as a magical item. It attunes only with those of virtue and honor, as determined by the GM. Once attuned, you gain a +1 bonus to attack and damage rolls made with the *warhammer of the worthy*, and you also gain access to its special powers. The warhammer has three charges and you may expend a charge as a bonus action to either add 18 (4d8) thunder damage to a successful attack or cast the spell *lightning bolt* (save DC 15). The *hammer of the worthy* regains charges when exposed to lightning, gaining a charge per bolt. You can hold the hammer aloft during a lightning storm to attract 1d3 bolts of lightning into it, causing no harm to you.

HEPTASCOPIC BLADE

Weapon (dagger), rare

This curved dagger has a handle inlaid with silver and small garnets, and a blade etched with an intricate geometric design. You gain a +1 bonus to attack rolls and damage rolls made with this dagger. If a successful attack with the dagger reduces a creature to 0 hit points, the *heptascopic blade* can be used to remove the creature's liver, a process that takes five minutes. The removed liver can be used to cast the *divination* spell.

HOPLOMACHUS' SPEAR

Weapon (spear), panoply (hoplomachus), very rare (requires attunement)

The hoplomachi wielded long spears as their primary weapon, though many carried a shortsword as a backup. The spears used for the magical panoply were of the finest quality, with shafts made of magically treated wood that was light yet stiff as steel, with heads enchanted to always remain sharp, and plumes of ostrich feathers affixed just behind the haft. If attuned to a *hoplomachus's helm*, you gain a +1 bonus to hit and damage with *hoplomachus's spear*.

If worn as part of a *panoply of the hoplomachus* with the *hoplomachus's manica*, as a bonus action you may grant your spear the Reach property until the end of your turn.

If carried as part of a complete set of *panoply of the hoplomachus*, as an action you may cast the *lightning bolt* spell. You may do this once and regain use of this feature following a long rest.

INTERROGATOR'S RAZOR

Weapon (sickle), uncommon

This long, slightly curved razor blade of folded steel is hinged to fit snuggly back into its handle. When you use it to make an attack, you gain a +1 bonus to attack rolls and a +1 bonus to damage rolls. While wielding the razor, you have advantage on Charisma (Intimidation) checks. If you use the razor during an interrogation of a helpless target, you may perform a ritual to cast *zone of truth*. You may do this once and regain use of this feature following a long rest. Use of this feature constitutes an evil act.

KILLED WEAPONS

Weapon (varies), conjunction (salt), rare

These magical weapons of ancient design are made of copper or bronze and feature a prominent hole drilled through their blades. *Killed weapons* are found only as axes, spears, and swords. You gain a +1 bonus to attack and damage rolls when using these weapons. Additionally, the weapons ignore any damage resistance or immunity to the type of damage they inflict and can interact with creatures that are ethereal, immaterial, or incorporeal.

JAWBONE OF SLAYING

Weapon (maul), conjunction (earth), unique

This jawbone, likely taken from a large herbivore such as a donkey or an ox, has been carved with an intricate set of symbols that pulse with blue energy. When you make an attack with the *jawbone of slaying*, you gain a +2 bonus to hit and damage. The enchanted jawbone has three charges and as an action you may expend a charge to make a single attack against every creature within reach. The *jawbone of slaying* regains all charges following a long rest.

LEAD ARROW

Weapon (arrow), rare

This arrow is of solid lead yet is as light and aerodynamic as a normal arrow of wood. The head is wickedly sharp, and the shaft is undecorated. A target hit by the arrow does not suffer any damage; instead, they hate the first person they see for the next hour. During this duration, the target feels great loathing toward the person and attacks if capable of doing so with any hope of success; otherwise, they use other means of causing harm such as insults, manipulations, or theft. The target must succeed at a DC 15 Wisdom saving throw or target their hated person with any attacks they make.

LEAFY SWORD

Weapon (longsword), uncommon (requires attunement)

This three-foot-long branch is roughly sword shaped with only a slight bend. A pair of leaves near one end give the impression of a hilt. After picking it up, you have an almost irresistible urge to swoosh it around and cut the heads off nearby dandelions. Once attuned to the *leafy longsword*, you may use a bonus action to transform it into a steel longsword that grants you a +1 bonus to attack and damage rolls or back into an amusing but innocuous stick.

LION-TAILED WHIP

Weapon (whip), rare

This long whip is made from a single lion skin with the end of the whip being the lion's tail. The handle is made from lion bones and tipped with a single fang. The whip grants you a +1 bonus to attack and damage rolls with it. Additionally, you may command the whip to light on fire for a minute once and regain use of this feature following a short rest. While lit, it inflicts an additional 1d6 + 1 fire damage with a successful hit, and targets hit by the whip are set on fire. A target set on fire by the *lion-tailed whip* suffers 1d4 fire damage at the start of its turn and may use an action to put out the flames.

MARLIN-SPIKED CUTLASS
Weapon (scimitar), uncommon

Like all of Mircanna the Shipwright's creations, the *marlin-spiked cutlass* is entirely utilitarian in appearance. To the casual observer, it is a well-used but sturdy cutlass of the type used by sailors across the world. When used as a weapon, it grants a +1 bonus to attack and damage rolls. However, its true purpose is to serve as a mobile tool chest for skilled artisans. By speaking a command word, the cutlass can transform into any desired tool from a single toolkit. You are considered proficient in the tool that the *marlin-spiked cutlass* takes the form of. If you are already proficient in that tool set, you may add your proficiency bonus twice to checks involving it. Each *marlin-spiked cutlass* can take the form of tools from a single toolkit; roll on the table below when the cutlass is found:

MARLIN-SPIKED CUTLASS TOOLS

1d6	Toolkit
1	Carpenter's tools
2	Cartographer's tools
3	Leatherworker's tools
4	Smith's tools
5	Woodcarver's tools
6	Navigator's tools

MAUL OF THE EARTH WARRIOR
Weapon (maul), panoply (earth warrior), conjunction (earth), rare

This finely crafted maul is forged from a solid piece of true stone found on the Elemental Plane of Earth. It is amazingly heavy for a weapon of its size. Once attuned to the *maul of the earth warrior*, you gain a +1 bonus to attack and damage rolls made with it. Additionally, the *maul of the earth warrior* may be used as a shovel to move up to 10 cubic feet of soil or stone per minute. Finally, as an action, you may slam the *maul of the earth warrior* into the ground and create a burst of energy that fills a 10-foot cube centered on you. All creatures (other than yourself, of course) within this area of effect must make a DC 15 Constitution saving throw. On a failure, the target takes 4d6 thunder damage and is deafened for one minute while on a success the target takes half that damage and is not deafened.

If you also wear the *sash of the earth warrior*, you are considered proficient in the following skills as long as you are wearing the sash: Animal Handling, Insight, Perception, and Survival. Additionally, you gain resistance to thunder damage.

If you wield the *maul of the earth warrior* with a complete *panoply of the earth warrior*, you gain a burrow speed of 30 feet. Also, you may use an action to cast one of the following spells: *conjure elementals* (earth only), *protection from evil and good*, and *magic circle*. You may use this feature only once and regain its use following a one-hour ritual that requires you to bury the *panoply of the earth warrior* in soil and leaves you with a level of exhaustion.

NINE ARROWS BOW
Weapon (longbow), very rare

This elegant recurved longbow is enchanted to string itself. When you fire an arrow from the *nine arrows bow*, you gain a +1 bonus to attack and damage rolls. If you drop a creature to 0 hit points with your attack, you may fire an additional arrow against another target. This arrow does an additional 1d8 piercing damage if it hits. You may continue to fire arrows upon successive killing shots up to a total of nine.

OX-HEADED MACE
Weapon (mace), very rare (requires attunement)

This ornate gold-chased mace has a head in the shape of an ox's head. It is a full metal mace with an iron shaft decorated with red and gold tassels. Centuries ago, kings carried the ox-headed mace as symbols of power. Most of these maces were lost, and each was unique in appearance in some way. Once attuned to the *ox-headed mace*, you gain a +1 bonus to hit and damage rolls with the weapon. The *ox-headed mace* has three charges, and you may expend a charge on the following properties.

Thunder. As a bonus action, you may command the mace to inflict an additional 2d8 lightning or thunder damage on your next successful hit with it, but if you do so, you must wait five minutes before being able to use this feature again.

Whirlwind. As an action, you may throw the *ox-headed mace* up to 50 feet. When it lands, it creates a small whirlwind with a five-foot radius that is 30 feet in height. This whirlwind lasts for as long as you concentrate on it, as if it were a spell. As a bonus action, you can move the whirlwind up to 60 feet on your turn. Any creature that enters the whirlwind or begins its turn inside the whirlwind must succeed at a DC 15 Strength saving throw or be restrained by it. When you move the whirlwind, any creatures restrained in it are moved as well. As an action, you may make a single attack with the *ox-headed mace* against all creatures restrained by the whirlwind.

Restrained creatures may attempt to escape from the whirlwind by using their action, or those outside the whirlwind may attempt to free those caught inside with a successful DC 15 Strength (Athletics) check. Any who attempt to help free someone caught in the whirlwind may be attacked by the *ox-headed mace* as if they were restrained by the whirlwind. You may use this feature once and regain use of it at the next sunrise.

QUILL OF THE ASSISTANT
Weapon (dagger), panoply (scholarly mage), conjunction (azoth), very rare (requires attunement by a wizard)

This large peacock quill has an ornate golden nib. It is always full of ink and can write on any surface. You may use the *quill of the assistant* as a magical dagger, gaining a +1 bonus to attack and damage rolls with it. The quill has three charges and regains 1d3 charges each sunrise. As an action you may expended one or more charges from the quill to cast the following spells, requiring no material components: *glyph of warding* (3 charges), *illusory script* (1 charge), *unseen servant* (1 charge).

If wielding the *quill of the assistant* while wielding the *staff of knowledge*, you may project up to three texts from the staff at once.

If wielding the *quill of the assistant* while wearing the *studious robes*, you do not need to expend a charge to cast *unseen servant* from the quill.

If wielding the *quill of the assistant* as part of a complete *panoply of the scholarly mage*, the quill can be commanded as an action to appear in a library you have folded up using the panoply and copy down a conversation, map a one-mile radius around you as you travel, or take dictation.

RAZOR OF BEAUTY
Weapon (sickle), uncommon (requires attunement)

This razor blade, of a type used by barbers, is lovingly etched along the blade with arabesque designs and the handle is similarly carved from rosewood. When you use it to make an attack, you gain +1 bonus to attack

CHAPTER TEN: WEAPONS | 41

and damage rolls. Your Charisma score increases by +2 while you are attuned to the *razor of beauty*. You may use the *razor of beauty* to cast *disguise self*, but doing so inflicts 1d4 + 1 slashing damage to you.

RETIARUS'S NET
Weapon (net), panoply (retiarius), very rare (requires attunement)

One of the signature weapons of the retiarius, whether the battle is being fought on land or in the water, is the simple fisherman's net. This could be used to entangle a foe but also to disarm opponents. Of course, the latter was of little utility when fighting against massive sharks or eyes of the deep. The *retiarius's net* is a six-foot-diameter circular net with an attached line that allows it to be reeled back in. Once you have attuned to the *retiarius's net*, you gain a +1 bonus on attack rolls with the net. Also, foes restrained by the *retiarius's net* require a DC 18 check to escape and the net cannot be cut.

If worn as part of the *panoply of the retiarius* with *retiarius's trident*, a creature hit by either *retiarius's net* or *retiarius's trident* suffers the effects of the *faerie fire* spell until the end of their next turn.

If worn as part of a complete set of the *panoply of the retiarius*, as a bonus action you can cause *retiarius's net* to tighten on a restrained creature to inflict 2d8 bludgeoning damage.

RETIARIUS'S TRIDENT
Weapon (trident), panoply (retiarius) very rare (requires attunement)

While the net used by the retiarius held a certain flair, the gladiators turned to the trident for the killing blow. Once restrained by the net, and hopefully lit by the magic of the panoply, the great sea beast or merfolk warrior facing the retiarius would be easy pickings for a few well-placed thrusts with an enchanted trident. The *retiarius's trident* is a five-foot-long ornate metal trident. Once you have attuned to *retiarius's trident*, you gain a +1 bonus on attack and damage rolls with the trident. Additionally, as a bonus action you can command the trident to return to your hand from up to 60 feet away.

If worn as part of the *panoply of the retiarius* with *retiarius's net*, a creature retrained by *retiarius's net* that is hit by *retiarius's trident* must succeed at a DC 15 Constitution save or suffer 1d8+5 necrotic damage.

If worn as part of a complete set of the *panoply of the retiarius*, as an action you can cast *lightning bolt*. You may do this once and regain use of it once *retiarius's trident* soaks in seawater for 24 hours.

SCEPTER OF THE HEAVENS
Weapon (mace), panoply (heavens), very rare (requires attunement)

Crafted millennia ago for the first caliph, the *scepter of the heavens* is war mace gilded in gold with the spikes carved like curling leaves. The mace, like the rest of the *panoply of the heavens* was lost when the Grand Caliph Rabi bin Ashkar Al Ammu and his entire court were slaughtered at the Battle of False Wells by the great wyrm Jalthranax. Once attuned to the *mace of the heavens*, you gain a +2 bonus to attack and damage rolls made with the *mace of the heavens*. Additionally, as a bonus action, you may command the mace to appear in your hand at the end of your turn as long as it is on the same plane as you.

If you are wielding the *mace of the heavens* while wearing the *crown of the heavens*, the mace inflicts an additional 2d6 bludgeoning damage against aberrations, celestials, elementals, fey, fiends, and undead.

If you are wielding the *mace of the heavens* as part of a complete *panoply of the heavens*, any creature not native to the plane you are on who is struck by the *mace of the heavens* must succeed at a DC 15 Wisdom saving throw or suffer the effects of a *banishment* spell.

SICKLE OF PARTHENOS
Weapon (sickle), rare

This silver-bladed sickle is much sought after by druids who serve rural communities. You can use it as a weapon, gaining a +1 bonus on attack and damage rolls, but the *sickle of Parthenos* is better served as an agricultural tool. You can harvest and process (threshing, sorting, or whatever the crop needs) up to 50 acres of produce in 24 hours. The produce created is of the finest quality, free of blight or blemish, and keeps for twice as long as it normally would.

SCORPION BOW
Weapon (shortbow), very rare

This unusual bow is oddly jointed and made of a chitin-like material, glossy black with red hints, with an organic appearance. The bow hisses slightly as it is drawn. You gain a +1 bonus on attack and damage rolls with the *scorpion bow*, and a target hit with an arrow fired from the bow must make a DC 15 Constitution saving throw, taking 2d6 poison damage on a failure, or half damage on a success.

SPEARHEAD OF THE THUNDERBOLT
Weapon (spear), rare

This bronze spearhead has a lightning bolt engraved down its middle. If attached to a wooden haft, it functions as a spear and grants you a +1 bonus to attack and damage rolls. When thrown, the spearhead and haft turn into a lightning bolt that inflicts an additional 14 (4d6) lightning damage on a hit. This consumes the haft and leaves a red-hot *spearhead of the thunderbolt* behind.

SPEAR OF JUMPING
Weapon (spear), rare

This ash spear is tipped with a finely crafted steel head. When wielding the *spear of jumping*, you gain a +1 bonus to attack and damage rolls with it. You may throw the spear and it reappears in your hand at the end of your turn. Furthermore, you may command the spear to perform a spear running. When you do so, you throw the spear as an attack. The spear splits into three spears that may target the same creature or up to three separate creatures. Make an attack roll and damage roll separately for each spear. You are magically compelled to run alongside the three spears, jumping from one to the other while they are in flight, ending within five feet of one of the targets. When you use this feature, you gain two levels of exhaustion.

SPEAR OF LENGTHENING
Weapon (spear), rare

This bamboo spear has a long tassel of silk below the metal tip. When you use the *spear of lengthening*, you gain a +1 bonus to attack and damage rolls. As a bonus action, you may speak a command word and cause the spear to extend, granting you a five-foot increase in your reach. This effect lasts until the start of your next turn.

SPINY LANCE
Weapon (lance), panoply (coral knight), conjunction (water), very rare

This lance appears to be a great spine as if from some massive fish's dorsal fins. When you wield the *spiny lance*, you gain a +1 bonus to attack and damage rolls made with it, and targets hit by the *spiny lance* must make a DC 15 Constitution saving throw. Thise failing suffer 2d6 poison damage and become poisoned for one hour, while those who succeed take half as much damage and are not poisoned. Additionally, as a bonus action you may cause the lance to spew forth a 15-foot-radius cloud of poisoned ink. You are immune to the effects of this cloud. The cloud of poisonous ink blocks all line of sight through it. Any creature that ends its turn in the ink cloud must make a DC 15 Constitution saving throw. On a failure the creature takes 2d6 poison damage and is poisoned for one hour, while on a success the creature takes half as much damage and is not poisoned. Creatures already suffering from the poisoned condition make this saving throw with disadvantage. You may use the ink blast property once and regain use of it at the next sunset.

If you wield the *spiny lance* while seated upon the *seahorse saddle*, you add twice your mount's strength modifier to any damage done with the lance.

If you wield the *spiny lance* while wearing the *shark-toothed necklace*, you may use an action to imbue the shark summoned by the necklace with the *spiny lance's* poison property, losing the extra poison damage from the lance attacks but adding the poison damage to the shark's attacks. The poison damage property returns to your lance when the shark is dismissed or dies, or when you use an action to cause it to do so.

If wielding the *spiny lance* as part of a complete *panoply of the coral knight*, you may throw the *spiny lance* up to 30 feet and make a ranged attack with it. The lance appears in your hand at the end of your turn.

SWORD OF THE DAWN STAR
Weapon (longsword), panoply (twin swords), unique (requires attunement)

This exquisite longsword has a blade forged of a reddish-orange metal. Arcane symbols are carved along its length that increase and decrease in radiance with the rising and setting of the sun. The crosspiece bears twin starbursts at the ends, and the pommel matches with a single ruby that diffracts sunlight to form a pattern of color and shadow on any flat surface much like a sunrise over a pleasant countryside. Once attuned to the *sword of the dawn star*, you gain a +2 bonus to attack and damage rolls with it. Additionally, as a free action you can cause the *sword of the dawn star* to shed or stopp shedding bright light in a 30-foot radius, with dim light extending out 30 feet beyond that. The *sword of the dawn star* has three charges. You may expend one charge to use one of the following properties.

Shed Daylight. As an action, you may use the sword to cast the *daylight* spell three times without requiring any material components. You regain uses of this ability following the next sunrise.

Sunfire. As a bonus action you can cause the sword to become engulfed in sunfire for one minute. While engulfed in sunfire, the sword inflicts an additional 2d6 fire plus 2d6 radiant damage. When engulfed in sunfire, the sword glows as above, and the sunfire counts as natural sunlight for any effects that require it.

If you are wielding the *sword of the dawn star* while wearing the *sash of the sun and moon*, you may use the *sash of the sun and moon's* lightstride ability three times, regaining uses of this ability through the usual means. Also, you are aware of any undead within 30 feet of you, but you do not know their type or location, just that an undead creature in within 30 feet of you and in what direction the creature is located.

If you are wielding the *sword of the dawn star* along with the *sword of the night orb*, your armor class increases by +1. Additionally, as a bonus action you may combine the two swords into one. This combined sword inflicts an additional 1d8 slashing damage and has all the powers of both swords, such as the sunfire and silver beam properties.

If you are wielding the *sword of the dawn star* as part of a complete *panoply of the twin swords*, you may cast the spell *sunbeam* once, requiring no material components, and regain use of this ability following the next sunrise.

SWORD OF THE FIRE WARRIOR

Weapon (longsword), panoply (fire warrior) conjunction (fire), rare

This finely crafted longsword is forged from solid flame found on the Elemental Plane of Air. It is amazingly heavy for a weapon of its size. Once attuned to the *sword of the fire warrior*, you gain a +1 bonus to attack and damage rolls made with it. Additionally, you may throw the sword as an attack (range 20/80 feet), and it returns to your hand at the end of your turn. Finally, you may use a bonus action to cause flames to form along the blade. These flames last for 1d6 turns before extinguishing. While the sword is lit, it inflicts an additional 1d6 fire damage and the target must succeed at a DC 15 Dexterity saving throw or be lit on fire, suffering 1d6 fire damage at the start of their turn until the flames are put out. Any creature can use an action to put out the flames.

If you also wear the *sash of the fire warrior*, you are considered proficient in the following skills while you are wearing the *sash of the fire warrior*: deception, intimidation, performance, and persuasion. Also, you gain resistance to fire damage.

If you wield the *sword of the fire warrior* with a complete *panoply of the fire warrior*, you may use the following properties:

Fire Walk. You may step into a fire and then step out of a different fire within 30 feet that you can see, using only five feet of movement.

Spells. You may use an action to cast one of the following spells: *conjure elementals* (fire only), *protection from evil and good*, *magic circle*. You may use this feature only once and regain use of it following a one-hour ritual that requires you to expose the *panoply of the air warrior* to open flames and leaves you with a level of exhaustion.

SWORD OF THE NIGHT ORB

Weapon (longsword), panoply (twin swords), unique

This exquisite longsword has a blade forged of a silvery metal. Arcane symbols are carved along its length that increase and decrease in radiance with the rising and setting of the moon. The crosspiece bears twin crescent moons at the ends, and the pommel matches with a single obsidian crescent that diffracts moonlight to form a pattern of color and shadow on any flat surface much like a full moon rising over a pleasant countryside. The *sword of the night orb* counts as a silver weapon. Once attuned to the *sword of the night orb*, you gain a +2 bonus to attack and damage rolls made with it. Also, as a free action you can cause the *sword of the night orb* to shed or stop shedding dim light in a 30-foot radius. The *sword of the night orb* has three charges. You may expend one charge to use one of the following properties.

Luna's Smile. You may use the sword to cast the *moonbeam* spell three times without requiring any material components. You regain uses of this ability following the next moonrise.

Silver Beam. As a bonus action you can cause the sword to become engulfed in a silver beam for one minute. While engulfed in a silver beam, the sword inflicts an additional 2d6 cold plus 2d6 necrotic damage. When engulfed in a silver beam, the sword glows as above, and the silver beam counts as natural moonlight for any effects that require it.

If you are wielding the *sword of the night orb* while wearing the *sash of the sun and moon*, you may use the *sash of the sun and moon's* shadowstride property three times, regaining uses of this property through the usual means. Also, you are aware of any lycanthrope within 30 feet of you, but you do not know their type or location, just that a lycanthrope is within 30 feet of you and in what direction the creature is located.

If you are wielding the *sword of the dawn star* along with the *sword of the night orb*, your armor class increases by +1. Additionally, as a bonus action you may combine the two swords into one. This combined sword inflicts an additional 1d8 slashing damage and has all the powers of both swords, such as the sunfire and silverbeam properties.

If you are wielding the *sword of the night orb* as part of a complete *panoply of the twin swords*, you may cast the spell *mass suggestion* once, requiring no material components, and regain use of this ability following the next moon rise.

SWORD OF SEVEN LIGHTNINGS

Weapon (longsword), very rare

This greenish-tinted, slightly curved longsword has patterns of lightning bolts etched along the blade and hilt. The pommel is a single large crystal through which one can peer to see flashes of lightning. When you wield this longsword, you gain a +1 bonus to attack and damage rolls. Additionally, the sword has seven charges and you can spend charges to use one of the following properties:

First Lightning. As a bonus action you can spend one charge to wreath the sword in electricity, inflicting an additional 2d6 lightning damage until the end of your next turn.

Second Lightning. As an action you can spend two charges to cast the spell *lightning bolt* (save DC 15) requiring no material components.

Third Lightning. As an action you can spend three charges to cast the spell *call lightning* (save DC 15) requiring no material components.

Fourth Lightning. As a free action you may spend one charge to cause the sword to deliver a sharp electrical jolt. The next time you hit a creature with the *sword of seven lightnings*, the target must succeed on a DC 15 Condition saving throw or be stunned until the end of their next turn.

Fifth Lightning. As a free action you can spend one charge to call the *sword of seven lightnings* to your hand as long as it is on the same plane as you.

Sixth Lightning. As a reaction, if you are hit by a melee attack, you may spend one charge to inflict 2d6 lightning damage on your attacker.

Seventh Lightning. As a reaction if you suffer lightning damage, you may attempt a DC 15 Dexterity (Acrobatics) check to cause the *sword of seven lightnings* to absorb all of the lightning damage, gaining one charge.

The *sword of seven lightnings* regains charges when struck with lightning, recovering one charge per strike.

TRIBUNE'S SPATHA

Weapon (longsword), panoply (tribune's panoply), very rare (requires attunement)

Bearing the heraldry of an imperial legion as well as the marks of the imperial smiths and the imperial college of wizardry, this muscle cuirass is decorated with intricate scenes of warfare and sculpted to resemble a heavily muscled torso. The creators spared no expense, and the armor is dripping with gold leaf and other adornments. The name of the tribune it was awarded to, as well as the date of awarding and the name of the emperor presenting it, are engraved along the blade in glowing script. The sword never tarnishes or rusts. Once you are attuned to the *tribune's spatha*, you gain +2 bonus to hit and damage with the *tribune's spatha*. Also, as a reaction when you are hit by a melee attack, you may make an attack roll and if your result is higher than the attack that hit you, that attack is parried.

If worn as part of the tribune's panoply with the *tribune's cuirass*, as an action you may cast *detect thoughts*. You may do this once and regain uses of this feature following a short rest.

If worn as part of a complete set of the *tribune's panoply*, as a bonus action you may summon the *tribune's spatha* to your hand at a range of 100 miles.

UNFINISHED DAGGER

Weapon (dagger), very rare (requires attunement)

This full tang jagged edged dagger lacks a hilt, handle, or other furniture. You add a +2 bonus to attack and damage rolls when you use the *unfinished dagger*. Furthermore, you may use a bonus action to cause the *unfinished dagger* to bite deep, inflicting an additional 22 (5d10) piercing damage with a successful attack. You may do this once and regain use of this feature after you slay a creature with the dagger.

Cursed. The *unfinished dagger* is cursed, a fact not revealed until you slay a living creature with the dagger. Once the curse is revealed, you

CHAPTER TEN: WEAPONS | 43

may not unattune to the *unfinished dagger*, nor may any magic short of a *wish* spell remove the curse. If you no longer have the dagger in your possession, it returns to your hand at the next moonrise. While under the effects of the curse, at every moonrise you must succeed at a DC 15 Wisdom saving throw or be compelled to murder a living creature in cold blood with the *unfinished dagger*. If you do not commit this murder before the next time you fail the Wisdom saving throw to resist, you lose 1 hit die. Once you have slain seven times in cold blood, the curse is lifted and the *unfinished dagger* teleports to a random location at least 1,000 miles away.

WAVE STEEL BLADES
Weapon (any dagger or sword), rare

Several cultures make these magical blades forged from rare steels and using a unique process. *Wave blades* receive their name from the wavy patterns that the forging process creates. These patterns are random and form along the length of the blade, and some magical smiths tint their blades to better display the patterns. You add +1 to all attack and damage rolls made with these weapons. Furthermore, *wave blades* will not break and inflict an additional 19 (4d8) slashing damage when used against an inanimate object or a construct.

WIND-SPLITTING SWORD
Weapon (longsword), rare (requires attunement)

This slightly curved longsword has an edge so sharp that you can see its danger from even six feet away. Once attuned to the *wind-splitting sword*, you gain a +1 bonus to attack and damage rolls made with the sword. Additionally, you have advantage on initiative rolls. You may use the *wind-splitting sword* to cast the *thunderwave* spell once and regain use of this ability following a short rest.

CHAPTER ELEVEN: WONDROUS ITEMS

A SUNNY DAY AT SOUTHDALE
Wondrous item, rare

This large five-foot-by-six-foot painting by Betran Ormian depicts a pleasant day at Southdale, a popular park-like spot. As the painting depicts, on sunny summer days city folk like to come here and enjoy the peaceful woods, beaches, and warm water. Picnickers can be spotted along the verge, small parties are on the beach, and bones lay underneath the trees.

Cursed. The painting is cursed, an accident created by Ormian. Once the command word is spoken, you and anyone within 30 feet are sucked into the painting where you appear among the animated throngs. Any creature trapped within the painting must succeed at a DC 15 Wisdom save or be overcome with lethargy and gain a level of exhaustion. Lying down in the shade of the fragrant trees, you just sit there until you die. Every 24 hours you may attempt another saving throw. If you succeed, you may exit the painting, and if you fail, you gain a level of exhaustion. You may not take a long or short rest while in the painting.

THE WORKS OF BETRAN ORMIAN

The famed painter of the last century, Betran Ormian established a studio famed across the land for its realistic portraits and landscapes. What few other than collectors of art or magic know is that many of the paintings that the master, and some of his students, created are enchanted. By issuing the right command, you can walk into the painting as if crossing a threshold into another room. Those on the outside can see you in the painting, and the painting comes to life while a person is inside of it. To use any of these enchanted paintings, you must hang them or otherwise properly display them; simply unrolling a canvas and laying it on the ground will not suffice. Any person inside one of Ormian's enchanted paintings when a painting is destroyed must make a DC 18 Constitution saving throw or drop to 0 hit points. Those who make their save lose half their hit points. In either case, the person (or their body) is cast into the mundane world.

ABA OF THE DANCING QUEEN
Wondrous item, rare

This loose chiffon robe of a style commonly worn by women in desert climes is bright white with a fine lace geometric design. It is uncommonly long and trails to the sides and behind the wearer but can be easily gathered up. When you wear this robe, you may perform one of the following dances:

Dance of Healing. During a short rest, you may forgo any other benefit of a short rest to perform this dance, and when you do so, all allies within 30 feet may add your Charisma modifier plus your proficiency bonus to each hit dice they expend.

Dance of Distraction. As an action, you may cast the *confusion* spell on one target (DC 15 spell saving throw). You may perform this dance once and regain use of it following a long rest.

Dance of the Dervish. As a reaction to being attacked, you may spin and leap. Until the start of your next turn, you gain a +2 bonus to your Armor Class.

ABA OF DISLOCATION
Wondrous item, very rare (require attunement)

Women in desert climes commonly wear this cotton robe. It is light colored with intricate geometric designs along the torso in darker contrasting colors. The aba is voluminous and roomy, comfortable in the heat but can be cinched tight in colder weather. Once attuned, you can issue a command word three times, regaining uses at sunset every night. When commanded, the *aba of dislocation* projects a magical illusion that makes it appear as if you are standing near your actual location, causing attack rolls against you to have disadvantage. If you are hit by an attack, this feature is disrupted until the end of your next turn. This feature is also disrupted while you're incapacitated or have a speed of 0. The effect lasts for one minute or until you cancel it.

ABA OF MISLOCATION
Wondrous item, very rare (require attunement)

Women in desert climes commonly wear this cotton robe. It is dark colored with intricate geometric designs along the torso in contrasting colors. The aba is voluminous and roomy, comfortable in the heat, but it can be cinched tight in colder weather. Once attuned, you may not be detected using magical means. Furthermore, you have advantage on Stealth checks.

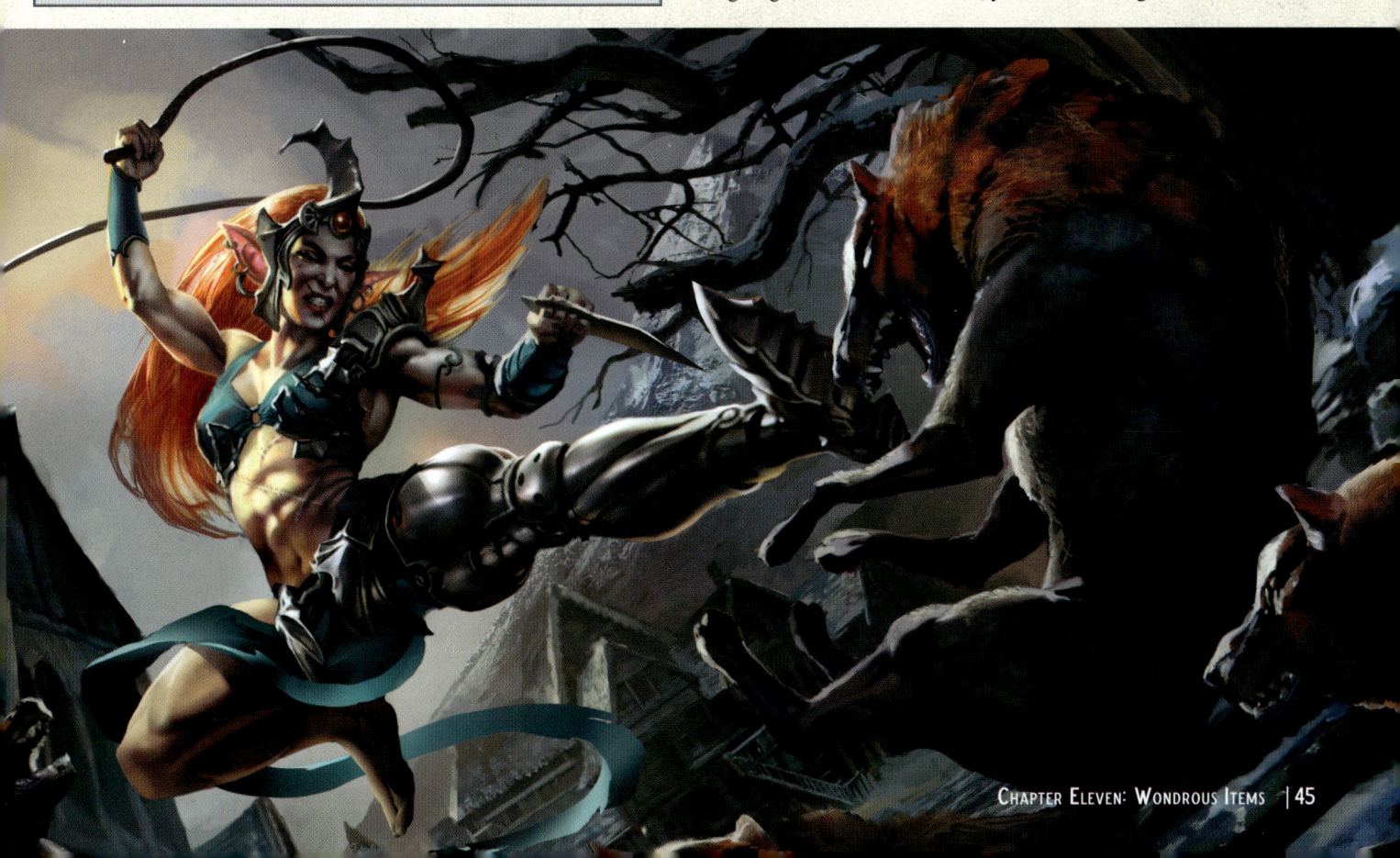

> ## THE CREATIONS OF ALBERT THE WIZENED
>
> Albert the Wizened was a retired adventurer who lived centuries ago. As he grew older, he found many of the common chores of adventuring to be increasingly tiresome, and so turned his arcane might toward creating items that could aid him. Once he retired to a small cottage far from the annoyances of other people, he created other items to aid in keeping up the cottage and for the pursuit of his new pastime: fishing.
>
> When Albert died, bandits raided his cottage and made off with many of his magical inventions. These have been sold and resold, and even copied by other mages. They might turn up in a tinker's cart, on the body of a dead adventurer, or in the keepsakes of a noble family.

ALBERT'S CHUM BUCKET
Wondrous item, uncommon

One of Albert's odder creations, the chum bucket is a silver pail with a golden handle. When the command word is spoken, the bucket generates a pound of fish, but only bait fish. While this raw fish can be eaten, it is by no means fresh and any attempts to consume it raw requires the eater to succeed at a DC 11 Constitution save or become poisoned for one hour. Once used, the bucket cannot be used to conjure fish again until after it spends five hours soaking in water.

The bucket has two additional features. It generates the perfect baitfish for the environment and the desired catch, and if the name of a species of fish is spoken directly after the command word, the bucket fills with the perfect bait. This grants advantage on any rolls to catch the desired fish. Also, should the golden handle be removed and the bucket inverted before the command word is spoken, the bucket continually generates a pound of fish a round for the next 24 hours, after which the magic is used up and the bucket becomes a normal silver pail.

AMULET OF PROTECTION FROM THE EVIL EYE
Wondrous item, uncommon (requires attunement)

This bronze amulet features a glazed glass eye in the center. Once attuned, you have advantage on saving throws against gaze attacks such as those from a medusa as well as curses such as the spell *bestow curse* or mummy rot. If targeted with a gaze attack or curses and your saving throw is successful, you may use your reaction to redirect the effects back at the creature that targeted you. This creature must succeed on a saving throw of the same type and DC as the one that targeted you or suffer the affects you avoided. If you use this feature and the target fails its saving throw, you may not use it again.

AMULET OF RESURRECTION
Wondrous item, conjunction (sulfur), very rare (requires attunement)

An *amulet of resurrection* is a large copper disk engraved with cuneiform markings detailing the quest of an ancient hero to find the secrets to immortality. The poem is well known to scholars of the Age of Strife, but little known outside of those rarefied circles. While wearing the amulet, you have advantage on death saving throws. Additionally, if you die while wearing the amulet and are attuned to it, you are targeted by a *resurrection* spell and the amulet alters to become an *amulet of false resurrection*. Attunement to the *amulet of resurrection* ends with your death.

AMULET OF RESURRECTION, FALSE
Wondrous item, conjunction (salt), very rare (requires attunement)

Appearing much like an *amulet of resurrection*, an *amulet of false resurrection* is a large copper disk engraved with cuneiform markings detailing the quest of an ancient hero to find the secrets to immortality. The long poem is the same as that on the *amulet of resurrection*, save that in the end the hero fails and dies. This alteration of a well-known myth from the Age of Silence can be deduced with a successful DC 15 Intelligence (History) check, provided you know how to read the ancient cuneiform script. While wearing the *amulet of false resurrection*, you have advantage on death saves.

Curse. This item is cursed, a fact that can be revealed through the use of an *identify* spell or once it is attuned. Attuning to the amulet curses you until you are targeted with a *remove curse* spell or similar magic. Removing the amulet does not end the curse. While wearing the *amulet of false resurrection*, if you die, you reanimate as an evil undead creature as determined by your level (see the table below). Your alignment and all statistics change to match the type of undead. Once you have been reanimated, the *amulet of false resurrection* drops from your body and you are no longer attuned to it. The poem changes to the version where the hero succeeds and the amulet becomes an *amulet of resurrection*. Also, while attuned to the *amulet of false resurrection*, you may not be the target of a *reincarnation*, *resurrection*, or other spell that returns you to life.

UNDEAD TYPES

Level	Type
1–5	Zombie
6–10	Wight
11–15	Wraith
16–20	Vampire

ANIMAL-HEADED CANOPIC JAR
Wondrous item, rarity by type

The wealthiest of the distant desert kingdom of Old Misra are buried with enchanted canopic jars. By far the most common of these are *animal-headed canopic jars*. The size of these jars depends upon the animal placed within. All are ceramic jars of the highest quality that are decorated with painted hieroglyphics depicting scenes of the animal in life as well as descriptions of how to use the jar's magic. The cap is a modeled and painted representation of the jar's contents, often with funeral headdresses, gold inlay, and lapis lazuli accents. Each *animal headed canopic jar* generates a single animal of a specific type. When active, this animal behaves as a smart and loyal animal of its type. If slain, the animal turns to ash and the ashes return to its jar, where they must rest for 24 hours before they can be activated again. Inside are the remains of the animal, often reduced to ashes. Several different kinds of *animal-headed canopic jars* exist:

Baboon (rare). When activated, the ashes in the jar swirl out to form a living **baboon**. The baboon serves you for eight hours, after which it must rest for 12 hours within the jar. The baboon can cast *alarm* as a ritual. If the *alarm* is triggered, the baboon raises a racket.

Cat (common). When activated, the ashes in the jar swirl out to form a sphinx **cat**. The cat serves you, or at least serves you as much as a cat can, for one hour before needing to rest in its jar for eight hours. The cat is oddly proficient with thieves' tools (effective +6 to any Dexterity checks made with thieves' tools) and can use its claws as such.

Crocodile (rare). When activated, the ashes in the jar swirl out to form a living **crocodile**. This crocodile serves you for six hours in any way that a crocodile normally can and then returns to its jar to rest for 12 hours. Once per use, the crocodile can cast *protection from evil and good*.

Dog (common). When activated, the ashes in the jar swirl out to form a living dog (use the stats for a **wolf**). This dog serves you for five hours as a loyal companion and then will return to its jar to rest for ten hours. Once per use the dog can cast *expeditious retreat* and *animal messenger* on itself.

Horse (common). When activated, the ashes in the jar swirl out to form a living riding horse. This horse serves you as a mount for eight hours and then returns to its jar to rest for 10 hours. If harnessed to a chariot, the horse can drive the chariot itself (effective + 6 to any Wisdom [Animal Handling] or Vehicles [land] checks.

Songbird (uncommon). When activated, the ashes in the jar swirl out to form a living songbird (use the stats for a **raven**). The songbird serves you loyally for six hours and then it returns to rest in its jar for six hours. If you take a short rest while the songbird is active, you add +4 to each hit dice you expend to recover hit points.

46 | Tome of Wondrous Items

ANCIENT KING'S HORNED HELM
Wondrous item, panoply (ancient king's), very rare (requires attunement)

The bronze helms of the long dead Ancient kings were simple affairs of bronze plates riveted to a leather backing and reinforced with a boar's tusks. A pair of horns, often taken from a great beast but sometimes just a large stag, adorned the helm and gave the wearer an even more fearsome mien. The helms rarely cover much of the face, though a few have been found with leather balaclavas reinforced with bronze rivets that can be pulled up over the nose. Once you have attuned to *ancient king's helm*, your armor class increases by +1.

If worn as part of a complete set of ancient king's panoply, as an action you charge a foe while moving your full speed and then make an attack with the horns of your helm. If you hit, you inflict 1d8 + 1 piercing damage and your foe must succeed at a Strength saving throw with a DC equal to 8 + your proficiency bonus + your Strength modifier or be knocked prone. Also, as an action, you may cast the *command* spell three times and regain one use of this ability every time you slay a foe.

ANCIENT KING'S PANOPLY

In ages before ages the Ancient kings ruled much of the land. These fractious, feuding, and often brutal tribal overlords sought any edge against each other they could get. Their mages practiced bizarre magics that might have been the precursor of modern magic but was at the same time more and less powerful.

The Ancient king who first had a panoply crafted is lost to time, but soon every petty tyrant wanted one of their own. In a time when magical items were rare or not easily transported, to have even a piece of the panoply afforded great power. The Ancient kings were buried with their panoplies, but these tombs are rarely looted for they are guarded by the restless hordes of the long-dead monarchs.

ANCIENT SPELL-STONE
Wondrous item, uncommon

Rune-covered *spell-stones* are still scattered across the world and harken to an ancient era. These are invariably large stones; the smallest are three to four feet tall and weigh several hundred pounds. Each stone is covered in ancient runes that cause a magical effect if properly read. As an action, the *ancient spell-stone* can be read by anyone who is proficient in this long dead language. After it is used, the stone cracks in half and becomes an inert lump of decorative rock. Each *ancient spell-stone* has a single spell carved into it (with a DC 15 saving throw if needed). Many of the spells carved into *spell-stones* have unusual powers, and the spells are cast with a spell slot 1d4 − 1 levels higher than the minimum.

Spell Level	Rarity
0–2	Common
3–4	Uncommon
5–6	Rare
7–9	Very Rare

ANCIENT PASS-STONE
Wondrous item, rare

These trinkets take many forms; some are simple stones carved with ancient runes, while others are necklaces, bracelets, or other pieces of jewelry. A rare few have been worked into swords or other weapons, though this is a poor choice given the nature of the *ancient pass-stone*. The item has little use beyond granting passage past animated ancient warriors of the same prehistoric culture that made the stones. If challenged by an ancient warrior, king, or other warrior that has been animated from an appropriate burial mound, you can present it to the leader of those buried there (or the highest-ranking person), and they will allow you to pass as long as you do not disturb their rest. Mind you, this is passage only; you may not tarry for more than 10 minutes without attracting their ire, nor may you disturb their barrow. You must give the *ancient pass-stone* to the leader to gain free passage.

However, some have discovered additional properties of the *ancient pass-stone*. If the runes carved into the stone are painted over with blood from an intelligent creature and the proper ritual performed (requiring a successful DC 13 Intelligence [Arcana] check), the stone can be used to distract undead of any type. To do so, the stone must be tossed at an undead creature. The targeted undead must succeed at a DC 15 Wisdom saving throw or become enthralled by the stone and unable to do anything but handle it (count as the stunned condition). The targeted creature may attempt a new saving throw at the start of its turn; if it succeeds, it breaks the stone into gravel and can act as normal.

ARMBAND OF THE RING GIVER
Wondrous item, rare (requires attunement)

This armband of gold has a running horse engraved along its outer surface. The horse is etched in such a way as to divide the armband into six roughly even pieces. While attuned to the *armband of the ring giver*, your Charisma score increases by 1 (to a maximum of 22), and you have advantage on Wisdom (Insight) checks. Additionally, the armband can be broken into six parts. You can break off a single portion or up to all six as an action. The broken piece disappears and a **berserker** appears within 10 feet of you. This berserker is loyal to you onto death, and has a name and a personality (at least as much personality as a berserker can). If a summoned berserker dies, it is not replaced. Once all six pieces of the *armband of the ring giver* are used to summon a berserker, the armband no longer has any magical abilities and ceases to function.

THE ASTROLOGICAL BOOK OF IBN FARABI
Wondrous item, very rare

While Abí ibn Farabi's works on the conjunction of heavenly bodies and the mystical arts are now part of magical instruction across the world, the pure form of these theories can be found only in the enchanted books ibn Farabi wrote. *The astrological book of ibn Farabi* is one such work, a thick Maghribian leatherbound tome filled with charts and a discourses on thaumatological theory. It takes one week to read and digest the information within this book, after which your Intelligence score increases by 2 (to a maximum of 22). Further study produces continued results, and if you spend a short rest studying *the astrological book of ibn Farabi*, you may recover an expended spell slot up to the highest level that you can cast.

ANTITHEIRKA MECHANISM
Wondrous item, legendary

Only one example of an *antitheirka mechanism* has been found, but scholars of imperial magics speculate that others are as yet undiscovered. The *antitheirka mechanism* consists of a set of interlinked bronze gears packed snugly together. Nine small handles protrude from the device and allow the various gears to be operated. When one gear is operated, it fits with several interlocked neighboring gears. Turning a single handle sets all 82 gears turning at their own rates and directions.

Unlike many other magical items, the *antitheirka mechanism* is not enchanted to provide directions to the user and must be experimented with. Each of the nine handles can be worked to align the gears in a variety of ways, creating a specific effect when the gears' ninth handle is pulled down. It takes one minute to properly align the gears to achieve a desired effect, but you can use an action to create a randomly determined effect. The following table lists the most well-known effects; additional effects are certainly possible as there are millions of possible permutations of gears. When an effect is generated, it must be activated; the *antitheirka mechanism* does not have an "off" switch. The handles are operated, the gears move, and things happen. The *antitheirka mechanism* has three charges and regains spent charges every 24 hours.

The various effects can be determined by experimentation or research. You must use the item and make note of what alignment of gears created an effect. This can be done with ease if you take a minute to operate the *antitheirka mechanism*; however, if you choose to randomly set the device, you must succeed at a DC 18 Intelligence saving throw to recall the precise alignment of gears. Many scholars have written about the *antitheirka mechanism*, and their works can certainly be found.

ANTITHEIRKA MECHANISM EFFECTS

1d100	Charges Used	Effect
1	1	You cast *comprehend languages*.
2	1	You and everyone within 30 feet of you are transported to Alfheim.
3	2	You cast *banishment*.
4	1	You and everyone within 30 feet of you are transported to Cymilard.
5	1	You cast *fly*.
6	1	You and everyone within 30 feet of you are transported to the Elemental Plane of Earth.
7	2	You adapt to underwater conditions, gaining the ability to breathe water and air as well as a swim speed of 30 feet. This lasts for 24 hours.
8	1	You cast *misty step*.
9	1	You and everyone within 30 feet of you are transported to the Plane of Elysium.
10	2	You cast *magic circle*.
11	1	You and everyone within 30 feet of you are transported to the nearest capital of a nation.
12	1	You cast *dimension door*.
13	2	You cast *contact other plane*.
14	1	You and everyone within 30 feet of you are transported to an entrance of the nearest dungeon.
15	3	You adapt to intense heat, gaining immunity to fire damage and the ability to breathe superheated air. This lasts for 24 hours.
16	1	You and everyone within 30 feet of you are transported to the plane of neutral good gods.
17	2	You cast *scrying*.
18	3	You adapt to extreme cold, gaining immunity to cold damage and the ability to breathe freezing air. You also ignore terrain that is difficult due to ice or snow and can burrow through ice and snow at a speed of 30 feet. This lasts for 24 hours.
19	1	You cast *protection from evil and good*.
20	1	You and everyone within 30 feet of you are transported to the Plane of chaotic gods.
21	1	You and everyone within 30 feet of you are transported to the nearest desert trading city.
22	3	You cast *phantasmal killer*.
23	1	You and everyone within 30 feet of you are transported to the Elemental Plane of Air.
24	1	You become resistant to poisons, gaining immunity to poison damage and the poisoned condition. This lasts for 24 hours.
25	3	You cast *planar binding*.
26	1	You and everyone within 30 feet of you are transported to the nearest open desert.
27	3	You gain a fly speed of 30 feet and immunity to thunder damage. This lasts for 24 hours.
28	1	You and everyone within 30 feet of you are transported to the inland trading city.
29	3	You gain a burrow speed of 30 feet and immunity to acid damage. This lasts for 24 hours.
30	1	You cast *locate creature*.
31	1	You and everyone within 30 feet of you are transported to the plane of chaotic evil gods.
32	1	You and everyone within 30 feet of you are transported to the plane of lawful good gods.
33	1	Two living creatures within 30 feet of you, chosen randomly, switch places via teleportation.
34	3	You are sent 1d4 years into the past and automatically return after 24 hours pass.
35	1	You and everyone within 30 feet of you are transported to the nearest port city.
36	1	You and everyone within 30 feet of you are transported to the Elemental Plane of Fire.
37	1	You and everyone within 30 feet of you are transported to the nearest gathering point of plains nomads.
38	1	Two living creatures within 1d100 × 10 miles of you, chosen randomly, switch places via teleportation.
39	3	You are sent 1d4 years into the future and automatically return after 24 hours pass.
40	1	You and everyone within 30 feet of you are transported to the nearest river bank.
41	3	One living creature within 1d100 × 10 miles of you, chosen randomly, is sent 1d4 years into the future and automatically returns after 24 hours pass.
42	3	One living creature within 1d100 × 10 miles of you, chosen randomly, is teleported to within five feet of you.
43	1	You and everyone within 30 feet of you are transported to the Elemental Plane of Water.
44	1	You and everyone within 30 feet of you are transported to the nearest farm.
45	1	You cast *locate object*.
46	1	One living creature within 30 feet of you, chosen randomly, is teleported to within five feet of you.
47	3	One living creature within 30 feet of you, chosen randomly, is sent 1d4 years into the past and automatically returns after 24 hours pass.
48	1	You and everyone within 30 feet of you are transported to the plane of lawful evil gods.
49	1	You and everyone within 30 feet of you are transported to the nearest underground city.

1d100	Charges Used	Effect
50	1	You and everyone within 30 feet of you are transported to the nearest arctic tundra.
51	1	You cast *pass without trace*.
52	1	You and everyone within 30 feet of you are transported to the plane of neutral evil gods.
53	1	You and everyone within 30 feet of you are transported to the nearest tropical island.
54	3	One living creature from up to 1d4 years in the past, chosen randomly, is teleported to within five feet of you.
55	3	You cast *demiplane*.
56	1	You and everyone within 30 feet of you are transported to an extra-planar city.
57	1	One living creature from up to 1d4 years in the future, chosen randomly, is teleported to within five feet of you.
58	1	You and everyone within 30 feet of you are transported to the plane of neutral gods.
59	1	You and everyone within 30 feet of you are transported to the nearest burial ground.
60	1	You and everyone within 30 feet of you are transported to the nearest temple.
61	1	You and everyone within 30 feet of you are transported to the nearest swamp.
62	1	You and everyone within 30 feet of you are transported to the top of the nearest mountain.
63	3	You gain darkvision 60 feet and immunity to necrotic damage. This lasts for 24 hours.
64	1	You and everyone within 30 feet of you are transported to the plane of chaotic neutral gods.
65	1	You and everyone within 30 feet of you are transported to the nearest fortress.
66	1	You cast *locate animals and plants*.
67	1	You and everyone within 30 feet of you are transported to the nearest forrest.
68	2	You cast *plane shift*.
69	1	You and everyone within 30 feet of you are transported to the oldest city in the world.
70	1	You and everyone within 30 feet of you are transported to the the top of the nearest hill.
71	1	You cast *pass without trace*.
72	2	You cast *dispel evil and good*.
73	1	You and everyone within 30 feet of you are transported to the nearest road.
74	1	You and everyone within 30 feet of you are transported to the plane of lawful neutral gods.
75	3	You gain blindsense 30 feet and immunity to radiant damage. This lasts for 24 hours.
76	3	One living creature within 1d100 × 10 miles of you, chosen randomly, is sent 1d4 years into the past and automatically returns after 24 hours pass.
77	3	One living creature within 30 feet of you, chosen randomly, is sent 1d4 years into the future and automatically returns after 24 hours pass.
78	1	You and everyone within 30 feet of you are transported to the nearest open plain.
79	1	You and everyone within 30 feet of you are transported to the nearest abandoned city.
80	2	You and one living creature within 1d100 × 10 miles of you, chosen randomly, switch places via teleportation.
81	1	You and everyone within 30 feet of you are transported to the nearest ocean shore.
82	1	You and everyone within 30 feet of you are transported to the nearest wizard's tower.
83	1	You and everyone within 30 feet of you are transported to the nearest freshwater lake.
84	1	One item you are carrying is teleported 1d100 miles away from you in a random direction.
85	1	You and everyone within 30 feet of you are transported to the plane of fey.
86	1	You and everyone within 30 feet of you are transported to the nearest prison.
87	2	You cast *astral projection*.
88	1	You and everyone within 30 feet of you are transported to the north pole.
89	1	You and everyone within 30 feet of you are transported to the nearest city-state.
90	1	You and everyone within 30 feet of you are transported to the nearest merchant.
91	1	You and everyone within 30 feet of you are transported to the nearest ship's deck.
92	1	You and one living creature within 30 feet of you, chosen randomly, switch places via teleportation.
93	1	You and everyone within 30 feet of you are transported to the south pole.
94	1	You and everyone within 30 feet of you are transported to the nearest jungle.
95	1	You and everyone within 30 feet of you are transported to the nearest throne room.
96	1	You and everyone within 30 feet of you are transported to nearest town.
97	1	You and everyone within 30 feet of you are transported to nearest village.
98	3	One living creature within 30 feet of you, chosen randomly, must make a DC 13 Wisdom saving throw or die and immediately be targeted with a *reincarnate* spell.
99	1	You and everyone within 30 feet of you are transported to the nearest reef.
100	1	Roll twice, rerolling further results of 100. Both effects happen at once, and the *antitheirka mechanism* is destroyed.

AUTOMATA CART
Wondrous item, rare (requires attunement)

Made of cast bronze with gilding of gold and silver, the *automata cart* was one of the more popular, but also more expensive, examples of Praxiteles' work. Once you've attuned to it, you may command the cart to follow a target at a speed of up to 40 feet. As a bonus action, you may direct the cart's movements to even the most minor detail. Finally, you may issue explicit directions to the cart to travel along a roadway at a speed of 10 mph, making up to three stops along the route for predetermined amounts of time. The cart moves on its own accord and does not need any draft animals. It does not float; it is made of bronze after all and weighs five tons. In all other respects, it behaves much like any other two-wheeled cart.

BAETYLUS
Wondrous item, very rare

This black stone is carved with golden letters in a dead language, but the words themselves are meaningless (though they can be deciphered with a successful DC 15 Intelligence [Arcana] check; the words are magical inscriptions). The stone is roughly the size of a child's fist and very smooth. Many pick these stones up and either toss them aside or keep them as oddities, ignorant of their true purpose.

A *baetylus* is a powerful magical item capable of great feats of healing. However, using it (and reusing it) is less than pleasant. The stone must first be activated by reading the inscription that covers it and then swallowed by the patient (an act requiring a successful DC 11 Wisdom saving throw). Once ingested, the stone acts as a *greater restoration* spell and allows the user to regain 4d10 + 15 hit points. The stone then becomes a lump of rock that cannot be used again until it passes through the digestive system. Cleaning between uses is highly recommended.

BAG OF SILVER
Wondrous item, very rare

This plain leather pouch contains 30 silver coins of unknown denominations. Their markings do not align with that of any modern or ancient coinage but look very much like legitimate coins. When found, the *bag of silver* has 1–30 silver coins within it. If you draw a coin from the bag, you are compelled by magical means to use all the silver coins at a minimum rate of one per week. Once all of the coins are used, the *bag of silver* disappears.

To use a coin, you must remove it from the bag and give it to someone. The target must willingly take the coin; you may not force it upon them or use magical means to suborn their will to get them to take the coin. Once the target freely accepts the coin from your hand, they must succeed at a DC 19 Wisdom saving throw or be subject to a *dominate person* spell with an eight-hour duration.

For every coin you use from the *bag of silver*, you gain a betrayal die. Betrayal dice are d6s if you are levels 1–5, d8s if you are levels 6–10, d10s if you are levels 11–15, and d12s if you are level 16 or higher. The GM can spend your betrayal dice to cause a follower or other NPCs to betray you by adding the result of the betrayal die to an NPC's attack roll or ability check, or by subtracting the result of the betrayal die from one of your attack rolls, ability checks, or saving throws. Once spent, a betrayal die is gone.

BANE JAR
Wondrous item, conjunction (air), common

These jars made of fired clay are incised with bands of cuneiform text. Each *bane jar* has a different incantation tied to the type of creature it is supposed to effect. The jar houses a trapped spirit of air, a minor elemental, that when released targets the creature hit with the jar. To use the jar, you must read the incantation and throw the jar as a ranged attack. If the jar hits the target, and the target is the type of creature to which the jar is tied, the creature must make a DC 15 Charisma save or suffer a 1d4 penalty on all saving throws and attack rolls for the next minute as the air spirit pesters and harries it. If the target struck by the jar does not match the jar's creature type, the *bane jar* bursts around it in a pulse of smoke. Each *bane jar* is typed to a specific creature type, such as aberrations, giants, or humanoids.

BANNER OF THE LION
Wondrous item, rare

This wide, flowing silk banner depicts a rampant gold lion on a field of green. If attached to a spear or lance and unfurled, you can speak a command word to grant 1d10 temporary hit points to all allies within 30 feet who can see the banner. These temporary hit points remain until used or for as long as you use a bonus action on your turn to hold the banner aloft. If you drop the banner, by choice or by force (including if you die), all allies within 30 feet who can see the *banner of the lion* must succeed at a DC 15 Wisdom saving throw or become frightened until the end of their next turn. The target of their fright is whatever foe they are currently fighting. You may willingly end the banner's effects as an action by carefully rolling the banner and putting it away, but if you do so, any temporary hit points the *banner of the lion* grants disappear. You may use the banner once and regain use of it following a long rest.

BATRACHITE STONE
Wondrous item, rare (requires attunement)

These colored stones are said to be taken from the hearts of giant frogs. Each type of *batrachite stone* protects against a certain type of damage depending on its color. To use the *batrachite stone*, you must swallow the fist-sized stone — no easy feat — which requires a successful DC 15 Constitution saving throw; if you fail, you may not make another attempt until you gain a level. Once swallowed, the *batrachite stone* remains inside you for a year and a day; it then passes in a perfectly natural but highly uncomfortable manner. The stone may then be reattuned and reused. Wash it first, please.

BATRACHITE STONE COLORS

Color	Provides Resistance to
Black	Necrotic
Blue	Lightning
Golden	Radiant
Green	Poison
Orange	Force
Purple	Psychic
Red	Fire
Speckled	Thunder
White	Cold
Yellow	Acid

BATTLE OF THE KING'S ROAD
Wondrous item, very rare

This massive painting by Betran Ormian is over eight feet long and five feet tall. It depicts the turning point of the Battle of the King's Road as Duke Elforth leads the charge of the royal household knights to break the enemy line. Duke Elforth is in the center foreground, with his horse rearing up to trample Lord Falfin, while the rest of the center foreground depicts the moment the royal household knights crash into the men-at-arms. The rest of the painting depicts the remainder of the battle, but with no great detail or accuracy. Scholars have pointed out that apart from the center foreground, the rest of the battle is much like other dramatic battlescapes created by Betran's studio. In truth, these parts are simply copied from other works by students and show a wide range of historical arms and armor.

Once you speak the command word, the painting can be entered, though the portal closes one minute after the command word is spoken. You are trapped in the painting if you do not leave within that time. Once the duration ends, the painting stops animating, and those trapped inside are petrified and appear as if part of the artwork. If you speak the command word while inside the painting before the portal closes, you may extend the duration by another minute, up to 10 minutes total duration, before the painting needs to rest on a wall for seven days.

50 | TOME OF WONDROUS ITEMS

Inside, the battle rages on and swirls about; you should be careful not to be caught up in the fighting. Arms, armor, and even horses can be freely taken out of the painting, becoming real, if mundane, copies of the original. People can be removed as well, though they are confused and disorientated for one minute. Up to 10 **guards** and 5 **veterans** can be taken out. However, anything taken out of the painting transforms into paint after 24 hours.

> ### MIRCANA THE SHIPWRIGHT
>
> The mage known as Mircana the Shipwright lived sometime during the last century, disappearing somewhere out on the sea years ago. Her magics focused on aids to sailors and the construction of magical ship furniture. Much of her work remains and can be found scattered across the world in the hands of various ship captains and maritime heroes. This is largely due to her gambling problem; she lost most of her work to debts or in the course of badly played hands of cards.

BINNACLE OF TRUE SIGHT
Wondrous item, uncommon

This compass and housing is designed to be mounted on a ship near the wheel so the helmsman and navigator can easily reference it. The *binnacle of true sight* allows one person within five feet of the *binnacle* to cast *find the path* once per day. In addition, while the *binnacle of true sight* is mounted on a ship, the helmsman gains darkvision 120 feet and can see through natural atmospheric disturbances such as mist, fog, and rain. Also, the helmsman's natural vision is enhanced and allows them to see to the horizon as if using a telescope (and thus extending their darkvision to the horizon). All these benefits apply only to the person currently at the ship's wheel; once they are more than five feet away, these benefits are lost.

BLADE OIL
Wondrous item, uncommon

This exquisitely carved stone jar features depictions of warriors slaying beasts and monsters. The jar contains thick, pungent oil that can be combined with a whetstone to clean and sharpen bladed weapons. Enough oil is in the jar to treat 10 weapons. A treated weapon is immune to rust, even the corrosive effects of a rust monster. Furthermore, the weapon is sharper and inflicts +1 damage. The blade oil lasts for 10 hours, after which its benefits fade away, like the oil itself. Once all 10 applications are used, the stone jar crumbles to dust.

BONE FLUTE
Wondrous item, rare

Most *bone flutes* discovered are tossed aside. These flutes, which are made from the hollow leg bones of larger birds, do not look like much. They tend to be well worn, weathered, dirty, and crudely made. However, in the right hands and to the right eyes, they are powerful magic items. Each flute is carved with minimalistic depictions of a species of animal, usually prey animals such as aurochs, deer, elk, or mammoths, but examples carved with lions, wolves, and other predators have been found.

As an action, you can play the flute to gain the effects of *speak with animals*, but only with the species the flute depicts. If you play the flute for one minute and succeed at a DC 13 Charisma (Performance) check, you can cast *conjure animals* once but may speak only with animals of the depicted species. You regain use of this feature following a long rest. As an action, you may play a single note and, if you succeed at a DC 15 Charisma (Performance) check, you may cast *dominate beast* once, but the target must be of the depicted species. You regain use of this feature following a long rest.

BOOK OF LIBRARIES
Wondrous item, very rare

This tome is bound in red leather and has gilt pages. An ornate arabesque design on the cover is worked in gold and decorated with semiprecious stones. Three silk bookmarks — blue, red, and yellow — are attached to the spine. The *book of libraries* has hundreds of pages; it is a very thick heavy book. The pages are blank until the *book of libraries* is given a command. It can be commanded to display the contents of any mundane book on the same plane or to display pages drawn from books covering a single topic. You can use the book to research a topic, which grants advantage on a single skill check related to that subject.

> ### PRAXITELES
>
> One of the more prolific creators of magical relics who lived during the empire, Praxiteles specialized in creating automata, living sculptures animated by magic. In addition to his enchanted statuary, Praxiteles also created many mundane statues and some bearing only minor enchantments such as *magic mouth*. Little is known of his early life or how he rose to prominence, but by his fortieth year, his studio was producing statues and automata for clients across the empire and beyond. In modern times, few of his great works can be found, but some say the Colossus and other legendary statuary are automata waiting to be awakened.

BOON JAR
Wondrous item, conjunction (earth), common

These jars of fired clay are incised with bands of cuneiform text. The jar houses a small spirit of the earth. As a bonus action you may break the jar or throw it at a target. Once the jar is broken, the spirit exits and forms around the body of the person who broke the jar or was hit by the jar if thrown. For the next minute, the sprit bolsters the target, granting a 1d4 bonus to all saving throws and attack rolls the target makes.

BOWL OF MISCIBILITY
Wondrous item, rare

This ceramic bowl has incised rows of geometric patterns around the outer rim and incised graduated lines around the inside. The entire bowl is coated in a purple slip glaze. You may pour up to four potions into the bowl, swirl it around, and then drink the contents as an action. When you do so, you gain the effects of all the potions.

BOX OF EVILS
Wondrous item, very rare

This plain wooden box has a firm lock that can be opened with a DC 18 Dexterity check using thieves' tools. If opened, the box it unleashes some form of plague that affects all creatures within a 10-square-mile area. Roll on the table below each time the box is opened to determine what plague strikes the land. Once the plague is released, the *box of evils* closes and locks.

BOX OF EVILS' PLAGUES

1d10	Plague	Effect
1	Blood	All water sources in the area of effect are turned to blood. This includes natural waterways and stored water such as in cisterns or waterskins. Flowing waterways clear in 1d3 days, while lakes and other standing water take 1d6 days.
2	Frogs	Hopping frogs cover the land. No one may take a long or short rest for the next 2d6 days. The frogs get into stored food supplies and ruin half of it. Furthermore, the frogs die in the end and leave rotting corpses all over the place, a perfect breeding ground for disease.
3	Gnats	Biting gnats swarm across the land. No one may take a long or short rest for the next 2d6 days. Every living creature within the area of effect must succeed at a DC 15 Constitution saving throw at each sunset or be poisoned until the gnats go away.
4	Wild Animals	Every wild animal in the area of effect becomes mad as if with rabies and violently attacks. This continues for the next 2d6 days.
5	Pestilence	Disease strikes the land. All living creatures in the area of effect must succeed at a DC 15 Constitution saving throw or suffer a disease as per the spell *contagion* (roll 1d6: 1, blinding sickness; 2, filth fever; 3, flesh rot; 4, mindfire; 5, seizure; 6, slimy doom).

CHAPTER ELEVEN: WONDROUS ITEMS | 51

1d10	Plague	Effect
6	Boils	All living creature must succeed at a DC 15 Constitution saving throw or contract horrid boils that last for 2d6 days. During this time, the affected creatures cannot take a short or long rest, are poisoned, and may not regain hit points through any means.
7	Hail of Fire	Burning hail falls from the sky across the area, starting fires and smiting folks. All creatures within the area of effect must make a DC 15 Dexterity saving throw, taking 4d6 fire damage on a failure, or half as much on a success.
8	Locusts	Millions of locusts descend upon the area, stripping it of vegetation and slaying any plant creatures.
9	Darkness	The sky turns darker than night with no stars or moons for the next three days.
10	Double Plague	Roll twice, rerolling results of a 10. The land suffers two plagues.

BRAZIER OF LIES

Wondrous item, uncommon

This three-legged bronze brazier has arcane symbols incised into its outside and cast handles in the shape of dragon heads. The *brazier of lies* appears as a different magical brazier to any spells used to identify it, such as *identify*.

Cursed. If you use the *brazier of lies* to cast a divination spell, the spell is disrupted. If the target of the spell can make a saving throw against its effects, it does so with advantage. Information that the spell returns is erroneous 50% of the time. If the spell cast already has a margin of error, that margin is doubled.

BRAZIER OF DIVINATION

Wondrous item, uncommon

This three-legged bronze brazier has arcane symbols incised into its outside and cast handles in the shape of dragon heads. If placed over a fire, you can use the *brazier of divination* to aid in the casting of your divination spells. The save DCs of any divination spells you cast while using the *brazier of divination* are increased by +1, the range and duration of the spells are doubled, and the information is 50% more reliable if there is a chance of error. Finally, when you use the *brazier of divination* to cast a divination spell as a ritual, it takes half the normal time.

BRICK OF BUILDING (STRUCTURE)

Wondrous item, rare

This plain, simple red brick bears arcane markings baked into its six faces. If a command word is spoken, you can throw the brick onto a level, clear surface such as an empty lot. The brick creates a copy of itself, and then another, and then another until it creates a sturdy brick building 10 feet wide and 15 feet long. This building has a five-foot foundation, a dirt floor, but no roof, doors, or windows. As the structure forms, you can designate up to two windows and one doorway per wall. The structure takes one minute to form.

If additional *bricks of building (structure)* are used in conjunction with each other or a structure created by a *brick of building (structure)*, the resulting structures form with a doorway connecting them or stacked on top of each other up to three stories tall.

You can remove the *brick of building (structure)* by drawing it from the weave of bricks. However, it must be found with a successful DC 15 Intelligence (Investigation) check. If it is removed, the entire structure created by that brick ceases to exist.

BRICK OF BUILDING (WALL)
Wondrous item, uncommon

This simple, plain brown brick bears arcane markings baked into all six faces. If a command word is spoken, you can throw the brick onto a flat or gently sloped (less than 10 degrees) clear surface. The brick creates a copy of itself and then another, and then another, until it creates 50 linear feet of wall that is three feet tall and two feet thick. The wall has a two-foot-deep foundation. This wall can have up to four 90-degree turns. The wall forms at a rate of 10 feet per round.

If additional *bricks of building (wall)* are used in conjunction with each other or a structure created by a *brick of building (structure)* or a wall created by a *brick of building (wall)*, the wall you create with this brick can connect them.

You can remove the *brick of building (wall)* by drawing it from the weave of bricks. However, it must be found with a successful DC 15 Intelligence (Investigation) check. If it is removed, the entire wall created by that brick ceases to exist.

BRICK OF BUILDING (WELL)
Wondrous item, uncommon

This simple, plain blue brick bears arcane markings baked into all six faces. If a command word is spoken, you can throw the brick onto a flat natural surface such as an open field. The brick creates a copy of itself and then another, and then another, until it creates a three-foot-tall circular well that drills itself down 15 feet. It fills with fresh, clear water. The well does not form with a winch, bucket, pulley, or other system. There is a 50% chance that the well forms with 1d100 cp at the bottom. The well takes one minute to form.

If additional *bricks of building (well)* are used in conjunction with each other, the depth of the well increases by 15 feet.

You can remove the *brick of building (well)* by drawing it from the weave of bricks. However, it must be found with a successful DC 15 Intelligence (Investigation) check. If it is removed, the well ceases to exist and the hole fills in to match the surrounding soil and stone.

BRONZE HIPPOI
Wondrous item, very rare

Second only to *golden watchdogs* in popularity but far more expensive, the *hippoi* are metal automata shaped like horses. Their materials and cost ranged from bronze, through silver, and on to gold, and rumors abound that a platinum *hippoi* was made for the emperor. When given the command word to animate, *hippoi* become metal horses capable of any action a horse normally could (treat as either a **riding horse** or a **warhorse**, depending on the statue, but with AC 18 due to natural armor). If slain, the *hippoi* reverts to inanimate metal and cannot be reanimated for 1d4 days. All *hippoi* may innately cast *expeditious retreat* on themselves three times and regain expended uses at the following dawn. More expensive *hippoi* have additional abilities, as described below:

Silver Hippoi: Treat as a **warhorse**. The *silver hippoi* may innately cast *unseen servant* once and regains use of this feature at the following dawn.

Golden Hippoi: Treat as a **riding horse**. The *golden hippoi* many innately cast *healing word* once and regains use of this feature at the following dawn.

Platinum Hippoi: Treat as a **warhorse**. The *platinum hippoi* many innately cast *levitate* once and regains use of this feature at the following dawn.

BRONZE WATCHDOGS
Wondrous item, rare (requires attunement)

The *watchdogs* of Praxiteles were his studio's most common creation. Despite the name, clients could order them in silver, gold, or platinum. Those made of precious metals were merely coated in the gleaming substances; the underlying statue was always bronze that was cast in the master's arcane foundries.

Once attuned, you can issue the *watchdog* a command that animates the statue. The animated statue (treat as a **wolf** but with AC 18 due to natural armor) is still made of metal, unlike some of Praxiteles' other creations that turn to flesh and bone. If slain, the *bronze watchdog* reverts to inanimate metal and cannot be reanimated for 1d4 days. The *bronze watchdog* patrols an area, attacks a target, and otherwise behaves much like a well-trained guard dog. Additionally, the *watchdog* can innately cast the *alarm* spell three times, regaining expended uses at dawn. More expensive *watchdogs* have additional abilities as described below:

Silver Watchdog: The *silver watchdog* may innately cast *burning hands* once and regains use of this feature at the following dawn.

Golden Watchdog: The *golden watchdog* may innately cast *hold person* once and regains use of this feature at the following dawn.

Platinum Watchdog: The *platinum watchdog* may innately cast *scorching ray* once and regains use of this feature at the following dawn.

BULL'S YOKE
Wondrous Item, rare

This gold- and silver-plated yoke is much like those used by oxen. It adjusts itself to fit any creature ranging in size from Tiny to Large sized. Once fitted, the *bull's yoke* allows you to pull weight as if your Strength score was 24 and your size was Huge. If attached to a plow, you can plow up to 50 acres a day, and the plowed fields sprout wheat that grows and ripens within 24 hours despite the fertility of the soil, the season, or the availability of seed.

BUST OF KELL
Wondrous item, very rare

This painted marble bust, often with only a few flecks of paint left on its worn surface, depicts a mature woman with a full helm pushed back on her head, coils of hair tightly wound peeking out from the rim of the helm, and a warrior's cloak pinned across her shoulders and neck. Long dead, or at least believed so, Kel was a goddess of wisdom, self-sacrifice, and protection. While many busts of her were created by philosophers and watch captains, a few were enchanted to aid in the pursuit of truth.

When given a command word, the bust animates, and her eyes open and gaze upon the world with piercing, inquisitive eyes. The bust asks the petitioner to state their question in clear terms and then waits impatiently for a response. She does not engage in conversation outside of what is needed to elicit a question and to answer it. Questions asked of the bust can cover a wide range of topics, but her answers come only after 1d10 × 5 minutes of quiet contemplation by the bust. If interrupted during this time, add an additional 1d6 × 5 minutes to the time before the answer. In all other ways, this functions as a *divination* spell. The bust can answer only one question and regains the ability to answer questions after it rests for 24 hours.

CADUCEUS OF THE LEGIONS
Wondrous item, very rare

The legions managed to conquer an empire with a swiftness that overwhelmed and confused many at the time and continues to puzzle scholars to this day. One of the aids to this conquest was the prevalence of enchanted items among the legions. The *caduceus of the legions* was carried by the medici cohortis, the medical officer overseeing a cohort of six centuries. While the mundane healing ability of the military medical corps was advanced, the ability to bring in the magical power of the *caduceus of the legions* enabled the legions to quickly recover battlefield injuries, stave off illnesses before they spread through the ranks, and keep conquering at breakneck speed.

You may use the *caduceus of the legions* to cast the spells *detect poison and disease* or *purify food and drink* without using a charge. As an action, you may expend one or more charges to cast the following spells: *cure wounds* (1 charge), *healing word* (1 charge), *lesser restoration* (2 charges), *mass healing word* (3 charges), *prayer of healing* (2 charges), *protection from poison* (2 charges), or *revivify* (3 charges). You can cast the spells at higher levels by expending additional charges, one additional charge per increased spell slot level.

A *caduceus of the legions* has up to 20 charges when discovered; roll 1d20 to determine how many. Charges are regained following a one-hour ritual, with each performance of this ritual restoring five charges. The ritual was a closely kept secret of the legions' medical corps but can be found in some older texts and is well known to this day by the priesthood of gods of war.

CENTAUR'S HALTER
Wondrous item, rare

This oddly shaped harness is designed to fit a humanoid torso with straps that go over the shoulders and around the waist connected front to back by horizontal strips of leather. When donned, it easily fits under armor or clothing. As an action, you may speak a command word and transform into a centaur with your torso, head, and arms. You remain transformed for eight hours and may use this feature once, regaining use following a long rest. At the end of the duration or if reduced to 0 hit points, you revert to your normal form. While in centaur form, your Strength scores increases by +2, you gain a +1 bonus to hit and damage with shortbows, you become a Large-sized creature, and your speed increase to 50 feet.

CHAPTER ELEVEN: WONDROUS ITEMS | 53

CANOPIC URN OF REVENGE
Wondrous item, rare

This large ceramic urn is decorated with hieroglyphics that depict the death and resurrection of a body and include instructions on how to use the urn. Investigations of the urn, such as the use of an *identify* spell, reveal it to be a *canopic urn of undead, greater*. However, this item is cursed. When found, there is a 50% chance that the urn is already occupied.

Cursed. When you first attempt to use this item, you must succeed at a DC 13 Constitution save or be slain as your body and soul are sucked into the urn. You are dead, but good news, you are now mummified. The *canopic urn of revenge* now functions as a *canopic urn of the undead, greater*. However, if your mummified corpse is summoned out of the urn, you are not under the control of the owner of the urn and instead attack that person. Your soul is trapped inside the urn or your mummified body, as appropriate, and you cannot be raised by any means until your mummified corpse is destroyed and the urn is crushed.

CANOPIC JAR OF ETERNAL LIFE
Wondrous item, very rare (requires attunement)

This ornate ceramic jar is finely painted with hieroglyphs that depict life, death, and resurrection, as well as offering instructions for the use of the *canopic jar of eternal life*. The attunement process involves an eight-hour ritual at the end of which you remove your still-beating heart and place it within the jar, inflicting 4d10 slashing damage to yourself in the process. Your heart continues to beat within the jar. If you die while your heart is still in the *canopic jar of eternal life*, you cannot be resurrected in any way. Instead, your body reforms itself next to the jar within the next 2d4 days, fully healed of all damage and without any conditions such as poisoned or petrified as per the spell *resurrection*. If the jar is destroyed, your heart is destroyed as well and you die immediately with no chance of resurrection. Should someone open the jar, they have your heart in their hands and can destroy it at will, killing you with no chance of resurrection.

CANOPIC URN OF THE UNDEAD, LESSER
Wondrous item, rare

This large ceramic urn is decorated with hieroglyphics that depict the death and resurrection of a body and include instructions on how to use the urn. By placing a desiccated humanoid heart and the cremated ashes of its body within the urn and then treating all with an alchemical mixture, the necromancer fashions a portable undead servant. When the urn is opened and a command word spoken, the corpse's body swirls out of the urn to serve whoever possesses the vessel. The corpse is a **skeleton**.

The skeleton serves until it or its urn is destroyed. If the skeleton is destroyed, a new skeleton can be placed within the urn or sucked in. An urn that does not have a skeleton assigned to it can be used to capture a skeleton and place it under your control. The target skeleton must be within 30 feet of the urn and succeed at a DC 15 Charisma saving throw or be sucked into the urn. If the urn is destroyed while the skeleton is active, the skeleton becomes uncontrolled.

CANOPIC URN OF THE UNDEAD, GREATER
Wondrous item, very rare (requires attunement)

This large ceramic urn is decorated with hieroglyphics that depict the death and resurrection of a body and include instructions on how to use the urn. By placing a desiccated humanoid heart and the cremated ashes of its body within the urn and then treating all with an alchemical mixture, the necromancer fashions a portable undead servant. When the urn is opened and a command word spoken, the corpse's body swirls out of the urn to serve whoever possesses the vessel. The corpse is a **mummy**, and you are immune to the conjured mummy's *dreadful glare* attack.

The mummy serves until it or its urn is destroyed. If the mummy is destroyed, a new mummy can be placed within the urn or sucked in. An urn that does not have a mummy assigned to it can be used to capture a mummy and place it under your control. The target mummy must be within 30 feet of the urn and succeed at a DC 15 Charisma saving throw or be sucked into the urn. If the urn is destroyed while the mummy is active, the mummy becomes uncontrolled.

CAULDRON OF SWARMS
Wondrous item, rare

This wrought-iron cauldron has loops to allow it to be hung over an open fire. When hung over a fire and filled with water and special ingredients, the cauldron generates a swarm per round for the next six rounds. These swarms are under your control and remain for 24 hours or until slain. You can use a bonus action to perceive the world through the senses of a swarm created by the cauldron. You know the distance and direction of the swarms you create and can issue mental commands to them. Several types of *cauldrons of swarms* exist, and each creates a different type of swarm (see table below):

CAULDRON OF SWARMS

Swarm Type	Decoration	Special Ingredient
Bats	The loops are bat heads with open mouths	100 ounces of guano
Poisonous Snakes	The loops are shaped like two snakes rearing up to strike a full moon	100 mice
Rats	The sides are decorated with beady-eyed rats in relief	100 ounces of cheese
Ravens	The loops are shaped like ravens taking flight	100 eyeballs
Spiders	The sides are decorated with spider webs	100 insects

54 | Tome of Wondrous Items

CAVE PIGMENTS
Wondrous item, rare (requires attunement)

Found in caves across the world, *cave pigments* are a set of painter's tools that date back to an earlier time. They consist of several shallow, dish-like shells decorated with carvings of wild animals. Some of these shells are seashells, while others are those of turtles or other riparian creatures. The shells generate pigments in bright earth tones of ochre red, dusty yellow, and various browns and blacks when used. Anyone can dip a brush or even their hand into the pigment and use it to paint on surfaces or daub it on their bodies. In the hands of a skilled painter, cave pigments are much more powerful. Anyone attuned to a set of *cave pigments* who is proficient with painter's supplies can use any of the following properties of the *cave pigments*:

Draw Animal. As an action you can draw an image of a natural animal (even a giant version of that animal) and gain the effects of a *speak with animals* spell with the species you drew.

Draw Scene. You may take one minute to draw a scene of animals in their natural environment and cast *conjure animals*. If you do so, you cannot use any other features of the *cave pigments* until the next full moon.

Fearsome Visage. You may take one minute to paint a person with fearsome designs. Until the pigments are removed or the target takes a long rest, the target gains a +1 bonus to armor class and advantage on any saving throws to resist fear effects. You may paint up to six figures from a set of *cave pigments*. If you use this feature, you may not use any other feature of the *cave pigments* until the next sunrise.

CHARIOT OF THE SUN
Wondrous item, very rare

This small chariot (speed 65 mph, crew 1, passengers 1, cargo 10 pounds, AC 15, 50 HP) is of a type meant for racing and hunting, not war. It is heavily ornamented in gold and rare gold and copper alloys, with a bright sun in relief on the front of the cab. When activated with a command word, two horses (treat as **riding horses** but with immunity to fire and radiant damage) appear alongside the yoke. The chariot can move along the ground as normal, achieving speeds many would consider reckless. It practically floats above the ground and skips over any obstruction less than two feet high and ignores difficult terrain. However, when on the ground it cannot cross water with a depth of more than two feet.

A second command word allows the chariot to take flight (speed 85 mph). It can fly only during the day and even then only if moving generally westward. As the sun sets, the chariot loses its speed to fly, dropping speed by 1 mph every minute during the last hour of daylight. You had best land before the sun sets, as once the last rays of the sun no longer pass above the horizon, the chariot loses its ability to fly.

CAPSTAN OF THE MISER
Wondrous item, uncommon

This capstan is made of brass and wood and shows signs of long but well-cared-for use. When anchored to a ship or other stable surface, the capstan acts as a regular capstan: It turns and winches up a line, greatly increasing the strength of those using it and allowing up to four people to combine their muscles. When the command word is spoken, the *capstan of the miser* turns on its own as if four strong sailors were working it. The name comes from the belief that any captain using the *capstan of the miser* is only doing it to cut the payroll by four common sailors.

CENTURION'S GALEA
Wondrous item, panoply (centurion's), rare (requires attunement)

Crafted by the imperial smiths and enchanted by imperial wizards, the *centurion's galea* is a finely wrought helm that features a short brim, cheek guards, and a transverse crest of red horsehair. Gold chasing frames the wearer's face, and many helms have decorations depicting legionary numbers and heraldry. It is not unusual to find the name of the centurion the helm was made for inside the helmet in inlaid gold script. The helm never tarnishes. When you are attuned with the *centurion's galea*, you gain a +1 bonus to your armor class and advantage on saving throws to resist fear effects and immunity to the frightened condition.

If worn as part of the centurion's panoply with the *centurion's lorica segmentata*, you can project your voice up to 300 feet away. Also, as an action you may issue a command to any ally within 30 feet. That ally may use a reaction to attempt a saving throw against any condition they are currently suffering. You may do this once and regain use of this feature following a short rest.

If worn as part of a complete set of the centurion's panoply, as an action you may issue a command to any ally that can hear you. That ally may use a reaction to attempt a saving throw against any condition they are currently suffering. You may do this once and regain use of this feature following a short rest.

CHESSBOARD OF THE LONG MOMENT
Wondrous item, rare

This chess set has a board of inlaid ivory and onyx, with two sets of pieces carved from green serpentine and red sandstone. The pieces include a king, advisors, chariots, elephants, knights, and footmen. The entire set is enclosed within an ornately carved box with a scene depicting two people sitting at a table playing chess on the lid. You may open the box as an action and challenge one creature you can see and that can hear you within 30 feet. That creature must succeed at a DC 15 Wisdom saving throw or be compelled to sit and peacefully play a game of chess with you. You are likewise magically compelled to play the game and may not make a save to resist the effect.

While compelled, you and your opponent must complete the game of chess to the best of your abilities. Neither may make attacks, cast spells, or otherwise act other than to do what is necessary to complete the game. Others might attempt to attack you and your opponent or target you with spells, and to do so they must succeed at a DC 15 Wisdom saving throw. If either you or your opponent is successfully attacked or has a spell cast upon them, the game is ruined and the effect ends. A game of chess lasts for one hour unless either player is proficient with chess and succeeds at a DC 15 Intelligence check to end the game earlier. In that case, the game ends in 1d4 × 10 minutes.

CINNABAR ROUGE
Wondrous item, uncommon

This small round porcelain container is filled with red cinnabar paste. When you apply it to your face, your skin becomes pliable and can be remolded to any shape you desire. You can use this to create a disguise as per the spell *alter self* (but only the change appearance option). You can also use the *cinnabar rouge* to give yourself fangs (granting a bite attack that inflicts 1d6 piercing damage), alter your eyes to grant you darkvision 60 feet, or change your nose so that you can detect scents as well as a dog. These alterations are not subtle and make psychical changes that are readily apparent to any viewer. The container can hold up to 10 applications of *cinnabar rouge* and when these are gone, the magic fades away.

CITY IN A BOTTLE

Wondrous item, rare (requires attunement)

This four-foot-diameter terrarium contains a model of a small city complete with outlying farmland. The model is in exacting detail. If you peer though the carefully blown glass's natural magnification you can see tiny models of people and animals at work and play. The terrarium is so well made that clouds of mist regularly gather at the roof and produce small rains, and miniature plants grow in copses and fields. The longer you stare, the more real the model looks.

Once attuned, you may speak a command word and transport yourself and up to six other living creatures into the bottle. When you do so, the model comes to life as the people animate and move about and can be communicated with. However, they lack true sentience and limited knowledge. Most have only a few lines of dialogue they can speak before repeating themselves, but the nobles and court officials of the city are more advanced and can fool you into thinking they are real. However, any food or drink you consume inside the bottle replenish and refresh you as if they were real. The models can make repairs on mundane goods and produce basic goods for use within the bottle, but anything made within the bottle cannot be taken out of it (anything from the outside world repaired inside can be taken out and remains repaired). There is no set day-night cycle within the model; all lighting comes from outside.

While in the city, you are the lord and master of the city and are treated as such. You may speak a command word to bring yourself or any creature you have brought into the city out of it. There is also a small prison for those who offend your majesty. You and those with you do not age within the city.

CITY IN A BOTTLE, CURSED

Wondrous item, rare (requires attunement)

This terrarium appears much like a *city in a bottle* and even spells such as *identify* do not detect the difference. However, once you have attuned to the *cursed city in a bottle* and entered it, you become subject to its curse.

Curse. You and anyone you bring into the bottle may not leave until complete some grand task. You do not know what that task is, but you do know that you must complete it to exit. The models do not treat you as the lord of the city as a default; how they treat you depends on the nature of your grand task. Once the grand task is completed, you and everyone who entered the bottle with you is sent back out, and you are no longer attuned to the *cursed city in a bottle*. The GM can create a grand task or roll on the table below:

CURSED CITY IN A BOTTLE GRAND TASK

1d10	Task
1	Overthrow the tyrannical lord of the city.
2	Save the city from a rampaging monster (CR at least 4 higher than the person attuned to the *cursed city in a bottle*).
3	Gain the love of the adult child of the ruler of the city.
4	Resist the attempts of an evil advisor to usurp your rule.
5	Root out a secret cult, tribe of wererats, or other insidious foe.
6	Fight off an invading force (invaders seem to appear at edge of terrarium already in a horde).
7	Stop an epidemic or famine and locate its supernatural source.
8	Find an ancient relic lost ages ago and hidden within the city.
9	Steal the crown jewels of the city's ruler and escape to a hidden location in the countryside.
10	Find a spouse, settle down on a farm, and live out a long, happy life.

CLAY SEAL
Wondrous item, conjunction (azoth), uncommon

These disks of unfired clay have cuneiform inscriptions that ward off a specific type of creature. The back of the disk is wetted and the seal is affixed to a structure such as a door or window, after which the inscription must be read to activate the *clay seal*. As long as the *clay seal* is affixed to the structure, up to a 30-foot cube within the structure acts as if under a *magic circle* spell with a DC 15 spell save.

CLOAK OF THE DEAD
Wondrous item, conjunction (salt), rare (requires attunement)

This cloak of vulture feathers reeks of a week-old corpse left out in the sun. Maggots crawl across the feathers and tend to wander onto the person wearing the cloak. The cloak has three charges. Once attuned, as an action you may expend one charge from the *cloak of the dead* to use one of the following properties:

Flight. You gain a fly speed of 30 feet, but your flight is ungainly and you suffer disadvantage on any Dexterity (Acrobatics) checks.

Wight Friend. You gain advantage on all Charisma (Persuasion) checks involving undead for the next 10 minutes.

Sheltering Wings. You gain resistance to necrotic damage for 10 minutes.

Spells. You may cast *animate dead*, *chill touch*, *false life*, or *speak with dead*, requiring no material components.

The *cloak of the dead* regains 1d3 charges after the wearer spends one hour lying with the cloak among a pile of at least 10 hit dice worth of corpses.

CLOAK OF THE DWARVEN KING
Wondrous item, Panoply (dwarven king), unique (requires attunement by a dwarven king)

Created by the power of the *ideal forge*, the *cloak of the dwarven king* is even more important than the other pieces of the *panoply of the dwarven king* — even the *crown of the dwarven king*. While the *hammer of the dwarven king* is a mighty weapon and the *crown of the dwarven king* grants powerful defensive abilities and aids in rulership, the *cloak of the dwarven king* brings prosperity to the clan that made it.

Woven from fibers taken from the hair of every member of the clan at the time of its making, the cloak is a multihued tapestry that records the lineage of the clan in one place. As new clan members are added or born, their hair is added to the *cloak of the dwarven king*. The greatest dwarven kingdoms have cloaks that trail behind their kings for a dozen feet or more.

Once you attune to the *cloak of the dwarven king*, you become a conduit between the gods of the dwarves and your people. You may speak with the gods as if talking to a person sitting next to you, though the gods choose if they answer or not. You can also communicate with any person who has died whose hair was woven into the cloak. Finally, you know the lineages and history of your clan perfectly.

If you wear the *cloak of the dwarven king* while also wearing the *crown of the dwarven king*, you may use three spikes of the crown at a time.

If you wear the *cloak of the dwarven king* with a complete set of the *panoply of the dwarven king*, you may wrap up you clan's *ideal forge* and carry it in the cloak. While doing so, you gain a level of exhaustion per day and may not take a long rest.

CLOAK OF MANY WEAPONS
Wondrous item, rare

This old cloak is the color of old leather, stiff as if washed too many times, and blemished with splotches that could be identified as blood if they weren't such old stains. The inside of the cloak has a dozen pockets, all empty until you put your hand into one. The pockets open up into extradimensional spaces similar to that used by *bags of holding*. However, these spaces can hold only weapons. You can store a weapon, no matter how large, in any of the dozen pockets. The cloak always weighs five pounds and appears as if no weapons are hidden within it. When the *cloak of many weapons* is found, the pockets contain 1d10 random weapons.

CLOAK OF DISARMING
Wondrous item, rare

This old cloak is the color of old leather, stiff as if washed too many times, and blemished with splotches that could be identified as blood if they weren't such old stains. The inside of the cloak has a dozen pockets, all empty until you put your hand into one. The pockets open up into extradimensional spaces similar to that used by *bags of holding*. However, these spaces can hold only weapons. You can store a weapon, no matter how large, in any of the dozen pockets. The cloak always weighs five pounds and appears as if no weapons are hidden within it. When the *cloak of disarming* is found, the pockets contain 1d10 random weapons.

Curse. The *cloak of disarming* operates in all ways like a *cloak of many weapons* save that when you go to draw a weapon from the cloak, there is a 50% chance the weapon has disappeared into the ether.

> ### PANTO'S HATS
> Panto is a famed, some would say infamous, hat maker whose pure passion for haberdashery led to the enchantment of some of his creations. Untrained, Panto studies ancient tomes of haberdashery, gleaning a few arcane secrets along the way. His taste is somewhat suspect, as he seems to have no idea of the concept of over-ornamentation and his fascinators are truly, if not fascinating, something to behold. Entrancing might be the proper term, though some would argue repellant.
>
> Panto operates the Hilltop Emporium in his small town far off the beaten track and sells his hats to dealers and a large number of fey. He is open to special commissions, though even Panto does not know what makes a hat magical or tasteful.

COMMANDER'S SHAKO
Wondrous item, rare (requires attunement)

This tall conical military hat by Panto features an abundance of gold braids, bear skins, tartan swatches, a massive medallion of silver encrusted with semiprecious crystals in the middle of the crown, and a hanging fringe of leopard skin in the back that almost makes the hat look like an enlarged kepi. Once attuned to the hat, you gain a +1 bonus to your armor class and radiate an aura that encourages your allies. All allies within 30 feet have advantage on Wisdom saving throws. Furthermore, you may use a command word to grant 5 temporary hit points to all allies within 30 feet. You may do this once and regain its use following a long rest during which the hat is placed within a protective box.

COOLING FAN
Wondrous item, uncommon

This silk hand fan features an ivory handle and an elaborate painting of a wind-tossed sea and a ship nearing rocks. When the fan is held in a hand and the command word spoken, it floats free and gently fans the head and face of the user. The fan orbits the user's head and provides a cool breeze that negates any hazards due to heat. It also disperses smoke, mists, fogs, and gases within five feet of the user. The fan does so for eight hours or until commanded to stop. Either because its duration expired or it was commanded to stop, the fan must thereafter rest for eight hours before being used again.

COTTAGE OF CONFINEMENT
Wondrous item, very rare

This small metal trinket is much like those worn on charm bracelets. It depicts a peasant cottage in great detail. The cottage is obviously well kept and well loved, with flowers around the door and a roof well thatched. When you hold the *cottage of confinement* and name a specific creature you can see within 30 feet, that creature must succeed on a DC 15 Wisdom save or become trapped inside the *cottage of confinement*.

Creatures trapped inside the *cottage of confinement* do not age, cannot be harmed by any force outside the *cottage of confinement*, and are unaware of the outside world. Time passes oddly for them; the windows grow brighter and darker with the normal progress of the sun and moon, and the seasons change at the same rate as they do in the real world. However, the days seem to slide together in memory, and it is difficult to keep track of how long one has been in the *cottage of confinement*.

Being trapped within the *cottage of confinement* is not deadly in itself but it is not entirely pleasant. The temperature and atmosphere are comfortable for the time of year. The three rooms of the cottage — living room, kitchen, and bedroom — are spartan but sufficient. Food and drink (plain but nourishing) appear in the cupboards every morning, and dirty dishes are magically clean by the next sunset. The chamber pot empties itself every sunrise.

The *cottage of confinement* can hold up to four creatures at a time. If at capacity and a new creature becomes trapped, one of the current residents

CHAPTER ELEVEN: WONDROUS ITEMS | 57

is released (chosen at random). A resident can be released by anyone holding the *cottage of confinement* who speaks the proper command word. Released residents appear within five feet of the *cottage of confinement*, though they do not appear if the conditions are dangerous. The *cottage of confinement* can be destroyed (AC 20, 50 hit points), and doing so releases all current residents.

THE FAILURES OF TALVAN

Now known as the Mad Lich, Talvan of Reme was once a prolific creator of magical items and a great experimenter in arcane mechanics. His adventuring years were spent in the far west, but he retired to his tower in the city after suffering a debilitating injury from a poisoned arrow. Secluded with none but his loyal construct servants (and rumors at the time of a mass of undead servitors), Talvan became enthralled with the pursuit of mastering esoteric conjunction. As the years went by and his physical condition worsened, Talvan isolated himself further. During his last two decades residing in the city, he was never seen. Many thought he had died, with his servants merely carrying on due to their programming.

Thieves broke into his tower one night. Many died as Talvan's defenses and constructs fought off the intruders. In the end, the authorities intervened to keep the battle from spilling out into the city. Once the dust settled, they found an abandoned tower wracked by the battles, vast amounts of treasure left untouched for decades, and several magical items with odd properties. Of Talvan there was no sign for decades until a tower erupted from the earth and the Mad Lich began subjugating the local orc population.

Several of Talvan's failures have surfaced in the past centuries. Some were liberated by the thieves who attacked his tower, while others passed into the hands of various corrupt authorities before being lost or sold. Others lack a provenance tied to the tower, and show that work on esoteric conjunction continues at the Tower of the Mad Lich.

CUBE OF THE TOWER

Wondrous item, conjunction (earth), rare

This one-inch-square cube of stone is covered in eldritch runes and fine lines that swirl around the letters. When held in a living hand, the lines pulse with green light in time with the heartbeat of the holder. The *cube of the tower* was an attempt to create a magical item closely tied to the elemental earth but lacked the conjunction many earth-tied magical items have. While it is closely tied to elemental earth, it is strongly resonant with that type of elemental energy.

As an action you toss the *cube of the tower* onto open ground. When it lands, it quickly roots itself into the ground and into the Elemental Plane of Earth. Once this process begins, nothing save the hand of a god can move the cube. At the beginning of your next turn, the *cube of the tower* multiplies itself to form a circular wall 10 feet high with a 20-foot diameter. The following round, the wall becomes 50 feet tall and 40 feet in diameter. On the third round after it lands, the wall is 90 feet tall and 50 feet in diameter.

At the start of your next turn after the cube forms a wall of maximum dimensions, a wave of acid is extruded from the base of the wall in a 60-foot sphere. Any creature caught in this wave must make a DC 15 Dexterity saving throw, taking 4d6 acid damage on a failure, or half damage with a success. The wall then encloses itself with a wooden ceiling and begins filling in the tower, creating nine floors that are 10 feet high each. A new floor is created every five minutes. A single stairwell winds up one interior side and allows access to the floors and the roof. The bottom floor is pierced with a single door of banded oak and a sturdy lock (which can be picked using thieves' tools with a successful DC 15 Dexterity check). The upper floors have four narrow windows each facing the cardinal directions. The *cube of the tower* does not provide any furnishings. Talvan made multiple *cubes of the tower* and tested them across the wolrd before abandoning the project. Many of these tests still stand and have become homes to settlers or lairs for various monsters. So far, none have discovered the command to revert a tower back into a *cube of the tower*.

If carried along with another magical item with earth esoteric conjunction, the *cube of the tower* gains the following properties.

Furnished. As each floor of the tower is built, you may add furnishings. These furnishings are drawn from the Elemental Plane of Earth and are made of substances common to that plane such as soil or stone.

Reshape. You can shape the structure the *cube of the tower* builds but must retain the same base volume of wall.

CUP OF PHYRGA

Wondrous item, very rare

Said to be modeled after the cup carried by the cupbearer of the gods, the *cup of Phyrga* is an alabaster cup with a gold rim. You can command the cup to be filled with eight ounces of any potable liquid. However, the cup is enchanted to never spill, meaning that the contents can be removed only by drinking from it.

CURSE BAG

Wondrous item, uncommon

This leather bag is often decorated with red or black dyes, beads, or quills. A locking bead on the drawstring holds it tight. Inside are six small items: a ball of wood, a stone, a piece of crinoid, a chunk of quartz, a cube of copper, and a glass pyramid. These items correspond to the die sizes of a d20, a d12, a d10, a d8, a d6, and a d4.

As a bonus action or a reaction, you may draw an item from the bag and subtract its corresponding die from any one attack roll, ability check, or saving throw made by a creature you can see within 30 feet of you. You must choose to draw and add the die to the roll before you know the results of the roll. Once an item is drawn from the *curse bag*, it loses its power.

CROWN OF THE DWARVEN KING

Wondrous item, panoply (dwarven king), unique, requires attunement (by a dwarven king)

The rightful king of a dwarven hold can attune to this exquisite crown of metal and gems. Anyone other than the rightful king who dons the *crown of the dwarven king* dies (no save) and may not be resurrected by any magic short of the intervention of a dwarven deity. The crown has five spikes that extend from a headband of a unique alloy of copper, gold, mithril, platinum, and silver. Each spike is topped with a different gemstone the size of a closed fist (a dwarven fist at that): a ruby, an emerald, a diamond, a sapphire, and a topaz. Once you have attuned to the *crown of the dwarven king*, you may use an action to activate the powers of one of the gem-tipped metal spikes. Only one spike may be in use at a time, and the power of a spike lasts until another spike is activated or you die.

Diamond-Tipped Mithril. Your armor class increases by +3.

Emerald-Tipped Gold. You may command creatures of elemental earth. You must be able to see an elemental within 60 feet, and it must be able to hear you. The elemental must succeed at a DC 18 Wisdom saving throw or obey your commands as per the spell *dominate monster* for as long as the emerald-tipped spike is active.

Ruby-Tipped Copper. You may command creatures of elemental fire. You must be able to see an elemental within 60 feet, and it must be able to hear you. The elemental must succeed at a DC 18 Wisdom saving throw or obey your commands as per the spell *dominate monster* for as long as the emerald-tipped spike is active.

Sapphire-Tipped Platinum. You may mentally communicate with any of your subjects who is within the hold you are the rightful ruler of. You may not invade their mind, and they do not have to reply to you. You can communicate with them as if speaking to them and must share a common language to understand each other.

Topaz-Tipped Silver. You create a halo of power around you that affects all allies within 30 feet. Those affected gain advantage on saving throws and may use their reactions to recover 1d8 hit points.

If the *crown of the dwarven king* is worn while wearing the *cloak of the dwarven king*, you may have two spikes active at a time.

If the *crown of the dwarven king* is worn as part of a complete *panoply of the dwarven king*, you gain the following when you activate a spike:

Diamond-Tipped Mithril. You gain resistance to bludgeoning, slashing, and piercing damage from nonmagical attacks that are not mithril.

Emerald-Tipped Gold. You may summon a creature from the Elemental Plane of Earth. The creature may not have a challenge higher than half your level, rounded down. The summoned creature appears within 60 feet of you.

Ruby-Tipped Copper. You may summon a creature from the Elemental Plane of Fire. The creature may not have a challenge higher than half your level, rounded down. The summoned creature appears within 60 feet of you.

Sapphire-Tipped Platinum. You may use the spell *detect thoughts* on any of your subjects as long as they are within the hold you rightfully rule. There is no save possible for this effect.

Topaz-Tipped Silver. Those affected by your aura of power regain 1d6 hit points at the start of their turn.

PANOPLY OF THE HEAVENS

The current ruler of the caliphate does not offer a reward for the return of the pieces of his predecessors' panoply. Instead, anyone found in possession of the *panoply of the heavens* suffers arrest, torture, and eventually death. However, it is rumored that one of his advisors does offer a reward, though none know for what purpose. Legends say that the current caliph is not the true and rightful ruler, and once the panoply returns, it will be in the hands of the next caliph.

CROWN OF THE HEAVENS
Wondrous item, panoply (heavens), very rare

Crafted millennia ago for the first caliph, the *crown of the heavens* is a simple crown of a platinum headband holding a single sapphire the size of a hen's egg. The crown, like the rest of the *panoply of the heavens*, was lost when the Grand Caliph Rabi bin Ashkar Al Ammu and his entire court were slaughtered at the Battle of False Wells by the great wyrm Jalthranax.

Once attuned to the *crown of the heavens*, you can use the following properties of the *crown of the heavens*.

Hear Petitioners. As an action, you gain the benefits of a *detect thoughts* (DC 15 spell save) spell that automatically targets anyone you speak with or who speaks to you. This can be very distracting.

If you are wearing the *crown of the heavens* while sitting upon the *throne of the heavens* you gain the following:

Hear Subjects. As an action, you can use the *detect thoughts* (DC 18 spell save) ability on anyone within a region you are the lawful ruler of.

If you are wearing the *crown of the heavens* as part of a complete *panoply of the heavens*, you gain the following:

Watch Subjects. As an action, you may use the *scrying* (DC 20 spell save) spell upon a target anywhere within a region you are the lawful ruler of.

DANCER'S ANKLETS
Wondrous item, panoply (dancer's) rare (requires attunement)

These golden anklets have strings of tiny bells attached to them. Two anklets are in the set and both must be worn for their magic to have any effect. The anklets were made for Caliph Aziz ibn Hasram's favorite court dancers as part of the larger *dancer's panoply*. As a dancer won the caliph's approval, he bestowed another part of the *dancer's panoply* on them. With the death of Aziz ibn Hasram and the ascension of his reform-minded brother Hafiz ibn Hasram, the practice was ended. After their discharge from the palace, the dancers returned to their homes and further adventures, and the pieces of the *dancer's panoply* spread with them.

Once you attune to the *dancer's anklets*, your Dexterity score increases by 2 to a maximum of 22 and you gain proficiency with the Acrobatics skill. If you already have proficiency with that skill, you may add your proficiency bonus twice to checks involving that skill. Finally, you suffer disadvantage on Dexterity (Stealth) checks as the bells jingle all the time.

If worn alongside the *dancer's castanets*, as an action you may perform a one-minute dance that causes the effects of one of the following spells: *bane*, *bless*, or *heroism*.

If worn as a complete set of the *dancer's panoply*, as an action you may perform a dance that causes the effects of the *irresistible dance* spell with a DC 15 spell save. However, you must dance along with the target and are subject to the same effects.

DANCER'S CASTANETS
Wondrous item, panoply (dancer's) rare (requires attunement)

These chestnut castanets are adorned with inlaid gold and mother of pearl. There are two castanets in the set, and both must be carried for their magic to have any affect. The castanets were made for Caliph Aziz ibn Hasram's favorite court dancers as part of the larger *dancer's panoply*. The *dancer's castanets* were given to the harisu, the select group of the caliph's court dancers. These dancers served double duty as the caliph's secret bodyguards and as secret police within the caliph's court dancers.

Once you attune to the *dancer's castanets*, your Wisdom score increases by 2 to a maximum of 22 and you gain proficiency with the Perception skill, and if you already have proficiency with that skill, you may add your proficiency bonus twice to checks involving that skill.

If worn alongside the *dancer's veils*, as an action you may snap the castanets together to cast the *shatter* spell with a DC 15 spell save.

If worn as a complete set of the *dancer's panoply*, as a reaction you may snap the castanets together to cause any damage just suffered by one ally within 30 feet whom you can see to affect you instead.

DANCER'S VEILS
Wondrous item, panoply (dancer's) rare (requires attunement)

These silk veils are brightly colored and nearly transparent. The veils were made for Caliph Aziz ibn Hasram's favorite court dancers as part of the larger *dancer's panoply*. The *dancer's veils* were given to the greatest of the caliph's dancers, and many who were gifted with this magic item went on to become one of the caliph's wives. By far the rarest of the *dancer's panoply*, one set is still held in the treasury of the caliph in Hava for use by the caliph's wife. Another set is worn under the armor of Princess Adelet, according to some who say this at great risk of their tongue. Once you attune to the *dancer's veils*, your armor class increases by +2 and you gain proficiency with the Performance skill. If you already have proficiency with that skill, you may add your proficiency bonus twice to checks involving that skill.

If worn alongside the *dancer's anklets*, as an action you may cast the *enthrall* spell with a DC 15 spell save.

If worn as a complete set of the *dancer's* panoply, as an action you may use the veils to cast the *confusion* spell with a DC 15 spell save.

DECONJUNCTIONIFIER
Wondrous item, unique (requires attunement)

Talvan created several *deconjunctionifiers*, but he destroyed them as all were failures. One was left behind in his tower and recovered by the grand duke. A century later, it was stolen from the ducal treasury and turned up in a distant city at an auction. Its purchaser reported it lost a decade later. Most recently, it was discovered in the treasure hoard of a giant in the north country.

The *deconjunctionifier* is supposed to remove esoteric conjunction from a magic item, but it fails to do that. Once you are attuned to the *deconjunctionifier*, it suppresses all esoteric conjunction of any other magic items you are attuned to. If you are no longer attuned to an item that is having its esoteric conjunction suppressed, its esoteric conjunction returns. Likewise, all suppressed esoteric conjunction returns if you lose attunement to the *deconjunctionifier*. Finally, the *deconjunctionifier* is cursed. When you attune to it, roll 1d12; that is the number of years before you lose the *deconjunctionifier* through some means.

DESERT PRINCE'S KEFFIYEH
Wondrous item, panoply (desert prince's), rare (requires attunement)

This cotton headdress is held on by a goat's hair agal threaded with gold wire. There have been several *desert prince's keffiyehs*, each dyed to contrast with the accompanying *desert prince's thawb*, though the one made for the Black Prince Faisal ibn Nassir is black with a white agal. Of all the pieces of past *desert prince's panoplies*, the keffiyeh fared the worst. Most were lost over the centuries and if the headdress is separated from the agal, neither has any magical power. Many tribal leaders wear part of a *desert prince's keffiyeh* and offer a large reward for someone who can locate the missing piece. Once you have attuned to the *desert prince's keffiyeh*, your armor class increases by +1 and you gain advantage on Charisma (Intimidation and Persuasion) checks.

If worn with the *desert prince's scimitar*, as an action you may issue a single command to all within 30 feet who can see and hear you. Those in the area of effect must make a DC 15 Wisdom saving throw or spend their next action paying attention to you. This includes looking, listening to your words, and weighing their veracity. This does not make them believe you or follow your orders. You may do this three times and regain expended uses at sunrise.

If worn as part of a complete *desert prince's panoply*, as an action you may glare at one creature within 30 feet who can see and hear you. This creature must make a DC 15 Charisma saving throw. On a failure the atrget takes 6d8 psychic damage and is stunned until the end of your next turn, while on a success, the target takes half this damage and not stunned.

DESERT PRINCE'S SADDLE

Wondrous item, panoply (desert prince's), rare (requires attunement)

This leather saddle is ornamented with silver conchos — silk tassels that contrast with the color of the matched *desert prince's thawb* — and fine scriving. The saddle can be placed on any horse, camel, or a similar creature. Of all of the pieces of the *desert prince's panoply* created, over time the *desert prince's saddles* are the ones that survived the best. Mostly this is because while the personal items of a great hero are buried with them, lost in battle, or taken as trophies, their saddle and mount are often passed to a close relative. While you are the one attuned to the saddle, you must place it on a mount to gain its benefits. Once you have attuned to the *desert prince's saddle*, your mount's AC increases by +2 and its speed increases by 20. Also, your mount ignores difficult terrain that is rocky, sandy, or steep. Finally, your mount's attacks count as magical attacks.

If used with the *desert prince's keffiyeh*, your mount may cross water as if on solid ground. It may cross up to 100 feet of open air provided it begins and ends its move on solid ground.

If worn as part of a complete *desert prince's panoply*, you and your mount may become incorporeal for 10 minutes. Any equipment you wear or carry becomes incorporeal as well. While incorporeal, you can move through living creatures and objects as if they were difficult terrain, but if you end your turn within a living creature or object, you are shunted aside and suffer 1d10 force damage. Additionally, while incorporeal you may not physically interact with the material world such as opening or closing doors, attacking with weapons, or manipulating objects. You may cast spells as normal. While incorporeal, you are immune to bludgeoning, piercing, and slashing damage from nonmagical attacks and have resistance to acid, cold, lightning, thunder, necrotic, and radiant damage. However, you are vulnerable to force damage. You may do this once and regain use of this feature the next dayat midday.

DESERT PRINCE'S THAWB

Wondrous item, panoply (desert prince's), rare (requires attunement)

This light cotton robe has long sleeves and reaches to the knees. There have been many *desert prince's thawbs* made over the centuries and while most are dyed white, some are brown, blue, or in the case of the thawb made for the Black Prince Faisal ibn Nassir, deep black. The desert tribes have long held that a great prince will rise up among them and reunite the scattered sons and daughters of the Assurian Empire. When a likely candidate arises, their claim to the long lost throne is cemented when a collection of tribal leaders gifts them with the *desert prince's panoply*. To date, none has succeeded, but recent events in Pelshtaria reignited this lost cause. Once you have attuned to the *desert prince's thawb*, your armor class increases by +1. The *desert prince's thawb* can be worn over armor, and you are immune of the effects of extreme heat, dehydration, and sunburn. Finally, you gain resistance to fire damage.

If worn with the *desert prince's saddle*, you may call your mount to you from any distance. If your mount is farther away than the distance it can run in one turn or if something is blocking its movement to you, the mount appears next to you at the end of your next turn.

If worn as part of a complete *desert prince's panoply*, you may twirl around to create a small, short-lived sandstorm. This storm covers a 100-foot cube centered on you. You may designate any allies within the cube to be unaffected by the sandstorm. Those affected must succeed at a DC 15 Constitution saving throw or be blinded while they are within the sandstorm. The sandstorm lasts for one minute. You can use this feature three times and regain expended uses at sunset.

DIADEM OF THE SPIDER

Wondrous item, rare (requires attunement)

This silver headband features a spider carved from a single ruby in the center. The workmanship is exquisite, and the carved spider looks as if it might crawl off the diadem and down the wearer's face. Once attuned, you can use any of the following properties of the *diadem of the spider*.

Skitter and Hide. As a bonus action you may take the Dash or Hide action.

Spells. As an action you may cast one of the following spells: *conjure animals* (but only spiders), *darkvision*, *spider climb*, or *web*. You may cast any of these spells once and regain use of this property at the rising of the moon. Additionally, you may cast *speak with animals* and *animal messenger* any number of times, but in both cases the target animals must be spiders.

DRUMS OF SUMMONING

Wondrous item, varies

These animal skin drums have wooden bodies decorated with abstract geometric designs. When played, they can be used to summon creatures, though the skill of the player determines what type of creatures are summoned. Summoned creatures obey the summoner for one hour, after which they gain free will and might be rather upset they were summoned. To summon a creature, you must play the drums for 10 minutes and make a Charisma (Performance) check. The result of this check determines the type of creature you summon, although you may summon a creature of a lesser check result if you prefer. Playing the *drums of summoning* is hard work; you gain a level of exhaustion at the end of the performance.

DRUMS OF SUMMONING

Charisma (Performance) check	Creature
10	**Giant hyena** or **dire wolf**
13	**Saber-toothed tiger** or **glyptodon** (see **Appendix A: New Monsters**)
15	**Prehistoric honey badger** (see **Appendix A: New Monsters**) or **prehistoric beaver** (see **Appendix A: New Monsters**)
18	**Megalonyx** (see **Appendix A: New Monsters**) or **cave lion** (see **Appendix A: New Monsters**)
20	**Mammoth**

EAGLE THRONE

Wondrous item, very rare (requires attunement)

This exquisite throne of gold leaf-covered wood, plush silk cushions, and arching eagle wing back would suit even the most discerning monarch. A great eagle's head arches up from the back to peer over your head and glare at those supplicating themselves before your majesty. Once attuned to the *eagle throne*, you must change your character flaw to arrogant. The *eagle throne* has six charges. You can issue a command word to have the *eagle throne* use one of the following properties of the throne:

Call Eagle. Expend two charges to summon a **giant eagle**. This eagle serves you faithfully for eight hours.

Flight. Expend three charges to have the wings of the throne animate and carry you off at a speed of 40. The throne flies for eight hours.

Majesty. Expend one charge to gain advantage on all Charisma (Intimidation), Charisma (Persuasion), and Wisdom (Insight) checks for one hour.

The *eagle throne* regains 1d4 + 1 charges at each day at sunrise.

ELLIDI

Wondrous item, unique (requires attunement)

This longship of northern style is well made, sturdy, and decorated with a smiling, helmeted woman on its bow stem. Sleek and narrow, the ship is built as a raider but can also carry a decent amount of cargo or plunder. Her keel is shallow and even the most untrained eye can see that *Ellidi* could easily slip up a river and into a port.

Attuning to *Ellidi* is no easy task. She must accept her new companion. Any living creature of good alignment may attempt to impress *Ellidi* with their worth. This requires three successful ability checks displaying the petitioner's worth. First, the petitioner must prove to be knowledgeable of ships and the sea, both of which can be proven with a DC 15 Intelligence check (either using proficiency in water vehicles or Nature). Next, the petitioner must prove capable and brave by displaying to *Ellidi* the head of some great beast (a monster of Challenge 6 or higher) they have slain. Finally, the petitioner must display knowledge of poetry and song with a successful DC 15 Charisma (Performance) check.

Once attuned, *Ellidi* serves her new companions to the best of her abilities. She is a sentient magic item. She is honorable in thought and deed, has a special interest in small furry animals, and expects to be treated as a valued ally. She can speak the common tongue of the north, can hear and see with darkvision to a range of 1,000 feet, and has Intelligence 14, Wisdom 18, and Charisma 14. She is proficient with water vehicles (+8), and has Insight + 6, Nature +4, and Perception +6. As a longship, she has AC 16 and 400 hit points, with a damage threshold of 20. She can carry up to 100 people and 10 tons of cargo.

In addition to the above, *Ellidi* has the following properties:

Common Spells. *Ellidi* can cast *comprehend languages* and *speak with animals* as rituals requiring no components and targeting herself.

Dragon Head. Her bow stem decoration can be taken off and replaced with a dragon-headed one (which is kept in a locker near her tiller), a process that takes one minute. She cannot speak, cast spells, recover hit points, regain expended spells, or generate a fog cloud while this dragon head is on. She gains a breath attack that affects all creatures within a 30-foot cone originating from *Ellidi's* bow stem. All creatures caught within this cone must succeed at a DC 15 Dexterity saving throw or suffer 6d10 fire damage. She may use this flame breath three times and regains uses every sunset.

Limited Spells. *Ellidi* can cast the following spells as rituals requiring no components and targeting herself: *find the path*, *invisibility*, *locate animal or plant*, *locate creature*, *locate object*, *nondetection* (which can cover her entire body, not just a 10-foot area), and *pass without trace*. She can cast spells three times and regains a use of this ability at each sunrise.

Sailing. She has a sailing speed of 3 mph. This can be increases by +1 mph if sailing with the wind and/or if at least 40 people are rowing. *Ellidi* can move without sails or oars if she so desires.

Summon Fog. *Ellidi* can summon a fog that enshrouds her, causing disadvantage on any checks to detect her within the fog or target her with a ranged attack. This fog lasts for one hour.

Ellidi recovers 2d10 hit points worth of damage every day at sunrise.

EVERCHANGING DRESSER

Wondrous item, uncommon (requires attunement)

This wooden cabinet stands eight feet tall and is three feet wide. Two large doors open outward above a set of three shelves. Inside a main compartment are a series of hooks, shelves, and a long mirror. Once attuned, the dresser can be ordered to produce any article of clothing the user desires. The clothing is fitted to the user as if by a tailor and displays any heraldic badges or other decorations the user might specify. Accessories such as jewelry, scarves, and hats are also produced. The dresser has a fine eye and balks at any unfashionable choices, but it still complies in the end.

The clothing and accessories produced by the cabinet are magical in nature and radiate conjuration magic under *detect magic* or a similar spell. They are also ephemeral and disappear after five minutes if removed from the user. The dresser can produce one entire outfit every 12 hours.

EVERLASTING CART
Wondrous item, conjunction (salt), rare

Sages who have studied the career of Talvan mark the creation of the *everlasting cart* as the moment he began experimenting with necromancy. This two-wheeled cart is made from blackened wood and gleaming bone. The cart also features skulls for hubcaps and other adornments. When the command word is spoken, a skeletal horse appears in the cart's yoke. The horse can pull the cart with a load of up to 1,000 pounds indefinitely, and does not need to eat or sleep, nor does it get tired. However, the skeletal horse is nearly mindless and must be carefully guided, levying disadvantage on any Dexterity checks to manage the vehicle.

EYES OF CONJUNCTION DETECTION
Wondrous item, rare

Talvan tired of casting *analyze conjunction* (see **Appendix B: New Spells**), so he created these handy tools. Since they have a limited use, he made dozens of them, especially when one takes into account his general forgetfulness and tendency to lose his glasses. These heavily tinted lenses sit in rims of fine platinum wire. When donned, you can determine the conjunction of magical items as if using an *analyze conjunction* spell and do not need to provide the material components for the spell. The *eyes of conjunction detection* can be used once per long rest.

FAN OF CONCEALING
Wondrous item, uncommon (requires attunement)

This painted paper folding fan depicts scenes of court life on one face and scenes of country life on the other. The handle is lacquered a deep red and black with engraved cranes picked out in gold. Once attuned to the *fan of concealing*, you can use its powers to alter your appearance, render you invisible, and to misdirect your foes. As a bonus action, you may expend one charge from the fan to perform one of the following: You can cast the spell *disguise self* on yourself. You can hide yourself from scrying and other divination magics for up to one hour. You can expend two charges from the *fan of concealing* to cast the *invisibility* spell on yourself requiring no material components.

The fan has three charges and regains 1d3 charges each midnight.

FASCINATOR OF FABULOUSNESS
Wondrous item, rare (requires attunement)

This hat by Panto, which must be carefully pinned to your hair or it falls off, consists of a mesh veil, a constellation of pheasant tail feathers springing forth and curling like an exploding star, a cascade of flowers that trails down three feet behind your head, small stuffed birds pinned into the mix that bob about as you walk, and small sequins made from mother of pearl. Plus, some pearls. A little gold foil here and there. A sapphire buried in a ceramic recreation of a broken robin's egg as if hatching forth.

Once you have attuned to the *fascinator of fabulousness*, your Charisma scores increases by 2 to a maximum of 20. Furthermore, as an action you may cast the *confusion* spell (DC 15 spell save). You may do this once and regain use once you let the hat recover in a hat box during a long rest.

FIBULA OF ARMOR
Wondrous item, uncommon

This sturdy bronze cloak pin has a helmet cast into its body. When you wear this fibula, you gain a +1 bonus to your armor class. Additionally, you can cause an illusory suit of armor to appear upon you.

FIBULA OF BINDING
Wondrous item, uncommon

This bronze cloak pin has an intricate swirl cast into its body. As an action you may make a melee attack against a creature, and if you hit, you fasten the *fibula of binding* on the creature's clothing. The creature's clothing wraps around the creature and tightens, restraining it (escape DC 15). If the *fibula of binding* is removed, the effect ends and the creature is freed. A creature bound by the *fibula of binding* cannot remove the fibula itself other than by escaping its restraint.

FIBULA OF THE WARDROBE
Wondrous item, uncommon

This bronze cloak pin has a single chip of ruby embedded in it. You must be nude to use the *fibula of the wardrobe*. When you use the fibula to pierce your skin (inflicting 1 piercing damage), the *fibula of the wardrobe* conjures a suit of clothing around you. You can conjure any style or type of clothing you can imagine, including an exact copy of something that you have seen. Clothing conjured using the *fibula of the wardrobe* disappears if removed from your body.

FIGURINE OF WONDROUS POWER
Wondrous item, rarity by figure

A figurine of wondrous power is a statuette of a beast small enough to fit in the pocket. If you use an action to speak the command word and throw the figurine to a point on the ground within 60 feet of you, the figurine becomes a living creature. If the space where the creature would appear is occupied by other creatures or objects, or if there isn't enough space for the creature, the figurine doesn't become a creature.

The creature is friendly to you and your companions. It understands and obeys your spoken commands. If you issue no commands, the creature defends itself but takes no other actions.

The creature exists for a duration specific to each figurine. At the end of the duration, the creature reverts to its figurine form. It also reverts to a figurine if it drops to 0 hit points or if you use an action to speak a command word again while touching it. When the creature becomes a figurine again, its property can't be used again until a certain amount of time passes, as specified in the figurine's description.

Alabaster Crocodile (rare). This statuette of a great river crocodile can become a living **giant crocodile** for one hour. Once it has been used, it cannot be used again for seven days.

Baobabwood Rhinoceros (rare). This statuette of a rhinoceros is carved from the heartwood of a baobab tree. When activated, it can become a **rhinoceros** (immune to fire damage) for one hour. The *baobabwood rhinoceros* extinguishes any natural fires in its space that it comes in contact with, extinguishing a 10-foot-diameter area at the start of its turn. If the *babobabwood rhinoceros* is used, it cannot be used again for 12 days.

Basalt Tortoise (uncommon). This statuette of a tortoise carved from black basalt animates with saddle and pack harness, as well as baskets and saddlebags. Once it is used, it cannot be used again for two days.

Chert Scorpion (uncommon). This scorpion chipped from a large nodule of chert can become a living **giant scorpion**. Once it is used, it cannot be used again for two days.

Ebiarawood Manticore (very rare). The striated, multi-hued ebiarawood of this statuette beautifully follows the curves of the manticore's body. It can become a living **manticore** for one hour. Once it is used, it cannot be used again for seven days.

Mahogany Cheetah (uncommon). This statuette of a cheetah can become a living cheetah (use **panther**, but speed is 80) for eight hours. While in animal form, the figurine allows you to cast *animal messenger* on it at will. Once used, it cannot be used again for two days.

Mangowood Hippopotamus (rare). This statuette carved from mangowood can become a living **hippopotamus** (see **Appendix A: New Monsters**) for eight hours. The hippopotamus can carry up to two Medium or one Large passenger. Once used, it cannot be used again for two days.

Sandstone Sphinx (rare). Carved from sandstone, this rearing statuette can become a living **gynosphinx** for one hour. You may ask the sphinx one question and it answers as if using the spell *augury*. Once used, it cannot be used again for 12 days.

Soapstone Camel (uncommon). This statuette carved from soft soapstone can become a living **camel** for eight hours. The camel has a saddle and two full 10-gallon waterskins made from complete goatskins. Once used, it cannot be used again for two days.

FIRE CLOTH
Wondrous item, common

Fire cloth is woven from threads spun by the sulfur hornets of the Elemental Plane of Fire. It is usually made into a cloak, but other articles of clothing can be found. Fire cloth provides you with resistance to fire damage. However, it cannot be cleaned using water or other mundane means. One hour in a fire cleans the *fire cloth* and returns it to a pristine shimmering state.

> **FLAYED MAN'S PANOPLY**
>
> The creator of this horror is unknown, which might be a good thing as it means the secrets of their creation might be lost. Only the vilest beings would wear this suit of human skin, or at least that is the general attitude of those knowledgeable about magical items. That said, the panoply is powerful and a tempting item for those willing to dress themselves in human skin. Rumors abound that there are more than one of these and any flesh golem discovered is certain to cause imaginative theories that it is a suit of the flayed man.

FLAYED MAN'S COWL
Wondrous item, panoply (flayed man), rare

This cowl, much like those that can be attached or removed from cloaks and coats, is made of human skin stitched together with threads of sinew. The cowl is deep and those wearing it can easily hide their face in dim light by pulling down the cowl. The opening of the cowl is fringed in human hair and the back of the cowl has the dead face of the skin's previous owner. Once you have attuned to the *flayed man's cowl*, your armor class increases by +1. Also, you may not be surprised by someone behind you.

If you are wearing the *flayed man's cowl* as well as the *flayed man's gloves*, you may cast a spell into the *flayed man's cowl* up to the highest level you can cast. The spell remains locked inside the cowl until you use a bonus action to release it. When you release it, the face on the back of the cowl performs the casting and any effects originate from there. You may have only one spell stored within the cowl at a time.

If you are wearing the *flayed man's cowl* as part of a complete *panoply of the flayed man*, as an action you may pull the cowl down over you and become invisible. When you do so, you see the world as a hazy image as if peering through layers of gauze, and your point of view is behind you. You may move only at half your normal speed and have disadvantage on anything that requires you to see your hands and feet. However, this invisibility cannot be pierced even with spells such as *true seeing* and extends to cover blindsight and truesight effects.

FLAYED MAN'S GLOVES
Wondrous item, panoply (flayed man), rare

This pair of gloves is made from the carefully degloved skin of a human. The gloves are complete, and you can easily see the wrinkles of the palm and knuckles, hair on the back of the hand, and even the fingerprints and nails. The gloves fit easily, stretching to snuggly encase your hands in warm skin. Once you have attuned to the *flayed man's gloves*, you double your proficiency bonus with tool sets that require the use of hands, and as a bonus action, you may cast the spell *mage hand* at will, creating two hands instead of one. These two hands together can carry up to 20 pounds of weight.

If you are wearing the *flayed man's gloves* as well as the *flayed man's cowl*, as an action you may detach a glove to carry out your orders on its own. You must give the glove a task to perform, such as to pick a lock or choke a victim. The glove attempts to do so to the best of its abilities and continues to make the attempt until you tell it to stop. The glove is Tiny, has AC 18, speed 30, and your Strength, Dexterity, and Constitution. It is proficient with the tools you know. It may make a choke attack as an action that inflicts 1d8 bludgeoning damage. It has blindsight 120 feet. If you have a glove on detached duty, you generate only one hand when you use the *flayed man's gloves* to cast *mage hand*. You may detach both gloves, but if you do, you lose all other benefits of the *flayed man's gloves* until at least one returns.

If you are wearing the *flayed man's gloves* as part of a complete *panoply of the flayed man*, when detached, the gloves increase their speed to 60 and gain a climb speed of 30. They inflict 1d10 damage when they make a choke attack. Finally, you can use a bonus action to switch your view to or from the perspective of a detached *flayed man's glove*.

FLAYED MAN'S PANTS
Wondrous item, rare (panoply of the flayed man)

These trousers are made from the stitched together skin of a human. They are complete with wrinkles around the kneecaps, hair, and anatomical components best left unmentioned. The trousers have two pockets at the waist and loops for belts. Once you have attuned to the *flayed man's pants*, your armor class increases by +1. The pockets become extradimensional spaces. You may place any item in the pocket, and each pocket can hold up to 100 cubic inches of matter. The item need not be small enough to fit in the pockets but must have at least one corner or piece that can fit through the opening (the pockets expand to engulf the rest). As an action you can withdraw a stored item from the pockets. If searched by another, the pockets appear to be empty.

If you are wearing the *flayed man's pants* as well as the *flayed man's shirt*, as an action you may reach into the pockets and conjure out an item worth up to 1d10 + 10 gp or the same amount of coinage that is stored in the pockets. You may do this once and regain its use following a short rest. The item drawn from the pockets need not be small enough to fit in the pocket in the first place.

If you are wearing the *flayed man's pants* as part of a complete *panoply of the flayed man*, as an action you may hitch up the *flayed man's pants* and gain the ability to move across water as if it were solid ground. You must keep one hand hitching up the pants for this to work, and if you are unable to do so, the pants slide down and this effect ends.

FLAYED MAN'S SHIRT
Wondrous item, panoply (flayed man), rare

This long shirt is made from a single piece of human skin cut from a torso and stitched up the left side from the hem to the armpit. It is complete with hair, nipples, and other features. The shirt fits snugly to your torso but is loose around the arms. Once you have attuned to the *flayed man's shirt*, your armor class increases by +2, and as a bonus action, you may cause your arms to extend by 10 feet, increasing your reach. This effect lasts until the end of your turn.

If you are wearing the *flayed man's shirt* as well as the *flayed man's pants*, you may perform a one-hour ritual to cause the *flayed man's shirt* to grant you resistance to a type of damage of your choice. This choice remains until you perform the ritual again and change the type of damage you are resistant to.

If you are wearing the *flayed man's shirt* as part of a complete *panoply of the flayed man*, as part of an eight-hour ritual you may remove your heart and place it somewhere else. As long as your heart is removed, should you die while wearing the *panoply of the flayed man*, the panoply disappears and reappears around your heart. You now inhabit the *panoply of the flayed man*, growing your body inside the suit of clothing over the course of seven days. At the end of this time, you completely recover from death. However, while removed, your heart can be used to kill you. The heart has 20 hit points, is AC 10, and is vulnerable to all damage types. If the heart is destroyed, you die and the *panoply of the flayed man* animates as a **flesh golem**. You are dead, but your awareness is still trapped inside the flesh golem. You have no control over it and no way to interact with the outside world. If your heart is removed and you are no longer wearing the *panoply of the flayed man*, you die and may not be resurrected by any means short of a *wish*.

GIRDLE OF PASSAGE
Wondrous item, rare, (requires attunement)

This cloth belt of finely woven silk and golden threads can be lightly laid across a person's hips and closed with a simple buckle. Once attuned, once per long rest, you can use an action to become incorporeal for up to 10 minutes. Any equipment you wear or carry becomes incorporeal as well. While incorporeal, you can move through living creatures and objects as if they were difficult terrain, but if you end your turn within a living creature or object, you are shunted aside and suffer 1d10 force damage.

Additionally, while incorporeal you may not physically interact with the material world to do such things as opening or closing doors, attacking with weapons, or manipulating objects. However, you may cast spells as normal. While incorporeal, you are immune to bludgeoning, piercing, and slashing damage from nonmagical attacks and have resistance to acid, cold, lightning, thunder, necrotic, and radiant damage. However, you are vulnerable to force damage.

You may use the *girdle of passage* once and regain use of its power following a long rest. You can become corporeal again with an action, ending the effect.

GIRDLE OF THE TWINS
Wondrous item, rare (requires attunement)

This belt made of gold cloth is decorated with red tassels that hang down to mid-thigh. Each *girdle of the twins* is linked to another; once attuned, you can detect the direction and distance to your girdle's linked *girdle of the twins*, as well as if it is currently attuned or not. You always know the location, direction, and distance to the wearer of your linked *girdle of the twins*, as well as their general state of health and any conditions that are currently affecting them. While attuned to and wearing the *girdle of the twins*, you may do any of the following. During a short rest, you may expend your hit dice to allow the wearer of your linked *girdle of the twins* to recover hit points. As a bonus action, you may take the Help action targeting the wearer of your linked *girdle of the twins*. As an action, you may cast the *message* cantrip targeting the wearer of your linked *girdle of the twins*. As an action, you may cast the *aid* spell, but may target only the wearer of your linked *girdle of the twins*; you may do this once and regain use of this feature following a long rest.

GLADE WITH UNICORN
Wondrous item, very rare

This large painting is seven feet long and five feet tall. It depicts a well-lit forest glade surrounded by deeply shadowed woods. A bold unicorn grazes quietly on fresh grass in the middle of the glade. Meanwhile, hunters armed with spears and hunting dogs slip quietly through the shadows.

You may enter the painting once you speak the command word. Once inside, the 8 hunters (**scouts**) and 10 dogs (**mastiffs**) attack the unicorn. If you intervene, the hunters and dogs attack you as well. The unicorn is trapped by a net as soon as you enter and cannot defend itself. If you rescue the unicorn, the painting reverts to its original appearance. You may call upon the unicorn once within the next 30 days and it will serve you for 24 hours, provided you are of lawful good alignment. If not, the unicorn ignores your summons. Should you fail to rescue the unicorn or if it is slain while in your service, it slowly "regrows" brush stroke by brush stroke and returns to the painting within six months. If you die within the painting, you become one of the hunters, trapped to repeatedly attempt to slay the unicorn and face off against intruders for the rest of eternity.

GHOST STONE OF THE TOWER OF SCREAMS
Wondrous item, unique

The Tower of Screams was the abode of the dread lich Rathor the Flayer. During his centuries-long tenure as the lord of that accursed tower, he kidnapped hundreds, whom he tortured and killed, only to reanimate and torture them again. Of that multitude, seven managed to escape torment, but only by haunting a stone of the tower. Scholars debate how this came to pass. Was it an act of will? A result of the foul lich's experiments? Some twisted mercy for the gods?

Seven *ghost stones of the tower of screams* exist. Each has a soul bound to it that can manifest itself in some way, has a distinct personality, and offers service in exchange for the limited freedom their kind can enjoy. When one or more of the *ghost stones of the tower of screams* are embedded in the fabric of a structure, the inhabitant of that stone awakes. The awakening process takes 1d6 days, after which the inhabitant of the *ghost stone of the tower of screams* can use any of its abilities. If their manifested form is destroyed, the spirit from the stone must sleep in its stony home for 1d4 days. The stones themselves can be destroyed but that causes the inhabiting spirit to manifest and walk the earth as a normal creature of its type, although with its own personality.

Boots (CG). Boots is an orange tabby with white markings on the legs and throat. Boots manifests as a **ghost** (but Tiny sized, adjust hit dice to d4s and increase AC to 13) that likes to prowl the structure and hunt mice. If well treated, Boots keeps the structure free of vermin, no matter the size or ferocity. Any person who takes a long rest within the structure has a 25% chance of waking with Boots curled up beside them, in which case they gain advantage on death saving throws until they take a long rest. Boots is mercurial, curious, and easily offended (and goes off in a snit and sulks in the stone) but can also be affectionate and caring. Boots is as smart as any human but cannot speak and prefers to not be gendered, thank you very much. If angered by cruelty to cats or Gretchen (see below), Boots attacks.

Caolán of Cark (CG). A famed bard of two centuries ago, Caolán of Cark manifests as a **ghost**. If well treated, he likes to manifest in the evenings after meals and play his harp, granting all present the effects of a *lesser restoration* spell and providing for a pleasant evening. He can be called upon to converse on several topics if consulted involving the following skills: History, Nature, and Performance. This grants advantage on rolls during the consultation. Caolán of Cark is rather high-strung and tends to be passionate about any topic at hand, but most especially about Gretchen. Caolán of Cark manifests and attacks if angered by cruelty toward artists and artworks, if mocked, of if anyone is unkind to Boots or Gretchen (see below).

Eseld May (LN). Eseld May was a wealthy merchant Rathor the Flayer held for ransom, but her heirs failed to pay. Eseld May manifests as a **ghost**. If well treated, she keeps the books and accounts for the structure and those who reside within, and she personally guards any treasury present. Eseld May can summon 1d3 **specters** to aid in the defense of a treasury or other wealth kept in the structure. If consulted on negotiations and business, she grants advantage on a single Charisma (Diplomacy) checks made afterward. Eseld May is very particular about appearances and offers unsolicited advice about the structure and the people therein, which she takes to be constructive criticism. She manifests in anger only if the structure or its owner is attacked, if she hears of a ransom not being paid, or if someone commits theft inside the structure.

Gretchen (NG). Gretchen was a serving girl who caught the passing eye of Rathor the Flayed. When he recalled he was a lich and that such things no longer mattered to his undead state, he sent her to his dungeons. She manifests as a **ghost**. If well treated, Gretchen keeps the structure neat and clean, prepares accommodations for visitors, cooks meals, and brews a bold stout if materials are provided. She quickly becomes very protective of her structure and the cleanliness of it and its residents. Do not wear muddy boots onto her floor. Gretchen is aware of Caolán of Cark's crush on her but she does not reciprocate those feelings. Gretchen is angered if children, small animals, or women are harmed. This includes Boots, and she manifests to attack the perpetrators.

Master Kolonos (NG). Rathor the Flayer captured and tortured the scribe and scholar Kolonos for information. Master Kolonos now manifests as a **ghost**. If well treated, he can be consulted for advice on the following skills, granting advantage on their rolls during the consultation: Arcana, History, Investigation, Nature, and Religion. He is somewhat easily distracted and tends to go off on pedantic lectures that seem to have no end as he wanders from topic to topic. The structure he haunts has any of its books, maps, or scrolls organized. When left to his own devices, he writes scholarly tomes on whatever topic he can, assuming he is provided with the right materials and research aid. If any written work is intentionally damaged or if Boots is harmed, Master Kolonos manifests and flies into a rage.

Pallik the Kobold (LG). The kobold squire of Sir Archibald the Martyred, Pallik was captured when his master failed in the quest to slay Rathor the Flayer. Just a young kobold, he manifests as a **ghost** (but Small with d6 hit dice). If well treated, Pallik keeps all arms and armor in the structure well cared for and maintains horses and other baggage of war. Once per week, he does a particularly good job on one suit of armor or weapon, granting its user +1 AC or +1 bonus on attack and damage rolls with that item for the next 24 hours. Pallik is dutiful, honest, hardworking, and despite his suffering, still somewhat naïve. He has a huge crush on Caolán of Cark and cannot speak in his presence. The young kobold squire hates Boots, yet the cat seems to not notice Pallik at all. Pallik manifests and attacks if Caolán of Cark, Ritterin Walberga Scholz (see below), or anyone else he respects is harmed, or in the presence of an evil of some kind.

Ritterin Walberga Scholz (LN). A famed knight and one-time companion of Sir Archibald the Martyred, Ritterin Walberga Scholz was captured alongside the kobold squire Pallik. The knight manifests as a **wraith**. If treated well and if she respects the owner of the structure she haunts, she guards the structure, taking command of whatever defenses are in place and summoning 2d6 **specters** to aid her. She is commanding, noble, honorable, and willing to offer advice on military matters. She is very blunt. She utterly despises Caolán of Cark, barely tolerates Master Kolonos, ignores Gretchen and Boots, but has a soft spot for Pallik the Kobold (now her squire when they manifest together). She manifests in anger if the structure is attacked or if Pallik is harmed.

GOLDEN FIDDLE
Wondrous item, very rare (requires attunement)

This simple fiddle and bow are made of solid gold with platinum strings and silver fixtures. Despite this, it plays as one of the finest fiddles in the world. Once you are attuned to the *golden fiddle*, if you are proficient with the fiddle you add your proficiency bonus twice to any Charisma checks to play the *golden fiddle*. Furthermore, you may attempt to steal the soul of one living creature within 30 feet who can hear you play. You must make a Charisma check using the fiddle, and the result of this check becomes the DC of a Wisdom saving throw the target must succeed at or have a fragment of its soul stolen and placed in the fiddle. A creature can have only one soul fragment trapped in the fiddle, and the fiddle can hold up to five soul fragments.

A target whose soul fragment is stolen may not cast spells, may not be resurrected without your permission, and may not spend hit dice. The creature suffers disadvantage on Charisma and Wisdom saves. You can free a trapped soul fragment at any time. A creature that has a soul fragment expended from the *golden fiddle* permanently suffers these effects. If a soul fragment is released, the creature who lost that soul fragment no longer suffers the penalties listed above.

While a soul fragment is trapped in the *golden fiddle*, you may use an action to expend a soul fragment to cast one of the following spells using a spell slot one higher than the minimum: *confusion*, *dispel magic*, *fear*, or *shatter* (DC 15 spell save).

Cursed. As soon as you are attuned to the *golden fiddle*, you are subject to its curse. You may not willingly part with the *golden fiddle*. If challenged by a person to a fiddle contest, you must accept. Roll a contest of Charisma (plus proficiency bonus if proficient with fiddles). The loser has their entire soul trapped in the *golden fiddle*, which counts as five soul fragments (displacing any soul fragments currently in the *golden fiddle*) and dies.

GOURD OF CAPTURE
Wondrous item, rare

This hollow gourd is carved with abstract geometric designs. The *gourd of capture* has a hole in one face and a wooden stopper attached to a leather thong tied around its neck. As an action you may hold the gourd up and target one creature within 60 feet that you can see. That creature must succeed on a DC 15 Wisdom saving throw or be transported into the gourd. The stopper slams itself into the hole in the gourd and the trapped person is held inside (shrunk down, of course). An entrapped creature does not age or experience the passage of time while inside the gourd. If a creature is trapped within the *gourd of capture* and the stopper is withdrawn, the creature reappears within five feet of the gourd.

GRYPHON PEPPER POT
Wondrous item, uncommon

This rectangular golden box fits in the palm of the hand and features a small gryphon statue carved into its lid. If the user thinks of a type of spice and then removes the lid, they find that there is one ounce of that spice within the box. The pepper pot can create any type of spice or flavoring, even liquid ones or spice blends. However, it cannot create the same spice twice in a row. Any spice the pepper pot creates disappears after 24 hours.

> ### NOCIDERMUS THE SEVERED
>
> Nocidermus the Severed was one of the more enigmatic creators of magic items of the last few centuries. Little is known about this necromancer, though it is rumored that he hails from the heartlands. He would be largely unknown were it not for his tendency to sign his work. Each magical item he created bears a small tattoo of his sigil, often on the wrist but sometimes on the palm.
>
> His creations are all made from the severed hands of living creatures. The tattooed sigils are often applied postmortem. These hands run the gamut of intelligent humanoids: Some are from humans, others are from elves and dwarves, and a rare few are from orcs. The donors of these hands are often unknown; Nocidermus the Severed seemed to take them as he found them and left no witnesses. Scholars determined that the enchantment on the hands required lengthy rituals that occurred before the hands were severed, which required Nocidermus the Severed taking captives and holding them during this time.

Chapter Eleven: Wondrous Items | 65

HAND OF THE BEGGAR
Wondrous item, rare

This small dirty hand that once belonged to a small human or perhaps a halfling has a long fragment of bone sticking out of the wrist. A large tattoo of seven severed fingers arranged in a star pattern around a capital letter "N" is in the palm. If held out by the bone fragment toward a living creature, that creature must succeed at a DC 15 Wisdom saving throw or be compelled to place a coin of the highest denomination it has on its person in the palm of the hand. The target does not retain any memory of placing a coin in the palm of the hand. You may speak a command word to have the fingers close into the palm and then open, revealing that the coin has been duplicated. Two coins are now in the palm! The hand can be used to duplicate a coin once and regains use of this ability at sunset.

HAND OF DOOM
Wondrous item, rare

This severed orc hand drips blood from its ragged stump. A large tattoo of seven severed fingers arranged in a star pattern around a capital letter "N" is in the palm. The blood that drips from the hand is a corrosive venom. The dripping never stops and ruins any container into which the hand is placed, the floor below where the hand is stored, and other objects that come into contact with the dripping blood over the course of a few hours. As an action, any piercing or slashing weapon can be coated in the blood. The next successful hit with that weapon inflicts an additional 1d6 acid damage, and the target must make a DC 15 Constitution saving throw. A target who fails takes an additional 3d8 poison damage and is poisoned for one hour, while a creature who succeeds takes half this damage and is not poisoned. There is no limit to the number of times the *hand of doom* can be used to coat a weapon with blood, but every time a weapon is coated, the blood eats away at the weapon. On the first application, the weapon breaks if a 1 is rolled on an attack roll. This increases by +1 on each subsequent application of the blood from a *hand of doom*, with the weapon breaking on a 1–2 on the attack roll and so forth.

The blood from a *hand of doom* can also be used to taint food and beverage. The caustic nature of the blood makes it easy to detect in all but the strongest-flavored foods (requiring a successful DC 13 Wisdom [Perception] check to detect). A creature that ingests the blood suffers 2d6 acid damage and must make a DC 15 Constitution saving throw. A target who fails takes an additional 6d8 poison damage and is poisoned for one hour, while a creature who succeeds takes half this damage and is not poisoned.

Anyone handling the *hand of doom* must succeed at a DC 13 Dexterity saving throw, as does anyone carrying it on their person for more than an hour, or suffer 1d6 acid damage. A creature who fails the dexterity saving throw must also make a DC 15 Constitution saving throw. A target who fails takes an additional 3d8 poison damage and is poisoned for one hour, while a creature who succeeds takes half this damage and is not poisoned. This includes attempts to apply it to a weapon or deliver the blood as a poison. The blood from a *hand of doom* cannot be collected and saved for later; if it is not used (either applied to a weapon or dripped into food) within seconds of dripping from the stump, it becomes inert foul blood like that of a corpse.

HAND OF HOLDING
Wondrous item, common

This severed human hand bears a long surgery scar across the palm that looks like a healed and stitched-together wound. A large tattoo of seven severed fingers arranged in a star pattern around a capital letter "N" is on the wrist. If you use an action to stroke the surgery scar is stroked, the scar opens to display a six-inch-diameter hole like the opening of a small pouch. The interior of the *hand of holding* is an extradimensional space four feet deep that can hold up to 250 pounds with a total capacity of 32 cubic feet. The *hand of holding* weighs five pounds no matter how much is placed within. As a bonus action, you can order the hand to retrieve an item from its contents. The fingers stretch to open the palm and reach inside like five boneless tentacles. The item retrieved is placed in your hand and is ready to use.

If the *hand of holding* is pierced, overloaded, or torn, it is destroyed and its contents are scattered into the Astral Plane. The *hand of holding* can be turned inside out and its contents dumped, but it must be turned right side out to be used again. Breathing creatures placed within the *hand of holding* have enough air for a number of minutes equal to 10 divided by the number of creatures within the hand. They begin to suffocate after this time.

Placing a *hand of holding* inside another extradimensional space such as a *bag of holding* or a *portable hole* causes both objects to be destroyed and opens a gate to the Astral Plane. The gate originates where one object was placed inside another. Any creature within 10 feet is then sucked through and randomly deposited in the Astral Plane. The gate then closes. The gate is one-way and cannot be reopened.

HAND OF MANY HANDS
Wondrous item, very rare

This severed ogre-sized hand shows scars as if it was stitched together from several smaller human-sized hands. Each finger ends with a severed halfling hand that has been sewn onto the fingertip. A large tattoo of seven severed fingers arranged in a star pattern around a capital letter "N" is in the palm. To activate, you use an action to draw an intricate symbol on the seven-pointed finger-star on the palm; the choice of symbol determines which spell is cast. The hand can be used to cast one of the following spells: *Arcane hand* and *vampiric touch* may be cast once, and the *hand of many hands* regains the use of these spells at sunset. *Burning hands* can be cast three times, and the *hand of many hands* regains the use of this spell at sunset. *Chill touch* and *mage hand* can be cast an unlimited number of times.

HAND OF THE PRISONER
Wondrous item, very rare

This severed elf hand has a pair of manacles clasped around its wrist. A large tattoo of seven severed fingers arranged in a star pattern around a capital letter "N" is in the palm. If the dangling end of the manacles are attached to a living creature, that creature must succeed at a DC 15 Wisdom saving throw or fall under the effects of a *dominate person* spell. The spell retains its effects for as long as the manacle is attached. The spell ends if the manacle is removed. The manacle drops off if the creature ends the spell by succeeding at a saving throw.

HAND OF THE THIEF
Wondrous item, common

This severed human hand is missing its thumb. A large tattoo of seven severed fingers arranged in a star pattern around a capital letter "N" is in the palm. A set of lockpicks can be placed in the hand, and the hand can be held up to a lock. The hand attempts to pick the lock with an effective +8 to its Dexterity check. If the hand fails to pick a lock, it can be commanded to try again, each time removing one digit as the price of failure. When the hand is out of digits, it becomes an inert severed hand.

HALTER OF THE STEED
Wondrous item, uncommon

This halter is adjustable to be sized to fit any mount from the size of a warhorse to a donkey. You may use an action to utter a command word and cause a mount that would fit into the halter to appear in it, tack and harness on and ready to follow your commands. The summoned mount remains for eight hours and then disappears. You must wait eight hours before using the *halter of the steed* again. If the summoned mount dies, the halter must still rest before it can be used again.

PANOPLY OF THUNDER AND LIGHTNING

Said to have been created by a deity of the storm, the *panoply of thunder and lightning* is much sought after by temples dedicated to weather gods. Each claims that their divine patron is the one who created the panoply, and each might be right for there are credible reports of more than one *panoply of thunder and lightning* in the world. As recently as 30 years ago, a peasant rebellion in a distant kingdom was led by the priest of a storm god bearing the complete panoply.

HAT OF THE ETERNAL STORM
Wondrous item, panoply (thunder and lightning), rare

This plain and simple wide-brimmed hat is made from woven grasses. You gain a +1 bonus to armor class while wearing the *hat of the eternal storm*. Once attuned, you ignore difficult terrain caused by mud, puddles, standing water, and similar terrains created by atmospheric effects, and you cannot be moved by the wind, though your hair and clothing may be dramatically stirred. Even artificial winds have no effect on you. Finally, you may cast the spell *disguise self* at will, though you always appear as a plain, simple peasant of the local variety, a person of no significance who is beneath notice.

If you are wearing the *hat of the eternal storm* while wielding the *fan of lightning*, you may cast the spell *call lighting* once and regain use of this ability following a long rest.

If you are wearing the *hat of the eternal storm* while wielding the *fan of thunder*, as an action you may call down the thunder on a target. This target must be within 120 feet of you and you must be able to see the target. The target must make a DC 15 Dexterity saving throw, taking 3d10 thunder damage on a failure, or half as much with a success. This damage increases by 1d10 if the current weather conditions are stormy. Each round while the ability is active, you may cause the same target or a different target to be struck by the thunderclap as a bonus action. This ability lasts for 10 minutes.

If you are wearing the *hat of the eternal storm* as part of a complete *panoply of thunder and lightning*, you may cast the spell *control weather* requiring no material components. You may cast this spell once and regain use of it following a long rest. Also, you automatically know the weather for the next 24 hours and can predict weather patterns farther out with a successful DC 15 Wisdom check.

HELM OF THE CHOOSERS
Wondrous item, very rare (requires attunement)

This winged spangenhelm always shines as if polished to a high sheen. Once attuned, it increases your armor class by +1 and grants you a fly speed of 30 feet. As an action, you may touch one creature that has 0 hit points and stabilize them. Additionally, as a bonus action you may issue a command that causes the *helm of the choosers* to emit a cacophonous sound as if a hundred musical instruments were playing the same tune in conjunction. All foes within 30 feet who can hear this sound must succeed on a DC 15 Wisdom saving throw or become frightened of you until the end of their next turn. You may use this feature once and regain use of it following a long rest.

HELM OF THE AIR WARRIOR
Wondrous item, panoply (air warrior), conjunction (air), very rare

This ornate helm is forged from whisper steel found only on the Elemental Plane of Air. When you become attuned to the *helm of the air warrior*, you gain advantage on Intelligence checks and Intelligence saving throws, and your armor class increases by +2.

If you wear the *helm of the air warrior* with the *sash of the air warrior*, you may use the *sash of the air warrior's* body of living air ability twice and regain use following a long rest. Also, you may cast the spell *locate object* as a ritual, but the target must be a cloud, gas, or other substance tied to the elemental concept of air.

If you wear the *helm of the air warrior* as part of a complete *panoply of the air warrior*, your Intelligence score increases by 2 (to a maximum of 22). Also, you may spend one minute in quiet meditation, after which you may add your proficiency bonus twice to any one skill check.

HELM OF THE FIRE WARRIOR
Wondrous item, panoply (fire warrior), conjunction (fire), very rare

This ornate helm is forged from liquid bronze found only on the Elemental Plane of Fire. When you become attuned to the *helm of the fire warrior*, you gain advantage on Initiative rolls, Dexterity checks, and Dexterity saving throws, and your armor class increases by +2.

If you wear the *helm of the fire warrior* with the *sash of the fire warrior*, you may use the *sash of the fire warrior's* body of living fire ability twice and regain use of the ability following a long rest. Also, you may cast the spell *locate object* as a ritual, but the target must be a fire or other substance tied to the elemental concept of fire.

If you wear the *helm of the fire warrior* as part of a complete *panoply of the fire warrior*, your Dexterity score increases by 2 (to a maximum of 22). Also, you may spend one minute in quiet meditation, after which your speed for the next 10 minutes is doubled.

ELEMENTAL PANOPLIES
Created by cults dedicated to elemental powers, these four panoplies were meant for the cult's champions. A few have been lost or stolen, a black mark in any elemental cult. Every 592 years, the planes shift to a rare alignment and the elemental panoplies call out to a chosen few. Be they cultists or not, they are compelled to meet in a grand tournament of elemental warriors. Those with the panoplies battle one after another until only one is left alive. The victor becomes a creature of their patron element and rules on that plane for the rest of eternity. At least, that is what the legends say.

HELM OF THE EARTH WARRIOR
Wondrous item, panoply (earth warrior), conjunction (earth), very rare

This ornate helm is carved from a single diamond. When you become attuned to the *helm of the earth warrior*, you gain advantage on Constitution checks and Constitution saving throws and your armor class increases by +2.

If you wear the *helm of the earth warrior* with the *sash of the earth warrior*, you may use the *sash of the earth warrior's* body of living stone ability twice and regain use of the ability following a long rest. Also, you may cast the spell *locate object* as a ritual, but the target must be a gem, mineral, type of soil, stone, or other substance tied to the elemental concept of earth.

If you wear the *helm of the earth warrior* as part of a complete *panoply of the earth warrior*, your Constitution score increases by 2 (to a maximum of 22). Also, you may spend one minute in quiet meditation, after which you recover 10 hit points per minute and regrow lost body parts for the next 10 minutes.

HELM OF THE WATER WARRIOR
Wondrous item, panoply (water warrior), conjunction (water), very rare

This ornate helm is carved from permanent ice. When you become attuned to the *helm of the water warrior*, you gain advantage on Strength checks and Strength saving throws and your armor class increases by +2.

If you wear the *helm of the water warrior* with the *sash of the water warrior*, you may use the *sash of the water warrior's* body of living water ability twice and regain use of the ability following a long rest. Also, you may cast the spell *locate object* as a ritual, but the target must be a liquid or other substance tied to the elemental concept of water.

If you wear the *helm of the water warrior* as part of a complete *panoply of the water warrior*, your Strength score increases by 2 (to a maximum of 22). You may also spend one minute in quiet meditation, after which you may cause a natural body of water to rise or fall, increase or decrease flow, or erode an area of up to 10 acres.

HENNIN OF THE PRINCESS
Wondrous item, rare (requires attunement)

This conical hat is covered in gleaming samite and features a veil of silver wire, and a strip of gold hangs down from the crown to fall across your shoulders. It is worn perched on the back of the head and extends to a point two feet behind and above you. Once attuned to the *hennin of the princess*, you have advantage on any Charisma (Performance) checks that involve dancing. Also, as an action you may cast one of the following spells (DC 15 spell save): *animal friendship*, *charm person*, *unseen servant*. You may do this once and regain use of the ability following a short rest.

CHAPTER ELEVEN: WONDROUS ITEMS | 67

HOPLOMACHUS'S HELM
Wondrous item, panoply (hoplomachus), very rare (requires attunement)

One of the heaviest armed and armored of the gladiators, the hoplomachus wore a heavy metal helmet that enclosed the entire head. This helmet often sported elaborate and distinctive crests of creatures such as gryphons and hydras. While the vast majority of gladiators fought with weapons of common quality, a rare few used magical weapons. This practice was reserved for major events such as coronations and even then only the most experienced fighters wielded them. Once attuned to a *hoplomachus's helm*, your armor class increases by +1.

If worn as part of a hoplomachus's panoply with the *hoplomachus's shield*, as a bonus action you may command the helm to have the animal on the crest make a breath attack. The helm projects a 15-foot cone, and all creatures in the cone must succeed at a DC 13 Dexterity saving throw or suffer 2d8 damage. Possible damage types are acid, cold, fire, and lightning. Each helm was created to project a specific damage type. You may use this feature once and regain use of it following a long rest.

If worn as part of a complete set of the *panoply of the hoplomachus*, as an action you may cast the *sanctuary* spell once per long rest.

HORN OF FOG
Wondrous item, rare

This small bugle allows you to blow forth a thick cloud of heavy fog similar to that of a *fog cloud* spell. The fog covers a 10-foot cube next to you each round you continue to blow the horn; a fog cloud travels 10 feet each round in a straight line from the emanation point unless blocked by something substantial such as a wall. The device makes a deep, foghorn-like noise, with the note dropping abruptly to a lower register at the end of each blast. The fog dissipates after three minutes. A moderate wind (11+ mph) disperses the fog in four rounds; a strong wind (21+ mph) disperses the fog in one round.

HORN OF PRICUS
Wondrous item, rare (requires attunement)

This set of gold-chased goat's horns is held together by a band of metal much like a circlet. Once attuned, you can spend an action to change between a land- or water-based creature. As a land-based creature, you can breathe air (but not water), gain a speed of 30 feet (losing any water-based speed you might have as your tail splits to become two legs), and are not hampered by difficult terrain. As a water-based creature, you gain a swim speed of 30 feet (losing any land-based speed you might have as your legs merge to form a tail), can breathe water (but not air), and are unhampered by difficult terrain. Additionally, no matter which form you are in, you can ingest and gain sustenance from any organic matter.

HONEYED HEAD
Wondrous item, varies (see below)

This humanoid head has been coated in a thick layer of enchanted honey that preserves the head and also doesn't make a mess of the place by dripping honey all over. Each *honeyed head* is unique and possesses different personalities and skills. A *honeyed head* was an expert in life in one particular skill or skill set. As an action you may request the *honeyed head* to give you advice, and when you do so, you gain advantage on the next skill check that involves one of its expert skills. Even when not being asked for advice, the *honeyed head* might make unsolicited comments, brief asides, and rarely lengthy expositions. It is aware of its surroundings and may speak at any time unless ordered to be quiet, and even then it is only muted for one hour.

HONEYED HEAD SKILLS

Rarity	Skills
Common	Any one skill
Uncommon	Any two skills; may be related
Rare	A set of three related skills such as Arcana, Nature, and Religion or Deception, Sleight of Hand, and Stealth

HONEYED HEAD PERSONALITY

1d20	Personality	1d20	Personality
1	Authoritarian	11	Stubborn
2	Pedantic	12	Argumentative
3	Bored	13	Cowardly
4	Mischievous	14	Cheerful
5	Sycophantic	15	Enigmatic
6	Lazy	16	Treacherous
7	Dolorous	17	Aggressive
8	Sanguine	18	Melancholic
9	Curious	19	Phlegmatic
10	Distracted	20	Cheerful

HORN OF THE GREAT FEAST
Wondrous item, uncommon

This horn of a very large bull aurochs is banded in gold and has a steel chain that allows it to hang from a belt. When commanded, it produces a copious amount of food that flows from the mouth of the horn. This food takes the form of oatcakes, bunches of berries, pies, haunches of roast meat, and similar items. In addition, mead can be poured from the point of the horn. Enough food and drink is produced to feed 10 people.

The food and drink is enchanted and speeds recovery. If a short rest is spent consuming the meal, all who partake recover one expended hit die and remove a level of exhaustion. However, the entire meal must be consumed for the horn to be used again. Leftovers that are not consumed but instead left to rot can make the horn permanently inactive. Spilled mead, dropped crumbs, and cleanly picked bones count as consumed as long as the wastage was not intentional.

HORN OF WARNING
Wondrous item, rare

When this ivory horn is sounded, it alerts all allies within 50 miles to your location. You can choose this alert to be audible or a silent empathic sense, but you must choose when you blow this horn and it is the same for all targets.

THE GREAT TEACHER ABÍ IBN FARABI

Known as one of the greatest scholars that the world has produced, Abí ibn Farabi lived three centuries ago. Little is known about his early life other than that he spent 30 years traveling the world searching for knowledge. Many stories have crept up about these years, but all are deemed apocryphal. Abí ibn Farabi returned from this long journey to his home city and settled in there, living simply while he worked on magical inventions and wrote books that would become the cornerstone texts of astronomy, chemistry, mathematics, philosophy, and thaumatology. He was found dead in his apartment and the authorities confiscated his belongings due to the lack of a will or next of kin. Abí ibn Farabi's writings were studied by the court's favorite scholars and then rapidly published despite many of Abí ibn Farabi's conclusions overturning long-held standards in their respective fields. His magical inventions were lost; some say the sinister Zuma Qulldishi stole them, while others claim the aging scholar sold them off to make rent. Several folktales mention a mysterious bearded scholar granting a magical item of unique power to a worthy impoverished protagonist, but these are often dismissed as more apocryphal tales of the scholar known in the Caliphate as the Great Teacher.

IBN FARABI'S PLANAR ASTROLABE

Wondrous item, very rare

This five-inch-diameter disk of bronze is etched with intricate patterns of circles and lines. The device is a quarter-inch thick and has several geared components that can be turned to produce different settings. When one geared component is turned, it effects the movement of others. *Ibn Farabi's planar astrolabe* is used to calculate the movement of the planes in the greater cosmos, predict the conjunction of planes and thus the appearance of planar portals, and to detect the presence of creatures not native to the mortal plane.

Ibn Farabi's planar astrolabe projects a permanent *magic circle* around itself (DC 15 spell save) that you cannot dismiss. Additionally, you may cast the spell *detect evil and good* at will while you hold the astrolabe. Ten minutes and a successful DC 15 Intelligence (Arcana) check allows you to use the astrolabe's other features. If the check is successful, you can perform one of the following: cast the spell *banishment* (DC 15 spell save) once or determine the direction and distance to the nearest planar portal as per the spell *find the path*. Or you may instead determine the direction and distance for a specific aberration, celestial, elemental, fey, or fiend, or a type of the above, as per the spell *find the path*.

IBN FARABI'S PEN

Wondrous item, common

Ibn Farabi created several of these magical ink pens and of all of his inventions, this one has been verified by scholars as one that the Great Teacher readily parted with, once even gifting an *ibn Farabi's pen* to a young street urchin. The pen consists of a simple tapered hollow metal cylinder with a nib at one end and a small lever at the other. The plainness of *ibn Farabi's pen* is shocking — one would assume that a magical item would at least be gilded — but the Great Teacher preferred to spend his money on other things. You can write with *ibn Farabi's pen* as you would any other pen though the unique design allows you to draw ink into the hollow tube. Once filled, the ink never dries out and is constantly replenished by magical means. Furthermore, when writing with the pen, you can enchant your writings as per the spell *illusory script*. Finally, the pen can write on any solid surface and leave a clear mark.

IDEAL FORGE

Wondrous item, Relic of the Age of Dragons (requires attunement, by a dwarven clan)

It is said that the *ideal forge* was given to the dwarves by their gods. Its location is lost to time, even to the long-lived dwarves. It was first owned by Karam Ezun the Wyrmkiller around 15,000 years ago. The *ideal forge* resided in the hold of the Wyrmkiller for a thousand years, but when that kingdom fell to the forces of the Goblin Witch Rathastar, the *ideal forge* was taken deep into the mountains. Since that time, rumors have circulated that one party or another has moved it across the world.

The *ideal forge* consists of the tools and large machinery needed to run a massive forge. There are crucibles large enough to melt ingots the size of mammoths, anvils that can hold sheets of metal the size of houses, and bellows whose output is like that of a great beast risen from the deepest depths. Intricate triphammers, water and wind wheels, and other machinery allow the movement of material the size of small hills as well as the processing of incredible amounts of raw material into finished objects. These massive components are the most impressive, but the true wonder of the *ideal forge* is the plethora of normal-sized forge furniture, enough that a thousand master smiths and their helpers can work side by side without bumping into one another.

The furniture and tools are of the highest quality, and each fits the user's hand perfectly, even when passed from one user to another or from one hand to another. Everything is clean and orderly and seems to make itself clean and orderly almost on its own. The *ideal forge* almost has a mind of its own and magically repairs damaged parts over time.

A single person cannot attune to the *ideal forge*, and without attunement it is merely a very fine, and massive, forge. An entire clan of dwarves, and only dwarves, are needed to attune to the *ideal forge*. This clan cannot simply be a gathering of dwarves; they must be formerly incorporated as a clan by blood and oath.

The members of this clan must all have an open attunement slot. As a whole, all who will be attuned to the *ideal forge* (minimum 250 dwarves) must perform a 12-hour ceremony in order to complete the attunement.

Once this process is complete, the clan can work the forge to gain the following benefits:

Giant-Slaying Axe. Using the *ideal forge*, the clan can attempt to forge a *giant-slaying axe*. Only one *giant-slaying axe* can be in existence at a time. This massive undertaking requires the entire clan's work, 10 pounds of mithril, as well as 100,000 gp worth of other materials. It takes the clan 1d100 + 100 days to complete the work. At the beginning, middle, and end of this period, the head of the clan must succeed at a DC 22 Intelligence check using smith's tools (the perfected work feature of the *ideal forge* does not apply). If all three of these checks are successful, a *giant-slaying axe* is forged. If any of these checks fail, the entire project is scrapped, the materials are wasted, and the *ideal forge* is unusable for 1d20 + 10 days as it needs to be reset and re-consecrated.

The Ironshaker. Using the *ideal forge*, the clan may attempt to create an *ironshaker*. This massive undertaking requires the entire clan's work for one year to complete, as well as 1,000 pounds of mithril and other materials valued at 1,000,000 gp. At the beginning, middle, and end of this period, the head of the clan must succeed at a DC 28 Intelligence check using smith's tools (the perfected work feature of the *ideal forge* does not apply). If all three of these checks are successful, an *ironshaker* is forged. If any of these checks fail, the entire project is scrapped, the materials are wasted, and the *ideal forge* is unusable for 1d20 + 20 weeks as it needs to be reset and re-consecrated.

Panoply of the Dwarven King. Using the *ideal forge*, the clan may attempt to create the *panoply of the dwarven king*. This massive undertaking requires the entire clan's work for six months to complete, as well as 200 pounds of mithril and other materials valued at 500,000 gp. This creates one piece of the panoply. At the beginning, middle, and end of this period, the head of the clan must succeed at a DC 20 Intelligence check using smith's tools (the perfected work feature of the *ideal forge* does not apply). If all three of these checks are successful, one piece of the *dwarf king's panoply* is forged. If any of these checks fail, the entire project is scrapped, the materials are wasted, and the *ideal forge* is unusable for 1d10 + 8 weeks as it needs to be reset and re-consecrated.

Perfected Work. While working at the *ideal forge*, a dwarf who is attuned to the forge gains advantage on any skill or proficiency checks involving crafting, forging, mending, or researching metalwork, stonework, and gems. Furthermore, their projects take half the time and use half the materials normally needed.

Portal to the Home of the Dwarven Gods. Using the *ideal forge*, the clan may attempt to create a *portal to the home of the dwarven gods*. This massive undertaking requires the entire clan's work for two years to complete, as well as 2,500 pounds of mithril and other materials valued at 2,000,000 gp. At the beginning, middle, and end of this period, the head of the clan must succeed at a DC 28 Intelligence check using smith's tools (the perfected work feature of the *ideal forge* does not apply). If all three of these checks are successful, a *portal to the home of the dwarven gods* is forged. If any of these checks fail, the entire project is scrapped, the materials are wasted, and the *ideal forge* is unusable for 1d100 + 5 weeks as it needs to be reset and re-consecrated.

THE IDOL OF TINDLEHAVEN

Wondrous item, rare (requires attunement)

Farmers clearing new land outside the town of Tindlehaven found the *idol of Tindlehaven*. This small limestone figuring depicts a naked woman late in pregnancy, her head and face covered in coiled braids that resemble a beehive. The limestone is well worn and shows hints of red paint and darker red stains that can only be blood. While the *idol of Tindlehaven* is the most familiar, a dozen similar idols have been found across the world. The *idol of Tindlehaven* is in the grand ducal collection of a powerful noble and similar idols can be found in private collections and museums across the world.

The idol needs to be activated by soaking it in at least a pint of fresh blood for an hour and then burying it at moonrise in clean earth. The idol can then be unburied at the next sunrise when it gains its full powers. Once activated, the idol has three charges and regains spent charges through the same process required to activate it. As an action, the idol's charges can be spent to perform the following effects:

Increase Fertility. One charge may be spent to increase the fertility of one willing target you can see within 30 feet. The next opportunity the target has to generate offspring succeeds.

Spells. One or more charges can be spent to cast the following spells: *animal messenger* (1 charge), *conjure animals* (2 charges), *cure wounds* (1 charge), *dominate beast* (3 charges), *purify food and drink* (1 charge), *speak with animals* (1 charge), *speak with plants* (2 charges).

IMPERIAL DEATH MASKS

Wondrous item, uncommon

It was a common practice during the heights of the empire to make a mask of the recently deceased. These masks were then kept in locked cases, sometimes hung on a home altar in remembrance, and more often than not enchanted. A wide variety of these masks exist. Some are simple plaster with a few brush strokes, while others are ornate golden masks encrusted with gems. No matter if an *imperial death mask* is made for a pauper or an emperor, the magic works the same.

You can use an action to issue the mask a command and use it as the spell *speak with dead*, but only with the person from whom the mask was made. Keep in mind that the masks were made for for residents of a long collapsed empire; without knowledge of their language, little information can be gleaned from an *imperial death mask*. Each mask can be used once and regains its use following the next full moon.

When an *imperial death mask* is found, and if the subject of the mask is not known, roll on the table below to determine the subject of the mask:

IMPERIAL DEATH MASK SUBJECTS

1d12	Subject	1d12	Subject
1	Common laborer	7	Merchant
2	Legionnaire	8	Criminal
3	Noble	9	Child
4	Craftsperson	10	Centurion
5	Philosopher	11	Tribune
6	Sailor	12	Artisan

THE IRONSHAKER

Wondrous Item, unique (requires attunement, see below)

The *ironshaker*, a feared dwarven war machine of ancient eras, is a towering hundred-foot-tall golem powered by dwarven magic and controlled by a team of dwarves who ride inside. Its outer armor is composed of mithril alloy, its inner workings a complex set of gears and a frame of mithril-infused stone, and its power source an arcane engine that draws from the elemental planes of fire and earth. The *ironshaker* is capable of going toe to talon with the eldest of dragons, the mightiest of giants, and according to legends, the gods themselves.

The golem must be attuned to eight dwarves of the same clan bound by blood or oath. Each must give up an attunement slot to bond with the machine. If bonded during the process of forging an *ironshaker*, this attunement takes place during that process. If a new dwarf needs to be attuned — for example, if an attuned dwarf is lost in battle — the process requires an eight-hour ritual involving all the dwarves attuned to the *ironshaker*.

THE IRONSHAKER

Gargantuan construct, lawful good

Armor Class 22 (natural armor)
Hit Points 290 (20d20 + 80)
Speed 50 ft., burrow 30 ft.

STR	DEX	CON	INT	WIS	CHA
28 (+9)	8 (−1)	18 (+4)	1 (−5)	1 (−5)	1 (−5)

Saving Throws as own or highest of crew's
Damage Resistances acid, cold, fire, lightning, thunder
Damage Immunities poison, psychic; bludgeoning, piercing, and slashing from nonmagical attacks that aren't mithril

Condition Immunities charmed, frightened, exhaustion, paralyzed, petrified, poisoned
Senses darkvision 120 ft., tremorsense 60 ft., passive Perception as highest of crew's
Languages none
Challenge 10 (5,900 XP)

Crewed. The *ironshaker* has a crew of eight dwarves attuned to it. Each attuned dwarf may use its action to operate the *ironshaker*, either by having the *ironshaker* move or by taking one of its actions. The crew has complete cover from attacks originating from outside the *ironshaker*. However, they are spiritually linked to the *ironshaker*. On any turn where a dwarf has used its action to operate the *ironshaker*, the dwarf suffers one-tenth the damage (rounded up, minimum 1) that the *ironshaker* suffers that turn.

Immutable Form. The *ironshaker* is immune to any spell or effect that would alter its form.

Magic Resistance. The *ironshaker* has advantage on saving throws against spells and other magical effects.

Mindless. The *ironshaker* lacks a mind or will of its own. It cannot take actions on its own accord and must be given actions by its crew.

Siege Engine. The *ironshaker* deals double damage to objects and structures.

Actions

Multiattack. The creature makes one Fist attack and two Stomp attacks, or one Stomp and four Ballistae attacks.

Ballistae. *Ranged Weapon Attack:* +3 to hit, range 400/1,200 ft., one target. *Hit:* 10 (2d10 − 1) piercing damage.

Fist. *Melee Weapon Attack:* +13 to hit, reach 15 ft., one target. *Hit:* 34 (4d10 + 9) bludgeoning damage.

Stomp. *Melee Weapon Attack:* +13 to hit, reach 20 ft., up to three targets. *Hit:* 42 (6d10 + 9) bludgeoning damage.

Fire Breath (recharge 4–6). The *ironshaker* projects a 50-foot cone of fire from its powerful furnaces. Each creature in the area must make a DC 18 Dexterity saving throw, taking 55 (10d10) fire damage on a failure or half as much on a success.

The Knidian

Wondrous item, unique

The Knidian is perhaps the greatest automata created by the famed mage-sculptors. This life-sized and lifelike marble statue painted in the colors of living flesh is in the form of an attractive woman bending to prepare for her bath. Her hair is coiled neatly about her head, and she is smiling as if pleasantly surprised to see the viewer. When inanimate, the Knidian serves as an exquisite piece of sculpture of priceless value.

Once given the command word to animate, the Knidian comes to life. Her painted marble becomes living flesh, and her eyes glow briefly with blue light. While animated, she is treated as a **noble** (though unarmored with AC 11, Charisma 20, is unarmed, and speaks an ancient language instead of Common). If slain while animated, she reverts to marble and will not animate again for a year and a day.

While animated, the Knidian serves as a companion and advisor to whoever spoke the command to animate her. While she follows orders, she has a mind of her own and is neutral good; the Knidian will not act contrary to her nature. If given an order she does not wish to fulfill, the Knidian attempts to pervert the order so she can ethically follow the command, and failing that, she flat out refuses.

The Knidian was created to serve as a companion and helper to Praxiteles. While animated, she has the following abilities:

Assistance. She grants advantage on checks using artisan's tools when she assists and is proficient with all artisan's tools.

Consultation. She grants advantage on Intelligence (Arcana), Intelligence (History), and Intelligence (Nature) checks with which she assists. Additionally, she is considered proficient in these skills and can research topics or answer questions.

Lesser Spells. The Knidian can innately cast the following spells at will: *comprehend languages, detect magic, detect evil and good, locate creature, locate object, unseen servant*. The Knidian does not require spell components to cast these spells.

Greater Spells. The Knidian can innately cast the following spells once and regains use of cast spells following a long rest: *animate objects, disguise self, dispel magic, identify, sending*. She does not require spell components to cast these spells.

Knight Errant

Wondrous item, very rare

This two-foot-by-three-foot portrait depicts a knight-errant in gleaming armor from the waist up, her lance bearing a partially furled banner, the bright summer sun shining from the upper left corner. Upon speaking the command word, you may step into the painting. The knight-errant (use the stats for a **knight**) issues a challenge to you and faces off against a backdrop of a very common countryside. She offers to make three passes on horseback against you with lance, and the winner of the best two out of three passes gains a boon. If you lose, you are stuck in the painting for a fortnight, appearing in it as the knight's squire, and are petrified. Should you win, both you and the knight-errant are transported out of the painting. She arrives with her warhorse and serves you for a week and a day before returning to the painting. If she is slain while outside of the painting, her service ends and she returns to the painting.

Knot of Worldly Attachment

Wondrous item, rare (requires attunement)

This intricate knot of gold-threaded rope cannot be unraveled by mortal minds. Once attuned to the *knot of worldly attachment*, you cannot willingly move from the plane it is tied to, nor can you be forced to shift to a different plane.

Planes of Existence

1d20	Plane	1d20	Plane
1	Plane of lawful good deities	11	Ethereal Plane
2	Plane of chaotic good deities	12	Plane of neutral deities
3	Plane of neutral good deities	13	Plane of lawful evil deities
4	Plane of lawful neutral deities	14	A Prime Material Plane
5	Astral Plane	15	Plane of neutral deities
6	Elemental Plane of Air	16	Plane of chaotic evil deities
7	Elemental Plane of Earth	17	Fey Realm
8	Elemental Plane of Fire	18	Shadow Realm
9	Elemental Plane of Water	19	Demiplane
10	Plane of chaotic neutral deities	20	Roll twice, the knot of worldly attachment is tied to two planes

Kohl of Clear Sight

Wondrous item, uncommon

This small jar of alabaster has a tight-fitting lid. Inside is a black oily ointment of a type that many desert people apply around their eyes. It takes one minute to properly apply the kohl to your eyes (two if you want your eyes to be smoky). You can have only one enchanted kohl application applied to your eyes at a time, and the kohl must be applied to every eye (you cannot mix and match to gain multiple effects). Once applied, *kohl of clear sight* removes the blinded condition and prevents you from suffering the blinded condition until you take a long rest or until your face is doused with water. The jar contains 1d8 + 2 doses of *kohl of clear sight*.

Kohl of Far Sight

Wondrous item, common

This alabaster jar has a tight-fitting lid. Inside is a black oily ointment of a type that many desert people apply around their eyes. It takes one minute to properly apply the kohl to your eyes (two if you want cat eyes). You can have only one enchanted kohl application applied to your eyes at a time, and the kohl must be applied to every eye (you cannot mix and match to gain multiple effects, sorry). Once applied, *kohl of far sight* grants you the ability to see to the horizon with great details as if using a powerful telescope. This negates any penalties to ranged attacks due to distance or the size of the target. The effects last until you take a long rest or until your face is doused in water. The jar contains 1d8 + 2 doses of *kohl of far sight*.

KOHL OF NIGHT SIGHT
Wondrous item, common

Inside this plain alabaster jar is a black oily ointment of a type that many desert people apply around their eyes. It takes one minute to properly apply the kohl to your eyes. You can have only one enchanted kohl application applied to your eyes at a time, and the kohl must be applied to every eye (you cannot mix and match to gain multiple effects, sorry). Once applied, the *kohl of night sight* grants you darkvision 60 ft. or if you already have darkvision, doubles the range of your darkvision. The effects last until you take a long rest or until your face is doused in water. The jar contains 1d8 + 2 doses of *kohl of night sight*.

KOHL OF TRUE SIGHT
Wondrous item, rare

This small bronze jar is decorated with a variety of reliefs showing the ancient gods. Inside is a black oily ointment of a type that many desert people apply around their eyes. It takes one minute to properly apply the kohl to your eyes. You can have only one enchanted kohl application applied to your eyes at a time, and the kohl must be applied to every eye (you cannot mix and match to gain multiple effects). Once applied, the *kohl of true sight* grants you the effects of the *true seeing* spell for one hour or until your face is doused in water. The jar contains 1d8 + 2 doses of *kohl of true sight*.

KRATER OF ENDLESS LIBATION
Wondrous item, rare

This large, two-handled drinking cup is decorated on the outside with scenes of satyrs, nymphs, and others frolicking in a bucolic paradise. These images are in stark black upon a red background and finely detailed. Bands of red and black inside the cup can be used to easily measure the amount of liquid inside, and the very bottom of the inside of the cup has a smiling satyr's face with a beard of grapes.

Upon command, the *krater of endless libation* produces two gallons of wine of a vintage of your choice. It must be completely emptied before it can refill itself. Each time it is emptied, the eyes in the face in the bottom droop a bit and its grin becomes slack. After 10 gallons of wine are produced, the face is restful and serene, its eyes closed, and the krater will not produce any more wine. To regain its magical abilities, the krater must be refilled with one gallon of wine from an outside source that must then be consumed by a single person in one long drink (which requires a DC 13 Constitution saving throw; failure results in the drinker not being able to complete the task).

LAUREL OF THE ATHLETE
Wondrous item, rare (requires attunement)

Awarded by the emperor to the greatest athletes of the empire, the *laurel of the athlete* is a horseshoe-shaped wreath of golden leaves. Each *laurel of the athlete* was individually crafted and engraved with the name of the recipient and the emperor. Once attuned to the *laurel of the athlete*, your Charisma score increases by 2, up to a limit of 22, and as a bonus action you may cast *expeditious retreat* and *jump* spells, but only targeting yourself. Also, as an action, you may grant yourself one of the following movement types for one hour: burrow 30 feet, climb 30 feet, or swim 30 feet for one hour. You may do this once, and you regain use of this feature following a long rest.

LAUREL OF THE CONQUEROR
Wondrous item, very rare (requires attunement)

The greatest generals of the empire's legions were rewarded with a triumph through the capital. At the end of this parade, a grateful emperor awarded the general the *laurel of the conqueror*. This horseshoe-shaped wreath of golden leaves adorned with blood red rubies was individually crafted and engraved with the name of the recipient and the emperor. Once attuned to the *laurel of the athlete*, your Charisma score increases by 2, up to a limit of 22, and your armor class increases by +1. Also, as an action you may cast the *heroism* spell once per a long rest.

LAUREL OF THE HERO
Wondrous item, rare (requires attunement)

Most common of all imperial laurels, the *laurel of the hero* was granted to those who excelled in some manner in service to the empire, but not as an athlete, conqueror, or poet. Often, those awarded this laurel were common adventurers who performed mighty deeds, though scholars and engineers who managed a great intellectual feat were also rewarded. This horseshoe-shaped wreath of golden leaves adorned with sapphires was individually crafted and engraved with the name of the recipient and the emperor.

Once attuned to the *laurel of the hero*, your Charisma score increases by 2, to a limit of 22, and you may cast *unseen servant* as a ritual.

LAUREL OF THE POET
Wondrous item, rare (requires attunement)

Awarded every decade to the greatest poet in the Empire, the *laurel of the poet* is one of the more common imperial laurels. The great competition of poets was the highlight of the decade-ending celebrations held in Boros and saw competitors from across the empire and even beyond. This horseshoe-shaped wreath of golden leaves adorned with diamonds was individually crafted and engraved with the name of the recipient and the emperor.

Once attuned to the *laurel of the poet*, your Charisma score increases by 2, to a limit of 22, and you may cast the *dream* spell as a ritual.

LIBRA OF JUSTICE
Wondrous item, rare (requires attunement)

Used by the magistrates of the empire to determine guilt and innocence in difficult cases, the *libra of justice* consists of a set of golden scales likes those used to weigh goods in the marketplace and a collection of small metal tokens of equal weight. The entire set was enclosed in an ornamented wooden box with a lock that only the magistrate assigned to the *libra of justice* could unlock. Today, a *libra of justice* is usually found on its own or in association with a few tokens, and sometimes the tokens themselves are found separately. A complete set of *libra of justice* and tokens is a rare find and of inestimable value.

The metal tokens come in two types: crimes and people. The set of crimes is limited and covers only the major crimes of the empire; the creators of the *libra of justice* did not see fit to worry about minor crimes such as petty theft or vandalism. A full set of crime tokens consists of arson, blasphemy, extortion, forgery, kidnapping, larceny, murder, perjury, rape, and treason. The people tokens, meant to represent the accused, are representative of the social classes of the empire and include an artisan, farmer, laborer, legionnaire, magistrate, senator, tribune, and a generic foreigner.

The *libra of justice* is used by placing the crime token in one bowl of the scale. A small slip of paper with the accused's name is inserted into their representative token, and the token is placed in the opposite bowl. The scale then weighs the truth of the crime. If the bowl containing the crime descends, then the accused is guilty; likewise, if it ascends, this represents innocence. False results are possible if the accused is guilty of a different crime or if the accused's token is inaccurate in some way.

LOTUS SANDALS
Wondrous item, rare (requires attunement)

These simple thong sandals have soles made of green lotus leaves that are always fresh no matter the circumstances and that never wilt or age.

72 | Tome of Wondrous Items

The *lotus sandals* have three charges, and each use consumes one charge. The sandals regain spent charges each day at moonrise. As a bonus action you may speak a command word that grants you one of the following abilities for one hour: you can walk on water as if it were dry land; you can climb vertically and across horizontal surfaces; you gain a speed of climb 30; you can stand and balance on any solid object, even a single leaf; or you can stand on open air and ascend and descend as if climbing up or down stairs.

LUTE OF DANCING

Wondrous item, rare (requires attunement by a bard)

This fine lute with golden strings appears as another magical lute, such as a *lute of suggestion*, to any attempts to identify it through magical means. A successful DC 18 Intelligence (Arcana) check reveals its true nature.

Cursed. If the lute is issued a command word, its curse comes into effect. You and all creatures within 30 feet of you at the start of your turn become subject to an *irresistible dance* spell with a DC 15 spell save. You may not attempt to save against the spell. Every round you move up to your full speed in a random direction while playing the lute. You are compelled to continue playing the lute at a frenetic tempo. For every hour of playing, you suffer a level of exhaustion; when you reach five levels of exhaustion, you pass out and sleep for 10 hours. When you awaken, you may attempt a DC 15 Wisdom saving throw, and if you fail, you must begin playing the lute and continue to do so until you pass out again. If the *lute of dancing* is not in your possession next time you wake up, it teleports into your hands if it is on the same plane as you. This cycle repeats itself until you succeed on the saving throw, after which the curse is lifted and you are no longer attuned to the lute.

LUTE OF SUGGESTION

Wondrous item, rare (requires attunement by a bard)

This fine lute with golden strings can be played by those proficient with lutes to generate a *suggestion* spell up to three times. You regain all uses of this feature following a long rest. The target of the spell must save against a DC 15 spell save. The target must be able to hear you for the spell to take effect. You do not need to sing the suggestion, but you do need to speak it, and you may disguise it as part of a song. When played normally, the lute has no effect other than to produce a truly sweet tone.

LUCK BAG

Wondrous item, uncommon

This leather bag is often decorated with dyes, beads, or quills. A locking bead on the drawstring holds it tight. Six small items are inside: a ball of wood, a stone, a piece of crinoid, a chunk of quartz, a cube of copper, and a glass pyramid. These items correspond to the die sizes of a d20, a d12, a d10, a d8, a d6, and a d4. As a bonus action or a reaction, you may draw an item from the bag and add its corresponding die to any one attack roll, ability check, or saving throw you make. You must choose to draw and add the die to the roll before you know the results of the roll. Once an item is drawn from the *luck bag*, it loses its power.

LUCKY DICE

Wondrous item, very rare (requires attunement by a worshipper of the goddess of luck)

Created by the temples of the goddess of luck as a reward for those who do a great service for the church, *lucky dice* are a pair of six-sided bone dice that bear the face of the goddess in place of the six. They may be attuned only by one of the faithful of the goddess; all others find the dice to be mundane dice. Once you attune to the *lucky dice*, you may choose to roll them in order to gain the goddess's favor, though be warned that the goddess of luck and gamblers is a fickle patron. Rolling the *lucky dice* involves an hour-long ritual that looks a lot like an illicit dice game and requires at least two to five other participants, each of whom may choose to be affected by the magic of the *lucky dice*. At the end of the ritual, roll on the following table for each participant to see how they are affected.

LUCKY DICE TABLE

2d6	Effect
2	The affected participant suffers disadvantage on all rolls for the next 24 hours.
3	The affected participant has disadvantage on ability score checks for the next 24 hours.
4	Every action the affected participant prepares to make is subject to the results of an *augury* spell but the answers are always wrong. This includes every action, even mundane things such as eating and walking, for the next 24 hours.
5	The affected participant carries ill luck like a plague. They suffer disadvantage on their next roll, and after that pass the misfortune on to the next person they touch, and so forth, down to the seventh person afflicted with the ill luck.
6	The affected participant loses 2d100 gp of wealth to another participating in the ritual, and if they do not have that amount, the goddess of luck garnishes their wages and transfers the debt herself.
7	The affected participant loses 2d100 gp of wealth, and if they do not have that, they owe the difference to the temple of the goddess of luck, and she *will* collect.
8	The affected participant carries good luck like a smile. They gain advantage on their next roll, and after that pass the fortune on to the next person they touch, and so forth, down to the seventh person bestowed with the good luck.
9	Every action the affected participant prepares to make is subject to the results of an *augury* spell. This includes every action, even mundane things such as eating and walking, for the next 24 hours.
10	The affected participant gains advantage on all ability checks for the next 24 hours.
11	The affected participant gains advantage on all rolls for the next 24 hours.
12	Roll twice and combine the effects, although they might cancel each other out. If you roll this result again, the dice vanish.

MANNA BOX

Wondrous item, uncommon

This wooden box has ornate carvings of trees, crops, and livestock on its lid and sides. The lid has a simple catch made of gold-plated bronze. Despite this simple catch, the box cannot be opened without damaging it except at sunrise. You may open the box for one hour after sunrise to discover several two-inch-long white flaky pastries inside. Each pastry is filled with a fine-grained mixture that has the texture of meat, vegetables, rice, and other consumables. Different people report different tastes. Eating a single pastry provides enough sustenance to last a creature for one day, including any need for water. The *manna box* produces enough pastries to feed everyone in your household, which includes yourself, any spouses or live-in romantic partners, any children you claim as your own, adults and children who are familial relations to you who live in close proximity, servants that dwell with you, acknowledged guests, and livestock. Any pastries created by the *manna box* decay the following morning at dawn.

> In some worlds, the *manna box* is nearly indistinguishable from the *box of evils*.

MEDUSA'S HEAD
Wondrous item, very rare

Said to be the master painter Betran Ormian's final creation, *medusa's head* is a two-and-a-half-foot round painting of a very realistic medusa's severed head. The eyes are open, and the realism is such that the head looks as if it might leap off the painting and sink its fangs into the viewer. Once the command word is spoken, the head animates and gazes around as it seeks targets. The head remains animated for 10 minutes, after which it must rest on a wall for three days before being able to animate again.

While animated, any creature that starts its turn within 30 feet of the painting and who can see it must make a DC 15 Constitution saving throw. If the saving throw fails by 5 or more, the creature is instantly petrified. Otherwise, a creature that failed the save begins turning to stone and is restrained. A restrained creature must attempt another saving throw at the end of its next turn, becoming petrified if it fails or ending the effect if it succeeds. The petrified condition persists until the creature is the target of a *greater restoration* spell or similar effect.

METATE OF THE THREE SISTERS
Wondrous item, rare

This flat stone has a wide trough down its middle and is often found with a matching cylindrical stone. The trough and the cylindrical stone have pitted surfaces and carvings showing grains in the field, grains being harvested, and ancient gods of fertility and agriculture. If grain, nuts, or dried meat are placed in the trough and then ground, the amount of ground meal produced quadruples the amount of foodstuffs placed within and is purified of any contaminants. It takes five minutes to grind down one pound of foodstuff.

If you are proficient with cook's utensils, you can use the magic in the *metate of the Three Sisters* and place one pound of dried meat, one pound of grains, and one pound of nuts in the trough and spend five minutes grinding it. At the end of this time, the *metate of the Three Sisters* produces 10 cakes of pemmican. Each cake feeds one person for one day and when consumed allows the consumer to recover 1 hit die. No person can consume more than one enchanted pemmican cake in a 24-hour period. The *metate of the Three Sisters* can generate 20 enchanted pemmican cakes and regains the ability to generate more at the next sunrise.

MIRROR OF REVEALING
Wondrous item, rare

This silver hand mirror is set in a simple gold frame. Any creature or object that appears in its reflection appears as if under the effects of the spell *true seeing*. Also, any celestial, elemental, fey, or fiend who sees their own reflection in the mirror must succeed on a DC 15 Wisdom saving throw or become frightened condition and flee the mirror at their fastest speed for 1d4 minutes.

MOSAIC OF FAR STEPPING
Wondrous item, very rare

This intricate and finely detailed mosaic of glass fragments has been artfully arranged to depict the known world at the time of its creation. Locations are clearly marked in the language of the creator and their exact locations on the map are based on what the creator knew at the time they crafted the *mosaic of far stepping*. You can issue a command word, place your right foot on a location, and be teleported to that location. Alternately, you may issue a different command word and trace a route across the map with one finger. If you do so, you are teleported along that route from start to finish, moving to a new location every seven days.

The *mosaic of the far stepping* may be removed from its location. To remove the *mosaic of the far stepping* requires 100 hours of work and a successful DC 15 Intelligence (Arcana) check as well as a successful DC 15 Dexterity check using jeweler's tools. If either check fails, the *mosaic of the far stepping* is rendered inoperative until it can be properly laid. If the *mosaic of the far stepping* is partially removed, it no longer functions but can be made to function again by the same process as laying it, provided all the pieces are present.

MOSAIC OF THE BEDCHAMBER
Wondrous item, panoply (villa), very rare (requires attunement)

This delightful mosaic of red and orange glass forms an intricate geometric pattern that hints at warmth and comfort. Once you attune to it, you may use an action to issue a command word to pick it up, and each piece flies off the ground and swirls into either your hand or an open container you designate. Likewise, you may issue a command word to have the mosaic lay itself out, swirling from your hand or a container to form on the ground.

You may order the *mosaic of the bedchamber* to cover a 15-foot-by-15-foot area. The following round on your turn, four walls and a roof spring up around the mosaic. You can have up to two doors and three windows pierce the walls as they form, with each door being of stout banded oak and the windows having sturdy wooden shutters. On your next turn, the room thus made fills with a comfortable bed, a side table with a pitcher of water and a basin, a chamber pot, a fireplace and chimney, up to three pairs of soft slippers next to the bed, and three dressing gowns upon the bed. The pitcher of water refills itself every sunrise, and the chamber pot empties itself every sunset. The fireplace never runs out of wood and can be lit or extinguished at your will. The air is always comfortable and breathable inside the *mosaic of the bedchamber*.

If you are attuned to the *mosaic of the dining hall* and it has been laid, the room formed by the *mosaic of the bedchamber* opens a doorway into the room formed by the *mosaic of the dining hall*. You may issue a command, and food or drink from the *mosaic of the dining hall* floats through the doorway to your hand.

If laid down as part of a complete *panoply of the villa* attuned to the same person, the *panoply of the bedchamber* produces an additional bedchamber per room formed by the *panoply of the villa* attached to it.

MOSAIC OF THE DINING HALL
Wondrous item, panoply (villa), very rare (requires attunement)

This simple mosaic of blue and yellow glass forms a plain geometric pattern that emits the slight smell of cooked food and good wine. Once you attune to it, you may use an action to issue a command word to pick it up, with each piece flying off the ground and swirling into either your hand or an open container you designate. Likewise, you may issue a command word to have the mosaic lay itself out, swirling from your hand or a container to form on the ground.

You may order the *mosaic of the dining hall* to covers a 20-foot-by-10-foot area. The following round on your turn, four walls and a roof spring up around the mosaic. You can have up to two doors and two windows pierce the walls as they form, with each door being of stout banded oak and the windows having sturdy wooden shutters. On your next turn, the room thus made fills with a long banquet table, two comfortable chairs, two padded benches, a chandelier of candles hanging from the ceiling, and eight place settings laid out on a table fit for a lord's feast. Three times per day, you can command a feast to be laid out on the table and it appears. Each feast has enough food and drink to feed eight people. The air is always comfortable and breathable inside the *mosaic of the dining hall*.

If you are attuned to the *mosaic of the garden* and it has been laid, the room formed by the *mosaic of the dining hall* opens a doorway into the room formed by the *mosaic of the garden*. Furthermore, anyone you grant entrance to the building created by the *panoply of the villa* can command the *mosaic of the dining hall* to lay out a small snack of honey, fruit, nuts, cheese, and light wine.

If laid down as part of a complete *panoply of the villa* attuned to the same person, the *panoply of the bedchamber* produces an additional bedchamber per room from the *panoply of the villa* attached to it. The *mosaic of the dining hall* stretches by 10 feet in length, adds six more sittings, and creates enough food to feed six more people.

MOSAIC OF THE GARDEN
Wondrous item, panoply (villa), very rare (requires attunement)

This mosaic of blue and green glass forms a vining geometric pattern that emits a strong odor of honeysuckle and spice. Once you attune to it, you may use an action to issue a command word to pick it up, with each piece flying off the ground and swirling into either your hand or an open container you designate. Likewise, you may issue a command word to have the mosaic lay itself out, swirling from your hand or a container to form on the ground.

You may order the *mosaic of the garden* to cover a 20-foot-by-20-foot area. The following round on your turn, four walls spring up around the mosaic. You can have up to two doors pierce the walls as they form, with each door being of stout banded oak. On your next turn, the room thus made fills with flowering plants, a long grape vine on a trellis, small fruiting trees, a patch of vegetables, two benches, and a large fountain in the middle that constantly pours forth clean, cool water. Anyone you permit may complete a short rest in the *mosaic of the garden* in only 10 minutes, although it feels as if a full hour has passed. The air is always comfortable and breathable inside the *mosaic of the garden*.

If you are attuned to the *mosaic of the treasury* and it has been laid, that room forms beneath the garden and displaces any material there into an extradimensional pocket. One of the benches in the garden can be lifted up to reveal a trapdoor that can be spotted with a successful DC 15 Intelligence (Investigation) check and one hour of searching.

If laid down as part of a complete *panoply of the villa* attuned to the same person, the *panoply of the garden* produces a private garden off the room you choose as your bedchamber, half the size of a normal garden room but that can be accessed only by you or a person you so designate. The room formed by the *mosaic of the treasury* may be placed beneath this private garden.

MOSAIC OF THE HIDDEN CHAMBER
Wondrous item, very rare (requires attunement)

This small five-foot-by-five-foot mosaic of pale red glass forms a repeating geometric pattern that seems to draw the eye into it, and into infinity. Once attuned, you may use an action to speak the command word that activates the *mosaic of the hidden chamber*. If it is laid on the ground or on a wall, you and anyone touching you may walk through the mosaic and into an extradimensional space. Inside is a five-foot cube of open space per person, and not an inch more. The air recirculates so that it is constantly refreshed, but there is no light other than a faint reddish glow. You may remain in the extradimensional space created by the *mosaic of the hidden chamber* for as long as you like, but there is no food or water except what you bring in with you and no chamber pots. You and anyone touching you may leave at will by simply walking out.

As long as the *mosaic of the hidden chamber* is placed, the extradimensional space continues to exist. You can easily and safely store items inside, though they still suffer the passage of time.

If the *mosaic of the hidden chamber* is removed, anything within the extradimensional space is destroyed and cannot be recovered short of divine intervention. Removing the *mosaic of the hidden chamber* requires 100 hours of work and a successful DC 15 Intelligence (Arcana) check as well as a successful DC 15 Dexterity check using jeweler's tools. If either check fails, the *mosaic of the hidden chamber* is rendered inoperative until it can be properly laid. If the *mosaic of the hidden chamber* is partially removed, it no longer functions but can be made to function again by the same process as laying it, provided all the pieces are present.

MOSAIC OF THE PROTECTED ROOM
Wondrous item, very rare (requires attunement)

This octagonal mosaic of brown and orange geometric patterns with strong lines and firm designs is 10 feet long on each edge. Once attuned, you may use an action to speak a command word to cause the outer lines to form 20-foot-tall walls of opaque energy (AC 18, 200 hp, immune to poison and psychic damage) along each edge. There is no roof. You and any creature you designate may pass through the walls of the *mosaic of the protected room*. You may subdivide the interior of the protected room to create up to eight smaller triangular rooms that meet in a point at the center. You may designate any of the walls of energy that form these rooms to be permeable or closed off, and that certain creatures cannot pass through certain walls. The walls created by the *mosaic of the protected room* remain until you lower them or until they are reduced to 0 hit points. To regenerate any of the walls, the entire mosaic must be canceled and allowed to rest for one week.

To remove the *mosaic of the protected room* requires 100 hours of work and a successful DC 15 Intelligence (Arcana) check as well as a successful DC 15 Dexterity check using jeweler's tools. If either check fails, the *mosaic of the protected room* is rendered inoperative until it can be properly laid. If the *mosaic of the protected room* is partially removed, it no longer functions but can be made to function again by the same process as laying it, provided all the pieces are present.

MUKISSI

Wondrous item, rarity varies by type (requires attunement, requirements vary)

Mukissi are small wooden statues that hold bound spirits. The style of the *mukissi* serves as a clue to the type of spirit bound within it. For example, demonic *mukissi* feature horrific visages and are often carved from harder woods, while those that hold ancestral spirits show the ancestor in a benevolent figure and are carved from softer woods. Once attuned, you can activate a *mukissi* as an action.

Ancestral (uncommon). These *mukissi* hold the spirits of powerful ancestors and take the form of a bust or three-quarters statue of the ancestor. They are often painted to a high degree of detail, and those attuned to them adorn their *ancestral mukissi* with offerings the ancestor enjoyed in life. These spirits willingly allow themselves to be bound shortly after death in order to continue aiding their lineage. Only a person of the ancestor spirit's lineage may attune to the *ancestral mukissi*; all others find that the process of attunement simply does not work.

Once attuned to an *ancestral mukissi*, you can call upon the ancestor spirit's wisdom and knowledge. Each *ancestral mukissi* is tied to a specific skill, tool, or vehicle proficiency. Once activated, the ancestor spirit manifests and guides you, allowing you to add its proficiency bonus (+4) as well as your own to checks involving the linked proficiency. The ancestral spirit remains manifest for one minute and must rest inside the *mukissi* until the next sunrise before it can manifest again. You can talk with the ancestral spirit at any time, even if it is resting, which is nice. Unless you are a disappointment to your lineage, in which case it can be very annoying.

Demonic (uncommon, rare, or very rare). These hardwood statues are carved with snarling demonic faces and show the demon in full form squatting or standing on the screaming bodies of mortals. Attuning to and activating a *demonic mukissi* is a challenge as the demon has a chance of escaping during the attunement process and when it is activated. It requires a successful DC 15 Wisdom saving throw to safely attune or activate a *demonic mukissi*. Failure results in the demon escaping for 1d6 + 1 hours.

Once activated, the *demonic mukissi* allows the trapped demon out for one hour or the completion of one service, whichever is shorter. The demon is a Challenge 5 for uncommon *demonic mukissi*, Challenge 9 for rare *demonic mukissi*, and Challenge 12 for very rare *demonic mukissi*. Once the demon is activated, you can return it to the *demonic mukissi* as a bonus action. The *demonic mukissi* may be activated once, and it must be fed the blood of a number of creatures whose hit dice equal double the demon's hit dice before it can be activated again. When not in use, the *demonic mukissi* whispers horrid words in your ears to urge you to commit terrible crimes, to sell your soul to dark powers, and to take what is rightfully yours from the pain of others.

Dog (Uncommon). This softwood statue depicts a two-headed dog standing on four legs. The left head snarls at an unseen presence, while the right looks straight ahead as if in expectation of a reward. When activated, this *mukissi* acts as if it has the *true seeing* spell for one hour. It communicates to you through body language, barks, and snarls to warn you of invisible, shapechanged, and ethereal creatures, to point out hidden and secret doors, and to otherwise use the full abilities of the spell. It helps to let the *dog mukissi* sniff something you want it to investigate. The *dog mukissi* may be used once and regains its abilities after it spends a long rest snuggled next to you. When not active, the *dog mukissi* whimpers, whines, and begs for food and pets.

Earth (uncommon). These carved softwood statues depict a female figure riding a wild boar. Once attuned, you may activate the *earth mukissi* to allow the spirit to cast one of the following spells: *augury*, *prayer of healing*, *protection from poison*. The *earth mukissi* can be activated once and must be buried under the earth for 24 hours before it can be activated again. When not in use, the spirit within the *earth mukissi* seeks to counsel you with calming words, ease your emotional hurts, and urge peace and caution.

Justice (rare). This hardwood statue depicts a warrior with a raised spear bound in an intricate braid of ropes. Once activated, it releases the bound spirit of justice (**deva** or other CR 10 lawful good celestial). The spirit remains active for one hour and avenges one crime or aids in the investigation of a single crime during that time. If activated by anyone who has committed a heinous crime such as arson, kidnapping, murder, rape, or treason, the spirit attacks the activator and fights until dead. The *justice mukissi* may be activated once and can be activated again following the next sunset, for justice hunts at night. When not in use, the *justice mukissi* cautions you against committing crimes, judges your actions and the actions of those around you, and offers legal advice.

Sky (rare). This hardwood statue depicts a warrior with a pair of swords held up in the air, its pose like that of a victorious fighter on the field of slaughter screaming defiance to the heavens. When activated, the spirit bound in the *sky mukissi* enters your body and imbues you with martial might. For a number of rounds equal to your Wisdom modifier, you gain 10 temporary hit point at the start of your turn and have advantage on attack rolls. However, if you leave the fight during this time (but not if you end the fight victoriously), the spirit castigates you, you lose any temporary hit points and the bonus to attack rolls granted by the *sky mukissi*, and furthermore suffer 4d10 psychic damage at the start of each of your turns until the *sky mukissi* ceases to be active. The *sky mukissi* can be activated once and regains use after it spends 24 hours in an exalted position beneath an open sky. When not active, the *sky mukissi* counsels you to seek victory at any cost, offers sound tactical advice, and tries to encourage you with hard words and biting remarks.

> ### ORNMATHUR THE WICKED'S IRON BODY
>
> The adventuring wizard Ornmathur suffered many terrible wounds in her long career chasing gold and glory in the depths of ruins. Unwilling to accept such minor inconveniences as losing an arm to a troll or an eye to dragonfire, she crafted replacements. Choosing to forgo the vagaries of the flesh, she researched the creation of golems and forged her replacements from golem-enchanted mithril. These replacements survived her and were stolen from her tomb. They later ended up in the hands (or as the hand, as the case may be) of several infamous villains such as the vampire lord Ormand and the reaving viking Sven of the Shining Eye. It is due to misunderstandings of history that Ornmathur has been given the appellation "the Wicked," for rumor spread and became truth to many that the long-dead wizard had crafted these items for use by villains.

ORNMATHUR'S ARM

Wondrous item, panoply (Ornmathur's iron body), very rare (requires attunement)

A troll ripped off Ornmathur's arm during the great Troll March. This left arm of gleaming mithril engraved with golden arcane runes features sapphire and emerald accents. It attaches at the shoulder and includes a fair amount of shoulder as well as arm. To attune to it, you must be missing your left arm and part of your shoulder. The match must be exact or the arm will not attune and attach. A successful DC 18 Wisdom (Medicine) check and three hours of painful preparation make sure the location is ready for attachment. This might cost up to a quarter of your maximum hit points depending on how much arm and shoulder need to be removed to fit *Ornmathur's arm*. Once attached and attuned, for your left arm only your Strength score counts as 18. You may use your left arm as a magic shield, increasing your armor class by +3, but if you do so, you may not use that arm to wield a weapon or manipulate objects in the same turn it is being used as a shield. Also, you may store a single spell of no more than 3rd level within the arm. This spell remains stored in the arm until it is cast. Finally, you may attack with the arm. It counts as a magical melee weapon that inflicts 1d8 bludgeoning damage.

If worn with *Ornmathur's leg*, you gain a swim speed of 30 feet.

If worn as part of a complete *Ornmathur's iron body panoply*, you gain a burrow speed of 30 feet.

ORNMATHUR'S EYE

Wondrous item, panoply (Ornmathur's iron body), very rare

Ornmathur and her companions slew the crimson-scaled dragon Halatrhx. During the battle, her right eye was melted from her head by dragonfire. While the scars from that horrible moment were easily recovered through use of carefully crafted illusions, the eye was lost. *Ornmathur's eye* is made from a ball of solid mithril, engraved with golden arcane runes, and has a single onyx set within a band of citrine serving as the pupil and iris. The eye must be placed in a cleaned and prepared socket. A successful DC 18 Wisdom (Medicine) check and three hours of painful preparation make sure the location is ready for attachment. This might cost up to an eighth of your maximum hit points depending on if your eye needs to be removed and the socket cleaned.

Once placed and attuned, you gain darkvision 60 feet. If you look just through *Ornmathur's eye* by closing your other eye, you are immune to gaze attacks but suffer disadvantage on all ranged attacks and ranged spell attacks due to the lack of depth perception. Additionally, you may store a single spell of no more than 2nd level within the eye. This spell remains stored in the eye until it is cast. The spell originates from the eye. Finally, you may remove the eye for up to three hours without losing attunement to it. While removed, you can still see through the eye and cast a spell stored in it. On its own, the eye has AC 20 and 45 hit points.

If worn with *Ornmathur's hand*, the hand can carry the eye as a rider without affecting the functions of the hand.

If worn as part of a complete *Ornmathur's iron body panoply*, you gain blindsight 30 feet.

ORNMATHUR'S HAND

Wondrous item, panoply (Ornmathur's iron body), very rare (requires attunement)

Years after she replaced her left arm, Ornmathur's right hand was bitten clean off by a rabid owlbear. She crafted this mithril hand as a replacement. The hand is of gleaming mithril with golden runes carved into it and five sapphires serving as the nails. The hand must be placed on a cleaned and prepared stump. A successful DC 18 Wisdom (Medicine) check and three hours of painful preparation make sure the location is ready for attachment. This might cost up to a fifth of your maximum hit points depending on if your hand needs to be removed and the site cleaned. Once placed and attuned, your Dexterity score with *Ornmathur's hand* is 18. The hand has a small compartment in the wrist. Any single set of tools, no matter how large, can be placed within the compartment. You are considered proficient with the tools inside the wrist. Also, the hand can store a single 1st-level spell. This spell remains stored in the hand until it is cast. The spell originates from the hand. Finally, you may remove the hand for up to three hours without losing attunement to it. While removed, you can cast a spell stored in it. On its own, the hand has a speed of 20, AC 20 and 100 hit points.

If worn with *Ornmathur's eye*, and if the hand and eye are within 30 feet of each other, as a bonus action you can order the hand to teleport itself and the eye back to their respective locations on your body.

If worn as part of a complete *Ornmathur's iron body panoply*, the hand gains a fly speed of 30 feet.

ORNMATHUR'S LEG

Wondrous item, panoply (Ornmathur's iron body), very rare (requires attunement)

After she retired from adventuring, Ornmathur was involved in a carriage accident and lost her right leg below the knee. Undaunted, she crafted a replacement made from mithril covered with golden arcane runes. The leg must be placed on a cleaned and prepared stump. A successful DC 18 Wisdom (Medicine) check and three hours of painful preparation make sure the location is ready for attachment. This might cost up to a quarter of your maximum hit points depending on if your leg needs to be removed and the stump cleaned. Once placed and attuned, your speed increases by 20 feet and you can jump using *Ornmathur's leg* as if affected by the *jump* spell.

If worn with *Ornmathur's arm*, your Strength score increases by +2 to a maximum of 20.

If worn as part of a complete *Ornmathur's iron body panoply*, you gain a fly speed of 30 feet.

OSTRAKA OF CURSING

Wondrous item, uncommon

Possibly the most commonly found imperial enchanted item, *ostrakas of cursing* are small broken pottery fragments that bear little hint of their true power. Each is found with 1d6 names written on them in an ancient tongue, although each name is crossed out with a strong quill stroke. The opposite side of the fragment shows part of a red painted vessel with black figures picked out in exquisite detail. It is thought that an *ostraka of cursing* can be made only from the finest ceramics that are then broken to produce multiple fragments.

You must write the name of a living creature on the back of the fragment in the same ancient tongue. Each fragment can hold eight names. After the eighth name is written, the fragment crumbles to dust. The target's proper name must be written; using a nickname, nom de plume, or other name simply uses up one of the eight uses of the *ostraka of cursing*. The target suffers from the *bestow curse* spell until the curse is dispelled or until the *ostraka of cursing* is destroyed.

NECKLACE OF MISSILES

Wondrous item, conjunction (air), rare

The project that started Talvan on his studies of esoteric conjunction, a *necklace of missiles* is a finely wrought golden necklace with a dozen silver charms in the shape of various missile weapons. Talvan tried in vain to create a *necklace of missiles* that lacked conjunction with air, but he always failed. Many of these failures were tossed aside, destroyed, or carelessly given away.

As an action, you may remove a charm from the necklace and throw it at a foe. The damage and range is based on the type of charm, and you add your Intelligence modifier to attack and damage rolls instead of Strength or Dexterity. When the last charm is pulled, the *necklace of missiles* crumbles to platinum dust worth 500 gp. When discovered, a *necklace of missiles* has 1d12 charms. Roll on the table below to determine the nature of each charm:

1d12	Missile
1	Shortbow arrow
2	Light crossbow bolt
3	Sling stone
4	Spear
5	Dagger
6	Dart
7	Handaxe
8	Javelin
9	Longbow arrow
10	Blowgun dart (poisoned, target must succeed on a DC 15 Constitution saving throw or suffer an additional 2d6 poison damage)
11	Trident
12	Heavy crossbow bolt

OXHIDE INGOT

Wondrous item, rare

This cast ingot of copper or tin is shaped like a stretched oxhide with handles at the four corners. It weighs about 45 pounds and is inscribed with arcane sigils. If placed in a melting pan or similar vessel and exposed to enough heat to melt the metal, you can draw out up to 60 arrowheads, 30 spearheads, or 15 axe heads from the *oxhide ingot*. The weapon heads drawn from the *oxhide ingot* count as magical weapons. Only one type of weapon head can be drawn at a time. The material drawn out of the molten metal does not reduce the metal in any way. After drawing out the weapon heads from the *oxhide ingot*, the ingot must be allowed to cool and return to its original shape before it can be used again, a process that takes 12 hours.

PATENT OF ENNOBLEMENT

Wondrous item, uncommon (requires attunement)

This thick piece of papyrus features rich decorations and fine calligraphy. Once attuned, you choose a language for the writing to appear in as well as a style that would be acceptable to a specific government, as well as a name of the bearer of the document. The blank patent of nobility changes to match these parameters and is indistinguishable from a true patent of nobility save through magical means.

CHAPTER ELEVEN: WONDROUS ITEMS | 77

PAPER LANTERN OF CONFLAGRATION
Wondrous item, uncommon (cursed)

This paper lantern is decorated with scenes of nature. It appears, even under an *identify* or similar spell, to be a different magical paper lantern. When lit, it rises 200 feet into the air, shedding bright light in a 20-foot radius and dim light for another 20 feet beyond that.

Curse. The *paper lantern of conflagration* is cursed. Anyone who holds it feels compelled to light it at the next possible moment when they are outside in clear weather. You must succeed at a DC 15 Wisdom saving throw or light the lantern. Once lit, the lantern rises as above but then begins to drift 1d4 miles in a random direction, moving at a rate of 10 mph. Once it drifts this distance, it descends and explodes into a ball of flame that fills a 50-foot cube. The lantern is destroyed in the process. All creatures caught in this area of effect must succeed at a DC 15 Dexterity saving throw or suffer 36 (8d8) fire damage, or half that damage on a successful save. Furthermore, any flammable objects within the area of effect catch on fire. The fires created by the *paper lantern of conflagration* are intense and cannot be put out without expending twice as much time and resources. The fires spread rapidly, covering a one-square-mile area in one hour, and increase this spread per hour exponentially. The fires burn until put out naturally or if it runs out of fuel.

PAPER LANTERN OF THE COURIER
Wondrous item, uncommon

This paper lantern is decorated with scenes of nature. Before you light the lantern, you must write the name of a specific creature or location on a slip of paper and place it within the lantern as well as a message of no more than 25 words. Once lit, the *lantern of the courier* rises 200 feet into the air, shedding bright light in a 20-foot radius and dim light for another 20 feet beyond that. The lantern can be seen from up to five miles away. It drifts toward the named creature or location and continues to drift toward the target at a rate of 10 mph until it is floating above it. If the target moves, the lantern moves as well. Once above the target, the *lantern of the courier* descends toward the target and settles to the ground within 10 feet of them. It then burns out and displays the message in bright flaming letters. The *lantern of the courier* remains lit for 24 hours and then goes out, falling to the ground where it can be recovered if found. It must be allowed to cool for one hour before being relit.

PAPER LANTERN OF SEEKING
Wondrous item, uncommon

This paper lantern is decorated with scenes of nature. Before you light the lantern, you must write the name of a specific creature or its location on a slip of paper and place it within the lantern. Once lit, the *lantern of seeking* rises 200 feet into the air, shedding bright light in a 20-foot radius and dim light for another 20 feet beyond that. The lantern can be seen from up to five miles away. It drifts toward the named creature or location and continues to drift toward the target at a rate of 10 mph until it is floating above it. If the target moves, the lantern moves as well. The *lantern of seeking* remains lit for 24 hours and then goes out, falling to the ground where it can be recovered if found. It must be allowed to cool for one hour before being relit.

PAPER LANTERN OF THE STORM
Wondrous item, uncommon

This paper lantern is decorated with the image of ship just offshore fighting against a mighty storm. Once lit, this lantern rises into the air, ascending to a height of 12,000 feet and shedding bright light in a 20-foot radius and dim light for another 20 feet beyond that. The lantern can be seen from up to five miles away. It rises at a rate of 1,000 feet per round. Once at maximum height, the lantern explodes into a massive thundercloud that drops six inches of rain an hour for the next 1d6 hours before dissipating. Thunder and lightning are constant, and winds reach 40 mph. The lantern is destroyed in the process.

PAPER LANTERN OF TRANSFORMATION
Wondrous item, varies

This paper lantern is decorated with images of a type of flying creature. Once lit, this lantern rises rapidly into the air, ascending to a height of 4,000 feet and shedding bright light in a 20-foot radius and dim light for another 20 feet beyond that. The lantern can be seen from up to five miles away. It rises at a rate of 1,000 feet per round. Once at its maximum height, the lantern transforms into a type of flying creatures (see table below). This creature is under your command, and you can issue it mental orders as a bonus action. It remains under your command for one hour and then gains freewill.

PAPER LANTERN OF TRANSFORMATION CREATURES

Creature	Rarity
Manticore	Common
Chimera	Uncommon
Wyvern	Rare
Roc	Very Rare

PAPER LANTERN OF WIND JOURNEYS
Wondrous item, rare

This paper lantern is decorated with natural scenes. Before lighting this lantern, you and up to six others may grasp the base of the lantern. Once lit, this lantern rises rapidly into the air, ascending to a height of 4,000 feet and shedding bright light in a 20-foot radius and dim light for another 20 feet beyond that. The lantern can be seen from up to five miles away. It rises at a rate of 1,000 feet per round and drifts in a direction of your choosing at a rate of 5 mph. The lantern remains lit for 24 hours and then slowly descends to land safely. It must be allowed to cool for one hour before being relit. While the lantern's magic makes it easy to hold onto, it does not protect travelers from environmental effects or attacks.

PAPER LANTERN OF TRUE LOVE
Wondrous item, uncommon

This paper lantern is decorated with scenes of nature. Before you light the lantern, you must write the name of a specific creature on a slip of paper and place it within the lantern. Once lit, the *lantern of seeking* rises 200 feet into the air and sheds bright light in a 20-foot radius and dim light for another 20 feet beyond that. The lantern can be seen from up to five miles away. It drifts toward the named creature's true love at a rate of 10 mph until it is floating above them. If the target moves, the lantern moves as well. The *lantern of true love* remains lit for 24 hours and then goes out, falling to the ground where it can be recovered if found. It must be allowed to cool for one hour before being relit.

PARASOL OF NINETY-NINE DEMONS
Wondrous item, uncommon

This oiled paper parasol is decorated with vibrantly colored images of oni, demons, and other creatures, their fearsome faces snarling toward the top of the parasol. As an action, you may grasp the handle of the parasol and work the mechanism to fold and unfold it. When you do so, any aberration, celestial, elemental, fey, or fiend within a 30-foot cone originating from the *parasol of ninety-nine demons* must succeed at a DC 15 Wisdom saving throw or become frightened of you for one minute. The affected creature may attempt the saving throw again at the start of its turn, canceling the effect on itself if it succeeds. As long as you continue to use an action to keep flapping the parasol open and closed, any creature frightened of you is forced to use its reaction to maintain the same distance from you it had at the start of your turn. This forced movement can place a frightened creature into a harmful or dangerous position.

PARASOL OF FLIGHT
Wondrous item, uncommon

The oiled paper of this parasol is painted in vivid colors depicting floral arrangements and flying birds. When you grasp the lacquered handle and use an action to utter a command word, you gain a flying speed of 60 feet, but only for as long as you hold onto the handle. While flying, the *parasol of flight* remains orientated roughly horizontally to the ground, though it may tilt slightly one way or the other.

PARASOL OF THE WATER STRIDER
Wondrous item, uncommon

The oiled paper of this parasol is painted in a detailed depiction of the common water strider on a calm pool with a lily pad nearby. When you grasp the lacquered handle and use an action to utter a command word, you may walk across water as if it were dry land. No part of your body may be submerged while you speak the command word. If you let go of the *parasol of the water strider* or fold it, the effect ends and you sink as normal.

PIPA OF WEATHER CONTROL
Wondrous item, rare

This four-stringed plucked lute is undecorated, allowing its varnish to pick out the intricate details of the wood grain and simple elegance of the clean lines of the instrument's body. When played, the *pipa of weather control* can drastically alter the weather patterns over a large area, for good or ill. However, the instrument's magic is not easily accessed. Anyone can sit and pluck the strings to create a minor weather effect, but a skilled player can generate a specific weather effect of greater power and duration. If you want to create a specific weather effect, you must make a Charisma check modified by your proficiency bonus if you are proficient with stringed instruments, and it takes one hour to play the tune to control the weather. The DC is determined by the effect you want to generate. The Charisma check must be made every hour of play, and if you stop playing, the weather effect dissipates within two hours per hour spent playing the *pipa of weather control*.

PIPA OF WEATHER CONTROL EFFECTS

DC	Effect
0	A minor effect occurs. These could include a swirl of wind, a brief break in cloud cover, a 1º Fahrenheit temperature change over a 100-foot area, or an increase in cloud cover to shade a 100-foot area. The effect dissipates 10 minutes after being created.
10	Dense fogs and misty rains limit visibility over a 10-square-mile area, or sunlight dries a fog or misty rain over a 10-square-mile area.
13	Light rain falls over a 10-square-mile area, or sunlight dries up standing water up to one foot deep (but not natural bodies of water) over a 10-square-mile area; it might instead drop one inch of snow over a 10-square-mile area.
15	Moderate rain over a 10-square-mile area that causes shallow (one foot or less) bodies of water and ditches to fill; sunlight dries standing water up to three feet deep (but not natural bodies of water) over a 10-square-mile area; a 5º Fahrenheit temperature change; or drop six inches of snow over a 10-square-mile area.
18	Heavy rains over a 10-square-mile area that cause widespread flooding; sunlight dries standing and running water up to three feet deep over a 10-square-mile area; a 10º Fahrenheit temperature change; one foot of snow drops over a 10-square-mile area.
20	Driving rains over a 10-square-mile area that cause devastating flooding; sunlight dries standing and running water up to six feet deep over a 10-square-mile area; a 15º Fahrenheit temperature change; drops two feet of snow over a 10-square-mile area.
23	Massive thunderstorm that creates winds in excess of 85 mph and drops enough rain to flood a 10-square-mile area per hour; baking heat that raises the temperature by 20º Fahrenheit; a blizzard that drops four feet of snow over a 10-square-mile area per hour and lowers temperature by 20 ºFahrenheit.
25	Make any of the changes above, but now those changes last for 2d6 days.

PIPES OF FLAME
Wondrous item, rare

These pan pipes are dyed deep red and have abstract flames carved into them that have been painted in black. You can use an action to play the pipes, causing them to shoot out a 15-foot cone of fire. All creatures caught in the cone must make a Dexterity saving throw with a DC equal to the Charisma (Performance) check made by you. Creatures that fail suffer 6d6 fire damage, while those that succeed take half this damage. You may use the *pipes of fire* to create a cone of flame once and regain use after playing the pipes peacefully for one hour.

PLOW OF REAPING
Wondrous item, uncommon

This plain simple iron plow never rusts or tarnishes. If hooked to a team of oxen or other draft animals (or pulled behind creatures with a combined Strength score of 18), the *plow of reaping* can plow up to a hide of land in eight hours, sowing that land behind it if you provide it with at least one seed of grain. The next morning, the field has been reaped and the grain is neatly stacked. The *plow of reaping* can till, sow, and reap a crop from nearly any soil and does not require water or even fertility to be a factor. However, no hide of land can be subject to the effects of a *plow of reaping* more than once per year.

POMEGRANATE SEED OF KNOWLEDGE
Wondrous item, conjunction (azoth), rare

This enchanted pomegranate seed is from a larger fruit created millennia ago. Rarely is more than a single seed found at a time, and even then it is unheard of for more than two seeds to be found in the same location. Despite being an organic item, the seeds do not rot or decay, indeed they are not even digested. Once consumed, the *pomegranate seed of knowledge* grants you advantage on all Intelligence and Wisdom ability checks, skill checks, and saving throws until you take a long rest. Once consumed, you cannot consume another *pomegranate seed of knowledge* until the next lunar month. However, the power of the seeds never fades and a single *pomegranate seed of knowledge* can be recovered and consumed again and again. Scholars believe that only one enchanted pomegranate was ever made and that all the seeds found today are from that one fruit, and that the seeds have passed through countless users over the years.

PORTAL TO THE HOME OF THE DWARVEN GODS
Wondrous item, unique

This 50-foot-diameter arch of mithril alloy is engraved with dwarvish runes of power. When created using the *ideal forge*, a mithril key is made to unlock or lock the *portal to the home of the dwarven gods*. This key is usually entrusted to the head of the clan or if part of a larger dwarf hold with a monarch, the ruling monarch. Without the key, the *portal to the home of the dwarven gods* is just a very expensive paperweight.

Using the key, the *portal to the home of the dwarven gods* can be connected to any elemental plane or the plane of a dwarven deity. The resulting portal is two-way and remains in place for one hour. Turning the key can close the portal at any time. If more than one *portal to the home of the dwarven gods* is in existence on a plane, the portal can be opened between the two portals.

POWDERED INSTANT DEATH WATCH BEETLE
Wondrous item, uncommon

This loose, gritty, greenish-black powder is the remains of a death watch beetle transformed by magic into a powdered form. The powder can be blown in the face of a creature within five feet of you as a melee attack. If you hit, the target suffers 6d6 thunder damage and must succeed at a DC 15 Constitution saving throw or be deafened condition until the end of their next turn.

Instead of using the *powdered instant death watch beetle* as a weapon, you can apply one gallon of water to the powder. If you do so, at the start of your next turn, the powder grows into a full-sized **death watch beetle** (see **Appendix A: New Monsters**) that obeys your commands for one hour, after which it gains free will.

Finally, you may use an action to snort the powder. If you do so, you may spend an action to disguise yourself in natural surroundings, gaining advantage on Stealth (Dexterity) checks for one hour. However, you must immediately upon snorting the *powdered instant death watch beetle* succeed at a DC 15 Constitution saving throw or be poisoned for one hour.

Any of these uses consumes the *powdered instant death watch beetle*.

POWDERED INSTANT GELATINOUS CUBE
Wondrous item, uncommon

This loose, gritty, yellowish-gray powder is the remains of a gelatinous cube transformed by magic into a powdered form. The powder can be blown in the face of a creature within five feet of you as a melee attack, and if you hit, the target suffers 6d6 force damage and must succeed at a DC 15 Constitution saving throw or be stunned until the end of their next turn.

Instead of using the *powdered instant gelatinous cube* as a weapon, you can apply one gallon of water to the powder. If you do so, at the start of your next turn, the powder grows into a full-sized **gelatinous cube** that obeys your commands for one hour, after which it gains free will.

Finally, you may use an action to snort the powder. If you do so, you become invisible for the next 1d6 × 10 minutes. However, you must immediately upon snorting the *powdered instant gelatinous cube* succeed at a DC 15 Constitution saving throw or be poisoned for one hour.

Any of these uses consumes the *powdered instant gelatinous cube*.

POWDERED INSTANT GORGON
Wondrous item, uncommon

This fine gray powder is the remains of a gorgon transformed by magic into a powdered form. The powder can be blown in the face of a creature within five feet of you as a melee attack, and if you hit, the target suffers 6d6 thunder damage and must succeed at a DC 15 Constitution saving throw or be petrified until the end of their next turn.

Instead of using the *powdered instant gorgon* as a weapon, you can apply one gallon of water to the powder. If you do so, at the start of your next turn, the powder grows into a full-sized **gorgon** that obeys your commands for one hour, after which it gains free will.

Finally, you may use an action to snort the powder. If you do so, your armor class increases by +2 for the next 1d6 × 10 minutes. However, you must immediately upon snorting the *powdered instant gorgon* succeed at a DC 15 Constitution saving throw or be poisoned for one hour.

Any of these uses consumes the *powdered instant gorgon*.

POWDERED INSTANT OOZE
Wondrous item, uncommon

This loose, gritty, brownish powder is the remains of an ooze transformed by magic into a powdered form. The powder can be blown in the face of a creature within five feet of you as a melee attack, and if you hit, the target suffers 6d6 lightning damage and must succeed at a DC 15 Constitution saving throw or gain a level of exhaustion.

Instead of using the *powdered instant ooze* as a weapon, you can apply one gallon of water to the powder. If you do so, at the start of your next turn, the powder grows into a full-sized **black pudding** that obeys your commands for one hour, after which it gains free will.

Finally, you may use an action to snort the powder. If you do so, you may bend and compress your body to fit through a Tiny or larger opening for the next 1d6 × 10 minutes. However, you must immediately upon snorting the *powdered instant ooze* succeed at a DC 15 Constitution saving throw or be poisoned for one hour.

Any of these uses consumes the powdered instant ooze.

POWDERED INSTANT SALAMANDER
Wondrous item, uncommon

This loose, gritty, yellowish-red powder is the remains of a salamander transformed by magic into a powdered form. The powder can be blown in the face of a creature within five feet of you as a melee attack, and if you hit, the target suffers 6d6 fire damage and must succeed at a DC 15 Dexterity saving throw or be set on fire, suffering an additional 1d6 fire damage at the start of their turn until the flames are extinguished (an action can be used to put out the fire).

Instead of using the *powdered instant salamander* as a weapon, you can set the powder on fire. If you do so, at the start of your next turn, the powder grows into a full-sized **salamander** that obeys your commands for one hour, after which it gains free will.

Finally, you may use an action to snort the powder. If you do so, you gain immunity to fire damage for the next 1d6 × 10 minutes. However, you must immediately upon snorting the *powdered instant salamander* succeed at a DC 15 Constitution saving throw or be poisoned for one hour.

Any of these uses consumes the *powdered instant salamander*.

POWDERED INSTANT SPELL PARROT
Wondrous item, uncommon

This loose, gritty, bright reddish-blue powder is the remains of a spell parrot transformed by magic into a powdered form. The powder can be blown in the face of a creature within five feet of you as a melee attack, and if you hit, the target suffers 6d6 psychic damage and must succeed at a DC 15 Constitution saving throw or be deafened until the end of their next turn.

Instead of using the *powdered instant spell parrot* as a weapon, you can apply one gallon of water to the powder. If you do so, at the start of your next turn, the powder grows into a full-sized **spell parrot** (see **Appendix A: New Monsters**) that obeys your commands for one hour, after which it gains free will.

Finally, you may use an action to snort the powder. If you do so, you may cast one 2nd-level Wizard spell of your choice, using Intelligence as your spellcasting ability score. However, you must immediately upon snorting the *powdered instant spell parrot* succeed at a DC 15 Constitution saving throw or be poisoned for one hour.

Any of these uses consumes the **powdered instant spell parrot**.

> Just add water!

POWDERED INSTANT TROLL
Wondrous item, uncommon

This loose, gritty, green-gray powder is the remains of a troll transformed by magic into a powdered form. The powder can be blown in the face of a creature within five feet of you as a melee attack, and if you hit, the target suffers 6d6 poison damage and must succeed at a DC 15 Constitution saving throw or be poisoned for one hour.

Instead of using the *powdered instant troll* as a weapon, you can apply one gallon of water to the powder. If you do so, at the start of your next turn, the powder grows into a full-sized **troll** that obeys your commands for one hour, after which it gains free will.

Finally, you may use an action to snort the powder. If you do so, you recover 5 hit points at the start of your turn for the next 1d6 × 10 minutes. However, you must immediately upon snorting the *powdered instant troll* succeed at a DC 15 Constitution saving throw or be poisoned for one hour.

Any of these uses consumes the **powdered instant troll**.

POWDERED INSTANT UNICORN
Wondrous item, uncommon

This loose, gritty, sparkling rainbow powder is the remains of a unicorn transformed by magic into a powdered form. The powder can be blown in the face of a creature within five feet of you as a melee attack, and if you hit, the target suffers 6d6 radiant damage and must succeed at a DC 15 Constitution saving throw or be blinded until the end of their next turn.

Instead of using the *powdered instant unicorn* as a weapon, you can apply one gallon of water to the powder. If you do so, at the start of your next turn, the powder grows into a full-sized **unicorn** that obeys your commands for one hour, after which it gains free will.

Finally, you may use an action to snort the powder. If you do so, you may once, as an action, touch another living creature and heal 2d8 hit points of damage. However, you must immediately upon snorting the *powdered instant unicorn* succeed at a DC 15 Constitution saving throw or be poisoned for one hour.

Any of these uses consumes the *powdered instant unicorn*.

POWDERED INSTANT WINTER WOLF
Wondrous item, uncommon

This loose, gritty, bluish-white powder is the remains of a winter wolf transformed by magic into a powdered form. The powder can be blown in the face of a creature within five feet of you as a melee attack, and if you hit, the target suffers 6d6 cold damage and must succeed at a DC 15 Constitution saving throw or be paralyzed until the end of their next turn. Instead of using the *powdered instant winter wolf* as a weapon, you can apply one gallon of water to the powder. If you do so, at the start of your next turn, the powder grows into a full-sized **winter wolf** that obeys your commands for one hour, after which it gains free will.

Finally, you may use an action to snort the powder. If you do so, you become immune to cold damage for the next 1d6 × 10 minutes. However, you must immediately upon snorting the *powdered instant winter wolf* succeed at a DC 15 Constitution saving throw or be poisoned for one hour. Any of these uses consumes the *powdered instant winter wolf*.

POWDERED INSTANT WRAITH
Wondrous item, uncommon

This loose, gritty, black powder is the remains of a wraith transformed by magic into a powdered form. The powder can be blown in the face of a creature within five feet of you as a melee attack, and if you hit, the target suffers 6d6 necrotic damage and must succeed at a DC 15 Constitution saving throw or be frightened until the end of their next turn. Instead of using the *powdered instant wraith* as a weapon, you can apply one gallon of water to the powder. If you do so, at the start of your next turn, the powder grows into a full-sized **wraith** that obeys your commands for one hour, after which it gains free will.

Finally, you may use an action to snort the powder. If you do so, you can move through other creatures and objects as if they were difficult terrain. You take 10 force damage if you end your turn inside an object. This effect lasts for 1d6 rounds. However, you must immediately upon snorting the *powdered instant wraith* succeed at a DC 15 Constitution saving throw or be poisoned for one hour. Any of these uses consumes the *powdered instant wraith*.

POWDERED INSTANT XORN
Wondrous item, uncommon

This loose, gritty, gray and red mottled powder is the remains of a xorn transformed by magic into a powdered form. The powder can be blown in the face of a creature within five feet of you as a melee attack, and if you hit, the target suffers 6d6 acid damage and must succeed at a DC 15 Constitution saving throw or be petrified until the end of their next turn. Instead of using the *powdered instant xorn* as a weapon, you can apply one gallon of water to the powder. If you do so, at the start of your next turn, the powder grows into a full-sized **xorn** that obeys your commands for one hour, after which it gains free will.

Finally, you may use an action to snort the powder. If you do so, you can burrow through nonmagical, unworked earth and stone for the next 1d6 rounds at your normal movement rate. While doing so, you do not disturb the material you move through. If you lose the ability while within stone, you die. If you are within earth, you are merely buried alive. Immediately upon snorting the *powdered instant xorn* succeed at a DC 15 Constitution saving throw or be poisoned for one hour. Any of these uses consumes the *powdered instant xorn*.

PRAXITELES' BIRDS
Wondrous item, conjunction (air), rare (requires attunement)

The Praxiteles' studio made hundreds, perhaps thousands, of these ornate bird-shaped devices. Each is a finely crafted bird carved from ivory and decorated with gold-leaf feathers and gemstone eyes. Other details are picked out in precious metals and semiprecious stones. The effect is rather lifelike despite the sparkling metal and glinting stones. This appearance of a living metal bird is only enhanced when *Praxiteles' bird* is activated.

While attuned to the *Praxiteles' bird*, you can use an action to issue a command word, bringing the bird to life. Each type of *Praxiteles' bird* can fly, attack, scout out an area and report back, and do anything a living bird can do. As a bonus action on your turn, you can issue it a command or a complex series of commands, as long as it can hear you. Keep in mind that it has the mentality of a highly trained bird. Once activated, *Praxiteles' bird* remains active for eight hours and then returns to its statue form to rest for another eight hours, recovering any lost hit points during this time. If slain while active, *Praxiteles' bird* ceases to function for seven days. If it suffers enough damage for *Praxiteles' bird's* body to be completely destroyed, such as being dumped into a pit of lava, it does not reactivate.

These are the most common types of *Praxiteles' birds*, though others might be found:

CHAPTER ELEVEN: WONDROUS ITEMS | 81

Anser. This golden goose can be set to guard a person or a 30-foot cubic. Once ordered to go on guard, it circles the target and actively looks for danger. If anything the goose thinks is threatening is spotted, the *anser* begins honking loudly and running about flapping its wings. Use the stats for an **eagle** (but with AC 15 [natural armor], 3d6 hp, and no talon attack).

Aquila. Sculpted to look like a mighty bird of prey, the *aquila* is best used to scout areas or to hunt small game. If so ordered, it flies off in search of prey and brings back a rabbit, squirrel, or other small prey within 1d4 × 10 minutes, assuming any can be found in the area. It can also be sent to scout an area using its incredible vision and flight to map a one-square-mile area per hour, returning when done to scratch a rough map in the dirt or if given access to a quill and ink, on a piece of parchment. Use the stats for an **eagle** (with AC 15 [natural armor] and 3d6 hit points).

Nocturna. While it can hunt, the nocturna is built as a companion more than a tool. It can be ordered to perform a variety of tricks such as fetching items or comically flapping about. If so ordered, it flies off in search of prey and brings back a rabbit, squirrel, or other small prey within 1d4 × 10 minutes, assuming any can be found in the area. It can also be commanded to offer its insights on a single question, as per the *augury* spell, once per activation. Use the stats for an **eagle** (with AC 15 [natural armor] and 3d6 hit points).

Oscen. These small songbirds are thought to have been the toys of the children of elite imperial officials. When activated, they settle on a shoulder or circle the head, sometimes lighting on an outstretched finger. The *oscen* knows hundreds of songs that it can whistle, providing its own harmony. These magical bird statues are trained to enhance the social graces and any entertainments you might pursue, and grant advantage on Charisma (Performance or Persuasion) checks that they assist in. Use the stats for a **bat** (with AC 13 [natural armor], and 3d4–3 hit [points]).

Struthio. The biggest of the *Praxiteles'* birds, the struthio are large clockwork mounts that bear a striking resemblance to ostriches. They can be ordered to carry a mount, attack a foe, or just follow along as a pack animal. Use the stats for an **axe beak** (with AC 15 [natural armor], 6d10 + 3 hit points, and replace the beak attack with a kick that does the same damage).

PUTTO
Wondrous item, rare (requires attunement)

Although attributed to Praxiteles, the *putti* (singular *putto*) date to a time after the master's death. The confusion is no doubt due to the many unknown magical sculptors who created the *putti* being either former students (or students of students and so forth) of Praxiteles or who used techniques he had founded. In either case, *putti* show the clear marks of the master, being sculptures that animate and serve a useful function, but are inherently works of art.

A *putto* is an animated statue of a small cherubic figure, sometimes with a fantastical head such as that of a falcon, goat, or lion, that sports a pair of angelic feathered wings. Many are sculpted with clothing that also animates and trails behind them. They are intelligent and often have strong personalities. Human-headed *putti* are playful and childlike, falcon-headed ones are focused and cynical, goat-headed *putti* are ponderous and grim, and the lion-headed *putti* are arrogant and predatory.

Once you have attuned to a *putto*, it animates and the marble of its body becomes flesh and bone. Treat as an **eagle** with Intelligence 14 and Charisma 18. If reduced to 0 hit points, the *putto* reverts to stone and cannot be reanimated for 1d4 days. Each *putto* is created with proficiency in one skill or tool. When found, roll on the table below to determine the *putto's* talents. Unless taught another language, *putti* speak their native tongue.

PUTTI TALENTS

1d12	Proficiency
1	Acrobatics
2	Animal Handling
3	Arcana
4	Investigation
5	Medicine
6	Nature
7	Performance
8	Religion
9	Sleight of Hand
10	One set of artisan's tools
11	A single musical instrument
12	Roll twice, rerolling further results of a 12

QUERN OF GRINDING
Wondrous item, rare

This hand-cranked set of grinding stones can be used to produce prodigious amounts of flour. For every bushel of grain ground, 120 pounds of flour are produced. A single *quern of grinding* can change the economy of an entire region, save a town from famine, or make a person incredibly rich. When one is found, wars have been fought, treasures spent, and blood spilled.

RAKE OF MEDITATION
Wondrous item, uncommon

This long-handled, three-tined rake is made of plain wood. The tines are wide and perfectly parallel. You can spend 10 minutes raking sand, loose soil, or even leaves with the rake. If you are not interrupted, at the end of this time you gain the benefits of a short rest. You may use the *rake of mediation* once, and regain use of it after you complete a normal short rest.

RANGER'S BERET
Wondrous item, rare (requires attunement)

This blue and orange plaid beret has a golden pompom, a side feather of purple-dyed ostrich, and a badge on the front of silver thread depicting a centaur firing a bow. No matter how you sit the hat on your head, it always slopes slightly to one side at a rakish angle. Once attuned, you may use an action to cast the following spells: *druidcraft* (at will), *longstrider* (once per short rest), *pass without trace* (once per long rest), and *speak with animals* (once per short rest).

RAT WHISKER SLIPPERS
Wondrous item, rare

These plain slippers are lined with gray fur inside and out. They have tiny whiskers coming off the toe and buttons that look a bit like eyes. While wearing the *rat whisker slippers*, you may become a mouse for one hour as per the spell *polymorph*. Each slipper can be used once to become a mouse and you regain its use at the next sunset.

You can use both slippers to become two mice. Your consciousness is divided between the pair, which must remain within 30 feet of each other. You hear, see, smell, taste, and touch through both mice and move your two bodies on your turn, taking a full set of actions with each. However, when you do this, the *rat whisker slippers* cannot be used again for one week. If one of the mice bodies is destroyed, it reverts to a slipper and you suffer 15 psychic damage.

RETIARUS'S GIRDLE
Wondrous item, panoply (retiarus) very rare (requires attunement)

While most of the gladiatorial fights that entertained the empire did not involve enchanted weaponry, there was a taste toward the later years for magically enhanced combats. These fights took place only on the most auspicious of days, such as the coronation of an emperor, and even then only if true champions of the arena were available to don these enchanted sets of arms and armor. A *retiarus's girdle* is a wide metal belt, heavily ornamented in gold and engravings, with an attached loincloth of pure white cloth edges in maroon. Once you have attuned to a retiarus's girdle, you gain a +2 bonus to your armor class. Also, you can breathe air and water and gain a swim speed of 30 feet.

If worn with a *retiarus's trident*, you gain resistance to cold damage. Also, you gain proficiency with the Performance skill, and if you already have proficiency with that skill, you may add your proficiency bonus twice to all checks involving it.

If worn as part of a complete set of *panoply of retiarus*, as a bonus action you can cast *conjure animals*; however, the animals conjured must be aquatic in nature. You may do this once and regain use of this feature after the girdle has soaked in seawater for 24 hours.

RIVER BOATMAN
Wondrous item, very rare

This three-foot-by-four-foot portrait depicts a boatman leaning heavily on a sweep. The a broad river is in the background, and several small villages as well as river traffic are finely detailed. The boatman and his boat fill the foreground and take center stage in the piece. The *river boatman* is painted in Ormian's realistic style and shows the master's fine hand and eye for lifelike detail.

Upon speaking the command word, you can enter the painting and emerge next to the boatman. While inside the painting, you cannot move beyond the boat, but if you give the boatman directions to any point along the depicted river, you travel there by boat with the landscape in the background scrolling behind you. You arrive within 2d10 hours, during which time you may not leave the painting. Once at your destination, you may leave the painting and appear next to the painting that is now hanging on a wall or other feature in the location to which you have traveled. Outsiders viewing the painting see you on the boat and the landscape scrolling behind you, and when you arrive at your destination, the painting vanishes to reappear at your destination.

RIVER BRIDGE
Wondrous item, very rare

This small landscape painting is only three feet by two feet. It depicts a river bridge during a midsummer day. The river painting is full of activity, with boats on the river, carts crossing the bridge, and the town sprawled across both banks lively with people going about their business. While small, the detail is impressive although the faces are a bit too small to show much individuality.

You can step into the painting once you speak the command word. The hustle and bustle of a very busy market town surrounds you. While the goods on sale are of fine quality, the people are hazy and lack definition. All interactions are very direct and seem to follow a prearranged script of buying and selling, or exchanging money for services. You can find any common mundane item for sale in the market as well as the services of a wide range of craftspeople. You must pay for any goods or services; the people in the painting are only vaguely simulations and cannot respond to threats or other "off-script" directions. The magic of the painting prevents you from taking anything out for which you have not paid. You may spend up to 24 hours inside the painting and may leave at any time. All goods you have purchased exit with you, and any services you commissioned are completed.

ROBE OF FLAILING
Wondrous item, uncommon (requires attunement)

This dark blue robe is embroidered with patterns of silver stars, moons, and comets. The inside has several pockets, each bulging as if filled, yet empty to all investigation.

Cursed. Once attuned, you suffer from the *robe of flailing's* curse. While under the robe's curse you cannot remove it, and whenever you attempt to cast a spell, you must succeed at a DC 15 Wisdom saving throw or the spell slot is lost, the spell is not cast, and you must use your action this turn to randomly flail your arms about.

ROBE OF THE HEAVENS
Wondrous item, panoply (heavens), very rare

Crafted millennia ago for the first caliph, the *robe of the heavens* is an ornate silk robe decorated with silver stars and crescent moons upon a red background. The robe, like the rest of the *panoply of the heavens*, was lost when the Grand Caliph Rabi bin Ashkar Al Ammu and his entire court were slaughtered at the Battle of False Wells by the great wyrm Jalthranax. Once attuned to the *robe of the heavens*, your armor class increases by +2. Every door within the palace of the caliph in Hava will open at your command, and the *robe of heavens* never soils or is torn.

If you are wearing the *robe of the heavens* while sitting upon the *throne of the heavens*, you gain resistance to poison damage as well as bludgeoning, piecing, and slashing damage from nonmagical attacks.

If you are wearing the *robe of the heavens* as part of a complete *panoply of the heavens*, as an action, you may disguise yourself as a common beggar. This disguise is near perfect and requires a DC Intelligence (Investigation) or DC 18 Wisdom (Perception) check to penetrate. The disguise lasts until the next sunrise or until you choose to end it.

SALMON OF TRUTH
Wondrous item, uncommon

These fish bones come from a large salmon. The skeleton is complete and cannot be separated. If the bones are placed in a natural body of water, flesh and skin regrows on the body to create a living, vibrantly colored, salmon. The salmon stays in roughly the same area as it was placed and must be caught using fishing gear and a DC 12 Wisdom check. Once caught, the salmon can be cleaned, gutted, and cooked. Anyone who eats the *salmon of truth*, even the smallest morsel, must succeed at a DC 15 Wisdom saving throw or be unable to lie, even lie by omission, for the next hour. Once all the *salmon of truth* is consumed, the bones are ready to be reused.

> Not to be confused with the carp of lies, they are full of …

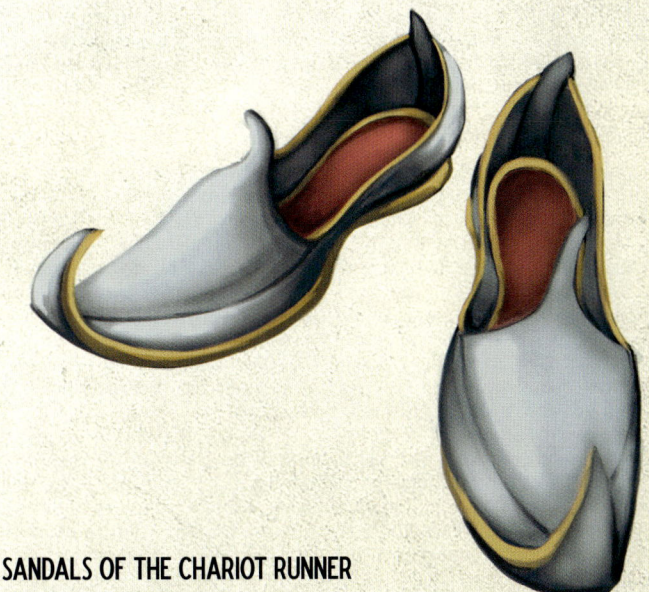

SANDALS OF THE CHARIOT RUNNER
Wondrous item, uncommon

Chariot runners, the supporting light infantry that runs alongside chariots, favor these sturdy sandals. Once donned, *sandals of the chariot runner* increase your speed to 400 feet (45 mph). Additionally, you may cast *expeditious retreat* up to three times while wearing the sandals and regain the use of this spell following a long rest.

SASH OF THE AIR WARRIOR
Wondrous item, panoply (air warrior), conjunction (air), rare

This gray and white silk sash is made from threads spun by the cloud wasps native to the Elemental Plane of Air. Once attuned to the *sash of the air warrior*, you may transform your body to living air for one minute. During this time, you gain resistance to acid, cold, fire, lightning, and thunder damage, as well as bludgeoning, piercing, and slashing damage from nonmagical attacks. You can move through other creatures and objects as if they were difficult terrain. You take 10 force damage if you end your turn inside an object. Additionally, you gain advantage on

CHAPTER ELEVEN: WONDROUS ITEMS | 83

Dexterity (Stealth) checks. You may do this once and regain use following a long rest.

If you wear the *sash of the air warrior* while wielding the *bow of the air warrior*, you may use the lightning attack ability of the *bow of the air warrior* twice and regain uses following a long rest. Also, the sash envelops you in a cloud of pure air that negates the need to breathe the foul stench of the world. This cloud encloses you but can be expanded to enclose up to a 10-foot cube centered on you, displacing the surrounding air for one minute. You may do this once and regain use following a long rest. You may also scent this air as you see fit. Rose petals are nice, but sophisticated people prefer a slightly musky citrusy scent with hints of clove and allspice.

If you wear the *sash of the air warrior* as part of a complete *panoply of the air warrior*, you may cast the *plane shift* spell as a ritual but may go only between the Elemental Plane of Air and the mortal realm, and you gain immunity to lightning damage.

SASH OF THE EARTH WARRIOR
Wondrous item, panoply (earth warrior), conjunction (earth), rare

This green and brown cotton sash is made from threads pulled from fluff rock found only on the Elemental Plane of Earth. Once attuned to the *sash of the earth warrior*, you may transform your body to living stone for one minute. During this time, you gain immunity to acid, cold, and thunder damage, as well as bludgeoning, piercing, and slashing damage from nonmagical attacks. However, you are vulnerable to lightning damage. While in this form you are immovable unless you choose to move and weigh 25 tons. You also grow in size as per the spell *enlarge/reduce*. Finally, if you stand still, you gain advantage on Charisma (Deception) checks to appear to be a statue. You may use this ability once and regain use following a long rest.

If you wear the *sash of the earth warrior* while wielding the *maul of the earth warrior*, you may use the thundering attack ability of the *maul of the earth warrior* twice and regain its use following a long rest. Also, your speed decreases by 10 feet; however, you ignore difficult terrain of any source.

If you wear the *sash of the earth warrior* as part of a complete *panoply of the earth warrior*, you may cast the *plane shift* spell as a ritual but may go only between the Elemental Plane of Earth and the mortal realm, and you gain immunity to thunder damage.

SASH OF THE FIRE WARRIOR
Wondrous item, panoply (fire warrior), conjunction (fire), rare

This red and orange metallic sash is made from threads of molten cinnabar and copper. Once attuned to the *sash of the fire warrior*, you may transform your body to living fire for one minute. During this time, you gain immunity to acid, cold and fire damage, as well as bludgeoning, piercing, and slashing damage from nonmagical attacks. However, you are vulnerable to cold damage. While in this form, any creature that begins its turn within five feet of you or hits you with a melee attack suffers 1d6 fire damage. Your own melee attacks inflict an additional 1d6 fire damage. Also, any flammable object you touch is set upon fire. You may use this feature once and regain use following a long rest.

If you wear the *sash of the fire warrior* while wielding the *sword of the fire warrior*, you may use the flaming blade ability of the *sword of the fire warrior* twice and regain its use following a long rest. Also, you may absorb heat and flame into the sash and use the energy to replenish your natural reserves. When you suffer fire damage (and before you apply either resistance or immunity to fire damage), you convert half of that damage into temporary hit points. However, if you suffer cold damage, you lose all temporary hit points generated from this ability and cannot use this ability until you complete a long rest.

If you wear the *sash of the fire warrior* as part of a complete *panoply of the fire warrior*, you may cast the *plane shift* spell as a ritual but may go only between the Elemental Plane of Fire and the mortal realm, and you gain immunity to fire damage.

SASH OF THE SUN AND MOON
Wondrous item, panoply (twin swords), unique (requires attunement)

This silk sash winds around your waist and contains loops to hold two longsword sheaths. The sash is finely woven from dyed thread to form two images. On one side is a pleasant landscape woven in bright threads that depict the rising, passage, and setting of the sun. On the other side is the same countryside woven in threads of dull color picked out with pools of silver that depicts the rising, passage, and setting of the moon in all its phases. Properly wearing the sash involves wrapping it so that it twists to reveal both images. Once attuned to the *sash of the sun and moon*, you gain a +1 bonus to your armor class. Also, you gain the ability to shadowstride once per day. To shadowstride, you must step into a natural piece of shadow that is edged on at least one side by natural light. As part of the same movement, you exit out of a similar pool of shadow within 100 feet of your point of origin. Additionally, you gain the ability to lightstride once per day. To lightstride, you must step into a natural ray of sunlight that is edged on at least one side by natural shadow. As part of the same movement, you exit out of a similar ray of sunlight within 100 feet of your point of origin.

If you are wearing the *sash of the sun and moon* while wielding the *sword of the dawn star*, you gain resistance to fire and radiant damage.

If you are wearing the *sash of the sun and moon* while wielding the *sword of the night orb*, you gain resistance to cold and necrotic damage.

If you are wearing the *sash of the sun and moon* as part of a complete *panoply of the twin swords*, as an action you may explode in a burst of energy and send out your material body in rays of light or darkness while your soul reforms your body in the place where you stood. Choose either fire and radiant or cold and necrotic. All creatures within 60 feet of you caught in this blast must make a DC 15 Dexterity saving throw. Thise that fail take 4d6 damage of each of the chosen energy types, while those that succeed take half as much damage. Undead creatures and lycanthropes suffer disadvantage on this saving throw. You reform at the end of your turn as if you had completed a short rest. You may do this once and regain use following the next conjunction of the moon and sun.

SASH OF THE WATER WARRIOR
Wondrous item, panoply (water warrior), conjunction (water), rare

This blue and white cotton sash is made from wool of the finned sheep native to the Elemental Plane of Water. Once attuned to the *sash of the water warrior*, you may transform your body to living water for one minute. During this time, you gain immunity to acid, cold, and lightning damage, as well as bludgeoning, piercing, and slashing damage from nonmagical attacks. However, you are vulnerable to fire damage. While in this form, you may flow through any opening that a Tiny creature can pass through, hide yourself in a liquid at least 10 gallons in volume as if using the spell *invisibility*, and any creature you grapple begins to drown. You may use this ability once and regain use following a long rest.

If you wear the *sash of the water warrior* while wielding the *axe of the water warrior*, you may use the ranged attack ability of the *axe of the water warrior* twice and regain its uses following a long rest. Also, you never thirst and are immune to ingested poisons. Once per day, you may touch any liquid and transform it into an equal-sized amount of any other liquid of up to 10 gallons in volume.

If you wear the *sash of the water warrior* as part of a complete *panoply of the water warrior*, you may cast the *plane shift* spell as a ritual but may go only between the Elemental Plane of Water and the mortal realm, and you gain immunity to cold damage.

> Sadly, these sashes tie instead of buckle; thus, you cannot wear one and become a *sashbuckler*.

SCARAB OF DEVOURING
Wondrous item, uncommon (requires attunement)

This palm-sized gold and lapis lazuli decorated copper scarab beetle looks much like other enchanted scarabs and appears as such under the scrutiny of *identify* and similar spells. However, once attuned, the scarab animates and burrows into your flesh. The scarab inflicts 4d6 necrotic and slashing damage at the start of your turn each round until removed. The scarab can be removed with a *remove curse* or similar spell, which produces an inert jeweled scarab ready to be attuned to someone else. You may also attempt to trap the scarab (requiring a successful DC 15 Dexterity [Sleight of Hand] check) in a limb or other part of your body and cut it out (or off if a limb), inflicting damage based on the weapon used (inflicting at least 10 hit points of damage if cutting it out or 30 hit points of damage if cutting off a limb), or with a successful DC 18 Wisdom (Medicine) check.

SCARAB OF EMBALMING
Wondrous item, uncommon

This palm-sized gold and lapis lazuli decorated copper scarab beetle has a pin on the back to attach it to cloth. If placed upon a corpse that has been dead for less than 24 hours, the scarab animates into a dozen similar-looking beetles and burrows into the corpse through the mouth, nose, and other openings. After one minute, the beetles clean and embalm the corpse, in the process removing the heart, liver, lung, and intestines for saving in canopic jars. The body does not rot and cannot be animated into an undead. However, the process also makes it impossible to raise the body with use of *true resurrections* or *wish*.

SCARAB OF MUMMIFICATION
Wondrous item, rare

This palm-sized gold and lapis lazuli decorated copper scarab beetle rests in the center of a wide copper necklace. When placed on a corpse that has been dead for less than 48 hours and if the command word is spoken, the corpse animates as a **mummy**. This mummy is under your control and remains animated for one hour or until it is destroyed. Once this duration elapses, the *scarab of mummification* cannot animate that corpse again, but it can animate a different corpse. Each time the *scarab of mummification* is used, one of the beetle's faïence legs breaks off. Once all six legs have been lost, the item is no longer magical.

SCARAB OF RESURRECTION
Wondrous item, very rare (requires attunement)

This small, jewel-studded golden scarab beetle looks lifelike. Once attuned, it animates and burrows into your flesh. It remains there, causing no damage other than occasional bouts of pain or nausea as it moves around. Others can see this movement if your skin is exposed, including your face, as the scarab likes to travel about. Following every long rest, roll 1d20; on a 5 or less, the scarab is visible in some way until you take a long rest. If you roll a 1, the scarab occupies an uncomfortable location and you suffer disadvantage on all rolls until the scarab moves. The scarab cannot be removed while you are alive; attempts to cut it out result in it burrowing deeper into your torso and coming to rest alongside a vital organ.

If you die while the scarab is inside you, you are resurrected within 1d6 + 4 hours. Once this happens, the scarab exits out of your nose and drops to the ground, becoming a piece of enchanted jewelry. You cannot attune to the same *scarab of resurrection* twice.

SEAHORSE SADDLE
Wondrous item, panoply (coral knight), conjunction (water), very rare (requires attunement by a paladin)

This saddle of fish hides decorated with coral and gold accents is shaped to fit a giant seahorse. Once attuned to the saddle, as an action you may summon a **giant sea horse** as a mount. The giant sea horse has double hit dice and AC 16. It obeys your commands and remains until slain or dismissed. If slain or dismissed, it cannot be summoned again until after the next full tide cycle.

If you are seated in the *seahorse saddle* and wearing the *coral plate*, the seahorse's attacks count as magical.

If you are seated in the *seahorse saddle* and wearing the *sharktooth necklace*, when you summon the **giant shark**, you may choose to ride the shark instead of the seahorse.

If you are seated in the *seahorse saddle* as part of a complete *panoply of the coral knight*, when you summon the **coral golem** (see **Appendix A: New Monsters**), you may choose to ride the coral golem instead of the seahorse.

SEAMLESS GLOBE
Wondrous item, unique (requires attunement, see below)

Often considered the greatest of Abí ibn Farabi's magical creations, the *seamless globe* has been lost for the past 50 years. Carried in the personal baggage of Qayid Usuf ibn al-Din, it is assumed lost when his ship went down in heavy seas. The *seamless globe* is an oddity among the inventions of the Great Teacher, for it is an ornate work. Made from the finest metals, encrusted with gems, and held in a gilded framework, the globe cost Abí ibn Farab a fortune to make. It is thought by scholars that the *seamless globe* was intended as a gift for the caliph, but the Great Teacher died before he could present it.

The *seamless globe* depicts the world when Abí ibn Farab created it, showing the continents and oceans, mountains and plains, and all the rivers of the world. Major cities are depicted as well, but political boundaries are absent. If you utter a command word and touch a point on the globe, you are teleported there. However, the *seamless globe* does not teleport with you. If you are attuned to the *seamless globe*, not only does it travel with you, but you may include up to six willing creatures within 30 feet of you in the teleportation.

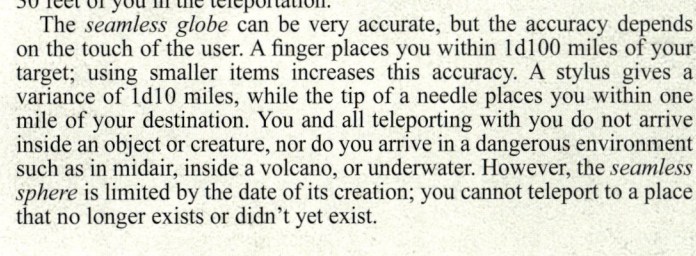

The *seamless globe* can be very accurate, but the accuracy depends on the touch of the user. A finger places you within 1d100 miles of your target; using smaller items increases this accuracy. A stylus gives a variance of 1d10 miles, while the tip of a needle places you within one mile of your destination. You and all teleporting with you do not arrive inside an object or creature, nor do you arrive in a dangerous environment such as in midair, inside a volcano, or underwater. However, the *seamless sphere* is limited by the date of its creation; you cannot teleport to a place that no longer exists or didn't yet exist.

CHAPTER ELEVEN: WONDROUS ITEMS | 85

SENATORIAL PANOPLY

Once elected or appointed as a senator of the long-dead empire that once ruled much of the world, the worthy person received a complete *senatorial panoply*. Gifted as tools to aid and protect the senator, most wore the entire panoply only when appearing in the senate. Because of this tradition, several pieces were stolen over the thousand-year course of the empire's history. Some of these have been found since, and are the only examples of the panoply that can be found today, for the senators of old had their panoplies destroyed after their death.

SENATORIAL SANDALS

Wondrous item, panoply (senatorial), very rare (requires attunement)

The emperor bestowed a set of enchanted items upon newly minted senators. While gifts from the emperor, it was assumed that these items would be used only in the pursuit of a senator's duties. Upon a senator's death, it was customary to destroy their *senatorial panoply*, though this practice declined in the later years of the empire. Senatorial sandals are finely made leather and wood sandals with thick soles that keep the wearer's feet out of the mud. The sandals are often made of gold thread enchanted to be as supple as leather. When attuned to the *senatorial sandals*, you ignore difficult terrain and are kept comfortably warm and dry in temperatures ranging from 20º Fahrenheit to 120º Fahrenheit.

If worn as part with the *senatorial toga*, as a bonus action you may cast *expeditious retreat* once per short rest.

If worn as part of a complete set of *senatorial panoply*, as an action you may cast the *water walk* spell once per long rest.

SENATORIAL STYLUS

Wondrous item, panoply (senatorial), very rare (requires attunement)

It was a senator's duty to make note of laws, lawbreakers, and issues that required attention by the state. Their stylus allowed them to perform these duties and helped serve as a last-ditch defensive weapon should assassins attempt to end a senator's term of service. The *senatorial stylus* is a long, thin piece of metal tipped in gold that is meant to etch letters into a wax tablet. When attuned to the *senatorial stylus*, the stylus can be wielded as a shortsword, gaining +1 to hit and damage, which increase by +1 to hit and damage per person adjacent to you wielding a *senatorial stylus* who is attacking the same person as you. Also, you can command the stylus to take down dictation, draw an object or scene you see, and otherwise write on a wax tablet as per your direction, thus leaving your hands free for other things.

If carried with the *senatorial tablet*, you may cast *detect magic*, *detect poison and disease*, *locate creature*, *locate object*, and *locate plants and animals* as rituals. The results of these spells appear on the *senatorial tablet*.

If carried as part of a complete set of a *senatorial panoply*, as an action you may cast the *glyph of warding* spell once per long rest.

SENATORIAL TABLET

Wondrous item, panoply (senatorial), very rare (requires attunement)

Senators carried a small wax tablet in an ornate leather-and-wood case that fit snuggly within the folds of their toga. These tablets were decorated with gold-engraved images of the senator's ancestors and the senator's name that were meant to encourage the swift and observant completion of one's duties. Inside the table was a safe place to keep a stylus, usually the matched *senatorial stylus*. When attuned to the *senatorial tablet*, you may cast the *augury* and *tongues* spells as rituals. The results appear on the *senatorial tablet*.

If carried with the *senatorial stylus*, you may cast the *zone of truth* spell as a ritual. The results appear on the *senatorial tablet*.

If worn as part of a complete set of *senatorial panoply*, you may cast the following spells as rituals; *divination*, *scrying*, and *true seeing*. If possible, the results appear on your *senatorial tablet*.

SENATORIAL TOGA

Wondrous item, panoply (senatorial), very rare (requires attunement)

No senator would appear in public without their toga, which served as their badge of office. While any citizen of the empire could wear a toga (and only citizens; foreign residents, and slaves were barred by law from wearing the garment), there were many varieties that denoted class and rank. The *senatorial toga* is a broad semicircular dark red cloth that must be carefully folded and held in place with a hand to be worn. Due to its bulk and design, it cannot be worn with armor. When attuned to the *senatorial toga*, your armor class increases by +2.

If worn with *senatorial sandals*, as an action you may cast *shield of faith* on yourself.

86 | TOME OF WONDROUS ITEMS

If worn as part of a complete set of *senatorial panoply*, you gain resistance to bludgeoning, piercing, and slashing damage from nonmagical attacks.

SHADUF OF IRRIGATION
Wondrous item, uncommon

This simple wood and fiber shaduf never breaks or shows signs of wear. It consists of a long crane and counterweight arm attached to a bucket. Water is raised by the bucket, swung around, and dropped into an irrigation channel. This enchanted shaduf does not need a water source to operate. Every time the bucket is lowered to the ground, it fills with 10 gallons of water. While this is a boon for desert dwellers, it is not of much use to desert travelers. The entire shaduf weighs 800 pounds, and the longest pieces (the legs and arm) are more than 10 feet long. It can be disassembled in three hours and set up in four hours, and it retains its enchantments if moved.

SHARBAT CUP
Wondrous item, uncommon

This gilded vessel of finely blown glass bears the marks of the caliph's personal glassblower. Hundreds of these were created, as it is customary for the caliph to gift *sharbat cups* to visiting dignitaries, as rewards to loyal followers, and even to random people whose actions reach the caliph's attention. The *sharbat cup* is a valuable piece of art in itself, but its true magic comes into play if you fill it with fruit juice and spices and then wave your hand across its open mouth. The fruit juice chills and partially solidifies to create a cool and refreshing drink. Some even include milk or yogurt alone or with their fruit juice, thus concocting a new taste.

SHARKTOOTH NECKLACE
Wondrous item, panoply (coral knight), conjunction (water), very rare (requires attunement by a paladin)

This necklace of coral and shark's teeth on a fish leather thong feels warm to the touch. While wearing the *sharktooth necklace*, you may use an action to summon a **giant shark** This shark remains for one hour and obeys your commands. If the shark dies, you use a bonus action to dismiss it, or if the duration expires, the shark disappears. You may do this one time and regain its use following the next sunset.

If you are wearing the *sharktooth necklace* as well as the *coral plate*, as a bonus action you may make a Strength-based bite attack that gains a +1 to the attack roll and inflicts 1d8 slashing damage.

If you are wearing the *sharktooth necklace* while wielding the *spiny lance*, the *spiny lance* inflicts an additional 1d6 slashing damage with each successful attack.

If you are wearing the *sharktooth necklace* as part of a complete *panoply of the coral knight*, you gain a +1 bonus to your armor class.

SHOVEL OF POSTING
Wondrous item, uncommon

This well-used shovel has a hickory handle and a spade-shaped blade of steel. When given the command word, the shovel flies 10 feet away and digs a small hole before moving on 10 feet and digging another. In digs one hole each round. The round after a hole is dug, it sprouts a wooden fencepost that links to the previous one by growing vine-like protrusions. The shovel can be directed where to dig the holes, but each hole must be directed separately. No hole can be dug without a fencepost sprouting out of it. The shovel continues to dig holes until directed to stop. The fence created by the shovel has AC 15 and 10 hit points per 10-foot length.

SHROUD OF REANIMATION
Wondrous item, conjunction (salt), rare

This tattered and dirty cotton shroud is much like that commonly used to wrap the dead before burial. If placed upon a fresh corpse, it animates the corpse as per the spell *animate dead*. The freshly risen zombie remains animated until the shroud is removed. Zombies animated by the *shroud of reanimation* may become incorporeal upon command. While incorporeal, the zombie is difficult to see, causing all Wisdom (Perception) checks to spot it to suffer disadvantage. While incorporeal, the zombie has resistance to the following damage types: bludgeoning, piercing, and slashing attacks from nonmagical attacks, and acid, fire, cold, lightning, and thunder. Furthermore, the zombie can move through other creatures and objects as if they were difficult terrain. It takes 5 force damage if it ends its turn inside an object.

SHROUD OF RESURRECTION
Wondrous item, conjunction (sulfur), very rare

This cotton shroud is much like that commonly used to wrap the dead before burial. If wrapped around a person who has been dead less than three days, the person is resurrected as per the spell *resurrection*. However, the person's visage is imprinted on the shroud and their soul is bound to it. Any spells or similar effects can use the *shroud of resurrection* to target the creature as if it were them.

The shroud has AC 18 and starts with 100 hit points, and is immune to bludgeoning and poison damage. The shroud regenerates 1d10 hp every day at sunrise. Any damage done to the shroud is passed to the creature. If the shroud is destroyed, the creature must succeed on a DC 15 Constitution saving throw or die. Every time the creature is forced to make a death saving throw, the shroud loses 1d10 hit points from its maximum. If the shroud is brought to 0 hit points this way, it is destroyed. Should the creature die, the shroud linked to them suffers 16d10 slashing damage. If the shroud survives, the creature's visage fades, the shroud's maximum hit points returns to 100, and the shroud regenerates 1d10 hit points every sunrise. Once the shroud is fully restored, it may be used again.

SILVER CANOE
Wondrous item, uncommon

This small silver canoe has a hook that allows it to be worn on a necklace or charm bracelet. The modeling is excellent, and a pair of small paddles can be discerned resting on the seats. If tossed in a body of water and an action used to speak the command word, the canoe expands to become a full-sized canoe capable of carrying two people and up to 500 pounds. The paddles can be separated from the benches and used. However, while its magic allows it to float and handle like a wooden canoe, the vessel is still silver and weighs 1,000 pounds if taken out of the water. A separate command word can be spoken as an action to return the boat to its pendant form. Each transition can only be used once per day.

SINGING HEADS
Wondrous item, very rare

These six stone heads are life-size and finely sculpted to represent individual people. They can be found in a variety of genders, races, and ages, but all are mounted on a single piece of stone often carved to resemble a branch or other natural feature. The entire assemblage is heavy, weighing 800 pounds, and must be complete to be used. Several broken and incomplete examples have been found, and these are best left alone.

When given a command word, the *singing heads* sing any song the user requests. The heads form a choir; any instrumental accompaniment must be provided for them. The *singing heads* can also be commanded to serve as backing singers for a musician or singer, granting advantage on Charisma (Performance) checks. The *singing heads'* performance drowns out other sounds, and if a creature is under the effects of a sound-based affect such as a harpy's song, they may attempt another save while within 30 feet of active *singing heads*.

Cursed singing heads. Incomplete sets of *singing heads* produce a discordant tone when commanded to sing. All creatures within 30 feet that can hear the heads must make a DC 15 Wisdom saving throw, taking 5d10 psychic damage on a failure, or half this damage on a success. The heads sing so loudly that they cannot be commanded to stop, though after 1d6 hours they fall silent of their own accord.

SKELETON OF INOVAX OF KRATIR
Wondrous item, unique (requires attunement, see below)

Any living creature except those native to other planes (such as celestials and fiends) can attune to the *skeleton of Inovax of Kratir*. The attunement process proceeds as normal until the end. The *skeleton of Inovax of Kratir* harness adjusts to fit its user, but if you are not a dragon or of a similar shape, it alters itself and your shape and size to fit. This process takes a few moments of extreme agony as your body bends, breaks, and cracks. Your flesh moves like clay under the ephemeral hands of some mad sculptor. Bones snap and reknit in new configurations. The *skeleton of Inovax of Kratir* often needs to make several attempts at matching a body to its frame.

When you attempt to attune to the *skeleton of Inovax of Kratir*, you must succeed on a DC 12 Constitution saving throw to complete the process. The DC of this saving throw increases according to the table below. If you fail the saving throw, you suffer 5d10 bludgeoning damage and your Strength, Dexterity, and Constitution scores all decrease by 2. You may reattempt to attune to the *skeleton of Inovax of Kratir* following a long rest, and frankly, with enough failures you end up needing the skeletal harness.

Once attuned to the *skeleton of Inovax of Kratir*, your ability scores increase while wearing the harness. Your Strength score becomes 27, your Dexterity score becomes 10, and your Constitution score becomes 25. If you take off the *skeleton of Inovax of Kratir*, your scores revert to their original scores. While wearing the *skeleton of Inovax of Kratir*, you gain a fly speed of 80 feet, a climb speed of 40 feet, and your speed becomes 40 feet. You gain blindsight 60 feet and darkvision 120 feet. Your armor class becomes 19, and you gain immunity to fire damage. As an action, you may make a Strength-based bite attack that inflicts 2d10 piercing plus 2d6 fire damage, and two Strength-based claw attacks that inflict 2d6 slashing damage. As an action, you may breathe a 60-foot cone of fire three times per long rest. Those caught in this area must make a DC 21 Dexterity saving throw, taking 18d6 fire damage on a failure, or half that damage on a success.

SKIRT OF MANY POCKETS
Wondrous item, very rare

This floral printed cotton skirt hangs in loose folds from an adjustable waist. The skirt has six pockets sewn into it. Five of these pockets are visible, but the last is hidden from all but you. Each pocket is an extradimensional space. You may place any item in the pockets, and each pocket can hold up to 100 cubic inches of matter. The item need not be small enough to fit in the pockets but must have at least one corner or piece that can fit through the opening (the pockets expand to engulf the rest). As an action, you can withdraw a stored item from the pockets.

SKY BARGE
Wondrous item, very rare

This river barge (speed 3 mph, crew 40, passengers 100, cargo 10 tons, AC 15, 200 hit points, damage threshold 10) can be rowed or sailed as normal. However, when you use an action to speak the command word, the barge can lift out of the water and float into the air. The *sky barge* flies much as it would ride across the water, with oars pulling and sails billowing, and has a top speed of 65 mph. The oars scratch the Ethereal Plane, which gives them purchase as they pull, and leave a trail of sparkling motes behind them with each sweep. The sail does not fill with any earthly breeze; it is driven by the ethereal wind.

The *sky barge* can land on water with ease and with a command act as a normal watercraft. It cannot land on the ground, but it can hover above while a ladder or rope is lowered. It requires a crew to operate; the *sky barge* will not fly on its own. Proficiency with vehicles (water) suffices to operate the *sky barge*. If damaged, it can be repaired as per a normal ship. If reduced to 0 hit points, the *sky barge* wrecks and its magic dissipates.

SKY GALLEY
Wondrous item, very rare

This ship of ancient imperial design (speed 5 mph, crew 40, passengers 100, cargo 10 tons, AC 15, 300 hit points, damage threshold 10) can be rowed or sailed as normal. However, when you use an action to speak the command word, the ship can lift out of the water and float into the air. The *sky galley* flies much as it would ride across the water, with oars pulling and sails billowing, and has a top speed of 65 mph. The oars scratch the Ethereal Plane, which gives them purchase as they pull, and leave a trail of sparkling motes behind them with each sweep. The sail does not fill with any earthly breeze; it is driven by the ethereal wind.

The *sky galley* can land on water with ease and can act as a normal watercraft with a command. It cannot land on the ground but it can hover above while a ladder or rope is lowered. It requires a crew to operate; the sky galley will not fly on its own. Proficiency with vehicles (water) suffices to operate the *sky galley*. If damaged, it can be repaired as per a normal ship, but if reduced to 0 hit points, the sky galley wrecks and its magic dissipates.

The empire used *sky galleys* as tools of war, advancing ahead of the legions in fleets to secure strategic locations, to break sieges, and to assault cities. Walls meant nothing to the armies of the empire. Because of this martial usage, *sky galleys* are equipped with a pair of ballistae on the fore and aft deck, as well as a corvus-style assault ramp that can be used to deposit soldiers directly onto buildings or city walls against which the *sky galley* is hovering.

SLIPPERS OF THE NIGHT'S WIND
Wondrous item, rare

These white silk slippers are supremely comfortable. You you can use an action to issue a command to the slippers that allows you to walk on thin air for one hour. You move on the air as if it were a solid surface, changing altitude as if ascending or descending stairs, and can even cross great gulfs of open space as if it were flat land. If you jump, you stick wherever in space the movement of the jump brings you. When you stand still, you stand as if on terra firma. The *slippers of the night's wind* can be used for one continuous hour and you regain their use following a long rest.

SLIPPERS OF THE NARROW GULF
Wondrous item, rare

These blue silk slippers are supremely comfortable. You use an action to issue a command to the slippers that allows you to walk on water for one hour. You move on water as if it were a solid surface, climbing up waterfalls as if ascending or descending stairs, and can even walk on choppy waves as if they were rolling hills. If you jump, you land on water as if landing on solid ground. When you stand still, you stand as if on terra firma. The *slippers of the narrow gulf* can be used for one continuous hour and you regain their use following a long rest.

SLIPPERS OF THE SMOKING INFERNO
Wondrous item, rare

These red silk slippers are supremely comfortable. You you can use an action to issue a command to the slippers that allows you to walk on fire for one hour. You move on fire as if it were a solid surface, changing altitude as if ascending or descending stairs, and can even cross lava as if it were flat land. If you jump, you land on fire as if landing on solid ground. When you stand still, you stand as if on terra firma. The *slippers of the smoking inferno* can be used for one continuous hour and you regain their use following a long rest.

SLITHERING ROPE
Wondrous item, uncommon (requires attunement)

This golden-colored flaxen rope is 50 feet long. It is exceedingly strong for rope (AC 18, 50 hp, resistance to slashing damage, immune to bludgeoning, piercing, and psychic damage). Once attuned, you can issue mental commands to the rope and it obeys. It can move (speed 30, climb 30 and across vertical or upside down over horizontal surfaces), knot and unknot itself, and even coil or uncoil itself. As a bonus action, you can command the rope to attack a target (*melee attack:* +6 to hit, reach 10 feet, one creature; *Hit:* target is grappled [escape DC 15]). If it has a creature grappled at the start of your turn, you can use a bonus action to command the *slithering rope* to restrain the creature.

STATUE OF TOWN DEFENSE
Wondrous item, very rare

This lifelike statue is designed to stand on its own on a pedestal of some kind. It is made from finely carved marble and, according to local tastes, may be painted or not. The *statue of town defense* must be set up in the center of a permanent settlement of at least 1,000 people. Once set on a pedestal, you must speak a command word that includes the name of the town in the local language to activate the *statue of town defense*.

Once active, the statue just stands there unmoving. If any citizen of the town (as defined by local law and custom) is attacked, the *statue of town defense* animates into a **caryatid column** (see **Appendix A: New Monsters**) and moves to defend the town's citizens, usually by slaying the attackers. If the attacker and the victim are citizens of the town, the *statue of town defense* attempts to separate the combatants and hold them for the authorities to deal with. Should there be a disaster affecting the town, such as a fire or oncoming flood, the *statue of town defense* sounds an alarm that can be heard from anywhere within the town and it animates to provide what assistance it can.

It should be noted that the *statue of town defense* has its own will and does not follow anyone's commands. It is by default lawful good in alignment and acts accordingly when an event triggers it to animate. Even when not animated, the *statue of town defense* is alert and observes the town and its citizens; the magic that allows it to protect the town grants it the ability to perceive anything occurring inside its town at any time. *Statues of town defense* are known to briefly animate to hold conversations.

If reduced to 0 hit points, the *statue of town defense* crumbles to dust. If injured, it recovers all of its hit points after 24 hours. If no citizens are within the town, the *statue of town defense* does not animate to defend the buildings or other inanimate objects in the town. If attacked while inanimate, the *statue of town defense* animates to defend itself. If the town it is defending is destroyed and its inhabitants slain or scattered, the *statue of town defense* becomes a statue and awaits a new town to defend, though there is a 10% chance the *statue of town defense* animates and seeks vengeance; this increases to 90% if the inhabitants of the town were mostly lawful good and treated the *statue of town defense* nicely.

STELE OF BINDING
Wondrous item, conjunction (azoth), very rare

This ornately carved stone monument stands six feet tall, is two feet wide, and weighs 600 pounds. Its surface is covered in complex geometric designs and cuneiform writing. Often *stele of binding* are found in groups of six aligned at the points of an imaginary star and facing inward. Only one *stele of binding* is required, but greater effects can be generated if more than one is put to use.

To activate a *stele of binding*, you must read the text inscribed upon the stele and perform the required ritual. This takes 10 minutes and requires a successful DC 13 Intelligence (Arcana) check to complete. Once complete, the *stele of binding* can be used to bind a single aberration, celestial, construct, elemental, fey, fiend, or undead creature. The target must succeed at a DC 15 Wisdom saving throw or be bound. The DC of this saving throw increases by 1 per each additional *stele of binding* used to bind the target, to a maximum of 20. Each stele remains active for one month, and then needs to be reactivated.

A creature bound by a *stele of binding* may not move, cast spells, or make attacks. Nor may it use spell-like abilities or other abilities that allow it to leave the area or plane of existence to which it is bound. The creature remains bound until it can succeed at a Wisdom saving throw with the same DC (possibly enhanced by additional stele as above) or until you release it. A bound creature may attempt a new saving throw every sunset and sunrise.

STELE OF COMMANDMENTS
Wondrous item, conjunction (mercury), very rare (requires attunement)

This ornately carved stone stands four feet tall and is a foot-and-a-half wide. It weighs 250 pounds. The surface displays scenes of followers paying obeisance and offering tribute to an enthroned figure of regal majesty. Once attuned to the *stele of commandments*, as long as you are within one mile of the stele you gain advantage on all Charisma (Intimidation), Charisma (Persuasion), and Wisdom (Insight) checks. Additionally, the *stele of commandments* has three charges. It regains expended charges each day at sunrise. You may take one minute to carve in the *stele of commandment* to expend one charge to cast one of the following spells: *command*, *suggestion*, *true seeing* (DC 15 spell save).

STELE OF EXORCISM
Wondrous item, conjunction (azoth), very rare

This ornately carved stone monument stands six feet tall, is two feet wide, and weighs 600 pounds. Its surface is covered in complex geometric designs and cuneiform writing. Often *stele of exorcism* are found in groups of five aligned at the points of an imaginary star and facing inward. Only one *stele of exorcism* is required, but greater effects can be generated if more than one is used.

To activate a *stele of exorcism*, you must read the text inscribed upon it and perform the required ritual. This takes 10 minutes and requires a successful DC 13 Intelligence (Arcana) check to complete. Once completed, the *stele of exorcism* can be used to exorcise the corrupting influence of aberrations, celestials, elementals, fey, fiends, or undead. The affected creature is placed in alignment with the stele or in the center of an alignment of multiple *steles of exorcism*. The creature targeted by the stele is no longer charmed, frightened, or possessed if the affecting creature is of one of the above listed types. An additional target can be exorcised for each additional *stele of exorcism* placed in alignment, up to five creatures total. When the exorcism is complete, the stele deactivates.

STAMP OF THE HEAVENLY EMPIRE
Wondrous item, very rare

This ornately carved square stamp can be used to impress a seal onto a document. The stamp must be inked to use. Whatever document the seal is stamped upon is a binding contract between two parties, both of whom are under the effects of a *geas* spell (DC 18 spell save) as if cast using a 9th-level spell slot. Care should be taken in wording the document, as the magic of the *stamp of the heavenly empire* obeys the letter, not the intent, of the contract.

Alternately, the *stamp of the heavenly empire* can be used to seal a compact between a person and a deity. Treat this as a *wish* spell, and the deity may or may not agree to the contract. If used in this manner, the *stamp of the heavenly empire* vanishes after it is used.

CHAPTER ELEVEN: WONDROUS ITEMS

STONES OF HARVA'ROTH

Although the creator of these stones is unknown, local legends credit a long-dead human druid by the name of Harva'roth. Six stones once stood on a hill 20 miles east of Bettlebridge in the Borderland Provinces. One stone, the dragon stone, was taken by the Great Red Wyrm Fratharex the Firebound to her lair in the Impossible Peaks. The remaining five stones still stand on the hill, although the giant stone and the wolf stone have toppled.

Today, locals consider the stones and their hill a convenient landmark, an interesting place to picnic, and often the source for horrid tales to frighten young folk and to annoy travelers. Shepherds graze their sheep on the hill's lower slopes and sometimes drive a herd within the stones to better contain them during inclement weather or lunch breaks. Most of the stones are so overgrown with moss and lichen, weathered, and in general disrepair that their true nature is all but forgotten.

STONES OF HARVA'ROTH RUMORS, LEGENDS, AND RESEARCH

1d8	Information
1	During the Age of Man, a powerful tribe that dwelt near the the coast erected a set of stones on a hill to protect themselves from the monsters that haunted the wilderness.
2	The Stones of Harva'roth have not worked in ages. Many believe their magic has long since dissipated.
3	A dragon stole one of the stones and took it across the continent to its lair somewhere in the west.
4	Moldy texts dating to the long dead empire mention that the stones could be used to capture and enslave monsters.
5	Six stones exist, with each bearing glyphs and a carving depicting the creature they affect. The six stones are bear, dragon, giant, lion, mammoth, and wolf.
6	The stones are a puzzle. To use them, they must be arranged in a specific pattern.
7	Fifty years ago, the wizard Garvan used the stones to summon a mammoth. He has since died. The wizard, that is. Not the mammoth.
8	The stones are more powerful as a set, but each should still work alone.

BEAR STONE OF HARVA'ROTH

Wondrous item, panoply (Stones of Harva'roth), legendary (requires attunement)

This six-foot-tall, three-foot-wide, and two-foot-thick blue stone pillar weighs 9-1/2 tons. It is well worn, and patches of lichen mar its surface. One face is roughly cut from the bedrock it once was part of, but the other long face was once smooth, though now it is somewhat pitted. The smoother face features an engraving of a bear standing on its hind legs, paws raised as if to attack, with a crown of antlers interwoven with holly branches upon its head. Two rows of petroglyphs whose meaning is lost to time circle this figure. Spells such as *comprehend languages* reveal that the rows describe the ritual needed to activate the stone in rather fanciful terms.

The stone must be set in the ground vertically on a high point and aligned so that the bear faces the rising sun. This alignment must be precise: The *bear stone of Harva'roth* must be placed facing southeast, and if the first rays of dawn do not strike the bear in the center of the crown, the stone cannot be activated. Thus, it requires a successful DC 13 Intelligence (Arcana) check to properly set the stone. Once set, a three-hour ritual requiring a fire, the heart and skull of a bear, and 500 gp worth of rare herbs and substances must be conducted. If the stone is moved, it deactivates and all effects end.

Once activated, while you are attuned to the stone, you gain the following abilities:

- You always know the distance and direction of the *bear stone of Harva'roth*.
- If you take a short rest within 20 feet of the *bear stone*, roll 1d20 for each hit die you expend, regaining that hit die on a roll of 10+.
- If you take a long rest within 20 feet of the *bear stone*, you need rest for only half the normal amount of time to gain the benefits of a long rest.

The stone can be used to create each of the following effects once and you regain each use the following day at each dawn. The stone casts one of the following spells: *animal messenger* (messenger is a bear), *cure disease*, *cure wounds*, *lesser restoration*, *remove curse*, *speak with animals* (bears only) on a target of your choice that you can see. The stone casts *magic circle* centered on the *bear stone of Harva'roth* that lasts until the next sunrise. The stone glows a bright blue color that can be seen for miles.

The stone has three charges that can be spent to create one of the following effects, and it regains a charge each time the ritual of activation is completed:

- Recast any of the spells listed above.
- Summon 1d4 bears of a type native to the region. These bears arrive within the next 2d6 hours and serve you for one lunar month.
- Create a 20-foot sphere that bars all bears and bear-like creatures, including chimerical creatures with bear features, from entering the area as per the spell *magic circle* but protects only against bears and bear like creatures.
- You can shapechange as if using a druid's wildshape ability, but only into a bear of Challenge 1 or less.
- You can dominate any bear, bear-like creature, or chimerical creature with bear features within 60 feet of the *bear stone of Harva'roth* as per the spells *dominate beast*, *dominate person*, or *dominate monster* depending on the target. The spell save DC is 13, and the effect lasts until the next sunrise.

If erected within 40 feet of another *stone of Harva'roth* and in alignment with the other stones, the *bear stone of Harva'roth* becomes more powerful. Aligning the stone with others in the panoply requires an Intelligence (Arcana) check with a DC equal to 15 + the number of stones being aligned. If aligned with other active stones attuned to the same person, the *bear stone of Harva'roth* gains an additional use of each one-time use effect and an additional charge per stone in the alignment. Also, the DC of any saving throws to resist the stone's effects is increased by +1 per stone in the alignment. Finally, the area of effect for the stone's effects are centered on the geometric center of the aligned stones instead of the stone itself.

The bear stone of Harva'roth remains active for one year or until it has no charges.

DRAGON STONE OF HARVA'ROTH

Wondrous item, panoply (Stones of Harva'roth), legendary (requires attunement)

This seven-foot-tall, three-foot-wide, and two-foot-thick greenish stone pillar weighs eight tons. It is well worn, and patches of lichen mar its surface. One face is roughly cut from the bedrock it once was part of, but the other long face was once smooth, though now it is somewhat pitted. The smoother face features an engraving of a dragon breathing fire upon a herd of cattle, the creature's tail arched over its back and touching its head. Circling this figure are two rows of petroglyphs whose meaning is lost to time. Spells such as *comprehend languages* reveal that the rows describe the ritual needed to activate the stone in rather fanciful terms.

The stone must be set in the ground vertically on a high point and aligned so that the dragon faces east inward toward the circle of aligned stones. This alignment must be precise. If the first rays of the equinox sun do not strike the point where the tail touches the head, the stone cannot be activated. Thus, it requires a successful DC 13 Intelligence (Arcana) check to properly set the stone. Once set, a 12-hour ritual requiring a fire, the heart and skull of a dragon, and 50,000 gp worth of rare herbs and substances must be conducted. If the stone is moved, it deactivates and all effects end.

Once activated, while you are attuned to the stone, you gain the following abilities:

- You always know the distance and direction of the *dragon stone of Harva'roth*.
- If you take a short or long rest within 20 feet of the *dragon stone*, your skin grows scales like that of a dragon, granting you an unarmored AC of 13 + your Dexterity modifier. This effect lasts until the next equinox.
- If you take a long rest within 20 feet of the *dragon stone*, you grow wings that grant you a fly speed of 40 feet. This effect lasts until the next equinox.

The stone can be used to create each of the following effects once, and you regain the use of each after the next equinox:

- The stone casts one of the following spells: *bestow curse, clairvoyance, nondetection, sending, teleportation circle* on a target of your choice that you can see. The spell save for any of these spells is a DC 13.
- The stone casts *magic circle* centered on the *dragon stone of Harva'roth* that lasts until the next equinox. The stone glows a bright purple color that can be seen for miles.

The stone has three charges that can be spent to create one of the following effects, and it regains a charge each time the ritual of activation is completed:

- Recast any of the spells listed above.
- You can summon an adult dragon of a type native to the region. This dragon arrives within the next 2d6 hours and serves you for 24 hours.
- You can create a 20-foot sphere that bars all dragons and dragon-like creatures, including chimerical creatures with dragon features, from entering the area as per the spell *magic circle* but protects only against dragons and dragon-like creatures.
- You can shapechange as if using a druid's wildshape ability, but only into a dragon of Challenge 9 or less.
- You can dominate any dragon, dragon-like creature, or chimerical creature with dragon features within 60 feet of the *dragon stone of Harva'roth* as per the spells *dominate beast, dominate person,* or *dominate monster* depending on the target. The spell save DC is 13, and the effect lasts until the next moonrise.

If erected within 40 feet of another *stone of Harva'roth* and in alignment with the other stones, the *dragon stone of Harva'roth* becomes more powerful. Aligning the stone with others in the panoply requires an Intelligence (Arcana) check with a DC equal to 15 + the number of stones being aligned. If aligned with other active stones attuned to the same person, the *dragon stone of Harva'roth* gains an additional use of each one-time use effect and an additional charge per stone in the alignment. Also, the DC of any saving throws to resist the stone's effects is increased by +1 per stone in the alignment. Finally, the area of effect for the stone's effects are centered on the geometric center of the aligned stones instead of the stone itself.

The dragon stone of Harva'roth remains active for one year or until it has no charges.

GIANT STONE OF HARVA'ROTH

Wondrous item, panoply (Stones of Harva'roth), legendary (requires attunement)

This 10-foot-tall, three-foot-wide, and four-foot-thick dark gray stone pillar weighs 15 tons. It is well worn, and patches of lichen mar its surface. One face is roughly cut from the bedrock it once was part of, but the other long face was once smooth, though now it is somewhat pitted. The smoother face features an engraving of a humanoid figure stepping on smaller figures, a large tree held above its head in its right hand. Circling this figure are two rows of petroglyphs whose meaning is lost to time. Spells such as *comprehend languages* reveal that the rows describe the ritual needed to activate the stone in rather fanciful terms.

The stone must be set in the ground vertically on a high point and aligned so that the giant faces west inward toward the circle of aligned stones. This alignment must be precise. If the last rays of the solstice sun do not strike the tip of the tree-club, the stone cannot be activated. Thus, it requires a successful DC 13 Intelligence (Arcana) check to properly set the stone. Once set, a 12-hour ritual requiring a fire, the heart and skull of a giant, and 25,000 gp worth of rare herbs and substances must be conducted. If the stone is moved, it deactivates and all effects end.

Once activated, the stone grants the following properties:

- You always know the distance and direction of the *giant stone of Harva'roth*.
- If you take a short or long rest within 20 feet of the *giant stone of Harva'roth*, your Strength score increases by +2. This effect lasts until the next solstice. After taking advantage of this effect, you cannot use it again until the next solstice.
- If you take a long rest within 20 feet of the *giant stone of Harva'roth*, you grow one size category larger. This effect lasts until the next solstice. After taking advantage of this effect, you cannot use it again until the next solstice.

The stone can be used to create each of the following effects once, and you regain each use following the next solstice:

- The stone casts one of the following spells: *banishment, contact other plane, dispel magic, flesh to stone, banishment* on a target of your choice that you can see. The spell save for any of these spells is a DC 13.
- The stone casts *magic circle* centered on the *giant stone of Harva'roth* that lasts until the next equinox. The stone glows a bright white color that can be seen for miles.

The stone has three charges that can be spent to create one of the following effects, and it regains a charge each time the ritual of activation is completed:

- You can recast any of the spells listed above.
- You can summon a giant of a type native to the region. This giant arrives within the next 2d6 hours and serves you for 24 hours.
- You can create a 20-foot sphere that bars all giants from entering the area as per the spell *magic circle* but protects only against giants.
- You can shapechange as the *polymorph* spell, but only into a giant of Challenge 9 or less.
- You can dominate any giant within 60 feet of the *giant stone of Harva'roth* as per the spell *dominate monster*. The spell save DC is 13, and the effect lasts until the next moonrise.

If erected within 40 feet of another *stone of Harva'roth* and in alignment with the other stones, the *giant stone of Harva'roth* becomes more powerful. Aligning the stone with others in the panoply requires an Intelligence (Arcana) check with a DC equal to 15 + the number of stones being aligned. If aligned with other active stones attuned to the same person, the *giant stone of Harva'roth* gains an additional use of each one-time use effect and an additional charge per stone in the alignment. Also, the DC of any saving throws to resist the stone's effects is increased by +1 per stone in the alignment. Finally, the area of effect for the stone's effects are centered on the geometric center of the aligned stones instead of the stone itself.

The giant stone of Harva'roth remains active for one year or until it has no charges.

LION STONE OF HARVA'ROTH
Wondrous item, panoply (Stones of Harva'roth), legendary (requires attunement)

This six-foot-tall, three-foot-wide, and two-foot-thick white stone pillar weighs eight tons. It is well worn, and patches of lichen mar its surface. One face is roughly cut from the bedrock it once was part of, but the other long face was once smooth, though now it is somewhat pitted. The smoother face features an engraving of a male lion turned to face the viewer and roaring in rage, a diamond shape on its forehead. Circling this figure are two rows of petroglyphs whose meaning is lost to time. Spells such as *comprehend languages* reveal that the rows describe the ritual needed to activate the stone in rather fanciful terms.

The stone must be set in the ground vertically on a high point and aligned so that the lion faces the south inward toward the circle of aligned stones. This alignment must be precise. If the first rays of the midday sun do not strike the diamond on the lion's forehead, the stone cannot be activated. Thus, it requires a successful DC 13 Intelligence (Arcana) check to properly set the stone. Once set, a three-hour ritual requiring a fire, the heart and skull of a lion, and 500 gp worth of rare herbs and substances must be conducted. If the stone is moved, it deactivates and all effects end.

Once activated, while you are attuned to the stone, you have the following abilities:

- You always know the distance and direction of the *lion stone of Harva'roth*.
- If you take a short or long rest within 20 feet of the *lion stone of Harva'roth*, any frightened condition you are suffering from is removed. Furthermore, when within 20 feet of the *lion stone of Harva'roth*, you are immune to the frightened condition and gain advantage on any saving throws made to resist a fear effect.
- If you take a long rest within 20 feet of the *lion stone of Harva'roth*, following the completion of your long rest, you gain advantage on your next attack roll.

The stone can be used to create each of the following effects once, and it regains use of the effect at each midday:

- The stone casts one of the following spells: *animal messenger* (messenger is a lion), *enhance ability*, *fear*, *heroism*, or *speak with animals* (lions only) on a target of your choice that you can see. The spell save for any of these spells is DC 13.
- The stone casts *magic circle* centered on the *lion stone of Harva'roth* that lasts until the next midday. The stone glows a bright yellow color that can be seen for miles.

The stone has three charges that can be spent to create one of the following effects, and it regains a charge each time the ritual of activation is completed.

- You can recast any of the spells listed above.
- You can summon 1d4 lions or other large cats of a type native to the region. These lions arrive within the next 2d6 hours and serve you for one lunar month.
- You can create a 20-foot sphere that bars all lions and lion-like creatures, including chimerical creatures with lion features, from entering the area as per the spell *magic circle* but protects only against lions and lion-like creatures.
- You can shapechange as if using a druid's wildshape ability, but only into a lion of Challenge 1 or less.
- You can dominate any lion, lion-like creature, or chimerical creature with lion features within the 60 feet of the *lion stone of Harva'roth* as per the spells *dominate beast*, *dominate person*, or *dominate monster* depending on the target. The spell save DC is 13, and the effect lasts until the next midday.

If erected within 40 feet of another *stone of Harva'roth* and in alignment with the other stones, the *lion stone of Harva'roth* becomes more powerful. Aligning the stone with others in the panoply requires an Intelligence (Arcana) check with a DC equal to 15 + the number of stones being aligned. If aligned with other active stones attuned to the same person, the *lion stone of Harva'roth* gains an additional use of each one-time use effect and an additional charge per stone in the alignment. Also, the DC of any saving throws to resist the stone's effects is increased by +1 per stone in the alignment. Finally, the area of effect for the stone's effects are centered on the geometric center of the aligned stones instead of the stone itself.

The lion stone of Harva'roth remains active for one year or until it has no charges.

92 | Tome of Wondrous Items

MAMMOTH STONE OF HARVA'ROTH

Wondrous item, panoply (Stones of Harva'roth), legendary (requires attunement)

This nine-foot-tall, three-foot-wide, and three-foot-thick reddish stone pillar weighs 10 tons. It is well worn, and patches of lichen mar its surface. One face is roughly cut from the bedrock it once was part of, but the other long face was once smooth, though now it is somewhat pitted. The smoother face features an engraving of a bull mammoth in full must, rampant facing the viewer. Circling this figure are two rows of petroglyphs whose meaning is lost to time. Spells such as *comprehend languages* reveal that the rows describe the ritual needed to activate the stone in rather fanciful terms.

The stone must be set in the ground vertically on a high point and aligned so that the mammoth faces due north into the circle of stones (if aligned with other stones). This alignment must be precise. If the first rays of the midnight full moon do not strike a point equidistant between the mammoth's tusks, the stone cannot be activated. Thus, it requires a successful DC 13 Intelligence (Arcana) check to properly set the stone. Once set, a three-hour ritual requiring a fire, the heart and skull of a mammoth, and 500 gp worth of rare herbs and substances must be conducted. If the stone is moved, it deactivates and all effects end.

Once activated, while you are attuned to the stone, you have the following abilities:

- You always know the distance and direction of the *mammoth stone of Harva'roth*.
- If you take a short rest within 20 feet of the *mammoth stone of Harva'roth*, you gain advantage on any Constitution saving throws or ability checks until the next high moon.
- If you and anyone else you are friendly with take a long rest within 20 feet of the *mammoth stone of Harva'roth*, everyone gains incredible fertility and creates a child the next time they are able to do so.

The stone can be used to create each of the following effects once, and you regain the use of each effect at next high moon:

- The stone casts one of the following spells: *animal messenger* (messenger is a mammoth), *detect poison and disease*, *enlarge*, *polymorph*, *speak with animals* (mammoths only) on a target of your choice that you can see. The spell save for any of these spells is DC 13.
- The stone casts *magic circle* centered on the *mammoth stone of Harva'roth* that lasts until the next high moon. The stone glows a bright red color that can be seen for miles.

The stone has three charges that can be spent to create one of the following effects, and it regains a charge each time the ritual of activation is completed.

- You can recast any of the spells listed above.
- You can summon one mammoth of a type native to the region. This mammoth arrives within the next 2d6 hours and serves you for one lunar month.
- You can create a 20-foot sphere that bars all mammoths and mammoth-like creatures, including chimerical creatures with mammoth features, from entering the area as per the spell *magic circle* but protects only against mammoths and mammoth-like creatures.
- You can shapechange as if using a druid's wildshape ability, but only into a mammoth of Challenge 6 or less.
- You can dominate any mammoth, mammoth-like creature, or chimerical creature with mammoth features within 60 feet of the *lion stone of Harva'roth* as per the spells *dominate beast*, *dominate person*, or *dominate monster* depending on the target. The spell save DC is 13, and the effect lasts until the next high moon.

If erected within 40 feet of another *stone of Harva'roth* and in alignment with the other stones, the *mammoth stone of Harva'roth* becomes more powerful. Aligning the stone with others in the panoply requires an Intelligence (Arcana) check with a DC equal to 15 + the number of stones being aligned. If aligned with other active stones attuned to the same person, the *mammoth stone of Harva'roth* gains an additional use of each one-time use effect and an additional charge per stone in the alignment. Also, the DC of any saving throws to resist the stone's effects is increased by +1 per stone in the alignment. Finally, the area of effect for the stone's effects are centered on the geometric center of the aligned stones instead of the stone itself.

The mammoth stone of Harva'roth remains active for one year or until it has no charges.

WOLF STONE OF HARVA'ROTH

Wondrous item, panoply (Stones of Harva'roth), legendary (requires attunement)

This six-foot-tall, three-foot-wide, and two-foot-thick blue stone pillar weighs 49-1/2 tons. It is well worn, and patches of lichen mar its surface. One face is roughly cut from the bedrock it once was part of, but the other long face was once smooth, though now it is somewhat pitted. The smoother face features an engraving of a pack of wolves chasing an elk. The lead wolf has a crown of light around its head. Circling these figures are two rows of petroglyphs whose meaning is lost to time. Spells such as *comprehend languages* reveal that the rows describe the ritual needed to activate the stone in rather fanciful terms.

The stone must be set in the ground vertically on a high point and aligned so that the wolf faces into an alignment of other stones. This alignment must be precise. If the last rays of sunlight before full sunset do not strike the wolf in the lead of the pack, the stone cannot be activated. Thus, it requires a successful DC 13 Intelligence (Arcana) check to properly set the stone. Once set, a three-hour ritual requiring a fire, the heart and skull of a wolf, and 500 gp worth of rare herbs and substances must be conducted. If the stone is moved, it deactivates and all effects end.

Once activated, while attuned to the stone, you gain the following abilities:

- You always know the distance and direction of the *wolf stone of Harva'roth*.
- If you and at least one other person take a short rest within 20 feet of the *wolf stone of Harva'roth*, any of the people taking the short rest may expend hit dice for each other.
- If you and at least one other person take a long rest within 20 feet of the *wolf stone of Harva'roth*, everyone completing the long rest gains advantage on attack rolls if they are within five feet of another person who took part in the long rest. This effect lasts until the next sunset.

The stone can be used to create each of the following effects once, and you regain use of each effect at the next sunset:

- The stone casts one of the following spells: *animal messenger* (messenger is a wolf), *darkvision*, *locate animals or plants*, *longstrider*, *speak with animals* (wolves only), or *windwalk* on a target of your choice that you can see. The spell save for any of these spells is DC 13.
- The stone casts *magic circle* centered on the *wolf stone of Harva'roth* that lasts until the next sunset. The stone glows a bright green color that can be seen for miles.
- The stone has three charges that can be spent to create one of the following effects, and it regains a charge each time the ritual of activation is completed:
- You can recast any of the spells listed above.
- You can summon 2d4 wolves of a type native to the region. These wolves arrive within the next 2d6 hours and serve you for one lunar month.
- You can create a 20-foot sphere that bars all wolves and wolf-like creatures, including chimerical creatures with wolf features, from entering the area as per the spell *magic circle* but protects only against wolves and wolf-like creatures.
- You can shapechange as if using a druid's wildshape ability, but only into a wolf of Challenge 1 or less.
- You can dominate any wolf, wolf-like creature, or chimerical creature with wolf features within 60 feet of the *wolf stone of Harva'roth* as per the spells *dominate beast*, *dominate person*, or *dominate monster* depending on the target. The spell save DC is 13, and the effect lasts until the next sunrise.

If erected within 40 feet of another *stone of Harva'roth* and in alignment with the other stones, the *wolf stone of Harva'roth* becomes more powerful. Aligning the stone with others in the panoply requires an Intelligence (Arcana) check with a DC equal to 15 + the number of stones being aligned. If aligned with other active stones attuned to the same person, the *wolf stone of Harva'roth* gains an additional use of each one-time use effect and an additional charge per stone in the alignment. Also, the DC of any saving throws to resist the stone's effects is increased by +1 per stone in the alignment. Finally, the area of effect for the stone's effects are centered on the geometric center of the aligned stones instead of the stone itself.

The wolf stone of Harva'roth remains active for one year or until it has no charges.

STUDIOUS ROBES

Wondrous item, panoply (scholarly mage), conjunction (azoth), very rare (requires attunement by a wizard)

These plain robes are stained on the sleeves by ink, patched in places, and very comfortable. Once you attune to the *studious robes*, you gain a +2 bonus to your armor class. You do not have to eat, drink, or breathe, and the robes keep you at a constant comfortable temperature. They also shed water and protect anything you wear under them. As a bonus action, you may command the robes to give you resistance from one of the following damage types, and you keep this protection until you use this feature again or until you dismiss it: acid, cold, fire, force, lightning, poison, psychic, or thunder damage.

If you wear the *studious robes* while wielding the *staff of knowledge*, you can choose two damage types to gain resistance to.

If you wear the *studious robes* while carrying the *quill of the assistant*, you may enter a book and reappear from another book within 100 feet of you. When you do so, you disappear. When you reappear, you occupy a space within five feet of the book from which you exit.

If you wear the *studious robes* as a complete set of the *panoply of the scholarly mage*, you may use an action to step into the extradimensional space occupied by a library you have folded up. When you do so, you disappear. When you return, you reoccupy the space you left, and if dangerous or occupied by a creature or object, you reappear within five feet of that space or in the nearest safe location. You may remain within the folded library's extradimensional space indefinitely.

SWAN HELMET

Wondrous item, rare (requires attunement)

This bowl-shaped bronze helmet has a cast swan as the crest, wings outspread, and head arched down toward your foe. While wearing the *swan helmet*, your armor class increases by +1. The *swan helmet* has three charges and regains spent charges each day at sunrise. You may spend one charge to use a bonus action to have the swan attack a creature adjacent to you (*melee attack:* +6 to hit, reach 5 feet, one creature; *Hit:* 6 [1d6+3] piercing damage). You may expend two charges to change shape into that of a swan as per a druid's wildshape class feature for up to six hours. Finally, you may expend three charges to gain a flying speed of 60 feet for one hour.

THAWB OF THE CITY DWELLER

Wondrous item, uncommon

This light cotton robe of a style worn by desert-dwelling men is bleached stark white and hangs loosely from the body. It does not stain or tear, and grants you resistance to piercing and slashing damage from nonmagical attacks. If you spend an hour inside a city or other urban location while wearing the robe, you learn its layout, major factions, rulers, and the general mood of its populace.

THAWB OF THE SAGE

Wondrous item, uncommon

This voluminous robe of a style worn by desert-dwelling men is made from wool and decorated with a geometric pattern in a lighter or darker color that contrasts with the wool. When worn, it grants you advantage on Intelligence (Arcana, History, Nature, and Religion) checks, as well as checks using chess sets. Additionally, the *thawb of the sage* allows you to enter a meditative state. It takes 10 minutes to enter this state, and the meditative state lasts for one hour. During this time, you must remain undisturbed; if interrupted, you lose the use of this feature and must begin again. At the end of the meditative state, you may cast the *augury* spell without needing any material components. You may do this three times and regain its use following an hour spent in a library or other place of learning.

THIMBLE OF MENDING

Wondrous item, uncommon

This small platinum thimble is paired with a platinum needle. It functions as the *mending* spell when used to repair any item. However, the thimble believes that many hands make fast work and that labor should be shared. Thus it will not work for anyone twice in a row on the same day.

THRONE OF THE HEAVENS

Wondrous item, panoply (heavens) very rare

Crafted millennia ago for the first caliph, the *throne of the heavens* is a massive ironwood throne adorned with intricate carvings depicting flowering plants and just dripping with gold leaf. The throne, like the rest of the *panoply of the heavens*, was lost when Grand Caliph Rabi bin Ashkar Al Ammu and his entire court were slaughtered at the Battle of False Wells by the great wyrm Jalthranax. Once attuned to the *throne of the heavens*, as an action you may command the throne to erect the royal tent. This fine silk tent easily houses 30 people, is divided into six rooms, has a carpeted floor, and comes fully furnished. Writing supplies are in the desks, food in the baskets, water in the ewers, and clothing in the hampers. All is of excellent quality and refreshes itself every dawn.

If you are sitting on the *throne of the heavens* while wearing the *robe of the heavens*, any creature that attempts to attack you must first succeed on a DC 15 Wisdom saving throw, and if they fail, their attack fails. Also, the throne radiates a constant *magic circle*.

If you are sitting upon the *throne of the heavens* as part of a complete *panoply of the heavens*, no one within 60 feet of you may speak or cast a spell without your express permission. Furthermore, you know if someone within this range is lying, even if it is a lie of omission.

TOKEN BALLS

Wondrous item, conjunction (mercury), uncommon

These small balls of unfired clay are by far the most commonly found magical item dating to the Age of Strife. The clay has hardened but is still rather fragile. Inscribed into each *token ball* is a single cuneiform word. The word describes the ball's contents but gives little clue as to how to use the item. If you speak the name of the item inscribed into the clay ball and use an action crack it open, the contained creature or object is released. The contents grow to full size within a round, becoming for all intents and purposes the object or creature held within the ball of clay. Once released, the magic is expended and the process cannot be reversed. Those who have investigated these items have discovered that a small, fired clay token representing the contents lies at the center of each clay ball. The contents of a *token ball* can be nearly anything, but the most common follow:

TOKEN BALL CONTENTS

1d12	Contents
1	1d2 oxen
2	1d6 + 1 goats
3	1d2 donkeys
4	A chariot
5	A plow
6	A shortsword, helm, shield, and breastplate of bronze
7	A sling and 20 stones
8	2d6 sheep
9	1d2 soldiers (as **guards**, with AC 12 due to leather armor)
10	1d2 scribes (as **commoner**, can read and write cuneiform)
11	1d4 + 1 musicians/dancers (**commoners**, with Charisma 14 and Performance +4)
12	A small house with dirt floors, adobe walls, thatch roof, a single bed, table, and four chairs

TRACKING FEATHER
Wondrous item, uncommon

The sharpened end of this gilded goose feather can easily pierce skin. If the command word and the name of a location or person are given, the feather can be tossed into the air as an action to hover at head level as it points in the direction of the target. The feather floats for 10 minutes before falling lazily to the ground; alternately, it can be snatched out of the air.

The feather has another use. If the sharp end is dipped in the blood of a living creature or used to prick the skin of a living creature (requiring an attack roll), the feather develops a small red stain. Afterward, if activated, the feather remains in the air pointing toward the target creature and follows the user at head level. Soaking the feather in caustic matter for two hours removes the stain and ends this feature.

TRIBUNE'S TOGA
Wondrous item, panoply (tribune's), very rare (requires attunement)

Worn by the tribunes of the empire as a formal uniform and considered part of their panoply, the *tribune's toga* was rarely worn in battle despite its benefits. This broad, semicircular white cloth has two purple stripes. Like other togas, it required one free hand to keep it from unfolding and falling off. The name of the tribune to whom it was awarded, as well as the date of awarding and the name of the emperor presenting it are sewn into the cloth so that it rests against the wearer's neck when the toga is properly worn. The toga never tears or frays. While you are attuned with the *tribune's toga* and wearing it, you have advantage on saving throws.

If worn as part of the *tribune's panoply* with the *tribune's baton*, as an action you may cast *magic circle* once per long rest.

If worn as part of a complete set of the *tribune's panoply*, as an action you may cast *banishment*. You may do this once per long rest.

TOME OF FATE AND PROPHECY
Wondrous item, unique

This thin, quarto tome is blank, and the covers are simple unadorned boards. Anything written in the *tome of fate and prophecy* is destined to happen at some point in the future, although how soon seems to vary. Each page can be written on once, and the writing becomes true in the fullness of time. When found, the *tome of fate and prophecy* has 1d4 pages of written text.

CHAPTER ELEVEN: WONDROUS ITEMS | 95

USHABTI LOCATIONS
Wondrous item, rare

These tomb models depict entire locations in fine detail. There are tiny wood, stone, and even adobe buildings, painted figurines of people and animals, and even terrain such as fields, rivers, and hills. The entire set needs to be present for the ushabti to function; if any of the pieces are missing, the models does not animate.

If you set the *ushabti location* on natural ground clear enough of obstructions to fit the unfolded model and use an action to speak the command word, the model grows to life-size and takes on the qualities of a real location, with the people and animals behaving as they would in life, and even the terrain magically melding to the natural terrain. Each type of *ushabti location* has a different duration and effect, but all can be returned to their model state with a command word (which requires them to rest for the listed amount of time). Any damage to the *ushabti location* while it is activated carries over to the model and vice versa, though damage can be repaired in either state as long as the majority of the whole is intact.

The people and animals created by the activated *ushabti locations* are brightly painted but often show few individual details, being abstract idolized forms rather than depictions of any single person. When the command word is spoken, they grow with the location to become life-sized and lifelike constructs. Treat *ushabti location* created people and animals as natural creatures, but change their creature type to construct and give them immunity to poison damage, and the charmed, exhaustion, frightened, paralyzed, and poisoned conditions. They do not need to sleep, eat, or breathe. If slain while animated, they revert to being small statues and must rest in that form for seven days before they can be reactivated.

Farm. This model unfolds to become a working farm with 40 acres of ripening grain, a small orchard of olives and dates, three cows, a dozen chickens, and several cats. There is a farmhouse, a threshing shed, a well, a dairy, and a stable. Eight people can comfortably live in the farmhouse, and eight horses can be stabled here. The model comes with a family of four, two adults and two children, who work the farm. The *ushabti farm* can remain active for seven days, after which it reverts to a model for seven days. Should it be activated on the spring equinox, the farm remains active until the fall equinox and produces grain and dairy products each month as if a full growing season had run its course.

Guard Tower. This model of a border watchtower unfolds to produce a 40-foot-tall sandstone and adobe tower with crenellations at the top, a reinforced wooden door, arrow slits spaced around its circumference, and a well in its basement. The tower has one main room on the first floor, a small basement cellar that is stocked to provide food and water for 30 people for 60 days, a set of stairs that leads up to a barracks floor, an armory, and then the top. The tower comes with 10 **guards** and a **veteran** to lead them. These people serve you with undying loyalty. The tower remains active for a fortnight and then reverts back to a model. It cannot be activated again for another fortnight. If you present the leader of the watch with proof showing your nobility, the tower remains active for a full month before reverting to a model to rest.

Inn. This model of a small roadside inn unfolds to produce a two-story inn of adobe, a stable, and a well. The inn comes complete with an innkeeper, a stable hand, and three servers, all of whom serve you loyally. The inn can seat 12 people in its common room and has eight private rooms on the second floor. The stable can house eight horses. The inn has a basement that holds enough food and drink to feed 20 people for 10 days, and a small brewery that produces 20 gallons of beer every week. The inn can stay active for two weeks and then reverts to a model to rest for two weeks.

Shrine. This model of a small shrine unfolds to produce a two-room shrine dedicated to a god. The shrine is of adobe and stone, and has a small altar room with a room for the single priest (treat as an **acolyte**) to dwell in. The priest serves you but is still a priest of its god and must balance the needs of faith and your orders. The shrine remains activated for 24 hours before it reverts to a model to rest for 24 hours. If you are a cleric, druid, paladin, ranger, or other class or background devoted to the shrine's patron deity, the shrine remains active for as long as you frequent it and perform at least one hour-long ritual in it per 24 hours.

Workshop. This model unfolds to produce an adobe workshop, as well as models of a master craftsperson and three apprentices. The workshop has all the required tools for a single craft, such as smith's tool or weaver's tools. The workshop can produce mundane goods associated with its craft, creating 1d20 + 10 gp worth of finished goods per 24 hours (this amount can be saved up to produce more expensive items over the course of several days). A person with proficiency in the appropriate tools can work in the shop and gains advantage on any checks related to their trade. The workshop remains activated for seven days before it reverts to a model to rest for seven days.

USHABTI PEOPLE
Wondrous item, rarity varies by type

These small statues are usually carved from stone, but ones made of ceramics or wood are not unknown. They are brightly painted but often show few individual details, being abstract idolized forms rather than depictions of any single person. When you use an action to speak the command word (which is often found painted on a statue's feet), they grow to become life-sized and lifelike constructs. Treat *ushabti people* as natural creatures, but change their creature type to construct and give them immunity to poison damage, and the charmed, exhaustion, frightened, paralyzed, and poisoned conditions. They do not need to sleep, eat, or breathe. If slain while animated, they revert to small statues and must rest in that form for seven days before they can be reactivated.

Herder (common). This *ushabti person* animates into a **commoner** (with Animal Handling + 2) clad in a shendyt and wearing a head wrap that protects them from the sun. They animate with a short goad and whip. The herder happily drives animals and provides whatever care those animals need, but has to be supplied with feed and other resources to do so. They animate for 10 hours and then must rest in statue form for six hours before being put to work again.

Laborer (common). This *ushabti person* animates into a **commoner** clad in a shendyt and wearing a head warp that protects them from the sun. They perform any needed task they are directed to accomplish, but lack initiative. You have to give them specific directions such as "pick up that stone and carry it to that location" for each stone they might need to move. They animate for 10 hours and then must rest in statue form for six hours before being put to work again.

Overseer (common). This *ushabti person* animates into a **commoner** (with Intimidation +2 and Persuasion +2) clad in a shendyt and wearing a nemes headdress. They animate with a rod and a whip. The overseer can direct the actions of up to 10 *ushabti laborers*. You can give the overseer complex orders, and the overseer sees that they are fulfilled. It animates for 10 hours and then must rest in statue form for six hours before being put to work again.

Performer (common). This *ushabti person* animates into a **commoner** (with Performance +2). It is dressed in an appropriate costume for their role and carries a musical instrument if so modeled. When you command it, the *ushabti performer* performs a routine from their catalog, which tends to be rather short and filled with its creator's favorites. They animate for two hours and then must rest in statue form for six hours before being called forth again.

Priest (rare). This *ushabti person* animates into an **acolyte** dressed in the religious garb of a Khemitian priest. They can cast spells and perform any rituals called for by their faith, but they balk at performing actions contrary to their patron deity's ethos. They animate for two hours and then must rest in statue form for 10 hours before being put to work again.

Sage (uncommon). This *ushabti person* dressed in a light gown animates into a **commoner** (with History +2, Nature +2, and Religion +2). They are knowledgeable on a broad range of affairs, but their knowledge stops at the time of their creation. They animate for four hours and then must rest in statue form for six hours before being put to work again.

Scribe (common). This *ushabti person* dressed in a light gown animates into a **commoner** holding a tablet and stylus. They can take dictation, draw a picture of something they can see, and copy documents. The scribe has only a single stylus and tablet, but additional writing material can be provided as needed. They animate for three hours and then must rest in statue form for seven hours before being put to work again.

Servant (common). This *ushabti person* dressed in a shendyt and light tunic animates into a **commoner**. While the servant has no special skills, it is highly trained in seeing to your needs. The servant mends your clothing and equipment, sets up and breaks down camp, cook meals, and offer advice on social situations (though from the perspective of a noble). They animate for 10 hours and then must rest in statue form for six hours before being put to work again.

Warrior (uncommon). This *ushabti person* animates into a **guard** dressed in a shendyt and wearing a nemes headdress. They serve you loyally unto death. The warrior can be ordered to guard a person or location, or simply be sent into a fight. It must have friend and foe carefully designated or it attacks anyone who is not you. They animate for four hours and then must rest in statue form for 10 hours before being put to work again.

USHABTI VEHICLES
Wondrous item, rarity varies by type

These wooden models depict common vehicles in great detail, right down to individual pegs and caulking. They are often found in burial tombs of the wealthy and powerful and are meant to aid them in the afterlife, or possibly in undeath. When activated, each model becomes a life-sized version complete with working parts, animals, and people as needed. The people and animals created by the activated *ushabti vehicles* are brightly painted but often show few individual details, being abstract idolized forms rather than depictions of any single creature.

When you use an action to speal the command word (which is often found painted on the vehicle), the statues grow to become life-sized and lifelike constructs. Treat created people and animals as natural creatures, but change their creature type to construct and give them immunity to poison damage, and the charmed, exhaustion, frightened, paralyzed, and poisoned conditions. They do not need to sleep, eat, or breathe. If slain while animated, they revert to being small statues and must rest in that form for seven days before they can be reactivated.

Barge (rare). This model animates to become a 150-foot-long and 20-foot-wide keelless wooden boat (speed 5 mph, crew 40, passengers 60, cargo 30 tons, AC 15, 200 hit points, damage threshold 10) that can be rowed or sailed. It has 40 sailors (**commoners**, with proficiency with water vehicles) ready to work the boat. The entire model can be animated for 10 hours, after which it must rest as a model for eight hours before being reactivated.

Barge, Royal (very rare). This model animates to become a 150-foot-long and 20-foot-wide keelless wooden boat (speed 5 mph, crew 40, passengers 100, cargo 10 tons, AC 15, 200 hit points, damage threshold 10) that can be rowed or sailed. It has 40 sailors (**commoners**, with proficiency with water vehicles) ready to work the boat, 20 **guards** ready to defend it, and 30 servants (**commoners**) to see to the needs of the passengers. The barge is ornately decorated and features all the possible comforts such as silk awnings, plush cushions, and enough food and drink for 140 people for 1 day. The entire model can be animated for 10 hours, after which it must rest as a model for eight hours before being reactivated.

Cart (common). This model animates as a standard cart complete with an ox to drive it. By far this is the simplest *ushabti vehicle*. The entire model can be animated for 10 hours, after which it must rest as a model for six hours before being reactivated.

Chariot, Racing (uncommon). This small chariot (speed 45 mph, crew 1, passenger 1, cargo 10 pounds, AC 15, 50 hit points) features a narrow wheel track, a yoke with two **riding horses**, and a charioteer (**commoner** with proficiency in Animal Handling and land vehicles). The chariot is painted in bright blues, reds, whites, and yellows. The entire model can be animated for five hours, after which it must rest as a model for 10 hours before being reactivated.

Chariot, War (rare). This chariot (speed 30 mph, crew 1, passenger 1, cargo 20 pounds, AC 16, 75 hit points) is designed for war and has high sidewalls, a wide wheel track, and an armed charioteer (**guard** with proficiency in Animal Handling and land vehicles). Two quivers holding 40 arrows each as well as two quivers holding six javelins each round out the equipment. The entire model can be animated for three hours, after which it must rest as a model for 10 hours before being reactivated.

WEATHER STONE
Wondrous item, uncommon

This plain gray stone is held in a cage of silver wire. When attached to a string and left to dangle, it predicts the weather for the next day. The stone gets warmer or cooler, drips water or is covered in a layer of frost and ice, and otherwise generates conditions that can be used to predict the next day's meteorological events. The stone even displays impending dangerous events such as electricity playing across its surface to denote lightning, swinging back and forth to show high winds, and pinging sounds as if being hit by hail. If the stone starts twirling in place, well, that is not a good sign.

WHEEL OF EARTH
Wondrous item, panoply (elemental wheels), conjunction (earth), rare

This cartwheel is made from a single piece of granite carved into a seven-spoke wheel. It can be attached to any wheeled vehicle such as a cart, chariot, or wagon. It takes one hour using carpenter's tools to attach the wheel and an additional hour to attune the wheel to the vehicle.

Once the *wheel of earth* is attuned to a vehicle, the vehicle's speed is increased by 50 mph, its AC increases by +2, and the vehicle's hit points increase by +50. Also, the vehicle may move at full speed over difficult terrain that is a natural feature, such as mud, sand, scree, or similar surfaces.

If attuned to a vehicle alongside a *wheel of water*, the vehicle does not leave tracks of any sort.

If attuned to a vehicle as part of a complete *elemental wheel panoply*, the vehicle can be driven through the ground and solid rock for one hour. If it is within the ground or solid rock at the end of this time, the wheel, the vehicle, and everything within it are destroyed.

WHEEL OF FIRE
Wondrous item, panoply (elemental wheels), conjunction (fire), rare

This cartwheel is made from a single piece of granite carved into a seven-spoke wheel. It can be attached to any wheeled vehicle such as a cart, chariot, or wagon. It takes one hour using carpenter's tools to attach the wheel and an additional hour to attune the wheel to the vehicle.

Once the *wheel of fire* is attuned to the vehicle, the vehicle's speed is increased by 50 mph, the vehicle's AC increases by +2, and the vehicle's hit points increase by +50. Also, the vehicle and everything within it are immune to fire damage. Finally, the vehicle can safely travel across lava, magma, and similar surfaces as if they were plain ground.

If attuned to a vehicle alongside a *wheel of air*, the driver of the vehicle can cause the vehicle to leave a trail of smoke as it moves along that rapidly disperses. This trail is a 15-foot-long cone that originates from the back of the vehicle. Any creature that begins its turn in the cone must succeed at a DC 15 Constitution saving throw or be poisoned for one hour.

If attuned to a vehicle as part of a complete *elemental wheel panoply*, once per day, the vehicle can teleport itself and everything within it as per the spell *teleport*. The driver of the vehicle must use an action to issue the command.

WHEEL OF WATER
Wondrous item, panoply (elemental wheels), conjunction (water), rare

This cartwheel is made from a single piece of granite carved into a seven-spoke wheel. It can be attached to any wheeled vehicle such as a cart, chariot, or wagon. It takes one hour using carpenter's tools to attach the wheel and an additional hour to attune the wheel to the vehicle.

Once the *wheel of water* is attuned to the vehicle, the vehicle's speed is increased by 50 mph, the vehicle's AC increases by +2, the vehicle's hit points increase by +50, and the vehicle can move across water as if it were solid ground.

If attuned to a vehicle alongside a *wheel of earth*, the vehicle can leave a trail of mud as it moves along. This mud is difficult terrain and lasts for about 24 hours, more or less depending on local environmental conditions.

If attuned to a vehicle as part of a complete *elemental wheel panoply*, the vehicle can be driven underwater as if flying through the air. The vehicle and everything within it are protected from water damage, and any living creatures in the vehicle (including the beast pulling it) gain the ability to breathe underwater. The vehicle may do this for eight hours and regains expended hours at a rate of two per hour spent above the water.

WHEEL OF WIND
Wondrous item, panoply (elemental wheels), conjunction (air), rare

This cartwheel is made from a single piece of granite carved into a seven-spoke wheel. It can be attached to any wheeled vehicle such as a cart, chariot, or wagon. It takes one hour using carpenter's tools to attach the wheel and an additional hour to attune the wheel to the vehicle.

Once the *wheel of wind* is attuned to the vehicle, the vehicle's speed is increased by 50 mph, the vehicle's AC increases by +2, the vehicle's hit points increase by +50, and the vehicle can move across gaps of up to 100 feet of open air as if it were solid ground. The vehicle must begin and end its movement on solid ground or it falls.

If attuned to a vehicle alongside a *wheel of fire*, the driver of the vehicle can command it to leap into the air, traveling up to 100 feet vertically and 50 feet horizontally. It must begin and end this leap on a solid surface.

If attuned to a vehicle as part of a complete *elemental wheel panoply*, the vehicle can be flown through the air as if traveling across solid ground.

WHISTLE OF THE MIDDLE-SKY
Wondrous item, very rare

This simple bone whistle is covered in ancient runes that speak of the middle-sky, a plane somewhere inside of or beyond the sky above and the earth below. As an action, you many blow this whistle to summon 1d4 + 1 **mi-go** (see **Appendix A: New Monsters**) that arrive within 30 feet of you. You do not have control over these creatures, but you may attempt to gain control of them by taking an action to play the *whistle of the middle-sky*. Each round you play, the mi-go must succeed at a Wisdom saving throw or become charmed by you. The DC of this saving throw is based on a Charisma (Performance) check you make using the *whistle of the middle-sky*. The mi-go remain charmed as long as you continue to play the whistle, and return to wherever they came from if slain or if you stop playing the whistle for five rounds.

WOTAN'S CLOAK
Wondrous item, rare (requires attunement)

This ragged wool cloak looks better on a beggar than on a noble. Once attuned to it, you may use an action to issue a command to change your form as per the spell *shapechange* into a **brown bear** or into a nondescript humanoid, but not into a specific humanoid. You may use the cloak once and regain use of its ability following a one-hour ritual.

APPENDIX A: NEW MONSTERS

CARYATID COLUMN

An exquisitely sculpted and chiseled statue of a beautiful female warrior adorns the area, longsword in her hand.

A caryatid column is akin to the stone golem in that it is a magical construct created by a spellcaster. Caryatid columns are always created for a specific defensive function. The caryatid column stands seven feet tall and weighs around 1,500 pounds. The caryatid column always wields a weapon (usually a longsword) in its left hand. The weapon itself is constructed of steel, but is melded with the column and made of stone until the column animates. When melded, the sword is likely to be overlooked (DC 20 Perception check to see it).

Caryatid columns are programmed as guardians and activate when certain conditions or stipulations are met or broken (such as a living creature enters a chamber guarded by a caryatid column). A caryatid column attacks its opponents with its longsword. It does not move more than 50 feet from the area it is guarding or protecting.

CARYATID COLUMN

Medium construct, unaligned

Armor Class 14 (natural armor)
Hit Points 45 (6d8 + 18)
Speed 20 ft.

STR	DEX	CON	INT	WIS	CHA
16 (+3)	14 (+2)	16 (+3)	2 (−4)	11 (+0)	1 (−5)

Damage Resistances piercing, and slashing damage from nonmagical weapons that aren't adamantine
Damage Immunities poison, psychic
Condition Immunities charmed, exhaustion, frightened, paralyzed, petrified, poisoned
Senses darkvision 120 ft., passive Perception 10
Languages understands the languages of its creator but can't speak
Challenge 2 (450 XP)

Immutable Form. The caryatid column is immune to any spell or effect that would alter its form.
Magic Resistance. The caryatid column has advantage on saving throws against spells and other magical effects.
Magic Weapons. The caryatid column's weapon attacks are magical.
Shatter Weapons. Whenever a character strikes a caryatid column with a non-adamantine, nonmagical weapon, the weapon must succeed on a DC 10 saving throw or shatter into pieces.

ACTIONS

Longsword. *Melee Weapon Attack:* +5 to hit, reach 5 ft., one target. *Hit:* 8 (1d10 + 3) slashing damage.

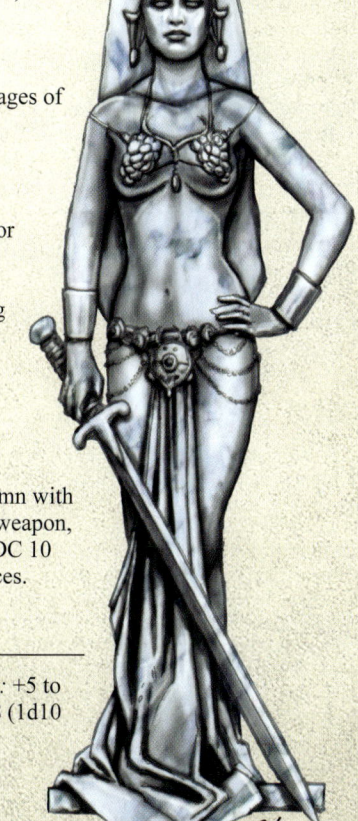

BEETLE, GIANT DEATH WATCH

This creature appears as a giant beetle with a dark green carapace and wing-covers. Its body is covered in leaves and sticks. Its mandibles are silver, and its legs are black.

The death watch beetle makes its lair in forests and uses a mixture of saliva and earth to stick rubbish (leaves and twigs, for instance) to itself in order to attack by surprise.

The death watch beetle begins combat using its death rattle ability. Any creatures that survive are bitten by the beetle's mandibles and devoured.

GIANT DEATH WATCH BEETLE

Medium beast, unaligned

Armor Class 14 (natural armor)
Hit Points 75 (10d8 + 30)
Speed 30 ft.

STR	DEX	CON	INT	WIS	CHA
20 (+5)	10 (+0)	16 (+3)	1 (−5)	10 (+0)	9 (−1)

Damage Immunities necrotic
Senses darkvision 60 ft., passive Perception 10
Languages —
Challenge 5 (1,800 XP)

ACTIONS

Bite. *Melee Weapon Attack:* +7 to hit, reach 5 ft., one target. *Hit:* 12 (2d6 + 5) piercing damage.
Death Rattle (recharge 5–6). The death watch beetle emits a clicking noise with a resonance frequency that affects creatures within 30 feet of it. Creatures in this area must make a DC 13 Constitution saving throw, taking 10 (3d6) thunder damage on a failed save, or half as much damage on a successful one.

CHAPTER ELEVEN: WONDROUS ITEMS | 99

CAVE LION

The prehistoric ancestor of the lion, or possibly the tiger, the cave lion is a truly massive beast standing 13 to 16 feet tall at the shoulder and weighing around a thousand pounds. More than just an enlarged lion, the cave lion has a shaggier coat, smaller mane, and shorter tail. Much like their descendants, they are social animals and live in prides of one to three males, four to six females, and numerous young.

Cave lions are not capable of long pursuits but they are excellent ambush predators. How they manage to hide such massive bodies in the grass beggars the intellect, but these canny hunters do just that. Like their name suggests, they prefer to lair in caves, but these lairs are only places to sleep and to keep the young protected. Do not expect to find a cave lion underground; the most likely encounter with one of these prehistoric predators is when one leaps out of the brush right behind you.

CAVE LION
Huge beast, unaligned

Armor Class 11 (natural armor)
Hit Points 68 (8d12 + 16)
Speed 50 ft.

STR	DEX	CON	INT	WIS	CHA
22 (+6)	10 (+0)	15 (+2)	4 (–3)	12 (+1)	7 (–7)

Skills Perception +3, Stealth +6
Senses darkvision 60 ft, passive Perception 13
Languages none
Challenge 4 (1,100 XP)

Keen Smell. The cave lion has advantage on Wisdom (Perception) checks that rely on smell.
Pack Tactics. The cave lion has advantage on an attack roll against a creature if at least one of the lion's allies is within five feet of the creature and the ally isn't incapacitated.
Pounce. If the cave lion moves at least 20 feet straight toward a creature and then hits with a claw attack on the same turn, that target must succeed on a DC 15 Strength saving throw or be knocked prone. If the target is prone, the lion can make one bite attack against it as a bonus action.
Running Leap. With a 10-foot running start, the lion can long jump 35 feet.

ACTIONS

Multiattack. The creature makes one Bite attack and two Claw attacks.
Bite. *Melee Weapon Attack:* +8 to hit, reach 5 ft., one target. *Hit:* 14 (2d8 + 6) piercing damage.
Claw. *Melee Weapon Attack:* +8 to hit, reach 10 ft., one target. *Hit:* 13 (2d6 + 6) slashing damage.

CORAL GOLEM

Coral golems are made from living coral, which gives them a colorful vibrance and lifelike presence. The coral polyps of the golem continue to live on even after the golem pulls itself off the seafloor, and every attack with its mighty fists includes a few minor stings. Being composed of living coral, these golems become a part of the local ecosystem and often attract fish, crabs, and other life.

Those who create coral golems tend to be nature-inclined magic-users, druids, and clerics. They know that pulling up part of the coral reef is not beneficial but they do so for the ability to protect the rest from harm. They often let their coral golems lie dormant as part of the reef. Not only does this limit the damage to the local ecosystem, but it makes for a cunning trap and great surprise for those who would harm the golem's creator or their natural charges.

CORAL GOLEM
Large construct, unaligned

Armor Class 16 (natural armor)
Hit Points 133 (14d10 + 56)
Speed 20 ft., swim 30 ft.

STR	DEX	CON	INT	WIS	CHA
20 (+5)	9 (–1)	18 (+4)	3 (–1)	8 (1)	1 (–5)

Damage Immunities poison, psychic; bludgeoning, piercing, and slashing damage from nonmagical attacks that aren't adamantine
Condition Immunities blinded, charmed, deafened, exhaustion, paralyzed, poisoned
Senses darkvision 60 ft., passive Perception 9
Languages can't speak but understands the languages of its creator
Challenge 9 (5,000 XP)

Berserk. Whenever the coral golem starts its turn with 60 hit points or fewer, roll a d6. On a 6, the coral golem goes berserk. On each of its turns while berserk, the coral golem attacks the nearest creature it can see. If no creature is near enough to move to and attack, the coral golem attacks an object, with preference for an object smaller than itself. Once the coral golem goes berserk, it continues to do so until it is destroyed or regains all its hit points. The coral golem's creator, if within 60 feet of the berserk coral golem, can try to calm it by speaking firmly and persuasively. The coral golem must be able to hear its creator, who must take an action to make a DC 15 Charisma (Persuasion) check. If the check succeeds, the coral golem ceases being berserk. If it takes damage while still at 60 hit points or fewer, the coral golem might go berserk again.
Cold Absorption. Whenever the golem is subjected to cold damage, it takes no damage and instead regains hit points equal to the amount of cold damage dealt.
Immutable Form. The coral golem is immune to any spell or effect that would alter its form.
Indistinguishable from Natural Coral. If not moving, the coral golem looks like a natural part of the reef.
Magic Resistance. The coral golem has advantage on saving throws against spells and other magical effects.
Magic Weapons. The coral golem's weapon attacks are magical.

Actions

Multiattack. The coral golem makes two Slam attacks.
Attack. *Melee Weapon Attack:* +9 to hit, reach 10 ft., one target. *Hit:* 16 (2d10 + 5) bludgeoning damage and the target must succeed at a DC 15 Constitution saving throw or suffer 9 (2d8) poison damage and be paralyzed until the end of their next turn.
Poison Breath (recharge 5–6). The coral golem exhales a cloud of poisonous ink that fills a 10-foot area and lingers for 1d6 + 1 rounds. This cloud blocks line of sight and each creature that ends its turn in the area must make a Constitution saving throw (DC 15), taking 22 (4d10) poison damage on a failure, or half as much on a success.

GIANT TORTOISE

Used in swampy and boggy regions as a pack and draft animal, the giant turtle might be slower than a horse but its utility lies in its ability to traverse mud and open water with ease. Standing five feet tall at the shoulder and nearly seven feet at the peak of its arched shell, those riding a giant turtle have an excellent position to stay out of the muck and mire. The turtle's broad shell provides a fine place to mount cargo nets, and its great shell and strength even permit a wooden platform to be affixed. Some lizardfolk tribes use giant turtles as mobile platforms for light ballistae.

GIANT TORTOISE
Large beast, unaligned

Armor Class 16 (natural armor)
Hit Points: 15 (2d10 +4)
Speed 15 ft., swim 40 ft.

STR	DEX	CON	INT	WIS	CHA
16 (+3)	8 (–1)	15 (+2)	2 (–4)	12 (+1)	4 (–3)

Condition Immunities prone
Senses passive Perception 11
Languages none
Challenge 1 (200 XP)

Muck Walker. The giant turtle ignores difficult terrain that is muddy, soft soil, or otherwise the result of sodden ground.
Shell. The giant turtle's shell is resistant to bludgeoning, piercing, and slashing damage from nonmagical attacks. Unless targeting the beast's legs or head, assume any attack targets the shell and thus apply this resistance. The giant turtle can draw its legs and head into its shell.

Actions

Bite. *Melee Weapon Attack:* +5 to hit, reach 10 ft., one target. *Hit:* 7 (1d8 + 3) slashing damage.

GLYPTODONT

Squat but massive, glyptodonts were heavily armored herbivores that wandered the forests and savannahs of ages long past. They had short, blunt heads, a rounded body covered in a thick carapace, and a long tail studded with spikes and rings of bone. Dermal plating extended along its neck, over its head, and along its tail. While only growing to be six feet tall, their bodies could be 13 feet long and nearly half as much wide.

The glyptodont's tail is its main threat, for it can strike with this armored, whip-like appendage with enough force to crush plate armor. The spikes on the tail create a natural mace of staggering power. The flexible tail can be wrapped around or over the body to hit creatures in front of the glyptodont, but its best use is to maximize its length and sweep from the rear to the sides, striking multiple targets and crushing them to the ground.

GLYPTODONT
Large beast, unaligned

Armor Class 16 (natural armor)
Hit Points 52 (7d10 + 14)
Speed 15 ft.

STR	DEX	CON	INT	WIS	CHA
18 (+4)	8 (–1)	15 (+2)	2 (–4)	12 (+1)	4 (–3)

Condition Immunities prone
Senses passive Perception 11
Languages none
Challenge 2 (450 XP)

Carapace. The glyptodont's carapace is resistant to bludgeoning, piercing, and slashing damage from nonmagical attacks. Unless targeting the beast's legs or head, assume any attack targets the carapace and thus apply this resistance.

Actions

Multiattack. The creature makes two Tail attacks.
Tail. *Melee Weapon Attack:* +6 to hit, reach 10 ft., 1–3 targets. *Hit:* 13 (2d8 + 4) bludgeoning damage.

HIPPOPOTAMUS

The hippopotamus is a grumpy, territorial animal native to tropical and subtropical wetlands. While a vegetarian, their massive jaws and long teeth can crack plate armor like a lobster shell and shred the soft flesh underneath.

HIPPOPOTAMUS
Large beast, unaligned

Armor Class 16 (natural armor)
Hit Points 13 (2d10 + 2)
Speed 20 ft., swim 30 ft.

STR	DEX	CON	INT	WIS	CHA
16 (+3)	10 (+0)	12 (+1)	2 (–4)	12 (+1)	7 (–2)

Senses passive Perception 11
Languages —
Challenge 1/2 (100 XP)

Hold Breath. The hippopotamus can hold its breath for 10 minutes.

APPENDIX A: NEW MONSTERS

Trample. If the hippopotamus moves at least 20 feet straight toward a creature and then hits with a Stomp attack on the same turn, that target must succeed on a DC 13 Strength saving throw or be knocked prone. If the target is prone, the hippopotamus can make one Stomp attack against it as a bonus action.

Actions

Stomp. *Melee Weapon Attack:* +5 to hit, reach 5 ft., one target. *Hit:* 12 (2d8 + 3) piercing damage.

MEGALOYNX

A mid-sized ground sloth, the megaloynx was 10 feet long and weighed around 1,000 pounds. It could rear up onto its hind legs and even walk short distances in this stance, much like a bear. It mostly ate leaves and bark, stripping branches bare long scythe-like foreclaws. It defended itself with these same foreclaws, and like most large herbivores, the megaloynx was not averse to a little carrion or opportunistic meat.

The megaloynx was hunted for its hide and copious, fatty meat. This was a heroic act, for facing an enraged ground sloth is a dangerous and often fatal undertaking. If wounded or cornered, the beast rises up on its short hind legs and brings its powerful claws into the fight, slashing open foes and rending bodies. The megaloynx's great bulk allowed it to shrug off all but the most-deadly of blows, and legends tell of these ground sloths fighting well beyond when they should be dead.

MEGALOYNX
Large beast, unaligned

Armor Class 14 (natural armor)
Hit Points 95 (10d10 + 40)
Speed 25 ft.

STR	DEX	CON	INT	WIS	CHA
20 (+5)	10 (+0)	18 (+4)	2 (−4)	12 (+1)	4 (−3)

Senses passive Perception 11
Languages none
Challenge 4 (1,100 XP)

Rage. If wounded or cornered, the megaloynx enters a rage. While in this rage, it gains resistance to bludgeoning, piercing, and slashing damage from nonmagical attacks, inflicts an additional +2 damage with its attacks, and continues to fight on even if it suffers a fatal wound. If reduced to 0 hp, roll 1d20. On a roll of 10+, the megaloynx does not drop to 0 hit points; instead, it gains 1 hit point and may make an attack as a reaction.

Actions

Multiattack. The creature makes one Bite attack and two Claw attacks.
Bite. *Melee Weapon Attack:* +7 to hit, reach 5 ft., one target. *Hit:* 9 (1d8 + 5) piercing damage.
Claw. *Melee Weapon Attack:* +7 to hit, reach 10 ft., one target. Hit: 14 (2d8 + 5) slashing damage.
Rend. As a bonus action, if the megaloynx hits the same target with both of its claw attacks in the same turn, it tears the target apart and inflicts an additional 7 (2d6) slashing damage.

MI-GO

Mi-go are giant lobster-like creatures with dorsal fins, membranous wings, and articulate limbs ending in pincers. Their strange heads are ellipsoids and sprout numerous short, tentacle-like antennae. They are eight feet long and stand six feet tall. While mi-gos primarily communicate by clicking their pincers, many of their species have learned Common to better convey their intentions. When they speak, their voices reverberate with a buzzing rasp many find annoying. Some believe the mi-go are planar travelers sent to mine other worlds of their resources and to test and examine the lifeforms they discover. Despite their monstrous appearance, the creatures are extremely intelligent and often employ odd technologies that confound adventurers.

MI-GO
Medium plant, neutral evil

Armor Class 17 (natural armor)
Hit Points 76 (8d8 + 40)
Speed 30 ft., fly 60 ft.

STR	DEX	CON	INT	WIS	CHA
16 (+3)	19 (+4)	21 (+5)	25 (+7)	15 (+2)	13 (+1)

Skills Arcana +10, Deception +7, Medicine +5, Perception +5, Stealth +7
Damage Resistances cold, radiant
Senses blindsight 30 ft., darkvision 240 ft., passive Perception 15
Languages Common, Mi-Go, Void Speech
Challenge 9 (5,000 XP)

Astral Travelers. Mi-go do not require air or heat to survive, only sunlight (and very little of that). They can enter a sporulated form capable of surviving travel through the void and return to consciousness when conditions are right.
Disquieting Technology. The mi-go are a highly advanced race and may carry items of powerful technology. Mi-go technology can be represented using the same rules as magic items, but their functions are very difficult to determine: *identify* is useless, but an hour of study and a successful DC 19 Intelligence (Arcana) check can reveal the purpose and proper functioning of a mi-go item.
Sneak Attack (1/turn). The mi-go does an extra 7 (2d6) damage when it hits with a Claw attack and has advantage on the attack roll, or when the target is within five feet of an ally of the mi-go that isn't incapacitated and the mi-go doesn't have disadvantage on the attack roll.
Spellcasting. The mi-go is a 10th-level spellcaster. Its spellcasting ability is Intelligence (spell save DC 19, +11 to hit with spell attacks). The mi-go has the following wizard spells prepared:

Cantrips (at will): *acid splash, fire bolt, minor illusion, poison spray, shocking grasp*
1st level (4 slots): *comprehend languages, detect magic, false life, shield*
2nd level (3 slots): *invisibility, magic mouth, suggestion*
3rd level (3 slots): *animate dead, major image, lightning bolt*
4th level (3 slots): *arcane eye, locate creature, stoneskin*
5th level (2 slots): *animate objects, dominate person*

Actions

Multiattack. The mi-go makes two Claw attacks.
Claw. *Melee Weapon Attack:* +7 to hit, reach 5 ft., one target. *Hit:* 14 (3d6 + 4) slashing damage, and the target is grappled (escape DC 13). If both Claw attacks strike the same target in a single turn, the target takes an additional 13 (2d12) psychic damage.

102 | Tome of Wondrous Items

PREHISTORIC HONEY BADGER

The prehistoric honey badger is no mere oversized weasel. Its thick skin and powerful jaws makes it a terrifying creature to contend with, and its fearlessness makes it more dangerous than many humanoids.

The prehistoric honey badger stands two feet at the shoulder and is over five feet long, weighing over 100 pounds. Strictly a carnivore, the fearless prehistoric honey badger hunts venomous or poisonous creatures, or humanoids, and even chases off larger creatures to steal their kills. Its jaws are capable of tearing through fresh meat like a cleaver and of crushing through bone without trouble.

Prehistoric honey badgers make their homes in dry grasslands and in moist forests. They dig burrows with their strong claws, where they lair alone, only nearing another honey badger to mate during the fall months. A honey badger's cubs are born in late winter, and after 6–8 weeks with the female honey badger, the cubs are left to fend for themselves.

PREHISTORIC HONEY BADGER
Medium beast, unaligned

Armor Class 14 (natural armor)
Hit Points 51 (6d8 + 24)
Speed 30 ft., burrow 30 ft.

STR	DEX	CON	INT	WIS	CHA
20 (+5)	12 (+1)	18 (+4)	7 (–2)	11 (+0)	5 (–3)

Skills Survival +2
Damage Resistances poison; bludgeoning, piercing, and slashing damage from nonmagical attacks
Condition Immunities frightened
Senses darkvision 60 ft., passive Perception 10
Languages —
Challenge 4 (1,100 XP)

Keen Hearing and Smell. The prehistoric honey badger has advantage on Wisdom (Perception) checks based on hearing or smell.

Relentless (recharges after a short or long rest). If the badger takes 14 damage or less that would reduce it to 0 hit points, it is reduced to 1 hit point instead.

ACTIONS

Multiattack. The prehistoric honey badger makes one Bite attack and one Crunch attack.
Bite. *Melee Weapon Attack:* +7 to hit, reach 5 ft., one target. *Hit:* 16 (2d10 + 5) piercing damage, and the target must make a DC 15 Strength saving throw or be grappled (escape DC 15).
Crunch. *Melee Weapon Attack:* +7 to hit, reach 5 ft., one grappled creature. *Hit:* The target suffers from broken bones and must make a DC 15 Constitution saving throw at the beginning of each of its turns. On a failed saving throw, the target cannot take any actions or reactions during that turn. The effect ends if the target receives magical healing or takes a long rest.

PREHISTORIC BEAVER

Although the tail is thinner than the average beaver, the prehistoric beaver is more than twice the size of its modern kin, with substantially larger canine teeth.

The beaver of prehistoric times averages over seven feet long and three feet at the shoulder. It is an herbivore that survives off tree bark and cambium, the soft tissue that grows beneath tree bark. It builds long, low lodges across large rivers. A family of prehistoric beavers can be the cause of an entire village's demise should they dam the river that passes near it.

A significant difference between a common beaver and a prehistoric beaver is the length of their teeth; suited to strip bark, the front incisors are more than five inches long, and the beavers use them to defend their lodges.

PREHISTORIC BEAVER
Large beast, unaligned

Armor Class 15 (natural armor)
Hit Points 52 (7d8 + 21)
Speed 30 ft., swim 40 ft.

STR	DEX	CON	INT	WIS	CHA
20 (+5)	12 (+1)	17 (+3)	3 (–4)	11 (+0)	5 (–3)

Skills Survival +2
Senses passive Perception 10
Languages —
Challenge 3 (700 XP)

Hold Breath. The prehistoric beaver can hold its breath for up to 20 minutes.
Siege Monster. The prehistoric beaver deals double damage to objects and structures.

ACTIONS

Bite. *Melee Weapon Attack:* +7 to hit, reach 5 ft., one target. *Hit:* 27 (4d10 + 5) piercing damage.

APPENDIX A: NEW MONSTERS

SCROLL FAMILIAR

An uncommon type of familiar, the scroll familiar is a construct created through careful use of a *scroll familiar* scroll. The construct created is a rolled up, three-foot-tall animated scroll covered with arcane sigils that form a faint impression of a face, and spindly limbs made from curling pieces of ribbon. Sometimes the sigils that form its face make expressions, especially a single raised eyebrow.

Scroll familiars are very loyal to their masters, but each has a unique personality. Some are curious, while others are skeptical. The most common seems to be a sarcastic pedantry that it directs at all and sundry, but most especially its master. They are knowledgeable on topics of arcane mechanics and often aid their master's research.

Some rare scroll familiars go rogue after their master dies. These might turn into vengeful figures that hunt down those who slew their master. If mistreated, many turn to petty theft of magic and. magic items to empower them. Rogue scroll familiars can be bound to a new master through the use of the spell *find familiar* and similar magics, but only if they are willing.

SCROLL FAMILIAR
Small construct, as master

Armor Class 13
Hit Points 7 (2d6)
Speed 35 ft.

STR	DEX	CON	INT	WIS	CHA
8 (–1)	16 (+3)	10 (+0)	14 (+2)	14 (+2)	14 (+2)

Skills Arcana +4
Damage Vulnerabilities fire
Damage Immunities poison, psychic
Condition Immunities blinded, charmed, deafened, exhaustion, paralyzed, poisoned
Senses blindsight 60 ft. (blind beyond this radius), passive Perception 12
Languages as master plus three others determined at the time of its creation
Challenge 1/2 (100 XP)

Immutable Form. The scroll familiar is immune to any spell or effect that would alter its form.
Spell Repository. The scroll familiar's master may cast a spell that they know into the scroll familiar. This spell does not take effect but is held in the scroll familiar until used. While within 100 feet of the scroll familiar, its master can use an action to cast a stored spell. Also, the scroll familiar may use an action to cast a stored spell. When a stored spell is cast, it uses the spell save DC and magic attack roll of the master when the spell was stored in the scroll familiar. The scroll familiar can hold up to three levels of spells. If the scroll familiar is destroyed or dismissed, any stored spells are lost.

ACTIONS

Paper Cut. *Melee Weapon Attack:* +5 to hit, reach 5 ft., one target. *Hit:* 4 slashing damage and the target must succeed at a DC 10 Constitution saving throw or be stunned by the pain until the end of its next turn.

SMOKE WYRM

Created by the *ring of the smoke wyrm*, these ephemeral constructs are made of living smoke and vapor. They can take any form the user of the *ring of the smoke wyrm* desires, but they always first flow out of the ring as a cloud of opaque gray vapor that bears a resemblance to the long neck, head, forelimbs, and wings of a dragon. The vapor fills a 10-foot-by-10-foot area but can lengthen to up to 20 feet long and three feet in diameter.

The smoke wyrm has no real thoughts or personality other than a cruel cunning. It is made to hunt down and slay a target its master designates, and when that task is complete, it returns to the *ring of the smoke wyrm* to await a new target. While it can be used in other ways, killing is the smoke wyrm's true purpose and even if assigned as a spy or used for common labor, it will seek out small vermin, animals, and even children to sate its bloodlust.

SMOKE WYRM
Large construct, unaligned

Armor Class 13
Hit Points 26 (4d10 + 4)
Speed 30 ft. fly 40 ft.

STR	DEX	CON	INT	WIS	CHA
16 (+3)	16 (+3)	12 (+1)	4 (–3)	10 (+0)	4 (–3)

Skills Perception +2, Stealth +7
Damage Resistances bludgeoning, piercing, and slashing damage from nonmagical attacks
Damage Immunities necrotic, poison
Condition Immunities charmed, exhaustion, frightened, grappled, paralyzed, petrified, poisoned, prone, and restrained
Senses darkvision 60 ft., passive Perception 12
Languages cannot speak but understands Common
Challenge 2 (450 XP)

Incorporeal Movement. The smoke wyrm and any creature it carries can move through other creatures and objects as if they were difficult terrain. It and any creature it carries take 5 (1d10) force damage if the smoke wyrm ends its turn inside a solid object.
Locate Target. If commanded to fetch, attack, carry a message, or locate a specific creature or target, the smoke wyrm knows the range and direction to that target.

ACTIONS

Multiattack. The smoke wyrm makes one Bite and one Claw attack.
Bite. *Melee Weapon Attack:* + 5 to hit, reach 10 ft., one target. *Hit:* 7 (1d8 + 3) piercing damage., plus 7 (2d6) psychic damage.
Claw. *Melee Weapon Attack:* + 5 to hit, reach 5 ft., one target. *Hit:* 3 (1d6 + 3) slashing damage.

104 | TOME OF WONDROUS ITEMS

SPELL PARROT

The bird appears to be an entirely ordinary parrot. When it speaks, however, it utters the words of a magical spell and arcane energy begins to swirl around it.

Spell parrots are an exceedingly rare and unexplained phenomenon. They look, think, and act primarily like parrots, despite high intelligence for an animal. No one knows why they are able to do what they do, though it is clear that the ability they possess is as likely to be a burden as a boon to them. When spell parrots first hear and mimic a spellcaster, they rarely seem to understand or expect the results of their mimicry. Older wild spell parrots have usually learned how to use their strange and unpredictable powers, but rarely do so unless threatened.

Spell parrots can be tamed as pets, but since they occur spontaneously (within any of the larger parrot species), it is difficult to discover one young enough to socialize it well. Only people with exceptional animal handling skills should attempt to keep a spell parrot around spellcasters, but careful training can result in a spell parrot that (usually) mimics spells only at a signal from a humanoid companion, and (usually) only targets spells as directed. Even a very well-trained spell parrot may occasionally choose to disobey a trainer, however. They can be cantankerous creatures, and moody, with questionable senses of humor.

Like mundane parrots, spell parrots often live a little longer than humans, and while they cannot become fluent in humanoid languages, they can memorize small vocabularies and engage in rudimentary verbal communication. Talking to a well-trained spell parrot is similar in clarity, depth, grammar, and logic to communication with a small toddler.

SPELL PARROT
Tiny beast, unaligned

Armor Class 15
Hit Points 12 (5d4)
Speed 10ft, fly 50ft

STR	DEX	CON	INT	WIS	CHA
4 (–3)	20 (+5)	10 (+0)	6 (–2)	18 (+4)	8 (–1)

Saving Throws Dex +8, Wis +7
Skills: Perception +6
Senses passive Perception 16
Languages see below
Challenge 3 (700 XP)

Innate Spellcasting. A spell parrot can innately cast one 0-level spell at will. The spell must have a verbal component, but can otherwise be of any type (example: *vicious mockery,* for which it always uses the exact same string of insults, whether or not they make sense in context). The spell parrot always casts without somatic or material components. Its spellcasting ability is Wisdom (spell save DC 14, +6 to hit with spell attacks). This one innate spell varies from parrot to parrot, but it cannot change throughout the spell parrot's life. Unlike mimicked spells (below), the spell parrot uses its one innate spell with as much logic and skill as can be expected of a bird.

Magic Resistance. The spell parrot has advantage on saving throws against spells and other magical effects.

Spell Mimicry. Spell parrots possess an innate ability to cast almost any spell they hear (arcane or divine) without material or somatic components, so long as it was cast with a verbal component. For spells of 0 level, the parrot can always cast the spell. For spells of 1st through 3rd level, the spell has a 50% chance of success. For spells of 4th through 6th level, the spell has a 33% chance of success. For spells of 7th through 9th level, the spell has a 10% chance of succeeding in a very limited way, usually equivalent to a related spell of 1st or 2nd level (for example, *control weather* might become *gust of wind,* or *true resurrection* might become *gentle repose,* and *wish* would depend on what was wished for). When a spell fails, nothing happens.

Each spell a spell parrot hears can be mimicked only once (even if it doesn't succeed). After that, the parrot may continue to "parrot" the verbal component, but nothing happens. Spell parrots can cast any given spell only within the first minute of hearing the verbal component. After that, the spell is lost to them. The spell parrot's effective spellcasting ability is Wisdom (spell save DC 14, +6 to hit with spell attacks).

Spell parrots choose their targets with sometimes clever but sometimes confused logic. If they fail to do something intrinsic to the spell's casting (such as touching the target in a touch-range spell), even a 0-level spell automatically fails. Older spell parrots usually know this, while younger parrots can figure it out with a DC 8 Intelligence check.

ACTIONS

Bite. *Melee Weapon Attack:* +7 to hit, reach 5 ft., one target. *Hit:* 6 piercing damage.

APPENDIX A: NEW MONSTERS | 105

APPENDIX B: NEW SPELLS

The following spells are on the spell lists for clerics, druids, sorcerers, warlocks, and wizards.

ANALYZE CONJUNCTION
1st-level divination (ritual)
Casting Time: 1 minute
Range: Touch
Components: V, S, M (a small brass pipe valued at 50 gp)
Duration: Instantaneous

You focus your inner eye on a magic item you are holding. You learn the item's esoteric conjunctions if it has any.

DRAIN CHARGE
3rd-level transmutation
Casting Time: 1 action
Range: Touch
Components: V, S
Duration: Instantaneous

You touch a magical item that possesses charges. If the item is currently being held by another creature, that creature may attempt a Wisdom saving throw to resist the spell, gaining advantage on the saving throw if they are attuned to the item.

You drain a charge from the item, using it to empower your own magic. For each charge you drain using this spell, you regain an expended spell slot level. For example, if you drain two charges, you may regain one second level slot or two first level slots. Items that may be destroyed when their last charge is used may be destroyed if you drain their last charge.

At Higher Levels. When you cast this spell using a spell slot of 4th level or higher, you may drain an additional charge of each slot level above 3rd.

FALSE ATTUNEMENT
4th-level illusion
Casting Time: 1 minute
Range: Touch
Components: V, S, M (ruby dust valued at 100 gp that the spell consumes)
Duration: Concentration, up to 10 minutes

You touch a magical item that requires attunement and fool it into thinking you are attuned to it. This does not last long, and you must follow all the normal rules of attuning to a magical item such as the number of items you can attune to or any esoteric conjunctions the item might have.

FUEL CHARGE
4th-level transmutation
Casting Time: 1 action
Range: Touch
Components: V, S
Duration: Instantaneous

You touch a magic item that requires charges, transferring some of your magical energy into the item. You expend your spell slots to power the item. For each level of spell slot you expend (beyond those used to cast this spell), the item gains one charge up to its maximum charges.

LOCATE PANOPLY
3rd-level divination (ritual)
Casting Time: 1 action
Range: Self
Components: V, S, M (a forked stick, an item that is part of a panoply)
Duration: Concentration, up to 1 hour

You focus on an item you are holding that is part of a panoply. For the duration of the spell, you know the direction and distance to the nearest item that is part of the same panoply.

MAJOR ENCHANTMENT
7th-level transmutation
Casting Time: 10 minutes
Range: Touch
Components: V, S, M (diamond dust valued at 1,000 gp)
Duration: Concentration, up to 1 hour

You touch an item of exquisite quality and transfer one spell you know of at least 1st level into that item to create a limited-use magical item. When you do so, you expend the spell slot of the spell you are transferring. You must designate a command word to activate the item. For the duration of the spell, anyone who holds the item can use an action to speak the command word, casting the spell from the item using your spell save DC and spell attack bonus, if applicable.

MINOR ENCHANTMENT
3rd-level transmutation
Casting Time: 10 minutes
Range: Touch
Components: V, S, M (diamond dust valued at 100 gp)
Duration: Concentration, up to 1 hour

You touch an item of exquisite quality and transfer one cantrip you know into that item to create a limited-use magical item. You must designate a command word to activate the item. For the duration of the spell, anyone who holds the item can use an action to speak the command word, casting the cantrip from the item using your spell save DC and spell attack bonus, if applicable.

SUPPRESS CONJUNCTION
4th-level transmutation
Casting Time: 1 action
Range: Touch
Components: V, S
Duration: Concentration, up to 1 hour

You touch a magical item that has an esoteric conjunction and suppress the conjunction for the duration of the spell. During this time, the item does not count as having an esoteric conjunction.

SUPPRESS ITEM
9th-level transmutation
Casting Time: 1 hour
Range: Touch
Components: V, S, M (powders and unguents valued at 1,000 gp that are consumed by the spell)
Duration: 24 hours

You touch a magical item and render it unmagical for the duration. You must be holding the item during the casting of the spell. While suppressed, the magical item cannot regain charges if it would normally do so. Artifacts and certain legendary magic items may resist this spell.

TRANSFER CHARGE
2nd-level transmutation (ritual)
Casting Time: 1 action
Range: Touch
Components: V, S, M (two magic items that require charges)
Duration: Instantaneous

You touch two magical items that require charges. You may transfer one charge between items.

At Higher Levels. When you cast this spell using a spell slot of 3rd level of higher, you may transfer an additional charge of each slot level above 2nd.

APPENDIX C: MAGIC TATTOOS

Magical tattoos are enchanted tattoos that are bonded to the user; they cannot be removed without destroying their magic. In many cultures, to receive one is an honor, to receive more than one marks a great hero. Other cultures use them to mark prisoners, show ideological or factional affiliation, or even abhor the decorating of the body through any means.

Painful to acquire, magical tattoos are made from minerals, herbs, and other pigments that are carefully forced underneath the skin using hammered needles by a skilled artist. It is a long and grueling process that can take days or even weeks to complete for more intricate tattoos. Magical tattoos require that the artist be a magic-user of some power as well as a skilled artist. The process takes longer and places a great strain on the bearer as the ink is not merely driven into their flesh, but into their soul as well.

To receive a magical tattoo, and assuming you have found someone willing and able to perform the ritual, you must spend at least a week per level of rarity in preparation (one week for a common tattoo, two weeks for an uncommon, and so forth). This preparation must be done following the guidance of the artists giving the tattoo and involves fasting, prayer, ritual dances, feats of self-denial, consumption of ritual herbs and drink, isolation, and some self-mortification. Once preparations are complete, the tattooing begins, a process that takes a week plus an additional week per level of rarity. At the end of this time, you must succeed at a DC 15 Constitution saving throw and a DC 15 Wisdom saving throw or the entire process is wasted. Any artist skilled enough to create a magical tattoo is capable of aiding in these saving throws.

Each magical tattoo must be placed on a specific body part. You cannot have more than one magical tattoo on any given body part, but the palm and back of the hand and similar arrangements are permitted. Once placed, the tattoo is linked to you physically and spiritually; should you lose that body part, you may still make use of the tattoo's powers as long as that body part is preserved. However, that body part is also linked to you and may be mystically used against you.

ARROWS
Wondrous item, rare (requires attunement)

These crossed arrows are usually done in black ink with intricate geometric designs on the feathers and heads. The *arrow tattoo* must be placed on the forearm of the non-dominant arm. When you grasp a bow with the limb bearing the tattoo, you gain a +1 bonus to attack and damage rolls with that bow, and your attacks count as magical. Furthermore, you may draw one of the arrows from the tattoo and shoot it. A target hit with the tattoo arrow must make a DC 15 Constitution saving throw, taking an additional 4d8 radiant damage on a failure, or half as much on a successful save. The removed arrow slowly fades into view over the course of one week, after which it returns to normal and can be used again. If you use the second arrow, you lose the magic of the tattoo until the first arrow reappears.

CLAN MARK
Wondrous item, common (requires attunement)

In some cultures, every member of a clan or faction receives a magical tattoo as a sign of initiation or adulthood. Each clan has a different set of marks, often a simple shape placed in threes on the chin shortly after birth. Unlike other magical tattoos, the recipient does not have to undergo a lengthy preparation. Instead, their sponsor stands in as your proxy during preparations. While you bear your *clan mark*, you can use a bonus action to know the location and general condition of anyone else bearing the same clan markings within 100 feet of you.

CLOAK CLASP
Wondrous item, uncommon (requires attunement)

This tattoo of a cloak pin is placed on your shoulder or upper breast. As an action, you may call upon it to clothe yourself in whatever outfit you imagine. The clothing appears real until it they leaves your body, at which point it disappears.

CROSSED WEAPONS
Wondrous item, rare (requires attunement)

This tattoo is normally placed on the back of the dominant hand, but it can be placed anywhere on either arm. The tattoo consists of a pair of crossed weapons, often a matching set such as two swords or two axes. As an action, you can cause one of the weapons to appear in your hand; the chosen weapon disappears from the tattoo when it does so. You can use another action to have the other weapon appear in your other hand. The weapons remain for one hour each and then return to the tattoo and cannot be called upon again until you take a long rest. You gain a +1 to attack and damage rolls with these weapons.

DRAGON
Wondrous item, uncommon (requires attunement)

This tattoo of a dragon's head and neck is placed on your neck and runs from the base of your neck to just behind either your left or right ear. The dragon may be of any color, and that color determines the powers of the *dragon tattoo*. You gain resistance to a damage type as well as a breath weapon you may use once per short rest. Creatures caught in the area of effect of the breath weapon must make a Dexterity saving throw with a DC equal to 8 + your Constitution modifier + your Proficiency bonus. On a failure, the creature takes the listed damage while on a success they take half this damage.

DRAGON TATTOO COLORS

Dragon Color	Damage Resistance	Breath Weapon
Black	Acid	15-foot line, 2d6 acid damage
Gold	Fire	15-foot cone, 2d6 fire damage
Green	Poison	15-foot cone, 2d6 poison damage
Red	Fire	15-foot cone, 2d6 fire damage
Silver	Cold	15-foot cone, 2d6 cold damage
White	Cold	15-foot cone, 2d6 cold damage

FALCON
Wondrous item, uncommon (requires attunement)

This geometric falcon tattoo spreads across your back, its wings unfurled to touch the tops of your shoulders. You may call upon your *falcon tattoo* to gain a fly speed of 30 for five hours, after which the tattoo must rest until the next moonrise before it can be activated again.

FANGS
Wondrous item, rare (requires attunement)

These tattoos of dripping fangs are placed on the inner lips, though some prefer to have them placed at the corners of the mouth. As an action, you may make an attack with the fangs, biting your foe. If you hit, you inflict 1d6 + your Strength modifier piercing damage and the target must make a DC 15 Constitution saving throw. On a failure, the target takes an additional 2d6 poison damage and is poisoned condition for one minute, while on a success, the target takes half as much damage and is not poisoned. A poisoned target can repeat the saving throw at the end of eah of their turns, ending the effect on a success.

FLOWERS
Wondrous item, rare (requires attunement by a spellcaster)

Flower tattoos tend to be brightly colored, some a singular bloom, others entire bouquets. The flowers fill with magical energy throughout the day and night, eventually accumulating enough to empower your spells. In areas where the thaumatological field is normal, the flowers accumulate enough magical energy every 24 hours to allow you to recover an expended spell slot of 5th level or lower. The time it takes to accumulate magical energy varies and may be longer or shorter depending on the local thaumatological auras. The flowers hold a finite amount of energy, enough for one use, and then must be allowed to refill.

GEOMETRIC
Wondrous item, very rare (requires attunement by a spellcaster)

The *geometric tattoo* is composed of several repeating geometric shapes stacked within each other. At the base is a triangle enclosed in a circle that touches all three points, itself enclosed within a square so that the four sides touch the circle at four points. At the four points of the square are four other squares, each touching the center square at a single vertex. Each of these squares has the same circle and triangle stacked within as the central square, The entire tattoo is placed on the chest so that the triangle rest directly over the heartbeat.

Your *geometric tattoo* acts as a permanent *protection from evil and good* spell. Furthermore, you may use the tattoo to cast the following spells: *augury, banishment,* and *true seeing* (DC 15 spell save) once each and regain use of each cast spell at the next moonrise. Finally, you may store up to four levels of spells you know within the tattoo, casting them as if you had prepared them.

HEART
Wondrous item, uncommon (requires attunement)

A heart tattoo over one's own heart creates an image of hearts within hearts spiraling into infinity. Once you gain this magical tattoo, you gain +1 hit points per hit die (retroactively, if needed) and advantage on death saving throws. However, the ink fades a little every time you fail a death save, and after seven failures, the tattoo disappears and becomes unusable.

HORSE
Wondrous item, common (requires attunement)

Often not much more than an impressionistic outline of a running horse, the tattoo is placed on the inner arm below the elbow so that the horse's head is pointing at the elbow. While you bear the *horse tattoo,* you gain advantage on Wisdom (Animal Handling) checks that involve horses, may speak with horses as with the spell *speak with animals,* and increase the speed of any mount you ride by 10 feet.

MOUNTAIN
Wondrous item, uncommon (requires attunement)

This abstract magic is little more than a few lines that denote the steep-sided chevron with hints of trees and clouds near the summit. Those who have performed great feats of strength and endurance are granted this tattoo. Your *mountain tattoo* increases your Strength score by 1 (to a maximum of 20) and grants you the ability to jump three times your normal height and distance.

PALM OF ENERGY
Wondrous item, rare (requires attunement)

This tattoo covers one of your palms and takes the form of a ball of energy colored to match the type of damage it inflicts. As an action, you may throw this ball of energy as a ranged attack, gaining +1 on the attack roll. If you hit, the target suffers 2d8 damage of the listed type. You can have one palm of energy per palm you have and each may be used once per long rest.

PALM OF ENERGY DAMAGE TYPES

Damage Type	Color
Acid	Green
Cold	White
Fire	Red
Force	Purple
Lightning	Blue
Necrotic	Black
Psychic	Yellow
Radiant	Golden
Thunder	Gray

RED EYES
Wondrous item, uncommon (requires attunement)

These painful tattoos cover your eyelids. When you close your eyes, you may choose to use the tattooed eyes instead, granting you darkvision 60 feet. However, your vision is strictly limited to 60 feet; you cannot see anything beyond that.

RIVER
Wondrous item, uncommon (requires attunement)

These three wavy lines are laid in a column upon your right chest. The *river tattoo* grants you the ability to breathe water, a swim speed of 30, and you are unhampered by aquatic environments and difficult terrain. You may share the water-breathing ability with one other living creature you can touch, but only as long as you are in physical contact.

SCROLL
Wondrous item, rare (requires attunement by a spellcaster)

You have the arcane words of a scroll tattooed on your body; it is hoped somewhere you can read it. The *scroll tattoo* can hold a spell of up to 3rd level and acts as a scroll of that spell save that it is not permanently used. When you read the spell from the *scroll tattoo,* it fades away and reappears slowly over the next 24 hours, at which point it can be used again.

SHIELD
Wondrous item, rare (requires attunement)

This tattoo of a shield is placed on the back of your non-dominant hand. As an action, you may cause the tattoo to manifest as a shield on that arm, ready to use. The shield remains for one hour or until you use an action to dismiss it. While wielding the shield, your armor class increases by +3. Once the shield has gone away, it cannot be used again until you complete a long rest.

SOCIETY MARK
Wondrous item, common (requires attunement)

Various crafting, healing, and military societies also have their own distinctive variations of *clan mark* tattoos that grant the same benefits. Each society has a different set of marks, often a simple shape placed in threes on the back of the left hand during initiation. While you bear your *society mark*, you can use a bonus action to know the location and general condition of anyone else bearing the same society markings within 100 feet of you.

SNAKE
Wondrous item, rare (requires attunement)

This massive tattoo of a snake wraps from your hip around your torso and rests its head on your upper chest. As an action, you may cause the tattoo to animate into either a giant constrictor snake or a giant poisonous snake. The snake obeys your commands and remains animated for one hour. The snake returns to your body as a tattoo if the snake is slain or if you use an action to command it to do so. Once the snake has returned to your body, you cannot call it forth again until you have completed a long rest.

SPEAR
Wondrous item, rare (requires attunement)

This tattooed spear starts at your armpit and extends to the palm of your hand. The tattoo grants you an unarmed attack that inflicts 1d6 piercing damage and counts as a magical attack. You may throw the tattooed spear, inflicting the spear's damage or your normal unarmed strike damage, your choice. The thrown spear disappears from your skin and reappears there at the end of your turn.

TIGER
Wondrous item, rare (requires attunement)

This stylized tiger mask covers your face and neck, extending over your head. Your *tiger tattoo* increases your Dexterity score by 2 (to a maximum of 22) and allows you to blend into natural terrain, granting you advantage on Dexterity (Stealth) checks in natural environments. You may use an action to lick your wounds and recover 4d8 hit points once per long rest.

THIRD EYE
Wondrous item, uncommon (requires attunement)

The third eye is tattooed on your forehead just above and between your eyes. The process is especially painful, but in the end you may cast one cantrip of your choice from any spell list. You choose the ability core you will use as the spellcasting ability score for this spell when the tattoo is applied.

WOLF
Wondrous item, uncommon (requires attunement)

These stylized wolf paw prints are placed on the palms of your hands and the soles of your feet. This tattoo is given to all initiates of the wolf soldier society. Your *wolf tattoo* grants you darkvision 60 feet and advantage on all Dexterity (Stealth) checks made in a natural environment. Additionally, if within five feet of an allied creature that is not incapacitated and who has *clan marks* or *society marks* that match yours, you and the ally both gain advantage on attack rolls.

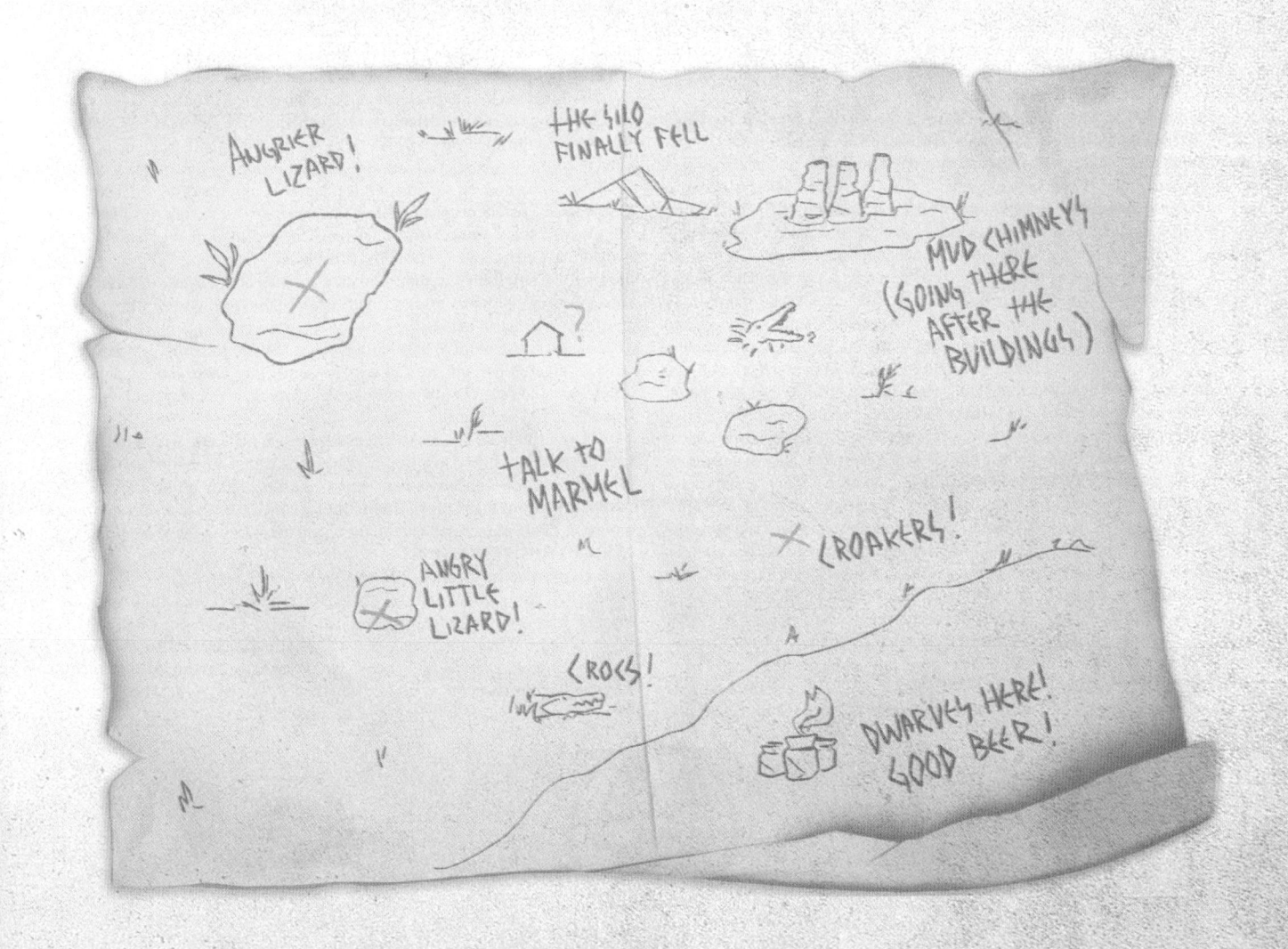

APPENDIX C: MAGIC TATTOOS | 109

Product Identity: The following items are hereby identified as Necromancer Games LLC's Product Identity, as defined in the Open Game License version 1.0a, Section 1(e), and are not Open Game Content: product and product line names, logos and identifying marks including trade dress; artifacts; creatures; characters; stories, storylines, plots, thematic elements, dialogue, incidents, language, artwork, symbols, designs, depictions, likenesses, formats, poses, concepts, themes and graphic, photographic and other visual or audio representations; names and descriptions of characters, spells, enchantments, personalities, teams, personas, likenesses and special abilities; places, locations, environments, creatures, equipment, magical or supernatural abilities or effects, logos, symbols, or graphic designs; and any other trademark or registered trademark clearly identified as Product Identity. Previously released Open Game Content is excluded from the above list.

Notice of Open Game Content: This product contains Open Game Content, as defined in the Open Game License, below. Open Game Content may only be Used under and in terms of the Open Game License.

Designation of Open Game Content: Subject to the Product Identity Designation herein, the following material is designated as Open Game Content. (1) all monster statistics, descriptions of special abilities, and sentences including game mechanics such as die rolls, probabilities, and/or other material required to be open game content as part of the game rules, or previously released as Open Game Content, (2) all portions of spell descriptions that include rules-specific definitions of the effect of the spells, and all material previously released as Open Game Content, (3) all other descriptions of game-rule effects specifying die rolls or other mechanic features of the game, whether in traps, magic items, hazards, or anywhere else in the text, (4) all previously released Open Game Content, material required to be Open Game Content under the terms of the Open Game License, and public domain material anywhere in the text.

Use of Content from Tome of Horrors Complete: This product contains or references content from the Tome of Horrors Complete and/or other monster Tomes by Necromancer Games. Such content is used by permission and an abbreviated Section 15 entry has been approved. Citation to monsters from the Tome of Horrors Complete or other monster Tomes must be done by citation to that original work.

OPEN GAME LICENSE Version 1.0a

The following text is the property of Wizards of the Coast, Inc. and is copyright 2000 Wizards of the Coast, Inc. ("Wizards"). All Rights Reserved.

1. Definitions: (a) "Contributors" means the copyright and/or trademark owners who have contributed Open Game Content; (b) "Derivative Material" means copyrighted material including derivative works and translations (including into other computer languages), potation, modification, correction, addition, extension, upgrade, improvement, compilation, abridgement, or other form in which an existing work may be recast, transformed, or adapted; (c) "Distribute" means to reproduce, license, rent, lease, sell, broadcast, publicly display, transmit, or otherwise distribute; (d) "Open Game Content" means the game mechanic and includes the methods, procedures, processes, and routines to the extent such content does not embody the Product Identity and is an enhancement over the prior art and any additional content clearly identified as Open Game Content by the Contributor, and means any work covered by this License, including translations and derivative works under copyright law, but specifically excludes Product Identity; (e) "Product Identity" means product and product line names, logos, and identifying marks including trade dress; artifacts; creatures and characters; stories, storylines, plots, thematic elements, dialogue, incidents, language, artwork, symbols, designs, depictions, likenesses, formats, poses, concepts, themes, and graphic, photographic, and other visual or audio representations; names and descriptions of characters, spells, enchantments, personalities, teams, personas, likenesses, and special abilities; places, locations, environments, creatures, equipment, magic or supernatural abilities or effects, logos, symbols, or graphic designs; and any other trademark or registered trademark clearly identified as Product Identity by the owner of the Product Identity, and which specifically excludes the Open Game Content; (f) "Trademark" means the logos, names, mark, sign, motto, designs that are used by a Contributor to identify itself or its products or the associated products contributed to the Open Game License by the Contributor; (g) "Use", "Used", or "Using" means to use, Distribute, copy, edit, format, modify, translate, and otherwise create Derivative Material of Open Game Content; (h) "You" or "Your" means the licensee in terms of this agreement.

2. The License: This License applies to any Open Game Content that contains a notice indicating that the Open Game Content may only be Used under and in terms of this License. You must affix such a notice to any Open Game Content that you Use. No terms may be added to or subtracted from this License except as described by the License itself. No other terms or conditions may be applied to any Open Game Content distributed using this License.

3. Offer and Acceptance: By Using the Open Game Content You indicate Your acceptance of the terms of this License.

4. Grant and Consideration: In consideration for agreeing to use this License, the Contributors grant You a perpetual, worldwide, royalty-free, non-exclusive license with the exact terms of this License to Use, the Open Game Content.

5. Representation of Authority to Contribute: If You are contributing original material as Open Game Content, You represent that Your Contributions are Your original creation and/or You have sufficient rights to grant the rights conveyed by this License.

6. Notice of License Copyright: You must update the COPYRIGHT NOTICE portion of this License to include the exact text of the COPYRIGHT NOTICE of any Open Game Content You are copying, modifying, or distributing, and You must add the title, the copyright date, and the copyright holder's name to the COPYRIGHT NOTICE of any original Open Game Content you Distribute.

7. Use of Product Identity: You agree not to Use any Product Identity, including as an indication as to compatibility, except as expressly licensed in another, independent Agreement with the owner of each element of that Product Identity. You agree not to indicate compatibility or co-adaptability with any Trademark or Registered Trademark in conjunction with a work containing Open Game Content except as expressly licensed in another, independent Agreement with the owner of such Trademark or Registered Trademark. The use of any Product Identity in Open Game Content does not constitute a challenge to the ownership of that Product Identity. The owner of any Product Identity used in Open Game Content shall retain all rights, title, and interest in and to that Product Identity.

8. Identification: If you distribute Open Game Content, You must clearly indicate which portions of the work that you are distributing are Open Game Content.

9. Updating the License: Wizards or its designated Agents may publish updated versions of this License. You may use any authorized version of this License. You may use any authorized version of this License to copy, modify, and distribute any Open Game Content originally distributed under any version of this License.

10. Copy of this License: You MUST include a copy of this License with every copy of the Open Game Content You Distribute.

11. Use of Contribute Credits: You may not market or advertise the Open Game Content using the name of any Contributor unless You have written permission from the Contributor to do so.

12. Inability to Comply: If it is impossible for You to comply with any of the terms of this License with respect to some or all of the Open Game Content due to statute, judicial order, or governmental regulation then You may not Use any Open Game Material so affected.

13. Termination: This License will terminate automatically if You fail to comply with all terms herein and fail to cure such breach within 30 days of becoming aware of the breach. All sublicenses shall survive the termination of this License.

14. Reformation: If any provisions of this License is held to be unenforceable, such provision shall be reformed only to the extent necessary to make it enforceable.

15. COPYRIGHT NOTICE

Open Game License v 1.0a © 2000, Wizards of the Coast, Inc.

System Reference Document 5.0 © 2016, Wizards of the Coast, Inc.; Authors Mike Mearls, Jeremy Crawford, Chris Perkins, Rodney Thompson, Peter Lee, James Wyatt, Robert J. Schwalb, Bruce R. Cordell, Chris Sims, and Steve Townshend, based on original material by E. Gary Gygax and Dave Arneson.

Tome of Wondrous Items, © 2022, Necromancer Games; Author Ken Spencer.